Chastity Morrow

**A PASSIONATE NEW LOVE STORY
BY ROSANNE KOHAKE
AVON'S NEW SUPERSTAR
OF ROMANCE NOVELS
AUTHOR OF
*FOR HONOR'S LADY***

AFFAIRE DE COEUR calls Rosanne Kohake "a welcome addition to the historic romance genre," and adds: "We await with pleasure more books from this talented new author."

ROMANTIC TIMES calls FOR HONOR'S LADY "an unforgettable love story which takes that step beyond entertainment and touches the heart . . . a romance novel you haven't read before, but you'll want to read again and again."

PUBLISHERS WEEKLY calls FOR HONOR'S LADY "a neat blend of fiction and accurate historical detail . . . a novel of style and taste."

Other Avon Books by
Rosanne Kohake

FOR HONOR'S LADY

Coming Soon

AMBROSIA

Chastily Morrow

Rosanne Kohake

AVON
PUBLISHERS OF BARD, CAMELOT, DISCUS AND FLARE BOOKS

AVON BOOKS
A division of
The Hearst Corporation
1790 Broadway
New York, New York 10019

Copyright © 1985 by Rosanne Kohake
Published by arrangement with the author
Library of Congress Catalog Card Number: 84-91209
ISBN: 0-380-88542-5

First Avon Printing, January, 1985

AVON TRADEMARK REG. U.S. PAT. OFF. AND IN OTHER COUNTRIES, MARCO REGISTRADA, HECHO EN U.S.A.

Printed in the U.S.A.

WFH 10 9 8 7 6 5 4 3 2 1

This book is dedicated
to my sister Geralyn
with all my love.

Prologue

Jonathon Stoneworth walked briskly along his favorite path through the Common, his serious eyes intent on the splashes of scarlet and copper in the green foliage above his head, his ears enjoying the pleasant crunch of crisp brown leaves beneath his feet. It had always been special to him, this place. He had come here often in his boyhood to dream and to think, to run, to feel the glorious freedom of wide open spaces—such a bitter contrast to the squalor of the North End.

He had survived on dreams throughout his boyhood, dreams nurtured by the rush of the tide, the spray of salt-sea air, and this special, almost magical place in the very heart of the city where he had been born.

Jonathon was no longer a boy. At the age of twenty-one he was a man full grown, tall, handsome, well educated, carefully bred in the tradition of the Stoneworths, who traced their line to the first English settlers of the Shawmut Peninsula. But Jonathon was just beginning to realize that the narrow, well-kept lanes and the neat red-brick sidewalks of Beacon Hill were in many ways even more confining than the tenements on the waterfront. And so he had come here to escape, just as he had so many years before. Finally he raised his eyes to the drab twilight sky, which hung low over acres and acres of brightly colored trees in the Common. Closing his dark brown eyes,

1

he drew a long, deep breath of sea-kissed autumn air. Then reluctantly, he turned and headed for home.

Jonathon hesitated before opening the huge polished wood door of the elegant bow-fronted house, one of several fashionable residences on the slope of Beacon Hill. Once inside he handed his hat to the ever-vigilant, impeccably clothed Jason, who offered his customary polite nod. "Good evening, Master Jonathon. I believe the cook might have kept something warm for dinner . . ."

"Thank you, Jason, but I'm not hungry. Where's Grandfather?"

"He's in the library, sir."

Jonathon nodded. His fingers felt nervously for the top button of his shirt to be certain that it was properly fastened. He checked the lay of his starched collar and jerked at the lower hem of his vest to straighten out its wrinkles. He wasn't looking forward to this. But it was something he had to do.

Jonathon's normally confident stride was noticeably lacking in arrogance as he approached the library's great oaken doors. He swallowed hard and lifted his chin. He knocked, then waited until his grandfather bid him enter.

Nathaniel Aaron Stoneworth, seated in his favorite worn leather chair, lowered a finely tooled morocco-bound volume as his grandson entered and closed the door behind himself. For an instant a hint of something warm touched his expression, but the warmth quickly fell victim to a slight scowl of annoyance. He rose and poured himself and Jonathon glasses of brandy from a nearby decanter. "Where have you been, Jonathon? . . . Or need I ask?"

Jonathon gratefully accepted the brandy and allowed the soothing liquid to slide down his parched throat before he responded. It was something his grandfather had taught him, that he ought never to answer even the simplest of questions without a pause for thought. "You didn't really have to ask, I suppose. I intended to tell you anyway." He paused. "I went to visit the O'Briens . . . to offer what help I could . . . to let them know that I haven't forgotten."

Nathaniel dropped into his chair with a sigh. "Just how long do you intend to go on with this foolishness?"

A sad, queer sort of smile twisted Jonathon's lips. "It's odd, sir, but this afternoon I posed the very same question to myself."

Nathaniel's brow darkened ominously. He disliked this newly acquired habit of Jonathon's, this way he had of avoiding any direct questions with a flippant remark. Of course, the boy's natural skill in verbal jousting was to be expected. Not only did Stoneworth blood flow in his veins, but he had also been tutored by a master—Nathaniel Stoneworth himself. Jonathon had all the makings of an excellent lawyer and a cunning politician, and his grandfather intended to see that he used them. After years of carefully molding the boy, Nathaniel had made great plans for him, plans that went much further than the partnership he'd just offered him in the family law firm.

But Nathaniel was becoming increasingly impatient with the recent rebellious shift of Jonathon's mind. For so long the boy had been so totally malleable, so eager to leave a shameful heritage of poverty and deprivation behind him. But suddenly it seemed that everything had changed. Of course he understood Jonathon's disappointment at losing his first court case, especially since the loss could be blamed entirely on a prejudiced judge who had refused to listen to words uttered by an "Irishman" in an American court of law. The fact that Nathaniel's grandson did indeed trace his parentage to the less than prestigious Irish county of Waterford was not a well-kept enough secret to allow him the free movement naturally accorded other members of elite Bostonian society. Jonathon's father had been a poor, uneducated Irish immigrant, and there were quite a few Brahmins who refused to forget it.

For a long while Nathaniel had pondered that problem, but then he had realized that Jonathon's heritage would be his greatest asset in the future. There was no stemming this flood of crude, famine-weary, ruddy-faced immigrants. The Know-Nothing movement had fallen by the way years ago, and the proper Bostonian who traced his ancestry back to the days of Puritan England was now a member of a minority—a powerful, wealthy minority, but a minority all the same. Numbers gave power to these Celtic laborers, and Nathaniel knew that someday soon the city of Boston would be run by the leaders of the Irish community.

And Jonathon Stoneworth, with his Harvard education, his quick-witted, clever intelligence, his personable appearance, and most important, his undisputed claim to Irish blood, had a chance to become the most powerful man in Boston. Nathaniel intended to see that he did. All in proper time; all in a rational, calculated process. Which was precisely the reason for Nathaniel's irritation. Jonathon's actions of late had been the result of emotion, not thought. It was the one aspect of his grandson's personality that worried Nathaniel to no end—that Jonathon had a hair-trigger temper, that he often reacted to his feelings on the spur of the moment. A Stoneworth always maintained his composure; always acted, never reacted; and was always in complete control of his emotions.

Nathaniel sighed and set his brandy aside, letting the back of his head rest comfortably against the chair. There was still plenty of time to rectify this flaw in his grandson, plenty of time. He watched Jonathon pace the library, back and forth, back and forth, like an animal in a cage. Something of great import was on his mind, Nathaniel knew. He waited in silence to find out what it was.

After several moments, Jonathon drained the last of the brandy from his glass and levelly met his grandfather's eyes. "I'm going to enlist, Grandfather. I made up my mind this afternoon. I'm not going to let you pay someone else to fight for something I believe in. It's my country, my duty to fight for it."

Nathaniel's brow rose the slightest bit, but his face showed no other trace of emotion. They had been over all of this before. "Be reasonable, Jonathon," came the cool reply. "Do you think one man will truly make a difference in this war?"

"It will make a difference to me," he answered quietly. "It will make a great deal of difference."

Nathaniel sighed deeply, thoughtfully pressing the tips of his long, straight fingers together, releasing them, and pressing them together once more. "You know very well you're being foolish about this, that you have everything to lose and nothing to gain."

"No. You're wrong about that, Grandfather. I consider my self-respect something very important, important enough to fight for."

"Self-respect?" His keen eyes lit with something that resembled amusement. "Will dying really buy you self-respect, Jonathon? If you think that, then you are a fool."

"I don't intend to die," he said strongly. "But I do intend to do my part—"

"Your part! Ah, now we have it. The crux of this discussion in a single pair of words—your part. Think a moment, Jonathon, and you will realize that your part in this is not that of a common soldier. You are a Stoneworth, boy! Not a—"

"Not a Donahue?" The words were flung back at him.

Nathaniel leaned forward to take a slow sip of his brandy. He had not expected this. He had thought the matter settled. "You are meant for greater things, Jonathon." Jonathon sighed and turned away from his grandfather's perfectly composed face. "I realize that the O'Brien boy's death came as quite a shock to you. But the death of a friend or an acquaintance always comes as a shock. And it really has nothing to do with your life, Jonathon. Forget it. Your future is much too valuable to cast to the wind just because some unimportant person died."

With his back to his grandfather, Jonathon closed his eyes and swallowed hard. He had no way of explaining how he felt about Jerry O'Brien's death. Just a few years ago they had been like brothers, living in the same waterfront tenement house, playing in the streets, sharing secrets, growing up together. Jonathon had almost forgotten those years . . . until he'd read the name in the newspaper. There it was—just a name. Just a tiny line of newsprint in the middle of a long list of similar names. Nothing more.

He fingered the heavy red velvet draperies, which hid the panes of a large picture window, and recalled the years of his childhood. For so many long years he had tried so hard to forget—he could hardly even remember his father's face anymore! But there were things he rememberd all too well, like the terrible feelings of hunger and hopelessness, the empty promises his father had made to his mother about having a fine house and wonderful stylish gowns. As a child Jonathon had believed those promises. His father had been a gentlehearted, loving man, full of hope and ambition and talent, and Jonathon had worshiped him as any child worships his father. But years had passed and Jonathon's father had never fulfilled his dreams, never given his wife and only son all the things he had promised. And in the end Jonathon had come to despise the man for his failure, to blame him for an adolescent disillusionment with the life of poverty that was his birthright. Only now was Jonathon beginning to understand the odds his father had fought against. And he was ashamed for having so easily condemned a man he had once loved, for having turned his back on the past for so long. He squared his shoulders and turned to face his grandfather. "My mind is made up. I'm leaving tomorrow morning."

For the barest moment a spark of disbelief lit in Nathaniel's eyes. But then the older man shrugged and his voice came as cool and dispassionate as before. "I cannot stop you from going. But I warn you, Jonathon, you can never come back. I will disown you the moment you cross that threshold."

Jonathon struggled to lift his chin. There was no doubt in his mind that Nathaniel would do exactly that. He was paying dearly for the decision he had chosen to make. He was turning his back on money and prestige, and everything that he had once sworn to have at any cost. For a fleeting moment a wave of uncertainty swept over him. But he knew that this was the only way to ease the guilt imbedded so deeply in his heart. He'd tasted this life of luxury and had found it bitterly empty. He needed more. "I—I had hoped you would understand," he said quietly. "I still hope that someday you will." He slowly released his breath and fixed the old man's face affectionately in his mind. Then he turned and left the library.

Chapter 1

The sun was rising with a hurting brilliance in the cloudless Nevada sky as Chastity Morrow settled herself comfortably on the leather seat of the rented coach. It had been a wet spring until yesterday, when unseasonably warm weather had taken over, burning the last traces of winter from the land. Chastity lifted a dainty, white-gloved hand to stifle a yawn as she scanned the long row of false-fronted buildings on Elko's main street, now classically silhouetted against a radiant sunrise.

She was a woman of striking appearance, with hair the color of both the sun's light and the moon's, and eyes that mirrored the blazing blue of a cloudless Western sky. There were other attractive, even beautiful aspects to her face—a high, intelligent brow; firm, determined lines to mouth and jaw; a smooth, straight nose—but her eyes triumphed over every other feature, reflecting the contrasts of Chastity's personality. Restlessness and confidence, alertness and apathy, the effervescence of a child entangled with the bitter disillusionment of growing up. An unhappy mixture. A struggling. A war within.

In many ways Chastity was still a child for all her nineteen years. She was swift to sit in judgment of others, though rarely critical of herself. (But then, for as far back as she could remember there had never been a shortage of derogatory comments about her behavior.) She offered explanations to no one.

Everyone assured Chastity that she was searching for

8

love . . . and she supposed that she was, if indeed it existed. After a long year and more of travel, of months spent visiting her cousins in St. Louis, she had yet to come across anything that even approached her idea of love. There had been plenty of men, of course, giving adequate testimony to Chastity's exceptional loveliness and often to the fortune which was synonymous with the Morrow name. But to Chastity, beauty and money were curses as well as blessings. While it gave her a feeling of power and worth to be sought after and promised the moon, those very same promises always left her feeling empty. She was tired of being measured by the number of proposals she had received, tired of being told that when she found the "right man" she would be perfectly happy bearing his children and catering to his whims. There had been no "right man" in St. Louis, and she had grown weary of listening to everyone extol the virtues of her suitors, men in whom she had no interest at all. There had to be more to life than just choosing the right man and living in that man's shadow, she thought. Chastity hated the idea of existing in anyone's shadow. Yet the few times she was frank enough to say that she was capable of something more than flirting and pouring tea and waiting for the right man to come along, her Aunt Susan had clucked her tongue and shaken her head in dismay. "There *is* no more for women, dear," she'd told Chastity time and again. And Chastity was beginning to think that her aunt was right. She certainly didn't want to be a spinster, a dried-up, withered old woman with nothing at all to show for her life. Yet it seemed to her that any man whose heart could be won with a simple smile or an intentional drop of her father's name was not worth the having. She continued to smile, though, and to flirt outrageously with those gentlemen who required the extra effort, because she did not really know any other way to prove herself. In a small way it was reassuring to know that she was desired and sought after, even if it was for the wrong reasons.

But she was never swept away by flowery compliments or pledges of devotion or poetry as other women might have been. Had any of the gentlemen who offered her such

gifts been able to see her true feelings, he would probably
have withdrawn his words and run away from her in horror. (At least that was what Chastity believed would happen.) She knew very well that she was not an easy person
to love, or even like, that she went to great lengths to get
what she wanted, that she was a very bad loser when
things did not go her way. She could count on a single finger the people she truly cared about—her father. The other
nine fingers and more could be used to count those she despised, or against whom she held grudges. But for Chastity it had all been a simple matter of survival. Anger and
frustration and hurt had all scarred her deeply in her
childhood, and she had learned to be cold and hard to survive.

Chastity imagined that her stepmother would be quite
disappointed when she returned to Virginia City without
a husband. But then, she thought wryly, her stepmother
would be quite disappointed that she returned to Virginia
City at all. But she didn't really care what Deborah or
anyone else thought at the moment. She was going home
because she belonged there. The Comstock was in her
blood.

The wealth and influence of Virginia City had provided
a catalyst for the creation of the state of Nevada. Just
nineteen years before, in the year of Chastity's birth, Nevada had been called Western Utah and had been important only as a means to the riches of California. But the
discovery of gold and silver at the Comstock had changed
all that, drawing fortune hunters by the thousands to Nevada itself, so that by 1861 it had become a territory and
in 1864 had entered the Union as the thirty-sixth state. A
few short years later the Central Pacific Railroad, which
ran through the state, linked up with the Union Pacific at
Promontory Point, Utah, just 150 miles to the east, to form
a railroad that spanned the continent. And the Pony Express, which had briefly provided mail service at the beginning of the decade, was made obsolete by the telegraph
lines that paralleled the track.

But to Chastity, Nevada's greatness did not lie in the
changes men had forced upon her soil. Nevada was alive

with natural beauty which too few eyes took the time to appreciate. From the peace of a springtime meadow blanketed in wild iris to the awesome glory of perpetually snow-capped mountains; from the untapped potential of the fertile Thousand Springs region to the barren, sunbaked alkaline sinks, where many had died on their way west; from valleys of sage grass and gorges of solid rock, from the heights of great mountains to the splendor of Tahoe—all this was Nevada, alive, ever-changing, home.

Chastity's gaze swept over the shadows of yellow and gold and brown that played on the rocky hills and mountains in the distance, and the strong bond that would always tie her to this land opened up a flood of bittersweet memories. She breathed deeply of the dry morning air dusted with the scent of sagebrush, and recalled a farmhouse, a tiny hearth, her mother and father sleeping peacefully in a bed near her own. There was a vague, childish memory of the woman who had been her mother—a soft voice, nimble fingers that had braided her hair, gentle hands that had touched her with love, smoothing over any troubles a five-year-old child might have had. She remembered that her father had been a farmer then, and she could still picture him in a field of wheat with stalks so tall and sturdy that the wind sent them billowing in all directions, like the waves on a choppy sea. That was the only memory she had of her father until much, much later in her life.

Samuel Morrow was a simple man whose life was guided by his heart and his dreams. In 1849, at the height of the gold rush, Samuel and his wife, Ruth, left their small farm outside of St. Louis and headed for California. But by the time the Morrows had reached Mormon Station, a small trading post on the Carson River just east of the Sierras, Ruth was well along in a difficult pregnancy and it was clear that the remainder of the journey would be impossible for her. The Morrows' first child, a son, was born dead a few months later, and Ruth began a lengthy convalescence on a farm they managed to purchase in the fertile Carson Valley.

The Morrows prospered in their new home, built with the generous help of Mormons who had settled in the area, and their dreams of instant fortune were forgotten along the way. Five years later, after a difficult labor, Ruth Morrow joyously gave birth to a healthy baby girl who immediately became the center of her and her husband's lives. There was no doubt in Ruth's mind that the tiny, screaming bundle had been worth every moment of her agony. But Samuel could not forget the toll his daughter's birth had taken on his wife, and he earnestly vowed that this child would be the last. Four years later, when Ruth Morrow died birthing a second stillborn son, Samuel Morrow was a broken man.

It was soon afterward that an old miner by the name of Henry Comstock publicly took credit for a gold strike in the Sierras just a few miles to the north. As soon as he heard the news, Samuel was swift to sell his farm, leave his daughter temporarily in the hands of friendly neighbors, and take off in pursuit of an old dream. His proximity to the strike gave him the opportunity to stake a prime claim in the area of the Comstock Lode even before the assayer's report found that the vein was far richer in silver than in gold.

But staking a claim and holding on to it proved two entirely different matters. That first winter at the Comstock was an extremely harsh one that found most of the miners "dug in" the mountainside, sheltered only by crude tents, blankets, or, in many cases, only the shirts on their backs. Sun Peak had long since been stripped of its trees, so there was no lumber for housing, no source of firewood or any other fuel. For months the roads were steeped in mud and snow, so that it was impossible for even the staples to be brought in. Food and water became so scarce that many men were forced to survive on whiskey alone, which was the only commodity in abundant supply.

Winter passed, and with the melting of the deep snows came thousands of hopeful prospectors to the mining camp on the eastern side of Mount Davidson. The expansion was too rapid, and because there was no established procedure for filing a claim on public land, the only way to defend one's property was at gunpoint. But peaceable men like Samuel began organizing and enforcing laws in the camp, clamoring for better territorial government and finally statehood for Nevada. The mining camp that had sprung up overnight became a thriving community of over twenty thousand people, and Virginia City's wealth gave birth to many famous American fortunes. Names such as Hearst, Mackay, Sharon, Sutro, and Morrow all were rooted in the riches of the Comstock.

As the mines bored ever deeper and the extraction of ore became more complex, individual prospectors sold their interests to larger mining companies. The mines were incorporated on the San Francisco Stock Exchange, linking the economies of the two greatest cities of the West. Many Comstock millionaires, or nabobs, chose to build elegant homes in San Francisco, spawning what became known as Nob Hill. But some who had come to love Mount Davidson, with the constant excitement of new bonanzas and the unfailing optimism that seemed a natural part of the Comstock, built and furnished elaborate residences in the westernmost section of Virginia City, the area of highest elevation. On Howard Street, just above A Street, Samuel Morrow built a huge three-story structure of painted yellow wood with mansard roof, excessively trimmed with popular jigsaw ornamentation. It was here, after years of being passed around a loose circle of well-meaning (but oftentimes resentful) families, that Chastity was reunited with her father.

Chastity's life instantly became a fairyland kind of existence, for after years of wearing hand-me-downs and being simply tolerated if not downright ignored, she suddenly had a father who adored her and doted on her every whim. Samuel did everything he could think of to make a home for his daughter, but he could never quite seem to satisfy her. The moment he gave her one thing, her heart's desire became something else. Samuel Morrow was now an important and respected man, a man who had made his dream of fortune come true. But he was also a lonely, unhappy man whose daughter was a demanding stranger and whose dead wife's memory still haunted his empty bed.

It seemed natural and wholly appropriate to all of Samuel's friends when he married for a second time, after over seven years of living alone. He had his pick of young and beautiful women—there were many who sought to share his fortune—but Samuel chose instead to marry a woman his own age, a woman by the name of Deborah Anne Garret. She was somewhat plain, with gray-streaked brown hair worn in a simple knot at the back of her neck, even features that seemed to soften as she spoke in a slow, gentle voice, and a pair of blue eyes that clearly mirrored her kind and generous heart. It was Deborah's first marriage, though she was well over thirty at the time. Her parents had come to San Francisco during the gold rush years and had left her a small, respectable boardinghouse, where Samuel had chanced to stay on one of his frequent trips to that city. Her quiet, affectionate nature perfectly complemented Sam's gruff facade and gave him back a part of himself he had feared lost forever. She cooked special meals for him, mended his shirts, and listened to every word he said, truly loving his company. No one could ever take the place of Chastity's mother, but Deborah offered Samuel a different kind of love and companionship, and most of all, an easing of his loneliness. The marriage seemed made in heaven except for one small complication: Samuel's twelve-year-old daughter.

To Chastity, Samuel's marriage to Deborah had been the ultimate insult, a painful announcement that a daughter's love was not good enough. She had wanted so much to be the center of his life, and his indulgence had made her almost certain that she was. But when he married Deborah, she felt she lost everything. Deborah was an agonizing reminder that her own love was inadequate, and this was something Chastity could not accept lying down. She rebelled, and for six long years tried every trick she could think of to force Deborah to leave her father. Nothing had worked. Deborah was a fountain of never-ending patience, and Samuel loved her dearly and needed her. For Chastity, that realization had been the deepest cut of all.

So what had she learned by running away from her defeat? she asked herself now as she let her glove glide over the worn leather seat of the stagecoach. Certainly she had grown up some. She had polished her manners and practiced her newly acquired womanly wiles on several men. But essentially she had to admit that nothing had changed. She was still angry with her father, she still hated Deborah, and she was still unhappy. But she wasn't going to travel all her life in an attempt to hide from the truth. She was going home.

The sun was lifting itself quickly from the horizon, exchanging its reddish-gold color for a blazing silver-yellow. Chastity sighed impatiently as the driver paused to mop his face with a calico kerchief for the third time in as many minutes. What was he doing? she wondered as he stood idle for a time, leaning heavily against the side of the coach. She grew even more anxious as the repeated delays of the last hundred miles flashed through her mind.

She had traveled by rail all the way from St. Louis to Utah without incident, but the train had scarcely crossed the Nevada border before it hissed and coughed to an unscheduled stop that had signaled a twelve-hour delay. Then just outside of Elko the engine had broken down a second time, and even before the defective part could be located, the telegraph had informed them that flash floods in the area had wiped out a good bit of track between there and the next stop. Rather than waiting out an indefinite delay, Chastity had chosen the only alternative, a hired coach. Thank goodness she had learned a long time ago to travel with enough money to cover any and all such emergencies.

The driver tossed a quick look at the sun and seemed to sense Chastity's impatience, for a moment later the suspension creaked loudly as he pulled his massive frame to his seat. He turned for a final check of the luggage and had taken reins in hand when a man dressed impeccably in a crisp, black broadcloth suit came into view, hailing the coach with one of two large suitcases. The driver heaved a tired sigh and put the reins aside, waiting for the man to reach the stage. His coach saw little use these days and he was anxious to have the money from yet another passenger, but he hadn't been feeling well this morning and he wanted the trip to be over and done with.

The gentleman in black conversed with the driver for several minutes before depositing his cases on the dirt street and counting out the agreed-upon fare. Then he hefted his cases one at a time to the driver.

The entire time Chastity was eyeing him with unmasked interest. He was decidedly virile, from his deeply tanned skin and jet black hair to his broad-shouldered, narrow-hipped physique. Though he was not an exceptionally tall man, his movements were smooth and confident and he lifted the cases with ease, though the jarring of the coach told her they were quite heavy. There was an almost regal air about him, a natural arrogance in the arch of his dark brows, an aristocratic definition to the line of his jaw, and a powerful magnetism in his cold blue-gray eyes. He watched as the driver fastened his luggage to the top of the coach, giving Chastity ample time to survey his every feature. She knew very well that it was improper to stare at him so boldly, but Chastity wasn't one to follow rules unless it was to her advantage to do so. In the case of men, she had found it very often to her advantage, but only when they were watching. This one was not.

There was definitely something about this man that ignited her interest, something challenging about his aloof, superior manner. She was studying him in silent concentration when he suddenly made a lurch for the top of the coach.

Chastity started and craned her neck to see what had caused the man's strange behavior, but it was impossible for her to see anything but his chiseled profile as he scrambled up the side of the coach.

"Are you all right?" she heard him ask the driver.

"Yeah . . . fine." The reply was thin and breathless. "Just want . . . t' get movin' . . . that's all."

The younger man drew back and repositioned his hat on his head, taking a long, hard look at the driver. "There's a doctor back at the hotel—"

"I'm fine. Just a little stomach trouble is all," the driver interrupted in a voice that sounded stronger already. "Let's get a move on. The lady wants to make it to Carlin before nightfall."

The man hesitated, then shrugged noncommittally and climbed into the coach, taking a seat opposite Chastity. He removed his hat and nodded the required greeting to her as the stage jerked forward and the horses settled into a steady gait.

"I hope you don't mind sharing your hired coach with me," he said in the same deep voice she had heard a moment before, "but I have some important business in Virginia City, and when I inquired about an alternative means of transportation, Mr. Jenkins at the hotel was kind enough to tell me about the coach . . . and just in time, I might add." He paused to flash her a small smile while his eyes appraised her with a frankness she had seldom encountered in the past. "Since the driver seems busy at the moment, I hope you won't object if I introduce myself," he went on evenly. "My name is Regan Spencer."

Regan Spencer, she repeated to herself, mimicking the smooth sound of his voice. She noticed that his speech was touched pleasantly with the easy fluidity of Southern breeding. Yes, she thought. It fit him. A very different name for a very different man.

"Chastity Morrow," she said, instinctively returning his smile before catching herself and casting her eyes demurely toward the window. She waited several moments. Then, having established her aloofness, she turned back to him intending further conversation. Instead she was just in time to see him remove a newspaper from his breast pocket. Chastity frowned and settled her head thoughtfully against the side of the coach to observe the man opposite, finding it difficult to believe that he would actually read a paper when he might converse with her, even if he had never heard the name Morrow before.

Mile after mile he stared at his newspaper, never once stealing a glance at her as she was certain he would. The newspaper must be a ploy, she rationalized to soothe her smarting ego. He was shy or embarrassed about making the first move. But there was still plenty of time, she thought confidently. When the coach made a stop, she would seek his assistance in alighting, lean against him a bit longer than necessary to catch her balance, and be certain of holding his attention for the remainder of the journey. With that thought, Chastity closed her eyes against the piercing brightness of the day and fell instantly asleep.

Regan raised his eyes from his newspaper, relaxing slightly when he saw that the other passenger had finally fallen asleep. He had been wondering just how long she would continue to stare at him, obviously expecting him to put the paper aside and concentrate entirely on entertaining her. She was a very beautiful woman, there was no denying that, but Regan had too much on his mind at the moment to be concerned with a woman like Chastity Morrow. He brushed a piece of lint from the starched lapel of his black broadcloth coat, liking the feel of the fine fabric beneath his fingers. He had never become accustomed to the clothing of inferior quality he had been forced to wear for so many years, and he had worked long and hard to be rid of them and the poverty that went with them. He gazed blankly at the treeless landscape with its stark formations of yellow-brown rock, remembering the sweet fragrances of thick, blue-green grass and magnolia blossoms after a spring rain. How far he had come in the past eight years, he thought, forcing his eyes back to his paper and willing away the memories that would always haunt him, no matter how far he traveled.

He would never forget the final crushing news of General Lee's surrender at Appomattox Court House, though the war had been lost for Regan long before then. His beloved home, *Regalia,* had been sacked and burned, the fields torn apart by weeks and weeks of blasting; even the family plot had been desecrated by General Sherman's butchers. But somehow Regan had survived the horrors of war, the deaths of everyone he loved, the end of the life of grace and beauty that was his birthright . . . only to find that the horrors of peace were worse. He bitterly remembered the hunger that had knotted his stomach day after day after day, the rags that had barely covered his back, the loneliness and desperation he had felt at being left alone to face a terrible, upended world. He had been forced to grovel to get a job at a Charleston dry goods store just to keep himself alive. But he had learned a great deal about the world since then, how to cheat and lie and take what ought to have been his all along. He sighed as his mind flitted past the memories that lay scattered between here and *Regalia*, memories of laboring like a field slave in the heat of the day, of bowing and scraping to Yankees and carpetbaggers and free darkies, of learning to get the better of them without their ever knowing it. He thought of Mrs. Simson, the wealthy middle-aged widow who'd taken a shine to him and lured him away from the streets of Charleston with the promise of pleasure and luxury. He had learned a great many things from that woman and had used her as ruthlessly as she had used him. There were times when he regretted the things he had been forced to do, when he grieved for the idealism that had been bred in him as a boy. He had been taught a code of honor, and then been forced to turn his back on all that was honorable and moral. It was the only chance he had of ever rebuilding the life the war had cost him. And it was a price he was resigned to pay, a temporary concession he made knowing that one day he would be rich again and respected, and then be the same kind of honorable gentleman his father had been, and his grandfather before him. One day . . .

But now Regan's tanned fingers ran nervously over the breast pocket of his coat, checking the thick stack of folded bills he had won in a high-stakes poker game in Natchez. His run of luck had been nothing short of incredible, and it had been pure luck, not the cunning finesse on which he regularly relied to win on a much smaller scale. It was a beginning. And the stock certificates he'd won in the same game, along with what he'd heard about Virginia City, had convinced him that a fortune was just around the corner. It had been a long, hard struggle. Very soon it could all be over.

Chastity woke with a start what seemed like moments later, frowning as the numbness of an uncomfortable nap eased away. The sun was high and her throat was parched, but it was a break in the rhythm of the movement of the coach that had caused her to waken. She glanced at the other passenger, who was staring intently at the passing rock formations, huge and stark in the full light of day.

"Do you think we'll be stopping soon?" she ventured pleasantly, taking hold of a leather strap fastened to the side of the coach to steady herself against the jarring.

"I think we ought to have stopped an hour ago to water the horses in this heat."

Chastity cocked her head and drew her brow in a confused frown. "What do you mean by that?"

He finally turned to face her, evenly meeting her expectant frown. "I mean that the driver ought to have stopped, but he hasn't. I'm beginning to think he'll try to drive straight through to Carlin without stopping at all."

"That's impossible," she returned with considerable annoyance. "The driver couldn't possibly expect us to go the entire day without a bite to eat. I made certain that the man at the hotel packed enough food for a generous lunch." She let her lashes sweep low as she added softly, "I would consider sharing my meal with a gentleman. . . ."

Regan let out his breath impatiently. "Back in Elko, when I tossed the driver my bag, he was having trouble breathing . . . turned white as a sheet for a moment or two. I knew something was wrong then, but I was anxious to leave." He shook his head with self-reproach. "If he stops this thing just once, I intend to drive it into Carlin myself."

Even as he spoke, the odd, bumpy break in movement occurred again, and Chastity suddenly realized that the coach had drifted off the side of the road and continued to pick up speed. "Why don't you do something?" she demanded, gripping the strap with both hands now as the vehicle bounced erratically over the rough uneven ground.

"What would you suggest?" he snapped indignantly. "If we were traveling any slower, I might attempt a climb to the top of this thing. But I'm no acrobat. I wouldn't have a prayer at this rate of speed." He drew a long breath and calmed himself. "There's always a chance that the driver will make it straight through," he added thoughtfully.

"But you don't think he will."

Instead of answering, Regan fastened a pair of cold blue-gray eyes intently on her face. He held himself steady with a single hand while the other hand reached pointedly into his pocket for his newspaper. As Chastity turned away in a huff, he cleared his throat and shook out the paper's folds. But it was utterly impossible for him to read a single word as he was jolted from side to side.

The coach was cutting its own path through patches of scrub grass, bouncing and jarring across the rocky terrain. Chastity felt it sway in one direction, and then, before she could take a firm enough hold on the strap, she was thrown across the coach directly into Regan's lap. She gasped and made a desperate attempt to raise herself, but just when she had almost succeeded, the right front wheel of the stagecoach ran over a fair-sized rock. Chastity let out a scream and clutched madly at Regan as the stage teetered precariously on its two left wheels. In that same instant, both of them saw the driver's body being hurled from the top of the coach, his skull smashing with a sickening crack against a huge rock.

Almost as if they sensed their freedom, the horses immediately picked up their pace until the coach was rattling insanely over the open range. "We've got to jump!" Regan snapped.

He pushed her to the floor and wedged himself lengthwise on the seat, bracing his feet against one side and his shoulders against the other. He groped for the door latch, found it and swung it open, only to have it slam again as the coach tipped to the opposite side. Chastity was flung toward the lower side and blindly grasped for Regan's arm as she slipped further and further down, trying desperately to keep from forcing the coach over.

"Jump clear, understand? Out, away, as far as you can."

The coach was balancing itself again as he screamed at her. But the tremendous speed and the terribly rough ground made it bob about like a wild stallion with a burr under his saddle. Before she even realized what was happening, the door was swinging open, and a hand on her rump was thrusting her firmly from the coach. And then she was falling, tumbling about in hot, sandy soil, which scraped and tore at her gloved hands as she lifted them to cover her face.

For what seemed like a long time she lay there unconscious, only gradually becoming aware of the sun's glare and of a voice she didn't recognize repeating her name.

"Miss Morrow? Miss Morrow? Are you all right?"

His voice sounded far away at first, and only by straining could Chastity see a blurry outline above her. Someone was lifting her shoulders and shaking her, and with the movement she felt the sting of countless bruises. Every muscle in her body was stiff with tension, and her head was throbbing in frantic rhythm with her heartbeat.

"Are you all right, Miss Morrow?" he repeated as he ran his fingers firmly along a tear in her sleeve, flexing her elbow.

"O—oh . . ."

"Does that hurt? It's just a sprain, and it doesn't seem to be a bad one. . . ." His fingers moved down her arm to test her wrist until she snatched it away, groaning with pain and finding her strength much diminished with the sudden move. Undaunted, Regan began his ministrations on her ankles. The man's familiar manner annoyed Chastity to no end. He was handling her like a horse being inspected before an auction, and she certainly didn't appreciate being touched in such a cold, offhanded way. When his hands moved to flex her knee, she promptly pushed him away with a well-placed foot.

He met her angry scowl with a look of surprise, then shrugged his lack of interest, rose, and began to walk away. With the realization that he meant to leave her, Chastity was outraged. Her head cleared instantly and her eyes flashed with righteous indignation. "Mr. Spencer!"

He half-turned to face her, with a good distance already separating them.

"You can't possibly mean to leave me here like this!"

Regan raised a single brow and narrowed his eyes.

"You're free to come along if you like," he stated tersely. "But I'm not waiting." He turned away again and began to walk.

Chastity's eyes widened in dismay as he took step after step without a backward glance. She stared after him in amazement. He actually meant to leave her here in the middle of nowhere! She scrambled to her feet and ran to catch up with him, her temper festering wildly in the midday heat. To think that she had actually offered to share her lunch with this—this scoundrel!

She paused for half a second and tried to catch her breath, noticing for the first time that Regan's lengthy strides followed the tracks of the runaway coach. Well, it certainly made good sense to follow it, to recover what they could in the way of supplies, and hopefully to ride the rest of the way into Carlin. The stage couldn't possibly have gone on much further at that wild speed. With any luck at all there would be at least one horse still able to carry a rider, even after the strenuous workout they'd endured this morning.

Chastity's muscles began to cramp after just fifteen minutes as a result of trying to keep up with Regan. She forced her legs to go on and on, straining, aching, wondering just how far she could go before she collapsed. It seemed they had walked for hours, over acres and acres of land barren but for sagebrush and tumbleweed. Then finally, as she followed Regan over a slight grade, her eyes caught sight of the stagecoach, overturned and smashed against a large rock formation. A few buzzards already circled the wreckage in greedy anticipation, but Chastity took no notice of them. What did catch her eye was the movement nearby—one of the horses had survived!

It was much easier to cover the next stretch now that an end was in sight. Besides lunch, there were canteens in the stagecoach, and Chastity was starting to feel weak from thirst as well as hunger. The last hundred yards or so Chastity actually ran. She thought of the canteens filled with water, the lunch she had ordered packed in Elko, and an end to the walking that was nothing less than torture. While still several yards short of the wreckage, Chastity abruptly stopped. All at once her mind registered what it was her eyes were seeing.

The coach had bounced off a hill of solid rock, crushing and mangling two of the horses beneath its battered frame. Another horse also lay dead, his finely muscled body twisted obscenely, his stomach split open by the sidebar of the coach. Blood and flesh lay spattered on everything nearby. The only sign of life came from the fourth horse, who jerked convulsively and filled the eerie silence with a pitiful whining sound. He had stumbled and been dragged along until most of the skin and muscle had been worn away from his legs and the underside of his belly. As her eyes fixed on him in horrible fascination, she felt the bile rising in her throat. She clasped a hand to her mouth and turned away, shivering with fear and revulsion.

The sight stopped Regan too, but only for a moment. If Miss Morrow had never had to cope with anything like this before, if she had been pampered and sheltered and knew nothing of the endless destruction of this world, then he envied her such innocence. He sighed impatiently and led her to a spot of shade, ordering her to wait until he retrieved the necessary supplies.

It seemed an eternity before a crack of gunfire put an end to the horse's agony, and Chastity sank weakly to her knees at the sound. A few moments later Regan returned to her and offered her a drink from one of the canteens. She stared at him in blank silence until he lifted it to her lips; then she greedily drew several long gulps from it before Regan stopped her. "That's enough," he said brusquely, assuming a distant air of authority, and reclaimed the flask. "I'm not sure how far we've strayed from the trail, so we've got to go easy until we get back to the river." He replaced the cap with unnecessary precision, pointedly avoiding her tear-stained face.

"Are you all right?"

She bit her lip hard and nodded, struggling for composure and not quite succeeding. "I—I'm sorry," she forced herself to say. "I—I never saw anything like—"

"Never mind," he cut her off. "We've about four hours of

daylight left. I want to reach the river by nightfall so that we'll be near a water source the rest of the way. I was able to salvage two canteens and some of the lunch you brought from Elko. . . ." He repositioned his dusty black Stetson further back on his head and examined the battered Winchester rifle that had belonged to the dead driver. "With any luck at all we'll make it to Carlin by early tomorrow."

He picked up his parcels, including one of his two leather cases, and for a second time that day he turned and walked deliberately away from her. Again Chastity took up mutely behind him, anxious to leave the site of the wreckage and more intrigued than ever by the man she followed. She had known immediately that he was different from other men. He said little, did as he pleased, and always looked out for his own interests first. He had learned to survive, Chastity thought, in the same selfish world as she. And, she admitted with a twinge of annoyance, he was the first man ever to have totally aroused her interest without displaying a shred of the same in her.

As she hurried behind him, Chastity raised her chin and squared her shoulders. That was a situation she definitely intended to see rectified.

Chapter 2

They sighted the river just before nightfall and camped within the sound of its current. Before daylight was lost, they gathered dried sagebrush to use for kindling a fire and shared a small portion of the food recovered from the wrecked stage. When Regan had finished eating, he sighed and propped his leather suitcase against a rock to support his back, tilting his hat low on his brow and thoughtfully fingering the rifle, which lay beside him. Damn, he was tired! He'd be sleeping well tonight in spite of this hard ground.

Chastity removed her traveling jacket and folded it into a neat square pillow as she attempted to find a comfortable position for the night. It had been a terribly long day, every joint in her body was aching, and her face had been burnt during the long hours of walking in the sun. But it was a troubled mind that kept her from sleeping, the countless frustrations which had piled atop one another in the past twenty-four hours. She wanted to be home. She wanted to see her father. She couldn't wait to see him, to fly into his thick, muscular arms and tell him about all the terrible things she'd endured. Even the thought of facing Deborah did not seem so bad anymore. She sighed softly and pressed her palms together to make a firmer pillow for her head. In the weak, flickering light of a dying fire she could see Regan's face, so handsome, so aloof, so unreadable. If he had been a different kind of man, he might have been more concerned about her comfort, would have seen to it before his own. She frowned thoughtfully, recounting the numerous attempts she'd made at conversation, the way he'd sidestepped answering even the vaguest questions, and the way he never returned those questions. He simply had no interest in talking with her, and he certainly hadn't wanted to divulge even the slightest clue as to who he was or where he had come from. She knew only that he was on his way to Virginia City, and that he had recently acquired quite a bit of mining stock. She had waited for him to mention the name of her father's mine, but it had never come up in their brief conversation. She stifled a yawn and once again her eyes wandered to his dark, handsome face, softer now in repose. The ground was already cold and uncomfortable, and for some strange reason she remembered the feel of his hands on her shoulders, the familiar way he had touched her earlier in the day. She began to wonder what it would be like to be held in Regan's arms, to be sheltered and warmed by that firm, masculine body. She closed her eyes and forced away the feeling. Tomorrow was another day, and there would be ample time for figuring out this man named Regan Spencer.

Chastity awoke at daybreak with a ravenous hunger. She was in the habit of eating a hearty breakfast, which she had missed for two days running now, and somehow the meager slice of dried-out roast beef and hard piece of bread Regan allotted her only made her hungrier. She grimaced as she washed down the last dry morsel with water from the canteen.

"Do you think we'll make it to Carlin by lunch—er, that is, noon?" she amended with some embarrassment.

"We should." He glanced at the morning sky, which was thick with pink-tinged gray clouds.

"I hope it doesn't rain," she said aloud, echoing his thoughts as he grunted and gathered up his leather case and rifle.

He took to the path along the green-gray river with Chastity close behind him, following in the footsteps of countless travelers who had come west via the Humboldt Trail. Now and again there were signs of others' passings,

names chipped crudely on the faces of rocks, cattle skulls
bleached white by the sun, graves marked by neat piles of
stones. Chastity thought of the scores of stories she'd
heard about this very trail, about the days before the railroad. Even her father spoke now and again about his journey from St. Louis to the Carson Valley, remembering
with pride that he had faced the unknown and triumphed
before the railroad had conquered this land of sun and
sand and tumbleweed and destroyed the mystery of its
vast emptiness.

After just an hour of walking, Chastity's eyes lifted reluctantly toward the sky. Shards of lightning were bursting in the clouds, and the wind was thrashing wildly over
the coarse, meager turf. Even before the rain began, Regan turned toward higher ground in search of some kind of
shelter. There were no trees anywhere, only hills of solid
rock and boulders piled one atop another, forming eerie
shapes and shadows as the sky exploded with light, then
darkened again. As the rain began in a heavy torrent,
they were forced to seek shelter in a small hollow between
two gigantic rocks which offered scarcely any protection
from the driving rain. Regan instinctively pulled Chastity
closer as the storm broke furiously about them, shaking
the earth beneath their feet as the thunder cracked and
rumbled and boomed. After an ear-shattering clap exploded directly above their heads, Chastity suppressed a
shudder of fear and realized, as Regan's fingers dug into
the flesh of her arms, that he was doing the same. In spite
of her fear and discomfort and weariness, the realization
of his closeness brought a rush of other sensations totally
foreign to her. His hard chest and masculine arms brought
a warm tingling to her breast, an excitement that was far
more pleasurable than anything she'd ever felt before.
How different this was from the clumsy embraces of other
men, embraces she'd quickly slipped from with a feeling of
revulsion. How different this was from anything she'd
even imagined or expected—and how much more wonderful! Long moments later when the rain stopped and the
sky seemed to brighten, Chastity sighed and lifted her
blue eyes to smile at Regan, fully expecting him to brush

his lips tenderly against hers. She would shyly break away from the kiss, of course, and blush furiously as any modest young woman would do. She felt a surge of elation as his eyes lingered on her full, perfect mouth, as his arms tightened about her, pressing her soft woman's flesh more intimately against his masculine frame. But as he tilted back her head and his blue-gray eyes darkened with a hunger she had never seen in a man's eyes before, she suddenly realized that he was playing a very different kind of game—a dangerous one. His mouth was lowering slowly toward hers when she suddenly gasped and twisted free, her cheeks coloring hotly and her breath coming short and labored though she didn't quite know why. She turned away from him in embarrassment.

Regan scowled as she backed away from the corner she'd been so eager to work herself into. He was fully aware of the games she was accustomed to playing and angry at himself for having been the least bit tempted to play along. She was bound to have a father or a brother or uncle or even a scorned suitor ready to kill the first man who touched her. She was a temptation he could not afford right now, not with the future he intended to build.

After a moment of calming herself, Chastity fixed a smile to her face and turned back to face him. "I—I love the air after a storm," she said softly, hoping that somehow she still held the advantage.

"Well, I hope you enjoy walking in the mud as much," he muttered irately. He abruptly stepped from the shelter and tested the ground outside, leaving Chastity frowning after him, wondering how she had managed to make him so angry. He was marching through the mire even faster than before, heading back toward the Humboldt River, and with a sigh of resignation she was forced to follow as quickly as she could. The incident had left her totally bewildered and emotionally drained. Regan Spencer had not acted at all like one of her proper suitors from St. Louis. And now she was left to wonder what had stirred all those delicious tingling sensations in her, and exactly what his eyes had been so hungry for.

The sky cleared partially, then clouded over again just

after noon. Its mass of shadowy clouds robbed the landscape of its rich brown-gold hues, blurring rock and grass
and soil into a drab, lackluster sepia. The air became
sticky, heavy with the promise of more rain, while the
mud from the morning's storm made walking messy and
all the more laborious. Large clods of mud clung tenaciously to their shoes, making each step more difficult
than the last. By this time, Chastity's feet were feeling the
effects of the long hours of walking. Blisters had formed on
her soles at the heel and on her smallest toes. It was a real
struggle to ignore the constant irritation, but she held her
tongue, sensing that Regan was already in a foul humor.
She gathered the bulk of her skirt to the side and lifted it
higher, frowning at the splotches of mud which had ruined
its fine new fabric. Several tendrils of her normally perfectly kept hair blew freely about her face; her jacket was
torn at the shoulder seam and had lost a button somewhere along the way; and her brand-new high button
shoes, nearly double their size with mud, were causing her
feet excruciating pain. She sniffed to hold back a tear and
impatiently brushed away a strand of hair that had blown
into her eyes. Regan had not even turned around to be certain that she was still following him. His new black suit
was also mud splattered and rumpled looking, but his posture was every bit as erect as when they'd started out, and
his stride was so arrogant and sure that she knew he
wasn't suffering nearly as much as she was. His travel attire and leather shoes were far better suited to absorbing
the rigors of walking than hers, she thought bitterly as
she hobbled after him, treading as lightly as possible under the circumstances and favoring her instep to avoid a
throbbing blister. Suddenly her foot caught the edge of a
wet patch of grass and caused her to slip and plunge head-
long into the slushy mess with a precipitate splat. At the
sound, Regan did an abrupt about-face and struggled to
keep from laughing at the sight. He came to help her to
her feet, gave her his kerchief so she could wipe off her
face, then turned away and started walking once more.

"I can't go any further!" she screamed after him. "Do
you hear me? I just can't!"

Regan muttered a low curse and continued walking, but only a few steps further. Then he bit his lip and scowled, wishing that his conscience would permit him to leave Miss Morrow right where she was. But something wouldn't let him do that, not after the hours and hours she'd trudged along behind him without complaint. He had thought himself capable of just about anything, but he wasn't capable of this. Reluctantly he returned to her side and pulled her hands away from her face. "What's the matter now?"

"I can't go on any further. It's my feet."

Regan tilted his hat further back on his head to contemplate her mud-caked shoes. They looked no worse to him than the rest of her at the moment. "What's the matter with your feet?"

"These shoes! They've worn my feet raw. They're not made for walking."

"Then take them off," he snapped at her.

Chastity's jaw slackened at the order, but the pain was so unbearable that she hobbled over to the nearest rock, took a seat, and numbly obeyed. She gingerly pulled the shoes from her feet, groaning at the sight of several blood-stains on her white cotton stockings. Regan did his best to hide his shock.

He swallowed hard and forced a casualness into his tone. "They aren't so bad. But you're better off without those shoes. Try it barefoot for a while. We've only about two miles or so left to go. You can make it if you put some extra effort forth."

Chastity searched his blue-gray eyes, but the expression she encountered assured her that he was serious. She flung one of her shoes angrily at his head, but, weighted as it was with mud, it fell short of its target. "I've been putting extra effort forth for the past three hours! If walking without shoes is such a marvelous idea, why don't you try it?" she screamed.

"Because you're the one with the sore feet!" he tossed back at her every bit as hotly. He let out a long breath through clenched teeth, which seemed to calm him considerably. "The way I see it, you have two choices. You can either try it barefoot for a while, or wait here until I send someone back for you."

She glared at him for a moment, then sent the other shoe flying at the same target as the first. This one also missed by a fair margin, but she felt some satisfaction when a bit of mud splattered on the brim of his black Stetson. She lifted her chin and lowered her feet into the thick muck with comical grace, causing Regan to turn away to hide a smile of wry admiration. She strode haughtily past him, ignoring his amused grin and resolving to walk the rest of the way into Carlin on her own if it killed her. It almost did.

Her feet did feel better for the lack of shoes, and the mushy ground was actually soothing, but it was also slippery. She was constantly sliding about, clutching at Regan's arm to keep from falling until he begrudgingly placed it about her waist and let her set the pace for the remainder of the journey.

The tiny town of Carlin could not have seemed more beautiful to Chastity had the simple frame buildings been formed in marble and the mud-rutted streets paved in gold. They found accommodations at the small hotel on Main Street, where the manager, with a wrinkle of his long, thin nose, demanded full payment in advance. Though the man's condescending attitude infuriated Chastity, she had to admit that neither she nor Regan appeared to be a good credit risk in their present condition. Both of them immediately ordered hot baths (for which the innkeeper charged them the unheard-of price of two dollars!), and Chastity sent at once for a seamstress, intending to dispose of her ruined clothing the moment it was off her back.

Four hours and twenty dollars later, Chastity descended the stairs with the arrogant step of a princess, willing away the hurt in her feet and noting that the innkeeper followed her every move as she approached his desk.

"Has the gentleman who arrived with me this afternoon gone to dinner yet?" The innkeeper did not answer, and when Chastity raised her eyes she found him still gaping. "Sir?"

"Uh . . . yes! Yes, he is. That is, he has. Er . . . the dining room is that way, miss . . ." He swept his arm to the right, toward a narrow, dimly lit hallway, upsetting the hand bell on the counter in the process. He was still fumbling about with the bell when Chastity murmured her gratitude and stepped daintily in the direction he had indicated, contentedly smiling with the knowledge that his eyes were still upon her.

Regan was one of three men in the dining room, a room that a score plus five persons would have filled to capacity. She paused at the threshold, taking in his crisp black suit and snow white linen shirt, and waiting until she had his full attention before she joined him at his corner table. He assisted her into a chair and resumed his own seat, then contemplated her steadily for a long moment.

"If there is one quality you are possessed of, Miss Morrow," he mused aloud, "that quality is resilience."

"I shall take that as a compliment, Mr. Spencer," she returned sweetly, daring to match his direct gaze.

"It was meant as one." He smiled leisurely into her eyes, toying with the bait she was once again dangling in front of his nose. At the moment he was very tempted.

"I'm absolutely famished!" she announced with a roll of her large blue eyes. "Have you eaten yet?"

"I was just about to order." He handed her a placard scrawled with the list of three available meals and their cost. "I'm having the beef stew. The woman told me it's the best item on the menu."

Chastity instinctively scanned the room for "the woman" to whom Regan referred. Her curiosity was satisfied when a portly middle-aged woman in a worn gingham dress entered with two steaming platters of food and placed them rather clumsily before the two men who occupied the table at the far side of the room. Chastity's blue eyes brightened at the sight. The hefty woman waddled over to their table and took their order for dinner, then returned quickly with a bottle of what appeared to be red wine. Regan poured two glasses of the liquid and proposed a toast to their adventure along the Humboldt Trail, and Chastity responded by eagerly raising her glass. She smiled and eyed Regan winningly as she took a sip of the wine. But her expression promptly tightened when she tried to swallow it. It was by far the strongest and most bitter liquid she had ever tasted. She cleared her throat and swallowed hard several times, trying to rid her mouth of its numbing effect so that she might take advantage of Regan's improved mood. "Well," she said brightly, "it looks as if you'll be in Virginia City within another day or two."

He nodded and sipped thoughtfully at the bad wine. She wondered how he could even swallow the stuff! "As will you, Miss Morrow. Tell me . . . why are you going to Virginia City?"

Chastity raised her brow and gave him a teasing smile. She had finally succeeded in drawing him into a conversation. Now to further her advantage. "Why do you think, Mr. Spencer?"

He placed his wine on the table and let his forefinger test the worn edge of the heavy glass. "I think . . . that you are planning to find a rich husband there."

Chastity's mouth dropped open in surprise, then clamped shut in anger. "If I were looking for a husband, Mr. Spencer," she said through clenched teeth, "which I most certainly am not, I would not find it necessary to travel all the way to Virginia City to get one!"

"That, Miss Morrow, is perfectly obvious to me. However, a rich husband is a bit more difficult to catch than a poor one, especially in these days of depression and ruin. Even such a lovely woman as yourself might find it necessary to travel in search of such a rare prize."

Chastity's eyes burned with her rising temper. "I am not the type of woman who would marry a man merely for the sake of his money!"

He seemed amused at having so easily ruffled her feathers. "Then why would you marry a man, Miss Morrow?"

"For love, of course," she told him promptly.

"And why would a man want to marry you?"

Chastity's eyes widened with embarrassment as she

caught the insinuation in his question. Everyone knew why men married, or at least everyone had a fairly good notion. But no gentleman would ever refer to such an unspeakable subject, particularly in the company of a young lady he hardly even knew. "I—I would hope that—that the gentleman would love me as well," she stammered after several moments, her cheeks burning with a painful blush.

"I would hope so too, Miss Morrow," he returned with a mocking smile tugging at his handsome mouth.

They were served their meal and ate in silence. Momentarily, Chastity had lost her desire to converse with Regan after the turn their brief conversation had taken. She nibbled sullenly at the bland food and flashed sidelong glances at the man who had caused her to lose her appetite, unable to fathom the reasons for his disinterest and growing all the more interested in him precisely because she didn't understand.

"The train will be here early tomorrow morning," he said, having cleaned his plate of food and placed his napkin on the table, "so I would suggest retiring directly after dinner." He paused to toy with the cork, which lay to one side of the bottle of wine. "I wired Elko about the stagecoach. They will send whatever baggage they can recover to Virginia City when the track's repaired. I told them the freight charges would be paid on arrival."

Chastity forced a smile, deciding to forgive his former rudeness. "Thank you, Mr. Spencer." She expected him to smile in return, but he did not. She watched him as he tapped the cork on the tablecloth and rolled it about beneath his finger. "Tell me, Mr. Spencer. What do you intend to do when you get to Virginia City?"

Regan set the cork aside and removed a long, thin cigar from the breast pocket of his coat. He raised a brow and waited for Chastity's nod of approval before he lit the cigar and took a lengthy draw on it. Then he met her deep blue eyes with a convincing lift of his chin. "I intend to become a wealthy man."

Chastity's mouth twisted skeptically. She had assumed that he was already wealthy, judging from his clothing and his mannerisms. "I don't think you're cut out to wield a pick, Mr. Spencer . . ."

"You are quite perceptive, Miss Morrow."

". . . and besides, the last I heard, miners were making only four dollars a day for their toils. Excellent wages these days, but not the stuff of which fortunes are made."

"You are also very well informed." Regan flicked an ash carelessly to the floor and drew another puff on his cigar while Chastity waited in silence. "There have been rumors about new bonanzas in several mines on the lode . . . particularly in the Consolidated Virginia. The man I met was a miner, and he swore that he'd seen it himself—the richest vein of silver in the whole lode. He said that it's a well-kept secret, but once it's out, the stock is bound to soar."

"There are always rumors being circulated about one mine or another," she scoffed.

He lifted the cork again and pretended to examine it closely, not knowing why he suddenly wanted to convince Chastity that he would leave Virginia City a wealthy man, not knowing why he wanted to tell her anything at all. "I've heard they struck silver ore two months ago, that ever since they've been bringing it up through an adjoining shaft . . . tons of it."

"And you believe that?" She couldn't hide her disappointment. Everyone in Virginia City speculated in mining stocks at one time or another, and nearly everyone who speculated eventually lost. To believe a miner's story was to be unbelievably gullible, and Chastity had no doubt that Regan would soon be wielding a pick or, worse, lighting the explosives used in the mines just to earn his passage out of town.

He placed the cork on the table and flicked another ash to the floor. It irritated him that Miss Morrow thought him a fool. He was certainly not one. He had studied the man's face long and hard before he'd accepted those stock certificates and the story he'd told, and he was certain that the man had not lied. "I believe it."

"Well, I wish you luck with your stock, Mr. Spencer," she told him flippantly. "But I certainly wouldn't get my hopes up. Unfortunately, those who speculate usually lose."

"And does that include you, Miss Morrow?"

A puzzled frown tugged at her brow. "I have never taken an interest in mining stocks."

"I wasn't referring to mining stocks," he countered quickly. "Your speculations concerning men." He took the cork and stuffed it abruptly back into the bottle. "I wonder if you've ever lost at your game, and if so, how much," he said arrogantly.

Chastity rose to her feet and tossed her dinner napkin on the table, then instantly showed him her back. "I wish you luck in your speculations, Miss Morrow," he called after her as she marched from the dining room. "But I certainly wouldn't get my hopes up. Unfortunately, those who speculate usually lose."

Chapter 3

Jonathon Stoneworth's dark brown eyes narrowed slightly at his first sight of the train, slowly chugging its way toward Virginia City Station. He wore a crisp beige business suit, perfectly tailored to his broad shoulders and chest, concealing the lean, well-defined muscles of powerful limbs and giving him a properly sober, professional appearance. His thick dark hair, tousled by mountain breezes now, framed a chiseled masculine face with straight nose, an angular chin, and a perfectly crafted, sensuous mouth. But it was an arresting pair of deep brown eyes accentuated by even darker, masculine brows that gave his face a certain indefinable strength, a magnetism complemented by every other feature. Those eyes, both alert and cool even under fire, reflected a rare blend of self-confidence and sensitivity and were marked with a maturity seldom found in a man of only a score of years and nine. His broad shoulders straightened and he cocked his chin the slightest bit. His arm muscles strained against the suit coat he wore and his brow furrowed in anticipation as the red and copper engine drew its long line of cars closer to their final destination. A part of him was anxiously looking forward to Miss Morrow's arrival, he admitted silently, his mouth suddenly hinting at a reckless smile. In spite of everything he'd heard about her, or perhaps because of everything he'd heard, he could hardly wait to meet Samuel Morrow's only daughter, even though there was good cause for him to anticipate some kind of trouble. After all, Deborah had painted a picture of her stepdaughter that resembled something of a cross between a wildcat and a shrew. Quiet, patient, peace-loving Deborah who got along so well with everyone hadn't gotten on at all with Samuel's daughter. That alone alerted Jonathon to the fact that Chastity's homecoming might add a further strain on an already worrisome situation. Samuel, on the other hand, had spoken of his only child with the blind devotion of a father whose daughter had been away for nearly two years. He had spoken of Chastity as if she were an angel, though even he frowned now and again and admitted that she was a "troubled child." The paradox had definitely aroused Jonathon's curiosity.

Jonathon's smile faded as he watched the train pull to a stop before the platform where he and Deborah waited, and he found himself remembering his own arrival in Virginia City less than two years before. He had been working for Nevada's senator, Bill Stewart, as an aide and courier of sorts, but he'd had enough of the glamour and intrigue of Washington, D.C., and enough of traveling as well. It seemed almost as if fate had led him here, and a single walk down C street convinced him to stay. Virginia City, Nevada, was a place quite unlike any other. There was a kind of restlessness in everyone's determined stride, a rhythmic madness in the constant clatter of stamping mills, hissing of huge hoisting works, whistles blowing at every hour, and muffled explosions from deep within the earth. The leading citizens of Virginia City made no claims to lengthy bloodlines or insignificant ties to royalty. They were Irish and Welsh and Mexican and German, Catholic, Protestant, and Jewish; not only the sons of immigrants, but oftentimes immigrants themselves. Millionaires walked the streets unnoticed in their dusty denims and worn miners' boots. And they all had unfailing optimism, a tongue-in-cheek way of accepting life as it came, all the while believing that something better was just around the corner. Among them Jonathon felt like a boy again.

He'd been in town only a few weeks when he'd struck up a friendship with Samuel Morrow and was offered a job defending the Morrow Mine against a recent surge of counterclaims. And he suddenly knew that this was what he had been looking for and took Sam up on the offer. Samuel Morrow was a gruff old miner with a heart of gold and a head full of dreams, a man who reminded Jonathon very much of his own father. There had been an instant kinship between the two men, an understanding that went beyond anything Jonathon could explain. But he knew that he was tired of traveling, and he was beginning to realize that he needed roots. Virginia City was a place where he felt certain he could grow them. And he was needed here now, with Samuel's sudden illness, and he knew that he had made the right decision in staying. He had come to care deeply for the man who was now his employer and for Deborah, his wife. He placed a comforting hand on Deborah's shoulder and gave her a warm smile of encouragement.

Deborah did her best to return Jonathon's smile. She was grateful that he had come here with her, that he stood so firm and supportive by her side. But the past three weeks had been extremely difficult ones for her, and Deborah was not a woman who concealed her feelings easily. She could not forget for a moment that her husband was critically ill, or that his only daughter, who had never bothered even being civil to her, would be home in another few minutes. Deborah was not looking forward to her arrival.

Just before the train entered a long tunnel, Chastity glanced behind her in a last effort to locate Regan Spencer. He had made himself scarce since their dinner in Carlin, barely nodding a greeting when they chanced to meet on the train. That had been a blow that weighed heavily on Chastity's pride at first. But now, as the temporary darkness engulfed the passengers on the last leg of their journey, she lifted her chin and firmly turned her mind to far more important matters than a disinterested male. There were many more like him, she assured herself, though she wasn't quite sure that it was actually so. Regardless, her father would be at the station waiting for her to arrive, and that was all that really mattered to her now. He was all that had ever mattered.

Chastity felt a surge of pride as the red-painted locomotive, trimmed elegantly in polished copper, flew out of the darkened shaft and chugged its way to the top of a steep incline. The Virginia & Truckee Railroad, built to connect Virginia City with the transcontinental railroad at Reno, reflected the wealth and prodigality of the Comstock in its powerful engines, its luxurious private cars, its carpeted and silk-shaded canary yellow coaches. It was the V&T that transported the Comstock's ore to the stamping mills, and the milled product on to the Carson City Mint; and the V&T that brought machinery, lumber, and supplies back to Virginia City. The building of a railroad to reach a city on the side of a mountain was in itself an engineering feat. Between Virginia City and Carson City, a distance of only twenty miles, the parallel silver threads of track made the equivalent of seventeen complete circles as they squiggled up the rugged terrain, scaling to breathtaking mountainous heights and disappearing now and again through the nearly twenty-five-hundred feet of tunnels.

The V&T was only one of the technological miracles brought by the men who plundered Mount Davidson of its precious metals. Citywide gaslights had turned night into day, fine homes had replaced the tents and hovels of earlier years, and soon seven miles of pipe being laid from the Sierras would give Virginia's population an unlimited supply of clean, fresh water.

Chastity's blue eyes brightened as the train rolled into Gold Canyon and made its final climb toward Virginia City Station. She could not restrain a smile as the familiar collection of buildings and dumps flowed past her window. She was home! Her heart pounded as the train slowed and she smoothed her hair nervously, wishing that she could have worn one of her better dresses for the occasion instead of an outdated gown hurriedly altered by the seamstress in Carlin. She couldn't wait to see her father!

Virginia City Station was bustling with its usual Sunday afternoon activity, with sightseers and vacationers anxious to be home and businessmen departing for Monday morning appointments in San Francisco, which was a little over twelve hours away by rail. A cloud of steam rose in the air as the engine hissed to a stop and passengers began to pour from the narrow exits of the cars. Chastity was one of the first off the train, her dark blue eyes searching a sea of faces before pausing momentarily on Deborah and moving on in obvious disappointment. Her father had to be here! He just had to be! Unless—unless something was very wrong . . . Anxious now that the thought had occurred to her, she pushed her way through the crowd in Deborah's direction, winning angry glares from several persons who did not appreciate being shoved aside.

With all the poise she could summon, Deborah forced herself to smile as she extended her hand. "Welcome home, Chastity."

Chastity's eyes flicked over Deborah's hand, but she made no attempt to take it. "Thank you," she said stiffly. "Where's Father?"

Deborah slowly dropped her hand. She had prayed so long and hard that Chastity's feelings toward her would change. Obviously her prayers had not been answered. "This is Jonathon Stoneworth, Chastity. Mr. Stoneworth is a lawyer who has been working for your father for over a year now."

She ignored Jonathon's hand just as she had Deborah's. "Where's Father?"

The older woman swallowed hard and was visibly distressed by her stepdaughter's behavior. Jonathon immediately moved to assume command of the situation. "Your father is at home, Miss Morrow. He wasn't feeling well, and—"

"Wasn't feeling well?" she repeated numbly. "What do you mean? Is he ill? What's happened to him?" She was suddenly breathing hard, her heart pounding against her ribs, her lip trembling with fear.

"Everything is under control, Miss Morrow, I can assure you," Jonathon told her gently, trying to sidestep her questions until they were somewhere more private. "But we thought it unadvisable to tell him of your arrival this afternoon—"

"You thought it unadvisable?" she repeated, glancing from Jonathon to Deborah and back again. She realized at once that he had avoided her question, and that only made her more afraid. Unable to cope with the panic that was taking hold, she felt a sudden surge of anger at this stranger who seemed to know so much about her father and be in such control. "Since when do you make personal decisions for my father, Mr. Stoneworth?" she demanded. Her voice rose to the point where she was attracting the attention of the crowd.

"I will be happy to answer all of your questions, Miss Morrow," Jonathon responded with calm authority. "If you will please come with us to the carriage. The driver is waiting."

For an instant her blue eyes clashed with his brown ones. He was a handsome man, a man she might have flirted with under different circumstances, but in her present state of mind none of that registered. She only knew that the homecoming she had dreamed of for so long had been snatched from her, and this Stoneworth fellow who was so all-fired sure of himself seemed the only person she could blame. But he was right, it served no purpose to argue with the man in public, even if he had overstepped his boundaries as a mere employee of her father. Who did he think he was, making a personal decision for Samuel Morrow? She frowned again as a tingling of uncertainty and fear began at the back of her neck. Father must have been very ill for anyone to assume such power.

"How many bags did you have?" Jonathon was asking. "I'll get them for you."

"None," she returned tersely, noting with satisfaction that a muscle in his jaw was twitching with restraint.

"All right then," he said, forcing a pleasant inflection into his voice, "we'll leave without baggage."

He offered Deborah an arm, which she gratefully accepted, and Chastity followed them out of the station. Jonathon gently assisted her stepmother into the coach, while Chastity narrowed her eyes in suspicion. He seemed overly concerned with Deborah's welfare and that didn't set well with Chastity at all. Nothing Deborah ever did set well with Chastity, and if this man as a friend of hers . . . She stiffened as his hand took hold of hers to lift her into the coach. His fingers were long and lean, and there was a strength to those hands—and to his entire body, Chastity realized—that was cleverly concealed by his tasteful beige suit. Their eyes locked for a moment and she was struck by the steadfastness of those eyes, by the totally confident way they held hers and measured her. She bent him a chilly stare as he entered the carriage and took a seat opposite, next to Deborah. They jolted forward with the sudden onset of motion and Chastity looked long and hard at Jonathon Stoneworth. A lawyer, Deborah had said, but there were scores of young lawyers here on the Comstock and Jonathon seemed to be something more. Before he spoke to her again, his cool brown eyes gave her an intimate perusal, missing not the slightest detail of her appearance, she was certain. Jonathon Stoneworth was not a shy man by any means, and she was beginning to wonder if he was even a gentleman. Under any other circumstances she might have blushed, but she was far too upset at this point, far too anxious. And he was calm, so calm that it actually made her angry because it put her at a loss. She knew nothing about her father's illness, nothing at all about what was going on. And she was totally dependent on this—this friend of Deborah's to give her some explanation.

"I know that this comes as a shock to you, Miss Morrow," he began in a quiet, richly masculine voice, "but your father is quite ill. He has been confined to his bed for the better part of a month, and it was quite impossible for him to come to the station today."

Chastity shook her head, trying to deny the confident authority in his voice, not wanting to believe his explanation or, for that matter, anything he said. Her father couldn't be that ill! He was too strong and healthy, and she loved him too much! "If my father has been ill for as long as you say," she argued, "an illness so serious as to confine him to his bed, then why wasn't I notified immediately?

Deborah knew exactly where I was." Her eyes left Jonathon's face to rake over her stepmother accusingly. "I can only assume, Mr. Stoneworth, that you are greatly exaggerating his condition, and that you made a decision for him that you had no authority to make."

His dark eyes leveled on her for what seemed like a long time before he responded evenly. "I only wish that were the case, Miss Morrow. But I will not lie to you. Your father's condition, while much improved, is still quite critical. You were not notified earlier because all this came about so suddenly, and we had hoped that—" He hesitated, letting out his breath and giving a brief shake of his head. "There was nothing anyone could do. And since Deborah knew that you planned to come home within a few weeks anyway, we felt that sending you such distressing news in advance would only cause you undue worry . . ."

In spite of Chastity's rude behavior, the man's words were calm and benevolently spoken. But their meaning was only beginning to penetrate Chastity's initial anger. Critical . . . we had hoped . . . nothing anyone could do . . . The words echoed in her mind and the fear was clearly etched in her expression. "What exactly are you trying to say, Mr. Stoneworth?" she interrupted him. "What is wrong with my father?"

There was an uncomfortable silence for a long moment, and she noticed that Deborah was blinking back tears. She felt a sickening tightness in her stomach.

"Your father has led a very full and active life," Jonathon began, "but he is no longer a young man and his heart is no longer that of a young man. A few weeks ago, when he was on his way home from his office, he stopped halfway up the steps between C and B streets, unable to catch his breath. And then . . ." His troubled eyes met Deborah's and he hesitated.

"And then what?"

"And then he fainted . . . and fell."

Chastity's face drained of all color as her mind's eye pictured the terrible thing happening. She suddenly remembered the driver of the coach she had hired in Elko, and the way he had seemed so well just before he . . . She closed her eyes and swallowed hard. Her entire world was suddenly falling apart. Her father was all she had, the only person she had ever loved.

"He was very lucky to have survived such a tumble at all," Jonathon went on, "but particularly without doing any irreparable damage. Dr. Perkins was amazed that he had no broken bones, only a few sprains and lots of bruises."

"He's going to be all right then?" she pressed hopefully.

Again Jonathon exchanged a quick glance with Deborah before he answered. "He sustained no serious injury in the fall. But the damage done to his heart is extremely serious. As Dr. Perkins explained it to us, a part of his heart has simply stopped working, and will never work again. That leaves all the more work for the rest of the heart. You can see why it is so very important for him to recover his strength gradually, and to remain calm and quiet."

"Yes . . . ," she mumbled distantly. She fixed her eyes on her hands, now primly folded in her lap.

For a long time Jonathon watched her, wondering what thoughts must be going through her mind. He could not help but notice the loveliness of that perfect face, so drawn now with concern for her father. She was by far the most beautiful woman Jonathon had ever seen, and he certainly hadn't expected that. She dressed and wore her hair so simply, but that only accentuated the dramatic color of her eyes, the softness of her almost silver hair. His eyes lingered on her flawless skin and dark blue eyes before taking in the soft, full line of her mouth, the ivory column of her throat, the perfect, feminine curves suggested beneath the plain cotton gown. For a long moment the only sounds to break the silence were the clip-clop of the horses' hooves and the crunch of gravel under the carriage wheels.

The coach turned off Taylor and onto Howard Street and rolled to a stop in front of the fine house. Chastity hurried up the steps to the main entrance, not bothering to wait for Jonathon or Deborah. She entered the front foyer, and with a steadying hand on the curved mahogany banister, she mounted the stairs, chin high, eyes fastened straight ahead. Only as she reached the closed door of her father's room did her courage flag. She hesitated. For a split second she wanted to turn and run away. But Chastity would never admit to being such a coward, and besides, where was there to run? Everything she cared about was here, in this house. She stared at the door and swallowed hard before she rapped on it sharply. She relaxed a bit when the door was opened by a familiar figure. Sarah had been the Morrows' housekeeper and cook for as long as Chastity could remember, and her round, ruddy face hadn't changed in all the time Chastity had been away. Sarah's eyes lit up with elation and she flung generous arms around Chastity for an instant, then gasped and clasped a hand to her mouth, drawing back in embarrassment. She was a servant, after all, and Chastity was a lady now, that was obvious at a glance.

Chastity gave her a half smile, her eyes flicking over the small, plump woman with a good deal of affection. She had always been fond of Sarah, even though Chastity's childhood years had been stormy ones touched by many differences of opinion and the clashing of wills. Sarah had a very clear but rather narrow view of what was right and what was wrong, and she had never minced words as to her opinion of Chastity's behavior. But Sarah cared for the girl more deeply than Chastity ever suspected, and was devoted to her in spite of her disapproval of many of the things she did. She followed the younger woman's eyes as they strained to make out her father's face in the darkened room. "He's restin' now, Miss Chastity. But he ought t' be awake soon," she whispered. "I'll leave you for a while if you like. If you need anything, I'll be just downstairs."

The shades were drawn tightly and the room was dark; Chastity's eyes were slow to adjust to the lack of light. She approached the bed timidly, her eyes blinking painfully at the sight of his pale face, heavily bandaged on the left side. He seemed so different from the man she remembered, so much older and more vulnerable. She took a seat in the chair next to his bed and waited, hardly believing the changes in him. Had she been gone so very long? she wondered. And had he missed her even a fraction as much as she had him?

Samuel's eyes lifted for a moment. He sighed and closed them again, turning his head toward the chair before he forced them open once more. Either Deborah or Jonathon was usually sitting there whenever he woke. As he squinted to make out the stranger who occupied the chair, he felt soft, warm fingers encircle his hand and lift it from the bed. He stared at the woman's face, so fair and lovely and delicate, at the silver-yellow hair coiled demurely at the nape of a long, swanlike neck. A thousand memories crowded his mind, and for a moment he was sure that he was still dreaming. "Ruth?"

"No, Papa. It's me. Chastity." Her throat was tight and burning as she forced out the words. "I'm home, Papa."

"Chastity?" He strained to see her better in the dim light. "Is it really you? Let in some light so that I can have a look at you!"

Chastity immediately dropped his hand and hurried to open the drapes and louvered blinds. She turned nervously so that he could view her, then smiled at the pleased expression on his face. His eyes were exactly as she remembered them. They hadn't changed at all since she was a little girl.

"They keep it real dark in here," he confided, "like night, even in the middle of the day. Dr. Perkins thinks it will help me to sleep."

"And does it?" she asked him with a curious raise of her brows. It was so unlike him to rest at all during the day; he had always kept himself so busy.

He snorted. "All I do is sleep!" he grumbled. Then he sighed and smiled at her. "Ah, Chastity. You're even prettier than your mother was at your age! You aren't my little girl anymore."

Her smile faded instantly and her eyes stung with tears. "Yes, I am!" she cried, running to lay her head upon his chest. "Yes, I am!"

He stroked her soft, silver-blond hair and remembered a hundred times in the past when he had done the same.

Yes, he thought wearily, she was still his little girl. She was crying openly now and he felt very close to tears himself. "I'm glad you've come home, Chastity. I've missed you so!"

"I missed you too, Papa. I—I didn't know about—what happened, or—or I would have—"

"I know. I know." He sighed, and his fingers lifted her chin. "Tell me all about your traveling," he said, eager to change the subject. "How are all the cousins? How is Aunt Susan? How is St. Louis?"

"St. Louis . . ." She sniffed and wiped her cheeks with the back of her hand. "St. Louis is green and wet and very boring. And the cousins are . . ." She paused for a bit, then giggled. "My cousins are just very boring! But I'll miss them, in a way. Not nearly as much as I missed this place, or you, of course."

He reached out to touch her cheek. "I'm so very glad you're home. Deborah has been burning the candle at both ends, and she really needs someone to look after her."

Chastity just barely kept a scowl from darkening her brow. "Deborah seemed fine to me."

"Well, she isn't fine. I'm worried about her," he said earnestly. Then he grinned and lifted a thickly bandaged arm. "Don't I look as if I need someone else to worry about?"

In spite of herself Chastity laughed, and his smile widened. "Tell me, Chastity . . . are there any special men in my little girl's life? Susan hinted as much in a letter a few months back."

"No one you would approve of," she teased. "But . . ." She frowned and nibbled thoughtfully at the tip of her finger. "As a matter of fact, there is one man in my life who's rather special. His name is Regan Spencer, and I met him on my way home from St. Louis."

"Spencer . . . Spencer . . . I don't believe I've heard of him."

Chastity told him that Mr. Spencer was a new arrival to the city, and then related a brief outline of her adventure with Regan, omitting most of the rather embarrassing details, including the fact that Mr. Spencer had shown no interest in her. ". . . and Mr. Spencer thinks he's going to get rich with a stack of stock certificates he recently acquired." She sighed with obvious disappointment. "He heard some story about a big strike in the Consolidated Virginia Mine, and he thinks it's going to be one of the biggest bonanzas of all."

"Well, he's in good company then. I've known John Mackay for a long time, and he and Jim Fair have got noses for sniffing out silver if there ever were any. I'll be very surprised if they don't come up with something from that mine of theirs. And Jonathon said the very same thing to me just the other day." His face brightened suddenly. "Have you met Jonathon yet?"

She bristled at her father's affectionate tone of voice when he mentioned the man's name. "I've met him," she said without enthusiasm. "And I wasn't at all impressed."

Samuel laughed a little at that, and Chastity was immediately angered and hurt at his light dismissal. "What are you laughing at?" she demanded.

"I'm sorry," Samuel returned with a grin that looked nothing like an apology. "It's just that you're the first person who *hasn't* been impressed with Jonathon. He's one of the brightest young men I've ever met."

She gave a snort and lifted her nose in the air. "Well, I don't see anything so wonderful as all that, Papa."

"You will, though," he insisted, "as soon as you know him a little better. He's a prince of a man, Chastity. And he's been almost like a son to me these past months . . . and so wonderful to Deborah."

Chastity felt a large lump in her throat as an explosion of jealousy tore at her heart. She was Samuel's daughter, his only daughter, and she wanted her father to love and need her alone, just as she needed him. Her resentment for this stranger who had suddenly driven a wedge between herself and her father was growing stronger every moment. He had taken things over so completely in so short a time. Surely he had ulterior motives, she was thinking. Surely he wanted more than just a close relationship with her father . . . and Deborah. "Mr. Stoneworth seemed to me the type of man who would—would take advantage of your—your present situation, Papa," she suggested. "I—I don't know exactly what kind of things you allow him to do for you, but I think that you ought to be very careful about trusting him," she finished stiffly.

The smile left Samuel's face when he saw his daughter's sincerity. He patted her hand and spoke in earnest. "Chastity, believe me. Jonathon Stoneworth is honest to a fault. I know. I worked with him closely for over a year."

"A year is not so very long a time," she insisted, envious of the way he defended the man. "And besides, people change when you aren't watching over them, when you allow them to handle too much responsibility."

"Not Jonathon. He's as reliable as the morning."

Chastity rolled her eyes doubtfully. "You aren't in a position to know that for sure at this moment, Papa," she argued, upset that her father trusted the man so completely. "I think it might be better if you got rid of him. There are plenty of other lawyers around to handle any legal problems we have. And after all, I'm home now. I can help you to do whatever else needs to be done. Correspondence or errands . . ."

Samuel sighed and closed his eyes. A few years ago he might have bowed to Chastity's wishes and hired another lawyer to handle his affairs simply because she had asked him to. But in his present situation he could not even consider it. Jonathon Stoneworth was an excellent lawyer, but he had become far more these past months. He had taken complete charge of Samuel's affairs when he had been unable to do anything for himself, and considering the precarious state of his health even now, he couldn't afford to let him go. Neither Chastity nor Deborah was prepared to handle things if the Lord saw fit to take Samuel tomorrow, but Jonathon was capable, willing, and honest. The Comstock could be stripped of its silver, the stocks could tumble to a penny a share, but as long as Jonathon managed the Morrow money, Deborah and Chastity would want for nothing.

"Papa, did you hear what I said?"

He opened his eyes and stared long and hard at his daughter, now a beautiful young woman. She had blossomed, but she still had so much growing up to do! "Chastity, you don't understand. Jonathon has taken over all of my work, has run the office all by himself—"

"Do you mean he's had access to the mining company accounts?" she broke in, aghast. It was becoming all too clear that Stoneworth was in a position to do a great deal of harm, perhaps even to ruin her father.

"Of course he has. And he's even made a report on my behalf to the stockholders. He was in San Francisco for a special meeting just last week." Samuel did not mention that the meeting had been called expressly to discuss the state of his health, that quite a few stockholders had wanted to completely reorganize the company so that very little depended on Samuel Morrow anymore. It had been Samuel's greatest fear, and the fact that Jonathon had convinced them of his employer's ultimate recovery and of his own ability to run things in the interim had given Samuel yet another reason for feeling gratitude for Jonathon. "He's done a marvelous job, Chastity—"

"But you don't know that!" she countered, truly concerned now that her father could easily be taken advantage of. "You have no way of knowing if he's cheating you, if he's being dishonest."

Samuel let out a weary sigh and shook his head. If only Chastity could see for herself what a fine man Jonathon was, if only she knew how hard he worked, how cleverly he handled things . . . His eyes brightened at the thought. She could do exactly that!

"I'll make a bargain with you," he said slowly. "If you can find one discrepancy in Jonathon's records, just one, any evidence of his having misused a single dollar of my money, I promise to discharge him immediately."

Chastity frowned thoughtfully. It was not exactly what she wanted, but if she were to look, she was certain she could find something dishonest in his records.

"I'll make it easier for you," he continued when she hesitated. "I'll tell Jonathon that I want you to help with the bookkeeping. He's been talking about hiring someone to help him at the office anyway. After a few weeks of working there, you'll be able to spot an error right away. You always were quick at figures."

That settled it. Chastity nodded just as Sarah knocked at the door and entered with a tray of steaming broth. As her father complained about his limited menu the past few weeks, Chastity planted a kiss affectionately on his forehead and promised to have a long visit with him the following morning. She was certain that he would be all right, now that she was home. She could not bear to think otherwise. Everything would be back to normal very soon, she assured herself. And she would take care of everything for him until then . . . including the matter of Jonathon Stoneworth.

Chapter 4

When Chastity arrived at her father's C Street office at half past seven the following morning, she was surprised to find that Jonathon was already behind his desk, buried beneath several piles of paperwork. He rose as she entered the office, his eyes reflecting something akin to surprise as they flickered over her every bit as thoroughly as they had the day before.

"Good morning, Miss Morrow," he said finally with what seemed to Chastity a disgustingly arrogant nod of approval.

"Good morning, Mr. Stoneworth," she returned stiffly, lifting her chin a notch. "My father said that—"

"Yes, he told me you'd be working here now that you're home," Jonathon interrupted. "It's just that I didn't expect you so soon, after your long trip home—"

"I've fully recovered from my journey, Mr. Stoneworth," she cut in haughtily, feeling a good deal of satisfaction at having caught him off guard. "And I am quite anxious to put the day to good use."

His eyes drifted over her a second time, making her seethe inwardly. He met her icy stare with a half-amused grin. He'd wondered why she had asked Sam if she could work in the office. He still wondered, but at least it was clear that she really did want to work. Now if she was only as good with figures as Sam had assured him she was . . .

"I believe you are, Miss Morrow," he assured her, "and I suppose we ought to begin with an explanation of just how

everything works in this office." His tone became serious
as he proceeded with a simple but thorough explanation of
the functions of the office, beginning with the basic prem-
ise that profits obtained from the mined ore had to equal
or exceed the costs of operating the mine and processing
the ore. If not, the difference had to be made up in assessments to the various stockholders.

"The invoices alone add up to quite a bit of paperwork,"
Jonathon told her with a wry smile, lifting a stack of papers from his desk and allowing them to drop again. "And
they are all paid through this office and kept on file here."

Chastity nodded. The costs of operating a mine came as
no surprise to her. The early days of the simple prospector,
pick and shovel in hand, were over. The Comstock of the
1870s had become a center of mechanical and technological advances, and the cost was staggering. Millions of feet
of lumber were gobbled up by the mines to support the
shafts from cave-in; candles were burned by the thousands, explosives by the ton. And the deeper the miners
probed, the fiercer the problems they encountered. A constant battle against flooding in the mines caused huge
hoisting works to be put into service. (The new pumps recently installed in the Morrow boasted an astonishing
pumping capacity of ten million gallons a month!) Elaborate ventilation systems had been installed, though these
hardly began to alleviate the heat in the lower levels,
which commonly soared past one hundred degrees. Miners
were forced to work shorter hours, and the daily allotment
of ice now approached eighty pounds per man.

"The payroll for the miners is worked up here at the end
of every week," he went on. "The wages are tallied from a
list Michael Murphy compiles of the men and their hours,
and the payroll records are filed here. . . ." He opened a
wooden file drawer and withdrew the payroll sheet from
the week before. He watched her closely as she scanned it,
then met his eyes. There was a determination in those
eyes which Jonathon couldn't help but admire. There was
much more to Chastity Morrow, he realized, than just a
pretty face. He cleared his throat and forced his mind back
to business. Beyond the payroll and the invoices, there

were also constant letters of inquiry coming in from companies with claims of valuable innovations in mining machinery, all of which (since her father's illness) were shown to Michael Murphy immediately, who then decided which ideas merited further inquiry and perhaps a presentation at the next stockholders' meeting.

"For the past year the ore from the mine has been low-grade, which has barely covered the cost of mining and refining. I keep a daily tally of everything that's been paid out, and at the end of each month I figure that amount against the amount of money the mine has actually earned for itself. From there it's determined whether or not the stock will pay out or call for assessments from the stockholders." He paused for a moment. "Is all of that clear?"

"Very clear," she responded matter-of-factly. She studied his face, surprised that he had not explained things in the patronizing manner she'd expected.

"Then I suppose you're ready to go to work," he told her promptly, lifting a stack of papers from his desk and placing them in her hands. "These are invoices I finished paying out this morning just before you arrived." Chastity glanced at them, wondering just how early he had arrived to have done all this. "And here's a sheet of paper so that you can work up a total," he continued. "Let me know what you come up with before you file them away."

Without a moment's hesitation Chastity took a seat at her father's desk and proceeded to go through the bills one at a time, over thirty of them, entering each one carefully on the sheet of paper Jonathon had given her, then figuring the total. Less than ten minutes later she placed the sheet on Jonathon's desk with a self-satisfied arch of her brow. "You seem surprised, Mr. Stoneworth," she remarked as he lifted the paper to scan her work.

"Not at all, Miss Morrow," he returned coolly, meeting her eyes a half second later. "Astonished is what I am," he admitted, "as well as very pleased." He handed the papers back to her with a warm smile. "While you're filing the others, you can put this with the daily accounts."

She accepted the paper with some surprise, searching

his face. "You—aren't you going to double-check this figure?"

His lips curved with amusement as his eyes drifted leisurely over her trim form. "I already have, Miss Morrow." He casually lifted a second sheet of paper from his desk and handed it to her without taking his eyes from her face. She glanced down at it and found a list identical to the one she had compiled a few minutes before. He met her indignant scowl with a nonchalant shrug. "I worked up my own tally earlier . . . just in case."

"And do you intend to do everything twice now that I'm here, Mr. Stoneworth?" she demanded, her blue eyes narrowed.

"Not unless you feel it's necessary, Miss Morrow," he returned pleasantly but with a definitely challenging lift of his brow.

She glared at him but said nothing as she made to file the stack of invoices away.

"This afternoon," Jonathon announced a few minutes later, "you can begin work on the payroll . . ."

Working at her father's office with Jonathon proved much less of a trial than Chastity had originally envisioned. She expected the work to be tedious and was certain that Jonathon would fill her hours with trivial chores like running errands or filing away papers. She did do those things, but she was surprised at the "important" tasks Jonathon also delegated to her, and was pleased to see that he trusted her accuracy . . . after the first few days of double-checking. There was so much more work than Chastity had ever realized, and Jonathon was obviously a very capable employee in seeing that it was done. But she reminded herself continually that his diligence was all a fraud, that he was taking advantage of her father at this very moment, and that she was the only person in a position to prove it before it was too late.

She had been working at the office for almost two weeks before she got the chance she'd been waiting for. The moment Jonathon left for an appointment at the bank, she scurried across the room and searched frantically about in the top drawer of his desk until she located the key to the larger bottom drawer, where he kept the ledger for the mine. A smile of triumph touched her lips as she inserted the key in the lock, opened the drawer, and removed the large black book. She placed it carefully on the desk and excitedly flipped through the pages. Her smile faded. She scanned page after page of numbers penned neatly in Jonathon's distinctive handwriting. There were long rows, thousands of numbers. She had hoped to discover some glaring error in his book work even before he returned from the bank, but she suddenly realized how foolish she had been. It would take a lot of time and a lot of effort to check the pages and pages of neatly recorded entries. She gnawed at her lip and sighed as she closed the book and thoughtfully replaced it in the drawer. Of course, Jonathon was much too clever to be caught so easily. But he wasn't clever enough to fool her. If it took a little more time than she'd originally planned to find something, then—

Chastity hurriedly tossed the key into Jonathon's desk drawer and jumped to her feet, assuming what she hoped was a casual stance just as the door to the office opened. She relaxed a bit when she saw that it was a woman who entered and not Jonathon. All the same, she returned to her father's desk, which she had been occupying these past two weeks and stood facing the visitor.

The woman was tall and her form was more than ample, so that the tightly fitted bodice of her bright green gown displayed a good bit of cleavage even though its neckline was not at all daring. She might have been attractive at one time—it was difficult to tell with all the false color on her mouth and cheeks—but she had certainly never been a raving beauty, and her best years were most assuredly behind her. Chastity was taken aback by the woman's almost resentful stare, but she returned it evenly, not giving an inch.

"May I help you with something?"

The woman's gray eyes flashed as she lifted her brow. 'Who're you?" she demanded.

Chastity smiled with cold politeness. "I was about to ask you the very same question."

The woman scowled at the curt response and drew herself up as she tried to mimic the younger woman's polished speech. "I am Rhonda Bates."

Bates . . . Bates . . . Chastity had heard that name often enough, but she couldn't for the life of her remember the connection. "Chastity Morrow," she acknowledged with a slight nod.

Rhonda pursed her generous lips and let her gaze sweep over the entire length of Chastity's body, as if sizing up an opponent. She gave a slight shrug. "I came t' see Jon—that is, Mr. Stoneworth. Where is he?"

"He's out at the moment," Chastity told her, adding an icy smile, "but I'll be sure and tell him you stopped by, Miss Bates."

Rhonda's eyes narrowed to hostile slits. "It's Mrs. Bates," she corrected stiffly. "I'm a widow woman. And thank you, but no thank you. I'll wait." Rhonda turned away from Chastity and began to pace the office, peeling off a pair of white gloves while she pretended to study the framed engravings of the Morrow mineworks hung about the room.

Chastity glared at her for a moment, then took a seat at her desk and angrily tore open an envelope from the morning's mail. The people who filter through this office! she thought indignantly. She mentally recounted the steady stream of needy souls who had poured through the doors within the past two weeks. There had been Mrs. Catha, a proud but obviously destitute widow whom Jonathon had promptly enlisted to do his mending as a great favor to him, though of course he had paid her generously for her trouble. A few days later she had rushed in breathlessly to thank him for the position he had found for her at Roos Brothers, one of the town's better clothing stores. Then there had been Jim O'Rourke, the injured miner whose benefits from the miners' union had long since ceased, who had hemmed and hawed until Jonathon offered him a loan to carry his family over hard times. And then there had been little Joey something-or-other, who had been ac-

cused of stealing a pair of boots from Banner Brothers and
who had been dodging the sheriff for over a week before he
came by to see Jonathon. Jonathon had accompanied the
boy to the sheriff's office and spent over an hour clearing
up what he claimed was a misunderstanding. Chastity
had no doubt at all that he had paid for the missing boots
in the end. Even Sister Fredricka had stopped in, asking
for help with mending the roof at the orphanage. And
there was Lo Chin, the skinny Chinese boy who never actually came into the office, but appeared out of nowhere to
deliver Jonathon's laundry and tag after him like a
shadow, always smiling a toothy smile and bobbing up
and down like an empty bottle on a lake. Jonathon attracted people like a magnet, and not a one of them ever
had to beg him for a favor. He was ready to offer help at
the slightest suggestion that it might be needed, and he always made it seem as if the recipient were doing him a
favor. It was no wonder that he came to the office early
and stayed late nearly every evening. It was amazing that
he kept the place running at all with the constant inter-
ruptions, she thought as her eyes flicked over the woman
who flounced so comfortably about the office, waiting for
him to return. Chastity made up her mind to hold her
tongue until Jonathon arrived, but she also intended to let
him have a piece of her mind the moment Mrs. Bates left
the office. It was obvious to her, if to no one else in this
town, that he was doing all these "good deeds" to keep his
character above reproach, so that no one would suspect him
of using his present situation for his own gain. But Chastity knew better. And this was an office, after all, not a
charitable institution, she fumed.

It was several moments later when an unsuspecting
Jonathon opened the door to the office and stepped inside.
He was completely unprepared for the large woman in
bright green who flew at him and burst into tears. Jonathon stared at her dumbly before tossing a stunned glance
at Chastity, who was momentarily as shocked as he. Mrs.
Bates had seemed perfectly calm just a minute or two before. Jonathon took hold of the woman's shoulders and

backed away to a more proper distance. "Is there something wrong, Mrs. Bates?"

She covered her mouth with her hand and shook with even more dramatic sobs. "It—it's Joey!" she choked out. "He—he's run away . . ." Her voice broke off with a shrill wail. "Oh, my baby!"

"How long has he been gone?" Jonathon inquired calmly.

"Three days," she sniffled. "Three long days and three longer nights. He ain't been home since supper last Monday."

Jonathon threw a sidelong glance at Chastity, wishing that he could speak to Mrs. Bates in private. He didn't want to make her look foolish with someone looking on, but then, she was already doing a fair job of it herself. He cleared his throat in embarrassment. "Well—um—I really don't see why you're so upset, Mrs. Bates. I know for a fact that Joey's run away before. Several times, as a matter of fact. And he's been gone before for more than three days—"

"Yes," she broke in, "but this time's different! I know it! This time he—he's gone for good . . ." She burst into tears again and abruptly fell against him, nearly sending him to the floor in the process. Only by hurriedly clasping a hand to the edge of his desk did he manage to maintain his balance, but he was still in a quandary about how to handle Mrs. Bates with Chastity watching his every move.

"Something's happened t' him," Mrs. Bates said raggedly. "I—I can feel it."

"Well . . ." Jonathon swallowed hard, then his eyes brightened as his mind began to function. "Have you spoken with the sheriff? Perhaps he's—"

"The sheriff!" she shrieked in outrage. "You know how he feels about Joey! After he accused my innocent boy of stealing those boots without a shred of proof, why, he'd probably love to find what's left of Joey in some abandoned mine shaft!" She was suddenly hysterical again and groping insistently for Jonathon, though he cleverly managed to elude her by circling his desk. He seemed calm and logical all the while he backed away, making two full circles around the desk. He was, however, more than a little upset that Chastity was observing. He could hardly be as blunt as he needed to be with such an audience. He was already far too embarrassed for the woman, not to mention himself. "Mrs. Bates, I'm certain that Joey is all right. He's quite an independent boy and he likes to take off on his own every now and again, but he'll be back. Probably around dinnertime. Three days is about as long as a boy wants to go without dinner." She was still coming at him. "I—I would go with you and help you find him now, but I—uh, am very busy just now and—" He stopped short when he caught sight of Chastity, who had dropped all pretenses of working on the mail and sat staring at him, brows raised expectantly, chin propped impertinently on her hands.

The moment Rhonda saw his eyes drift toward the pretty blond woman her momentary calm dissolved. She blinked more tears into her eyes and at the same time forced a brave smile. "It ain't necessary t' explain. I—I'm goin'."

"I'll be finished here in a few hours," Jonathon assured her, "and then I'll be happy to look for Joey."

She leaned forward, her face instantly bright, her ample bosom forcing him to sit on his desk to avoid intimate contact. "Would you?" she whispered.

"I'd be happy to do it."

"For me?"

He scowled darkly as he leaned back a little further. He didn't like being pushed, and if she pushed him another inch, he'd fall over backward, right off the desk. Then he really would lose his temper. "Mrs. Bates," he began sharply.

"No matter," Rhonda crooned sweetly. "I'll be eternally beholdin' t' you regardless." Before he could make another move, she had planted a bright red kiss on his mouth and whirled about. "Oh," she called over her shoulder just before letting herself out, "and plan on stayin' t' supper."

Jonathon watched the woman leave, feeling a mixture of relief and annoyance. He would stay to supper, all right.

And he would make it perfectly clear that nothing like this was ever to happen again.

"A friend of yours, I suppose?" Chastity questioned sarcastically as she rose from her chair. "Or is she a . . . business acquaintance?"

Jonathon said nothing as he wiped his mouth tersely with a clean linen handkerchief, but he shot a warning glance at her as he took a seat at his desk and began to rustle papers about.

"She appeared to be very interested in *your* business, Mr. Stoneworth," Chastity accused as she approached his desk. "Tell me, how quickly would you have left this office to go"—she paused to roll her eyes—"look for Joey if I hadn't been here observing?" She stood arrogantly before his desk, demanding an answer. He was silent. "I think perhaps my father would—"

Jonathon suddenly slammed his fist on his desk so hard that her head snapped back in amazement. She was even more surprised when he spoke in that very low, very controlled voice of his, for the venom burning in his eyes was unmistakable. "You have absolutely no basis for such accusations, Miss Morrow. And if you wish to carry tales to your father—"

"Carry tales? Hah!" Of course he wouldn't want her to mention this to her father, she thought. Papa thought him nothing less than a saint. But it only proved to Chastity what she had known all along. Her blue eyes sparked with temper and she stiffened haughtily before him. "That hussy . . ."

"Mrs. Bates is a widow woman, not a hussy."

". . . comes bouncing into this office and propositions you . . ."

"She did not proposition me."

". . . as if this place were a—a bawdy house! Anyone who would even associate with a woman like that is—is—"

He rose to his feet. "Is what?" he demanded hotly, his voice finally reflecting his anger.

"Is every bit as low as she is!" she articulated carefully.

"Oh, I see. I see." He nodded calmly, in complete control of himself once more. "Anyone who isn't part of the 'ac-

ceptable society' here in Virginia City is beneath the regard of a God-fearing, Christian woman like yourself.
Well, let me tell you something, Miss Morrow. There are a
lot of good people who happen to live below C Street, in
spite of what you might like to think. Of course their lives
haven't been quite as easy as yours has been. Many of
them have been on their own since they were children.
They've had to survive any way they could. They didn't
grow up with a doting father and they haven't been coddled and spoiled and—"

"Spoiled!" she repeated indignantly. She stared at him
in disbelief. What a pious hypocrite he was, accusing her
of being spoiled while he acted the part of the Good Samar-
itan just to get what he wanted! After all these days of
worrying about her father's vulnerability, after all the
work she'd already done to try to be rid of this scoundrel,
her patience snapped. She stamped her foot hard on the
floor and completely lost her temper. "How dare you accuse me of being spoiled!" She took a step toward him and
narrowed her eyes, and for an instant Jonathon actually
thought she might slap him across the face. "You know
nothing of my childhood, and if you did, you would never,
never accuse me of having been coddled! Do you think my
father doted on me when he was staking his claim on the
lode? No, Mr. Stoneworth! I was left behind! To be passed
around like an unwanted sack of goods! First there were
the McCulloughs—now there was a lesson in survival, Mr.
Stoneworth. To be thrust into a family of fourteen children, all of them older and much bigger than I. I was only
five years old but I was forced to work as hard as a field
hand, and I had to fight to get my share of the food at meal-
time. And when Mrs. McCullough decided that I was too
much of a 'burden' on the family, she passed me along to
the Porters." Chastity blinked as a tear stung her eye, but
the words continued to gush forth without a pause, like
water through a break in a dam. "There were only two
children in the Porter family, both of them girls just about
my age. But I didn't stay very long with them. Mrs. Porter
thought I was a bad influence on her little darlings, you
see, and so one day when I lost my temper and punched

one of them in the nose, I was immediately packed off to the Johnsons." She hesitated only long enough to take a much-needed breath, and Jonathon was painfully aware of the growing tightness in her throat. " 'A pitiful, homeless child,' Mrs. Johnson used to call me whenever she explained about all the trouble I'd caused her. And Mrs. Johnson told everyone and anyone who'd stand still long enough to listen—"

Chastity stopped short, gasping for breath. And suddenly she was struck by the strange look on Jonathon's face, that same compassionate kind of look she'd seen when he'd met Deborah's eyes, and she realized what she had just done. She rarely spoke of her childhood at all, but to have shared her most painful memories with a man she totally despised made her want to bite her tongue in two! The very idea that Jonathon might pity her filled her with disgust.

"I'm sorry," he said softly, his voice vibrant and masculine as he stepped toward her and instinctively sought to comfort her. She suddenly seemed so much like a lost child, so vulnerable, so full of hurt. But she instantly moved to keep a distance between them, and something in her eyes told him that she wanted no comfort from him. He searched about vainly for the words to say he understood, wanting very much to ease the pain in those dark blue eyes.

She stuck out her chin in defiance. "Don't you dare feel sorry for me, Jonathon Stoneworth! I don't want your pity or anybody else's!" She swallowed hard and brusquely wiped a tear from her cheek as she struggled to steady herself, resenting him all the more because he had seen a part of her she never allowed anyone to see. "I was merely trying to make a point," she stated much more calmly, "but there is no sense in arguing this any further." With a great deal of effort she turned away from him and casually gathered up her belongings. "Tomorrow I shall stay late and finish the work on my desk," she stated matter-of-factly. "Good day, Mr. Stoneworth."

Jonathon watched in silence as she left the office, dropping into his chair as the door closed soundly behind her.

His arms were still aching with the need to hold her; his heart was still full of the words of comfort she had not wanted to hear. He suddenly understood the stubborn persistence he had seen in her from that very first day at the train station. It was in fact vulnerability. The woman had never really come to terms with the childhood that had scarred her so deeply, and in spite of her beauty, her desirability, and even her exceptional intelligence, she was still trying desperately to prove to everyone—perhaps most of all to herself—that she was not an "unwanted sack of goods" anymore. In the past weeks he had seen evidence of it time and time again as she tackled a long column of figures or eagerly took on yet another duty with a spark of defiant determination in those beautiful deep blue eyes of hers. He had not known then what was driving her. Even so, he had been captivated by those eyes, had memorized the furrows that drew her brow whenever she was in deep concentration, and had come to admire her spunk. He let out a sigh as he leaned back in his chair, recalling that Samuel often referred to Chastity as his "little girl." The title, Jonathon realized now, was all too appropriate. For all her woman's body, Chastity still had a great deal of growing up to do.

Chapter 5

The sunny, mild days of May seemed brighter and warmer than those of April, and as spring poised on the threshold of summer Chastity grew restless and discontent with the quiet life she had been forced to lead since her return home a month before. The Howard Street house was so solemn these days, almost like a church with all the whispering and tiptoeing about to keep from disturbing her father's rest. In compliance with the doctor's orders, Samuel rarely had visitors, and Deborah, who had always been involved with an endless list of social and charitable affairs, had practically become a hermit in Chastity's absence. She sat by Samuel's bedside almost constantly these days, working on her needlepoint or on a patchwork quilt for the Orphans' Fair, declining all invitations to remain at home and see to her husband's care. That proved an unfortunate circumstance for Chastity, who had no proper escort and could hardly consider making an appearance at a public function all alone. At least for the present, Chastity's only escape from the house was her work at the office with Jonathon.

Though she certainly hadn't planned it that way, she came to enjoy the time she spent behind her father's desk and the office became a haven for her, a respite from the boredom of a silent house and her worries about her father. Oftentimes she found herself staying until dusk, finishing up a project just for the satisfaction of seeing it done. In less than three weeks she completely revamped the correspondence files which, it seemed to Chastity, her father had set up more according to whim than logic. She remembered the morning she announced to Jonathon in no uncertain terms that she was going to undertake the task, that a method of alphabetical filing would be far more workable than filing according to date received. She had stood before his desk, braced for an argument, completely unprepared for his look of pleased surprise. "Miss Morrow, you are a godsend," he had told her with enthusiasm.

Chastity had stared at that handsome, smiling face of his, still expecting him to say that she didn't know what she was getting into, that she was biting off more than she could chew, that she had no business trying to organize an office that had run perfectly well without her for years, or some such thing. Instead he had only repeated his initial pleased response.

In the days that followed, Chastity was forced to admit that Mr. Stoneworth was an easy man to work with. In spite of the fact that she was a woman, and few women were welcome additions to any kind of men's work, Jonathon worked with her as a peer. He expected a great deal from her, but he also gave consideration to her opinions and suggestions. That type of confidence in her ability was something she had never encountered in a man before. She might have actually felt friendly toward Jonathon if she had not been so certain that he was using her father's illness for his own gain. As it was, everything he did only deepened that conviction. He was trying too hard to win her over, she thought, to be everyone's friend, including hers. It was most apparent of all in the way he accommodated that plain, dowdy Maureen Murphy whenever she wanted to go somewhere and needed an escort. She remembered the first time Michael Murphy, the huge, red-haired Irishman who oversaw the extraction of ore from the Morrow Mine itself, had come by the office in his miner's boots and dusty denims to drop a none too subtle hint about his daughter wanting to attend a social. From his flustered stammering Chastity had easily guessed that either his wife or more likely Maureen herself had put him up to it. But Jonathon had made it so easy on him, insisting that he'd meant to invite Maureen all along. Why, any man worth his salt wouldn't have been seen in the company of that sour, ugly creature, Chastity thought indignantly. It amazed her to think that she was the only one clever enough to see through his saintly facade.

Chastity had been working at her father's office for just over a month when Jonathon casually mentioned that he would be attending a stockholders' meeting the following week in San Francisco and would be away for four days. Four days! Four whole, uninterrupted days for Chastity to go through his books and find evidence of his dishonesty. It was difficult for her to concentrate on her work in the interim. Her blue eyes would wander again and again to the locked drawer of his desk as she anticipated her ultimate triumph. Patience, she would counsel herself. Patience!

On the morning of Jonathon's departure, Chastity sat on the very edge of her chair sorting the mail. Her heart was racing and her eyes carefully avoided his as he packed his briefcase. When he finished and fastened the case shut, he turned and flashed her a handsome, guileless smile. She was certain that it was false, just as everything about him was false. "Well . . . I think I'm about ready to leave."

He expected her to smile in return, to say that she would miss his company or something to that effect, but instead she barely even glanced up before returning her attention to her work. He did not know that she refrained from saying anything for fear of betraying her own anxiety. "If anything urgent comes up while I'm gone," he added, "you can ask Mr. Murphy—"

"I know," she interrupted curtly, keeping her eyes fastened firmly to the bill she was opening.

He stared at her for a moment longer, attributing her behavior to nervousness at being left alone to keep things organized at the office. He would like to set her mind at ease, but a quick check of his pocket watch told him not to dally. He barely even had time to stop by the bank if he wanted to catch the early train for San Francisco. "Feel free to wire me if you need anything . . . anything at all. You know where I'll be staying—"

She raised a pair of indignant eyes. "Yes, I do."

That message was clear enough to Jonathon. She didn't want a patronizing lecture and he knew better than to give her one. She was capable enough to handle things in his absence, and if an urgent situation arose, she was surely intelligent enough to contact him. He sighed, then said a quick good-bye and hurried out of the office.

Chastity waited almost a full hour after Jonathon left her alone to be absolutely certain that he had caught the early train. Even then she approached his desk slowly, with much more caution than she had shown a few weeks before. She found the key in its usual place and easily unlocked the bottom drawer, removing the Morrow Mining Company ledger. She placed the book on Jonathon's desk and flipped through it until she found the page where her father's careless scrawl had been replaced by Jonathon's neat pen. She drew a deep breath and began to check each and every entry for accuracy. She worked the entire morning and well into the afternoon without a pause. As daylight began to wane on C Street, Chastity was almost ready to admit that Jonathon's records were flawless, that he had kept an accurate account of every penny of the company's money. But something drove her on, even as she neared the page of most-current entries, and finally her determination and perseverance were rewarded. Her eyes lit up when she saw it, and the fatigue and tension of long hours of work vanished. The very last entry in the book: Two hundred dollars! Jonathon had written himself a bank draft for two hundred dollars that very morning! She could hardly believe her luck as she stared at the entry. She smiled. She had been right about him all along.

Just as swiftly, her smile faded. Her thoughts of victory were suddenly jumbled with other considerations as the shadows fell more thickly and darkened the room. It

seemed too easy. Jonathon was far too clever to be caught
in such an obvious mistake. Yet there it was in black and
white for all the world to see. Of course, he hadn't expected
anyone to be checking up on him this way, she reminded
herself. He still did all the book work for the Morrow bank
account himself. She drew a deep breath and scowled at
the numbers written so neatly in line with all the others.
She was worried about her father's reaction to the news,
and for a moment she considered confronting Jonathon
on her own, insisting that he resign. But then she remembered that her father had called him "almost a
son." The words ate at her and filled her with bitter resentment. Jonathon had betrayed her father's trust and
for that he deserved to be discharged, even publicly dis-
graced.

It might be difficult, she realized, to find someone to
run the office as competently once Jonathon was gone.
She knew it would be months yet before her father could
return to work. But somehow, once Jonathon was out of
the picture, everything would work itself out, she was
certain of it. She liked to imagine what it would be like
some day in the future, working with her father here,
winning his respect and admiration. She closed the ledger and replaced it in the drawer, feeling that she was
doing the right thing for everyone by getting rid of Jonathon Stoneworth. She would have to stop by the bank
to verify that Jonathon had cashed the draft, of course.
But she was fairly certain that he had. And she would
need to plan what she would say to her father next Monday when Jonathon came to the house to bring him up to
date on the stockholders' meeting. She could just imagine the look on that scoundrel's face when she confront-
ed him with the evidence and demanded his immediate
dismissal. She tried not to think about the look on her
father's face. It would hurt him to find out the truth,
but perhaps even that hurt would be for the best. He
would be forced to see that blood was thicker than
water, that he should never have turned to an outsider
for help. Samuel had her, after all, and she was sure
she could fill any void Jonathon left behind if only he

would let her. This time he would not laugh away her suspicions, she knew. This time he would have no choice but to break with the man who had come between them.

Chapter 6

Early Monday morning, Chastity excused herself from the breakfast table and hurried up the stairs to her room for a final check of the ledger and a mental rehearsal of the indictment she would lay before her father. A quarter of an hour later, when she heard Jonathon greeting Deborah and making his way upstairs to her father's room, she gathered up the ledger, drew a long, steadying breath, and proceeded slowly according to the plan she'd worked out. At the door she hesitated, hearing her father's hearty chuckle over some remark Jonathon had made. She knocked quickly, anxious to interrupt their friendly exchange. Her father mumbled something in return before he responded to her knock, and she bristled when she heard them both laugh. She stepped inside and nudged the door closed behind her with an elbow, noting that her father's smile faded into a puzzled frown. "Is something wrong, Chastity?"

"As a matter of fact, Papa, there is." Her serious expression met Jonathon's eyes for a moment and her fingers tightened on the large black ledger she hugged close against her breast.

"Well, what is it?" Samuel growled, twisting his torso to fluff his pillows in order to give his back more support. He sighed and sat back comfortably, then frowned at the chill in Chastity's eyes. Only then did he notice what she held so tightly in her hands, and he felt a sudden weakness in his stomach as she deliberately approached his bedside.

He had begun to think that she had forgotten all about their bargain.

"I'm sorry to be the one to reveal this—this treachery to you, Papa, but such blatant evidence of wrongdoing cannot be ignored." She tossed an accusing glare at Jonathon, who seemed mildly surprised but still managed to look totally innocent. Not for long, she thought confidently as she continued. "I have no choice but to show you the evidence and then to insist that you discharge Mr. Stoneworth immediately."

Samuel's eyes flew helplessly from one face to another. Could Chastity possibly be right? No! He couldn't believe it! Not after all the boy had done for him, not after all he'd come to mean to him. The very thought made him feel nauseous and dizzy, and he had to swallow hard to relieve the discomfort in his throat.

"It's all here, Papa," she continued evenly, taking a seat beside him on the bed and placing the book in his lap. She opened it to the current entries. "Here is a bank draft for two hundred dollars which was cashed the day he left for San Francisco. I checked at the bank, and Mr. Simmons verified the fact that Mr. Stoneworth both wrote and cashed the draft."

Samuel scanned the long column of figures, pausing reluctantly on the draft in the amount of two hundred dollars. As Chastity had pointed out, it had been written and cashed the very day Jonathon had left for San Francisco. He closed his eyes, feeling absolutely weak with disappointment, and partially responsible, too, for having been the one to challenge his daughter to find a flaw in Jonathon's records. He sighed and forced himself to stare once more at the evidence before him, as if he could somehow change what was there in black and white. A silence fell on the room like a pall.

"Do I have the right to explain the draft?" Jonathon asked after a long, tense moment. "Or have I been found guilty as accused without benefit of a fair trial?" Chastity met his unblinking eyes, which surprisingly held only anger, not a trace of discomfort or fear.

"By all means," Samuel replied with a belated show of

good faith. "I have no doubt at all that there is a logical explanation for all of this."

Jonathon nodded calmly at his employer. "Thank you." Then he turned a bright, unyielding stare on Chastity and spoke with deliberate care, articulating each word with slow precision. "Your father has been ill for well over two months, Miss Morrow, and I have had to assume nearly all of his responsibilities. This has left me in a rather awkward position as to collecting my own salary." Chastity's smile of triumph froze on her lips. "I thought to delay the matter until your father had recovered, but for various reasons my savings have been depleted in the last few weeks, and I found it necessary to collect a portion of what was owed me."

"You're claiming the money was owed to you?" she repeated with obvious skepticism. "Two hundred dollars?"

"More than that, actually. I took only what I needed—"

"You are a liar!" She flung it at his face like a slap.

"Chastity!" Samuel slammed the ledger shut with nearly enough force to shatter its binding. He drew a long, shaky breath and stared firmly at his daughter. "You have made an error, Chastity," he said quietly. "To avoid any further embarrassment, let us leave it go at that."

She shook her head in disbelief. "But Papa—"

"I said, the matter is forgotten!" he barked back. His skin had gone deathly pale and a tremor in his voice made Jonathon bound forward from his chair just as Samuel clutched blindly at his chest.

"Deborah! Sarah!"

Jonathon's voice rang through the quiet house and several pairs of feet scrambled immediately up the long, winding staircase. Chastity stood watching helplessly as Jonathon removed the pillows from behind her father's back and settled his head gently down on the bed, repeating in a low, soothing voice, "Relax, Sam. Relax." She heard her father gasping for breath and she was terrified that he was dying, right before her eyes. Instinctively she raised a trembling hand to her mouth and backed away from his bedside until she stood against the wall. For a moment she stood frozen, unable to move. Deborah joined Jonathon at her father's side, and helplessly Chastity watched them leaning over him, his wife taking hold of his hand. And then, she did something she hated herself for doing—she turned and ran away.

It was all over so quickly that Jonathon could scarcely believe that it had happened at all. It had been much milder than the last; Samuel seemed to have recovered almost immediately. All the same, Jonathon insisted that Dr. Perkins be notified, and a slight nod to Sarah sent her scurrying from the room.

"Now, Jonathon, you know that isn't necessary," Sam told him in a tired but remarkably steady voice. "There's no need for all this attention."

Jonathon smiled softly at his objections, but the eyes that met Deborah's were not smiling. It was only after Dr. Perkins had done a thorough examination and received his usual gruff dismissal from Samuel that they relaxed and the worried looks disappeared from their eyes.

Locked in her own room, Chastity anxiously paced the floor for what seemed like hours, straining to catch any news of her father's condition yet unable to face anyone while the burdens of guilt and shame rested so heavily on her. At length she heard the doctor being shown down the stairs, heard Deborah speaking with him in a voice calm and collected, and even heard her father's voice, though she couldn't make out his words. She squeezed her eyes shut and began to cry. Thank God he was all right! He was going to live!

The moment he had rid himself of his "interfering physician," Samuel demanded a private word with Jonathon, and Deborah complied without argument. They were alone for several moments before either man spoke, and for the first time since he'd met Jonathon, Samuel was at a loss for words with him. But he knew he had to be honest with Jonathon, had to explain about his daughter's behavior so that he might understand, and perhaps forgive.

"I'm sorry I didn't mention my salary earlier," Jonathon said quietly, breaking the uncomfortable silence. "But I never thought that anyone—"

Samuel shook his head and stretched an unsteady hand until it rested on Jonathon's arm. "No, no! You mustn't apologize to me. It was my fault. All of this was really my fault." He sighed and reluctantly let the truth spill out. "This really has nothing to do with your salary, Jonathon. Chastity asked me to dismiss you the day she arrived home from St. Louis." He lowered his eyes with a guilty expression and missed the shock which registered on Jonathon's face. "Rather than say no to her, I challenged her to find fault with your records. That's why she has been working with you all these weeks." He raised his eyes apologetically. "I was sure if she had the chance to work with you, if she got to know you. . ." His voice trailed off weakly.

In spite of himself Jonathon smiled, a smile of self-reproach as much as anything else. All the while he had been trying to cultivate what he thought was a mutual friendship, she had been plotting to slit his throat! He had never even guessed; but then, it was difficult to imagine any subterfuge existed beneath that perfect, angelic face of hers.

"My daughter will apologize to you," Samuel said in a faraway voice. "I have never forced her to do anything before, but she owes you an apology and you will have one." He looked Jonathon straight in the eye and went on firmly. "You will also receive a raise—double your present salary—and from here on you will be paid entirely from my private account." He hesitated, hardly knowing how to say the rest of it. "You are much more than my lawyer, Jonathon. You handle my personal affairs, and I intend to pay you personally. I—I apologize for not seeing to these matters before."

Jonathon bit his lip as he lifted the ledger and placed it carefully in his briefcase. He momentarily considered rejecting the raise, but swiftly decided against it. Samuel needed rest now, not more arguments. "I know that you're tired, Sam, and if I could get your signature on just a few papers, then I can take care of things myself." He reached inside his case and removed the documents, which Samuel barely skimmed before signing. Jonathon replaced the papers in his case and extended his hand with his warmest smile. "Take care, Sam. I'll be here tomorrow morning, checking up on you."

"You have been a true friend to me, Jonathon," he said, blinking back a tear as he gripped the younger man's hand firmly between both of his own. "I—I thank you."

All along C Street the gaslights of Virginia City glowed like a neat row of soft yellow halos propped on the side of the mountain. In the shadows between two of the pale lights lay a cluster of smaller offices and businesses, all dark and deserted except for the office of Samuel Morrow, where Jonathon still sat at his desk. He had been there since late afternoon, but for all he had accomplished in those long hours he might as well have spent the day hiking up Mount Davidson. He lifted a hand to rub his eyes and massage his brow, willing away the image of soft moonlight hair and deep blue eyes. Chastity Morrow—a willful, selfish, thoughtless young girl . . . but also a very beautiful, desirable, intelligent woman. Jonathon made a fist and banged it hard against his cluttered desk. The more he thought about her, the more tightly the frustration coiled inside him. She had plotted against him, had cleverly sought to expose him as a villain to force her father to get rid of him, without a single thought to the consequences. He ought to be furious with her. He ought to be planning a way to make her pay for her actions, a way to teach her a lesson she wouldn't soon forget. But instead he was remembering the day when she'd actually cried about her childhood, and the broken, terrified look on her face today when she thought her father might die. She was still that frightened, lost little girl Samuel left behind so long ago, he thought, and ironically he was almost ready to blame himself for not being able to break through the wall she had built so effectively about a shattered heart. She was alone and afraid, Jonathon knew, but he had no idea how to reach a woman buried so deeply in her defenses that it seemed impossible she would ever grow and be free of them. If only he could touch her, if he could somehow make her see how much she had to give. He closed his eyes and sighed, imagining her in his arms, feeling her softness close against him, kissing her with a passion she returned measure for measure. But then he wondered just how many other men had thought of her that way, as some hollow object to be petted and used for pleasure. The thought made him angry. Everything about his feelings for Chastity seemed to make him angry because they were not emotions he had chosen at all. For the first time in his life he was caring much more than he wanted to care. And his feelings only seemed to grow, in spite of the instant dislike she'd shown for him, in spite of what had happened this morning. He sighed and once more attempted to force her face from his mind. He opened an envelope on the top of the pile of mail and was scanning the invoice when there was a knock at the door. He frowned, checked his pocket watch, and rose to answer it. He lifted the shade and his eyes brightened as the light from the office illuminated Chastity's face. Her skin was pale and her eyes were swollen from crying, and the anger Jonathon had felt a moment before instantly died. He fumbled with the door in his haste to let her in, worrying that Samuel might have suffered yet another attack. "Is your father all right?" he asked as soon as he had opened the door.

She entered the office and turned her back on his questioning stare. "Yes. That is . . . he is resting now, but . . ." She took yet another step away from him and drew a lengthy breath. For a moment she could not face him, could not face the fact that she had been so wrong, that she had acted in a way that had actually endangered the life of the man she wanted most to protect. She lifted her chin and forced herself to turn back to face Jonathon. "I—I didn't come here about Father. I came here to apologize."

Had her expression been only slightly less serious, Jonathon might have smiled. But she'd obviously suffered enough in the past hours without being made light of now. "It might have waited until tomorrow," he said, taking a step toward her so that the faint scent of her perfume reached him.

She shook her head. "No. I had to do it now. I—I wanted to do it now." She swallowed hard and lowered her eyes. He seemed to tall, so overpowering all of a sudden. "Papa explained about your salary— " she began.

"And he insisted that you apologize," he finished bluntly, annoyed to be reminded that the apology had been Sam's idea.

"Yes . . ." She raised her eyes to meet his and seemed to sense his annoyance. "But I would have done it anyway. Please believe that."

There was no room for doubt in those dark blue, pleading eyes. He nodded slowly and heaved a sigh of capitulation. "I do."

Chastity's face brightened for a moment; then she suddenly looked away. "I—I enjoyed working with you, Jonathon." She stopped short and her cheeks flushed a deep red. She had not meant to call him by his first name, but it seemed to have slipped out somehow. She stole a glance at him, hoping he hadn't noticed, but his eyes were lit with amusement and she knew he was holding back a smile. He had noticed, all right. She bit her lip nervously and took a step in the direction of the door. As she reached for the brass knob, she added hurriedly, "You're worth the raise, too. Every cent of it . . . and more."

Jonathon's hand closed over hers before she could open the door. His fingers were warm and strong, and she felt uncomfortably weak at his touch.

"Wait. There's something else I want to discuss with you."

Without meeting his eyes, Chastity nodded and awkwardly withdrew her hand. She waited in silence for Jonathon to proceed with a long lecture about her father and his present state of health, and about her unforgivable behavior that morning. She intended to endure it all with grace.

"Is there a reason why you and I can't declare a truce?" Her eyes lifted in confusion.

"I would like to be a friend of yours," he admitted,

wishing even as he said the words that he could be much more.

"Even after what's happened? But why?"

"Because I'm not comfortable having you for an enemy," he teased with an edge of seriousness. "As far as I can see, you're rather short on friends at the moment." He shrugged and grinned. "It's up to you, of course, but I wouldn't pass up an offer like this without thinking it over very carefully."

Unaccustomed to his teasing, and perhaps because it was the very last thing she had expected from him, Chastity immediately took offense. "I have many friends, Mr. Stoneworth," she retorted, "and I certainly don't need you to feel sorry for me."

"Sorry for you? Did I say that?" He frowned and shook his head, wanting to take her firmly by the shoulders and shake her hard—or kiss her, he wasn't really sure which at this point. "You really ought to learn to listen better, Miss Morrow. I was offering friendship, not pity."

"I already have lots of friends," she insisted, still not ready to accept his offer though she had no idea why. "Why, in St. Louis I was the most popular girl for miles around."

"I'll wager you were," he muttered under his breath. "But those weren't friends, Miss Morrow. Those were admirers. Ready to give you the world on a silver platter if you asked for it." The look on her face told him he was right. "But there's one thing I'll wager you never had with any of them."

"And what is that?" she returned skeptically.

"The freedom to be really honest."

Her forehead puckered thoughtfully. He was right about that, too. She had never really been honest with anyone, but she wondered just how he had known that, or why he cared, and more importantly, why he thought she could ever be honest with him, especially after what she had done. Her eyes drifted slowly upward from the open collar of his white shirt to the darkened skin of his face, and his deep brown eyes. For the first time she noticed the tiny flecks of gold that radiated from the cen-

ters of those eyes, and how thickly the dark lashes
framed them beneath mature, arched brows. The line of
his mouth softened a bit in a questioning sort of smile,
and a single brow rose in expectation. Almost at once
she realized that she was staring at him, and she
quickly turned away in embarrassment. It was several
moments before she said anything. "I—I would like to
be honest with you about one thing, Jonathon," she
forced out finally. She gulped and wrestled with her
mind to say the right words. "I think I would like to continue working here . . . with you." She turned to face
him with eyes imploring. "I promise I won't look for any
more discrepancies—"

"But I expect you to." He flashed her a stern expression.
"But I will also expect you to bring any mistakes to my attention and to listen to my explanations before you take
them to a higher court."

She nodded vigorously. "I will. I promise."

He smiled at her then, a flashing, white smile, which
for the first time she warmly returned. "It's settled
then. I'll expect to see you here first thing tomorrow morning. There's quite a lot of mail yet to be opened from today." He glanced out the window at the waiting carriage.
"Now you'd better be getting home. Deborah will be wondering what in the world has been keeping you all this
time."

Chastity bristled a bit at the mention of her stepmother, but her relief at having lived through the apology and retained her position at the office quickly
overcame her annoyance. "Can I drop you somewhere
along the way?"

He opened the door and followed her outside into the
cool evening air. "No, thank you. I have a few things to
finish up before I leave for the night. And besides, I
think I can use the walk tonight." He took hold of her
hand to assist her into the carriage, and she decided
that she was beginning to like the feel of his fingers, so
sure and strong and warm. "Tomorrow morning," he
repeated as she took her seat and he swung closed the
door. She nodded.

Jonathon bid the carriage driver a good evening and then watched in silence until the vehicle disappeared from view. He heaved a sigh and watched a moment longer before returning to the office to straighten his desk and lock up for the night.

Unnoticed in the shadows was another man, not quite so tall as Jonathon, a man whose crisp black suit blended easily with the darkness of the night. His blue-gray eyes scanned the gold block lettering on the office door just before Jonathon drew the blinds and blew out the lamp. Morrow Mining Company, Inc. His face lit with recognition. Morrow. Chastity Morrow! How had he failed to make the connection before? Of course, at the time it hadn't seemed to matter. He had thought to ride out his lucky streak and make a quick fortune, and be gone from this godforsaken place forever. But his luck had not been quite so good since his arrival in Virginia City. He had invested nearly all of his money in mining stocks, certain that news of a bonanza would hit and raise the value of those stocks. And though assessments for the Con Virginia had been waived at the last stockholders' meeting, the other holdings Regan had acquired were busily demanding money to continue with their drilling and blasting. Assessments would soon be due, and if he couldn't pay them, he would lose all the money he'd invested. He removed a cigar from his breast pocket, lit it, and drew on it thoughtfully. He hated to admit it, but his funds were quickly being depleted. He had been forced to check out of his suite at the International Hotel last week and take a room at a B Street boardinghouse. If his luck at the tables didn't improve soon, or if the stock didn't roar within the next month or so, he would desperately need an ace in the hole.

And perhaps he had just found one. His eyes skimmed over the gold lettering once more. Miss Chastity Morrow would surely be in attendance at the Sisters of Charity Benefit Social next week. Regan had read all about it in the newspaper, the *Territorial Enterprise,* and he was certain that all the pillars of Virginia City society would turn out en masse to help the good sisters with their work. He flicked an ash on the wooden walkway and sauntered toward a noisier, better-lit section of C Street in search of a saloon with a friendly game of poker. The Sisters of Charity had just sold themselves another ticket.

Chapter 7

The following morning at her father's office, Chastity lifted her eyes from the stack of payroll receipts she was filing to steal a glance at Jonathon. He was dressed in miners' clothing this morning rather than his usual suit, and the casual denim shirt he wore was opened at the collar to reveal a small V of crisp black hair. She paused to study his face, the firm, sculpted lines to his nose and chin; the full, chiseled mouth; the determined arch of brow over cool, intriguing brown eyes. Her eyes strayed to his hands, remembering the feel of those perfect lean fingers, strong but with an obvious capacity for gentleness, calloused the slightest bit as masculine fingers ought to be. She cocked her head, deciding that she liked the way he moved, with the agile sureness of an athlete, his tall, muscular body fit and controlled. It was as if she were seeing Jonathon Stoneworth for the very first time, and suddenly everything about him seemed to have changed.

Chastity had dressed with care and spent more time than usual preening before the glass this morning, feeling slightly uneasy about seeing Jonathon again even though everything had been settled between them the night before. It was only now that she decided that her uneasiness stemmed from the fact that she could not predict his reactions, that she knew too little about him. It had been so much simpler when she thought him a scoundrel. She had been perfectly comfortable with him then, not caring at all what he thought of her. But now she was suddenly aware of his manliness, of her own feminity. She cared what he thought and wanted very much to arouse his interest. She knew how to handle men, or thought she did. She simply smiled and laughed and flirted until they were falling at her feet. She'd missed that kind of attention since her return home and suddenly craved the reassurance of having a man pay court to her.

But this morning things were not going exactly as she'd planned. She'd smiled her most fetching smiles, been careful to pose prettily and perch her hand lightly on his arm at every opportunity. But there had been no trace of the interest she sought, and Jonathon had diligently turned away from her to attack the work at his desk as if she were not even there. She frowned, wondering if her cool behavior these past weeks would force her to use a more straightforward approach with him. Her eyes lit up with an idea, and her mouth curved into a small smile. The Sisters of Charity Benefit Social was only a week away. She had seen an article about it just yesterday in the *Enterprise*. And since Jonathon had been in San Francisco for most of the past week, it was very possible that Maureen Murphy hadn't wangled an invitation from him as yet. Perhaps if she were to bring the subject up and drop a hint or two . . .

"Did you see the article about the benefit social in the paper?" she asked suddenly.

Jonathon looked up in surprise, taking a long moment to digest her expression. It was the third time this morning she'd smiled at him that way, that overly demure little smile that showed off her dimples, those quick flutters of her long, dark lashes. After weeks of being just barely sociable, she was suddenly playing the part of a coquette. If her actions had been a lot less calculated, less false, Jonathon might have been taken in by them. But he realized at once that she was only playing a game she'd obviously played too often before. He didn't want any part of this game. "As a matter of fact, I did," he replied indifferently, returning his attention to his paperwork almost at once.

Chastity's smile faded quickly, then renewed itself as she lifted her chin and tried again. "The Sisters of Charity do so much wonderful work here in town," she gushed.

"Yes, they do . . . ," he mumbled as he sorted through a pile of letters, searching out one in particular.

"Deborah always works at their Orphans' Fair," she added hopefully.

"I know she does."

She frowned. He always made it so easy for Mr. Murphy; a single hint and he was eagerly requesting the "privilege" of Maureen's company. Why was he completely ignoring her?

"Do you think you'll be going?" she asked him bluntly, her frustration causing her temper to rise.

He fixed a blank expression to his face before he met her eyes. "Going where?"

She let out her breath through clenched teeth. "To the social!" she returned in exasperation. She had never done anything like this before; men were usually begging to take her places.

"I hadn't really given it much thought," Jonathon returned with a contemplative frown. "But now that you've brought it up . . ." He watched her eyes brighten, her lips curve into a catlike smile. He wondered if it was always so easy for her to get what she wanted. Or rather what she *thought* she wanted. "I think it might be a perfect opportunity for me to get Deborah out of that house," he continued after a slight pause, and he noticed that her smile promptly vanished. "She's been cooped up far too long, and with all the worry about Sam's health . . ."

For a long moment she stared at him in utter disbelief. "You—you're going to take *Deborah* to the social?" she repeated finally in despair.

"You'd be welcome to come along," he said with a slightly raised brow, holding back a knowing smile of his own.

Chastity scowled darkly and turned her attention promptly back to her filing. He was making everything impossible for her. Deborah, indeed! But then, she had gotten the invitation she'd wanted, even if it was as an afterthought. And if she played her cards right . . . Her face brightened again.

If the tension and anxiety about Samuel's illness made the days long and tedious for Chastity, they were even more taxing for Deborah, who had no outlet like the mining office to ease her troubled mind. For weeks she had all but lived at her husband's bedside, watching, worrying. When she did seek her rest, it was in an adjacent room that only made her feel lonely after nearly eight years of sharing a bed with her husband. They shared a closeness she had never expected to share with any man, even in her youthful, romantic dreams, dreams that had been put to rest long before she'd even met him.

Deborah had never been a truly beautiful woman, and a fierce devotion to an ailing father had kept her from encouraging any male attention she might have received when she was younger. At thirty-two she had resigned herself to spinsterhood and worked hard at the San Francisco boardinghouse, which was her only financial security at the time. She kept herself busy with friends and acquaintances, who became like family to her, people who came to love her dearly for her kindness and thoughtfulness. She was the type of woman who was always ready to sit with a sick friend, or care for someone's children, or bake a loaf of bread for the man next door who had just lost his wife. She never asked a favor of anyone in return.

She had been swept off her feet by Samuel's sudden devotion and had hardly believed it when he proposed marriage to her. At first there had also been fear to match the excitement and the joy. Deborah had never even kissed a man before she married Samuel. But once their vows were spoken, he had been kind and patient and far gentler than his gruff exterior had ever allowed her to hope. And he had held her and told her that he adored her, and spoken of his little girl who so desperately needed a mother like her. No one had ever spoken to her like that before, and Deborah had never loved anyone as she loved Samuel.

The strain of caring so much for him, of being so fearful of losing him these past few months showed clearly in Deborah's face. She aged quickly, almost before Jonathon's eyes, just as Samuel seemed to age. She was, as her husband had so aptly put it, "burning the candle at both ends" by refusing to leave the house. The ongoing conflict with Chastity added yet another burden to her slight, already sagging shoulders, though the tension between them was, for the most part, beneath the surface now for Samuel's sake. Chastity was polite to her stepmother at least, though she was still distant and cold enough to let Deborah know her feelings had not really changed.

It was Jonathon who finally put an end to Deborah's confinement by insisting that she make an appearance at the Sisters of Charity Benefit Social. Though the Morrows were devout Episcopalians, the sisters served all of Virginia City with a hospital, an orphanage, and a school and had always been one of Deborah's favorite charities. When Jonathon's prodding seemed to fall short of convincing her to attend, he gently reminded Samuel that Deborah's last outing had been to the train station to meet Chastity, and he enlisted the older man's help. Once Samuel made up his mind that Deborah needed the time away from the house, it was inevitable that she would agree. And there seemed no reason in the world why Chastity should not go along.

Chastity could hardly wait for the evening to begin—her very first social engagement since coming home. She had sorely missed being the center of attention, and tonight she intended to mark the end of a too-long period of exile. She ran her long, gloved fingers thoughtfully over the shockingly low neckline of her blue grenadine gown and smiled, anticipating the sensation it would cause this evening. In this town of "Washoe widowers," men who resided at the many boardinghouses around the city while their wives and families lived elsewhere, the men outnumbered the women by a sizable margin. And a woman like Chastity clothed in a gown like this would never lack for attention in Virginia City. She had ordered the dress just before leaving St. Louis, where it had taken an outlandish amount of money, hours of arguing, and a promise that she would never wear the thing within a hundred miles of her Aunt Susan before the seamstress had agreed to construct it according to her specifications.

Chastity playfully tossed her head, sending shimmers of light dancing over a perfectly arranged cascade of curls. She raised a brow flirtatiously at her reflection in the large, gilt-edged looking glass, pleased with the line of the elaborately draped tie-back skirt, which clung explicitly to the sleek curve of her hips. She would catch the eye of every eligible male in Virginia City tonight, she was thinking, and probably a few ineligible ones as well. It was just as well that her father was not escorting her and Deborah or she might not have had the courage to wear this particular gown at all.

At the sound of Jonathon greeting Sarah in the foyer, Chastity turned abruptly away from the mirror and snatched a matching blue satin mantle to toss over her shoulders. She didn't want Deborah to have a chance to object to her attire before she even arrived at the miners' union hall, where the social was being held. Not that she really cared what Deborah thought of the gown, or anything else for that matter. But it would be far more exciting and daring to wait until after her arrival and then enjoy the limelight. And that was exactly what she intended to do.

The hall had been gaily decorated with silk flowers and bright-colored paper streamers draped from the center of the ceiling to the corner of each wall. Laughter and music and animated conversation permeated the entire building, which was filled to capacity. Scores of gas jet lamps shed their soft, flattering light on hundreds of bright, excited faces.

Jonathon, Deborah, and Chastity had scarcely made their entrance before being assailed with questions from well-meaning neighbors and friends. How was Samuel doing? Was it true he intended to return to work as soon as he recovered? How long did the doctor expect that to take?

Jonathon would have stood politely at Deborah's side the entire evening, but after a mere quarter hour of introductions and listening to Deborah's responses to the same questions about Samuel's gradually improving health, Chastity was anxious to be free to pursue other matters. She intended to dance and flirt and have a marvelous time, and there was very little possibility of carrying out her plans if she remained among her father's middle-aged acquaintances. During an unobserved moment, she nudged Jonathon and tossed her head in the direction of the dance floor. He swiftly responded with the proper apologies to Deborah and a request that Chastity share a dance with him. She smiled and nodded, then turned her back to him and unfastened her wrap. She felt his fingers tense as she allowed him to remove it from her shoulders, sensing more than feeling his hesitation as his eyes beheld the stunning display of décolleté. From the corner of her eye she saw Deborah stiffen, saw the woman she was speaking with gasp in shock and wave a lace hanky furiously in front of her nose. Chastity stifled a smile and turned her head to observe Jonathon's reaction, very much aware of the murmurs of disapproval that were echoing all about her and even more aware of the eyes that could not look away. Much to her surprise, Jonathon's eyes lingered quite frankly on the curves of her breasts before rising slowly to meet her eyes. "Don't you like my dress?" she said with her prettiest pout.

He lifted a single, knowing brow. "I like what there is of it," he said with the barest trace of amusement. "And what's missing assures me that I'll be spending most of the evening with Deborah."

"There's not a man in the room anywhere near as handsome as you, Jonathon Stoneworth," she told him, smiling so that her dimples were shown off to best advantage.

He gave her a mildy reproving look, knowing full well that her smile was for the benefit of everyone watching as much as for him. "Miss Morrow, you are a terrible flirt," he accused. "If I didn't know better, I'd be down on my knees proposing marriage at this very moment."

"And why aren't you?" she asked him, slightly annoyed that he saw right through her, yet at the same moment almost glad that he had.

"Because something tells me that you're not ready to leave Howard Street and all its trimmings for my sorry residence and a feather duster and broom."

"You do make marriage sound so romantic," she returned with a roll of her deep blue eyes. "Still . . . ," she went on, toying with the buttons of her long white glove, "if you were to ask me—"

He scowled. "Come on. For now I'll settle for the dance you promised me."

She wondered exactly what he meant by "for now," but his face gave her absolutely no clue. They reached the dance area and waited a moment or two until the orchestra began a new song, this one a waltz. Chastity had not expected him to be such a marvelous dancer since she was used to making adjustments for clumsiness or timidity with just about every man she danced with. But there was no need with Jonathon. He had been taught well and had ample practice, which impressed Chastity as well as surprised her. She was also surprised at the mixture of amusement and annoyance in his eyes when she fluttered her lashes and smiled at him, though she had little notion what sparked either of those emotions. He confused her and left her feeling at a disadvantage in spite of all the attention she was receiving from everyone else in the room. Still, it was wonderful to be dancing again, to be gliding effortlessly along in his arms. She enjoyed the feeling immensely and was sorry when the music finally came to an end.

"Good evening, Miss Morrow." The greeting came the moment the music had stopped.

She spun about and her eyes lit with considerable excitement as she encountered its source. "Mr. Spencer! How nice to see you again!" She noted with satisfaction that Regan's eyes wandered freely over her attire before he gave reply. Now *that* was a look she readily understood.

"It's good to see you looking so . . . well, Miss Morrow," he understated casually. His eyes reluctantly drifted from her to the tall, dark gentleman who stood beside her, and Chastity hurriedly made an introduction. Regan seized advantage of the music and, nodding curtly to Jonathon, whisked Chastity off in his arms. There were several men who had stepped in her direction with that very same idea, and Chastity was careful to toss smiles in their directions, wanting to keep their interest fully aroused. For the first moments of the dance Regan did nothing but visually devour her, taking in every inch of her flawless skin exposed by the low, heart-shaped neckline. Chastity flushed with excitement. She had finally managed to get his full attention.

"If you're looking for a rich husband, there are quite a few likely prospects here tonight," Regan remarked pleasantly, noticing that she was intent on flirting with more than one man.

Chastity's eyes hardened a bit at his taunt, but her lips held a smile that reflected her confidence. "And just as many miners, Mr. Spencer. I told you before, I'm not looking for a rich husband."

"Come now, Miss Morrow. No woman wears a dress like that to catch the eye of a simple miner. You have higher goals in mind, whether or not you admit to them."

Chastity's mouth tightened and she resisted taking the next step in the dance. "If you intend to insult me, Mr. Spencer, then I will excuse myself—" She attempted to turn away from him, but he pulled her along in spite of her objections.

"I didn't intend to insult you," he interrupted.

She gave up struggling with him and turned her head to let her eyes scan the crowd of people lining the dance floor. "Then just what is your intention?"

"Well . . . actually, I . . ." He hesitated. Chastity Morrow was a stunning beauty, and tonight the lily was gilded to the extreme. There was no denying that she deserved the hungry glances that were tossed at her from all corners of the room. Regan would have preferred to spend the entire evening toying with her, arousing her interest by a series of strategic retreats and subtle advances, but there were simply too many others snapping at the bait. If he didn't make his move now, then he might not get another opportunity and the entire evening would be a complete loss. He had to play his cards now. "I wanted to invite you to the Miners' Union Picnic at the Bowers Mansion next Wednesday."

Her eyes flew to his face in bewilderment. This was the last thing she had expected him to do, and for the life of her she couldn't manage a proper reply.

"Well?"

"I—I—" She swallowed hard and did her best to hide her confusion while summoning enough poise to keep from giving him the advantage. "I'll have to check with Deborah and see if I'm free that particular day."

"Deborah?"

"My stepmother."

"Oh." His eyes narrowed and held hers for a long moment. "Does that mean yes or no?"

She lifted her chin and curved her lips in a slightly defiant smile. "It means perhaps."

"I see."

He did not say another word until the dance had almost ended. He simply held her eyes, unnerving her with his silent, accusing stare. When the music ceased, he loosened his arms from about her and finally returned her smile. Chastity sighed inwardly, certain that his smile was a symbol of victory, that she had played the game to perfection. Of course she intended to accept, but not right away. Perhaps if he coaxed her a bit, told her that it was truly important to him to see her again, perhaps during the next dance . . .

He bowed curtly. "In that case, Miss Morrow, I withdraw the invitation." He murmured a good-evening and turned away, leaving her standing alone in the center of the dance floor, a smile frozen on her lips.

It seemed to Chastity that she danced with at least a

hundred different men after that. First was a young miner who was so obviously uncomfortable in his fancy new suit of clothes that he continually ran a finger about his collar and winced at the tightness of his shoes. Next was the middle-aged miner who had doused himself in so much spiced cologne that Chastity had to restrain a grimace every time she drew a breath. After that came a flustered shopkeeper who stumbled through the entire dance trying desperately to keep his eyes from straying to Chastity's revealing neckline. And the schoolteacher whose breath smelled of cheap whiskey, and the liveryman who laughed at every word he said . . . and on and on. The evening seemed to last forever. Every man she met was anxious to impress her and win her, and not a one of them aroused her slightest interest. Even the very last dance, which Jonathon appeared from out of nowhere to claim, was marred by her thoughts' constant drifting to Regan Spencer. Who did he think he was, anyway? Withdrawing his invitation! Why, she had never heard of such a thing! she fumed. She'd had dozens of offers to attend that same picnic from gentlemen she'd met this evening—gentlemen ecstatic to know she was even considering their requests. She missed the next step in the waltz and mumbled an apology to Jonathon.

He frowned as they continued, noting her obvious preoccupation with something other than dancing, and having a fairly good idea just what—or rather who—was on her mind. He had been watching her closely this evening and had seen the stunned look on her face when Regan Spencer left the dance.

When the music finally ended, Chastity followed Jonathon to meet Deborah, trying all the while to decide which man she would allow the privilege of being her escort next Wednesday. It must be someone passably handsome, someone intelligent enough to make a decent impression but not too dreadfully boring—after all, she would be spending the entire day with him if Regan didn't show up to take his place. But she was fairly certain that he would be there, and she needed to choose an escort with care to be sure that Regan would be at least a little jealous. She mentally checked off most of the men she'd met tonight, finding obvious flaws in nearly every one. But as Jonathon slid her wrap deftly over her shoulders, her eyes suddenly brightened. "Jonathon . . . will the office be closed next Wednesday?"

He tossed her a puzzled frown.

"For the picnic at the Bowers Mansion," she explained.

He still seemed puzzled. "I hadn't given it any thought. Why? Are you planning to go?"

"Oh, yes!" she cried with an enthusiastic smile. She let that smile fade and gazed up at him with wide, pleading eyes. "That is, if I can find someone to escort me. . . ."

He measured her for a long moment until she lowered her eyes self-consciously. "Are you asking me to take you, Chastity?"

Her eyes lifted to face the amusement she had heard in his voice when he posed the question, and she felt a surge of annoyance. Why did he have to be so blunt about it? And how was it that he always saw right through her?

"I was hoping that *you* might ask *me*," she returned tartly, belatedly assuming a wide-eyed, hopeful look.

"And why is that?" he pressed, his eyes narrowed. He knew full well that she must have had a dozen invitations from other men to that same picnic tonight.

"Because you are the perfect escort," she returned sharply, no longer trying to hide her exasperation.

Jonathon lifted a skeptical brow. "Is that so?"

She let out a breath through clenched teeth. "Will you take me or not?"

He hesitated, then let his eyes drift over her quite thoroughly, almost as if he were trying to decide whether or not she was deserving of the invitation. "I'd love to, Miss Morrow," he said in a slightly teasing tone, just as she was about to tell him to forget the whole thing. "And I am so honored that you asked."

He smiled at her, but she only scowled and looked away. Now that she had an escort she was already deciding on a dress that would best display her assets in the bold light of day. Something a bit more subtle, she was thinking. But something flattering enough to insure that Regan wouldn't be able to forget her.

Chapter 8

The sun rose early and clear in Virginia City Wednesday morning, lifting from hills upon hills of purple and amber and setting the desert sands asparkle in the distance. Chastity woke early, smiling to herself as she planned the day that lay before her. She stretched her arms high above her head and breathed deeply of the spicy, sage-scented air. Today was going to be her day. Everything would go her way at the picnic—she could just feel it!

She ate her usual hearty breakfast and visited with her father before she returned to her room to dress with utmost care. Nearly an hour later she slowly descended the long, curved stairway in a cool, green linen dress, which clung snugly to every line of her graceful form. Her hair had been arranged in a sleek chignon with several colorful silk flowers about it, which contrasted attractively with the gown and Chastity's own coloring. She paused on the last step, stretching her white-gloved hand forward until it rested lightly in Jonathon's and smiling in reply to his warm nod of approval.

"I certainly hope it doesn't rain," he teased her. "I'd hate for you to be deprived of all the compliments you deserve today."

"It wouldn't dare rain today," she returned with a tart raise of her brow. "But I intend to have a marvelous time even if it teems." She withdrew her hand and took the last step, lifting her matching green parasol happily to her shoulder. She turned slightly to one side, allowing Jonathon a better view of her attire, and felt a new burst of confidence at his obvious entrancement. But a moment later, when Sarah hurried into the foyer with a large wicker basket fresh from the kitchen, Chastity lost her ardent admirer.

"Why, Sarah, you're looking prettier than ever," he said with only the barest hint of a smile in his eyes.

"Don't you be flirtin' with me, Johnny boy," the plump, middle-aged woman scolded, all the while smiling and loving every word. Her small dark eyes flickered over Chastity and she mumbled a comment about her gown before giving Jonathon another wide smile and handing him the basket. "I packed you plenty o' chicken, now, so you won't be givin' it all away an' havin' none for yourself. An' the tarts I made specially for you alone." Her tiny brown eyes narrowed as she leaned forward and whispered in his ear. "Blackberry."

His face lit up like a child's and he bent closer to mimic her conspiratorial tone. "I'll eat every one of them myself," he promised her, "and probably before the train reaches Gold Hill."

Chastity sighed impatiently and tapped her foot on the polished oak floor. If she hadn't been there to protest, he probably would have spent another half hour flirting with the housekeeper, she fumed in silence. There were times when Jonathon's friendliness was nothing less than a nuisance. She forced a smile and stepped forward to lay a hand on his arm. "It sounds like a marvelous picnic lunch, Sarah," she said a bit too sweetly. "I'd surely hate to miss the train and see it all go to waste."

Jonathon tossed her a scowling sidelong glance but relented when he sensed her growing impatience. "We really do have to hurry if we want to catch the early train." He took the basket in a single hand and escorted Chastity to the door, allowing her to exit and stepping outside himself before turning back and winking at Sarah. "You know who I'll be thinking of at dinnertime."

The carriage that would take them to the train station awaited them, the liveryman in his crisp black suit restraining a team of four bay mares. Chastity eagerly took a seat on the button-and-tufted soft leather upholstery, barely allowing Jonathon to take the seat opposite and swing shut the door before voicing her disapproval. "Why on earth do you waste your time flirting with a servant?"

He arched an amused brow. "Jealous?"

Her eyes hardened though she somehow managed a short laugh. "Of what?"

"Suppose you tell me."

She ground her teeth in silent frustration as the carriage jolted forward. "You really are impossible, Jonathon. I merely asked you why you bother being so friendly with Sarah."

"For the same reason you bother being so friendly with handsome young men," he returned, lifting the hinged cover of the wicker basket and greedily sniffing the feast that lay before him.

"Humph! You know it's not the same thing. You make an utter fool of yourself over a mere servant!" she accused.

He flashed her a reproving glare, which made her blush self-consciously when she realized its silent message. He was cleverly accusing her of making a fool of herself with her flirting. "You—you've scarcely said a word about my gown or my hair," she said, and began to pout.

He let the lid close with a sharp snap, but he spoke pleasantly. "Don't you already have all the eligible men of Virginia City groveling at your feet?"

She frowned and turned away. Not all, she thought wryly.

"I think perhaps you asked me to escort you to the picnic today precisely because I do not flatter you to excess, and maybe because I see that there is more to you than a pretty face."

She bit her lip hard, trying to take what he had said as a compliment even as she bristled at the reminder that *she* had been forced to ask *him* to this picnic. There were times when Jonathon was a bit too honest, when she would have preferred him to be a star-struck lover rather than a friend. Oh, she knew perfectly well that he would give her the shirt off his back if she asked him, but she also

knew that he wouldn't have a shirt to give if someone else
asked him first. She stared at the passing houses, wondering just what she would have to do to make him see her as
other men saw her, to make him desire her as—

"Wait! Stop the carriage!"

Chastity jerked to attention as Jonathon shouted the order, and her eyes dashed up and down Taylor Street
searching for the cause. "Jonathon, what—?"

"It's Joey Bates." As if that were explanation enough,
he swung open the carriage door and dropped from the
coach to greet the scruffy red-haired boy who had run to
catch up with them. "Aren't you going to the picnic today,
Joey?"

The boy scowled and kicked at the street with the toe of
a mud-caked, badly worn shoe. "Naw. I ain't goin'."

"Why not?"

"I ain't got the money t' go. An' Ma's still mad 'bout
me runnin' away last month. She said if they catch me
stealin' jus' one more time, she's gonna' let 'em put
me away fer good."

Jonathon assumed a serious expression as he inwardly
suppressed a smile. "That's too bad, Joey. Especially since
this is such a special day. Just about everyone in Virginia
City goes to the Miners' Union Picnic every year. Couldn't
you ask your mother for the money, and then pay her back
when—"

Joey rolled his eyes and folded his arms across his chest.
"Ya sure don't know nothin' 'bout women, Mr. Stoneworth," he told him in a condescending tone. "My ma ain't
got no money t' lend me. Every dime she gets is already
spent."

"Oh . . ." Jonathon did his utmost to hide his embarrassment. "I see . . ."

"I could hop the train like I usually do," Joey went on
candidly, "but the First Ward gang's out t' get me. One o'
them'd turn me in fer sure . . . before I could even make it
under the seat." He sighed his frustration as his eyes
drifted to the pretty woman seated in a fine carriage, obviously impatient to be off. He'd seen that lady before and
heard his ma talk about her, too. She was the one who had

something to do with Mr. Stoneworth's not coming around as much as he used to; at least, that's what his ma thought.

"You better get goin', Mr. Stonewoth. That train's not gonna' wait fer ya if yer late. An' it looks t' me like ya got yourself a mare that's chompin' at the bit."

Jonathon's brows shot upward and he tossed a glance at Chastity, who sat tight-lipped, face averted. Fortunately she seemed to have missed that last remark. But she was already in a less than perfect mood, Jonathon was thinking, and what harm in a little change in plans? He slapped an arm around Joey's shoulder. "How'd you like to come along with us today?"

That was a remark Chastity did not fail to catch. Her jaw dropped in utter astonishment. He was asking a boy—and not just any boy, but the most notorious juvenile troublemaker in town—to go along on their picnic!

Joey's eyes exploded with excitement. "Gosh, Mr. Stoneworth! You mean you'd pay fer me an' everythin'?"

"And everything," he affirmed. "Under one condition . . ."

The boy's face fell and he snorted. "Aw, there's always a condition." He scuffed his foot about in the dirt, debating whether or not to ask the question. "Well, what's the condition?"

"There's to be no trouble of any sort today. No fighting, no pranks, and *no stealing*. Is it a deal?"

One side of Joey's mouth pulled downward as he shifted his weight from one foot to the other, considering. "Gee . . . it might not even be worth goin' at all if yer gonna' treat me like a prisoner er somethin'." He stole a glance at Jonathon but found not the slightest bit of sympathy in his sharp brown eyes.

"It's entirely up to you, Joey. But like you said, the train won't wait forever."

Joey sighed and jammed his fists in his pockets. He didn't want to appear too eager. "Well . . . I guess I ain't got nothin' better t' do today, anyway . . ."

Jonathon stifled a smile and tightened the hand resting on the boy's shoulder. "Then let's go."

Joey scrambled up the side of the carriage and took a seat next to Chastity, testing the fine leather upholstery with his grimy fingers and wondering just how many pairs of boots he'd have to steal to buy one of these. Chastity cringed and gathered her skirts closer about herself, leaning away as if the boy were contagious.

"Come sit over here, Joey," Jonathon instructed, lifting the wicker basket and patting a place on the seat next to himself. "You don't mind another passenger, do you, Miss Morrow?" he inquired solicitously, now that the carriage was moving and she had very little choice. He flashed a reassuring smile at Joey, who was now openly scrutinizing the beautiful woman who was trying to ignore him.

"Are you hungry, Joey?" That got his attention.

"I'm always hungry!"

Jonathon chuckled and patted the wicker basket on his lap. "Good. Because we've brought along enough food to feed an army. Just wait till you taste Sarah's fried chicken."

Joey's eyes glowed with anticipation. "That's my favorite," he announced, staring at the basket with unmasked yearning.

"I'll just bet it is," Chastity muttered under her breath.

The comment was hardly audible, but its tone drew an instantly hostile look from Joey, and one only slightly less cold from Jonathon. The carriage halted at the station, where long lines of people already crowded the platform waiting for the train that would take them to the Bowers Mansion. At the sight of all those people, Chastity slumped low in her seat, mortified at having to make an appearance along with the town nuisance. Joey Bates! Of all the boys in Virginia City, why did Jonathon have to befriend this one? And why today, of all days! Chastity felt her chin quiver with frustration. She wasn't going to let him do this, she thought as she straightened her back and tightened her grip on her parasol. She just wasn't going to let him!

Jonathon put on his hat and jumped from the carriage with Joey less than a step behind. He turned, smiling, to offer Chastity assistance, but she ignored his hand and sat staring stubbornly at her parasol. Jonathon's smile froze on his lips. "You wait there for us, Joey," he said as he handed the boy the wicker basket and pointed to one of the few uncrowded benches. "We'll buy the tickets and meet you in a few minutes."

Joey took the basket but looked pointedly at Chastity before he obeyed the order. "Ya sure?"

Jonathon smiled. "I'm sure."

Joey couldn't resist making a face at her before he made his way to the bench Jonathon had indicated. Jonathon climbed back into the carriage and took a seat next to her. She drew a deep breath and raised her eyes to face him, but the hot, angry gleam in those large brown eyes made her falter and turn away.

"Well?" he said overpolitely, as if to a pouting child. "Are you coming?"

His indulgent tone rekindled her anger and she raised narrowed eyes to return his fiery stare. "Mr. Stoneworth," she pronounced through clenched teeth, "we made plans to attend this function several days ago. You and I. Not Joey Bates. And I certainly don't intend to waste my day playing nursemaid to a thieving, ragamuffin, eight-year-old boy!"

"Well, it seems we have quite a problem, then," he returned slowly, thoughtfully. "Because I certainly don't intend to waste my day playing nursemaid to my employer's spoiled brat." Despite her vicious snarl and clenched fists, he continued in the same patronizing tone. "You really ought to grow up, my dear. You're getting a little bit too old to pout and throw a tantrum just because things aren't working out exactly as you planned." He abruptly rose and jumped from the carriage, turning back to her for only a moment. "If you change your mind about going, I'll be in the ticket line." He sighed and shook his head with feigned regret. "It'd be a shame to let that lovely dress go to waste."

Chastity was left alone in the carriage without a single outlet for her smoldering temper. She nervously took a quick glance around the station. The place was bustling, people were shoulder to shoulder on the platform, and there were scores of children laughing, screaming, and running about. She sighed her frustration. She couldn't bear the thought of all those people seeing her in the company of Joey Bates. Her eyes shot daggers at his scraggly red head as she watched him covertly slip a piece of chicken from the basket and devour it in less than a minute. She bit her lip and considered the boy as he discarded the bone and contemplated taking another. Joey was small for his age, she rationalized, and he would mix easily enough in this crowd, even though quite a few people knew his face and his reputation.

"Have you decided to return home, Miss Morrow?" a rather confused driver turned to ask her.

She had to make a decision. "Yes. I mean no. I mean I'm going. Help me down."

A moment later she was making her way through the crowd until she stood beside Jonathon in the ticket line. "You've decided to come!" He seemed overly surprised. She kept her eyes glued to the plaid coattails of the man in front of Jonathon, gritting her teeth all the while. "I do hope your disposition improves somewhere along the way," he commented pleasantly.

Chastity held back an infuriated sigh and forced herself to smile, though she truly wanted to kill him. "There's nothing wrong with my disposition, Mr. Stoneworth," she managed in a tone that almost matched his. "I intend to have a perfectly marvelous time today."

He smiled a bit skeptically. "We all do."

She couldn't help but bristle at the reminder, but at this point there was little for her to do but make the best of the situation. As Jonathon paid the price of three fares, Chastity stepped aside and wondered again how she'd gotten herself into this mess. After the dozens of invitations to this picnic she had rejected! The most she could hope for now was that Jonathon wouldn't find any other misfits who wanted to go on a picnic today. She sullenly followed him to meet Joey, but before reaching him she remembered to paste on a smile. It was going to be a real struggle.

Joey straightened when he saw them coming toward him, and his folded hands took up an innocent perch atop the hinged lid of the wicker basket. His round blue eyes focused skyward with a dreamy, guileless sort of look, and he began whistling not a tune, but a strange progression of notes, which led Chastity to believe he'd eaten a lot more than one piece of chicken. She noticed a smudge of dark purple near his mouth, and had there been time she might have accused him of theft and seen to it that he was left behind. But the train was already boarding, and before she had a chance to say a word, Joey shot off through the crowd, ducking and twisting and pushing his way to the head of the line. Jonathon called to him, but his voice was lost in the noises of hissing steam and excited people. Chastity and he were forced to take their place in line and wait their turn.

A conductor stood at the entrance of the car taking tickets, and as Joey whisked by him with an arrogant thumb pointed over his shoulder, he quickly had the boy by the hair. "No stowaways this trip, sonny. It's a full train."

"I got a ticket!" he squealed as he was unceremoniously forced to retreat to maintain his scalp.

"Well, where is it?"

"Back there. Mr. Stoneworth's got it," he insisted, putting up quite a fight to stay on the train. The people behind him were pushing and complaining about the delay, and Jonathon was doing his best to pull Chastity through the throng, hoping to clear up the misunderstanding.

The conductor snorted in obvious annoyance. "You never paid a fare in yer life, Joey Bates. An' if the train wasn't so big as it is, an' didn't need itself a track, I daresay we could look fer it in yer pocket! Now move out of the way and let these people—" The old man sputtered to a stop as Jonathon, breathless from fighting through a hostile crowd, reached over Joey's shoulder and handed him three tickets.

"He does have a ticket today," Jonathon explained with an apologetic smile, hoping to expedite their boarding without any further scenes.

"Well, well," the man said as he collected them from Jonathon with a look of utter disbelief. "And so he does."

His heavily wrinkled eyes narrowed with resentment as Joey gave him a cocky "I told you so" grin. Then the boy whirled about and hurried off to claim a seat by the window.

With as much dignity as he could salvage after the episode, Jonathon led Chastity to the seat opposite Joey and sat down beside her with a pained sigh. "Joey—"

"Hey, Mr. Stoneworth!" Joey interrupted, his eyes fixed in wonder out the large glass window. "Ya sure can see more from up here than ya can from under the seat."

"Joey—"

"I sure am gonna' enjoy this trip. I'm gonna' sit up as tall as I can so everybody can see me—especially those First Ward kids." He straightened his back and lifted his chin, smiling from ear to ear. Chastity felt as if she might be sick. The seats were filling quickly now, gentlemen sitting with hats on their laps or offering their seats to ladies whose brightly colored skirts spilled over into the narrow aisle. Children were crawling over everyone and everything, it seemed.

"Joey," Jonathon began for the third time, "do you realize how many people were waiting in that line?"

"What line?" he asked innocently.

"The line to board this train."

"Oh, that line! . . . Probably a million," he answered after a slight pause for calculation.

Jonathon sighed at his utter lack of contrition. "Joey, don't you know that it's proper to wait one's turn in line? Even if one is at the end of that line?"

Joey's eyes widened in surprise, then narrowed in confusion. "But the ones at the end get the worst seats. They might even have to stand."

"That's right."

"Well, excuse me for sayin' so, but I think the ones who wait till the end are just plain stupid."

Jonathon tried not to show his exasperation. "Listen to me, Joey. Waiting in line is the polite and correct thing to do. And for the remainder of today you are to act like a gentleman, do you understand?"

Joey's mouth pulled down at the corners in obvious disapproval. "Yeah . . ." His face brightened. "We sure did get good seats this time, didn't we, Mr. Stoneworth?"

The train was filled to capacity and then some when it huffed a large cloud of smoke and began its descent into Gold Canyon. Two more cars overflowing with picnickers were added at Carson City before the train sped onward to Washoe and the Bowers Mansion.

An imposing two-story sandstone structure with an ornate balustraded front porch and numerous fountains and water pools, the Bowers Mansion was the pride of the first real Comstock millionaires. Sandy and Eilley Bowers, whose marriage had joined their claims on the lode, had once drawn thousands of dollars a day from their mine and had spent two glorious years in Europe buying every imaginable luxury for their home. But Sandy's death five years before had left Eilley to cope with expensive litigation over their claims, a heavily mortgaged mansion, and a declining production in their mine. Consequently the mansion had been turned into a resort, its lovely landscaped grounds and swimming pools were opened to picnickers, and its elegant quarters made available to all who could pay the price of admission. But the efforts by Mrs. Bowers to regain her fortune were failing, and the *Enterprise* had even announced a lottery planned for the autumn, with the grand prize being the mansion and its contents.

Today though, the train unloaded its passengers within a few hundred feet of the Bowers Mansion, and the picnickers hauled their baskets down the well-worn paths toward the lovely grass-covered grounds. Once they had reached their destination and chosen a shady spot beneath the poplars, Jonathon took a large red and white checkered cloth from the wicker basket and handed Joey a corner to help spread it on the ground. While Joey wolfed down four pieces of chicken and Jonathon attacked the fare almost as eagerly, Chastity picked at a single piece and kept a sharp eye out for Regan Spencer. Thank heavens he hadn't been on that train! But she had been so certain he would come. Perhaps he had decided against coming after she declined his invitation. And perhaps it was all for the best. She glanced down at her lovely green gown, then at Jonathon, then at Joey. Nothing was working out the way she'd planned, and it was all the fault of that red-haired little brat.

"Ya gonna' enter the archery contest?"

Jonathon blinked at him in surprise. "I don't know. I hadn't thought about it. I haven't the equipment—"

"Aw, they got plenty. Ya can borrow somebody's. If ya think ya have a chance t' win, that is."

"Well . . ." Jonathan turned to Chastity. "What about you? Have you ever shot a bow? The kind with an arrow, I mean," he amended with a grin.

She raised her chin at his pun and the challenge, but didn't return his smile. "It has been a while, but I've done my share of shooting."

He eyed her closely, wishing that she would loosen up a bit. Joey was behaving admirably and there was no reason to ruin the entire day. "Do you mean you want to enter? The competition is usually close, if what I read in the *Enterprise* was correct. Perhaps you'd rather just try a game of croquet."

"I am not afraid of competition, Mr. Stoneworth, and I am quite capable of holding my own in any archery contest."

"Aw, I bet ya' can't hit the target once," Joey blurted out.

"And I'll bet I can hit it more than once," she snapped back at him. "In fact, I'll bet I can win that contest."

"Bet ya can't."

"Bet I can!"

Joey raised a brow in silent appraisal. "What'll ya bet?"

She snorted and lifted her nose in the air. "You couldn't match my wager, so why bother to ask?"

"Oh yeah? Well, I could work it off . . . if I lost, that is. But I ain't gonna lose. Not if ya got the nerve t' bet me."

Chastity considered a moment. "All right. Then I'll wager two dollars against eight hours of hard labor. You'll have to do whatever I ask." She'd ask him to walk all the way back to Virginia City!

"Or pay ya the money," Joey reminded her.

She nodded.

"Now wait a minute, you two. I don't think this is—"

"Ya never said nothin' 'bout bettin', Mr. Stoneworth. An' besides, the bet's been agreed on already. We can't take it back now." Jonathon frowned his disapproval first at one, then the other, but neither seemed concerned with what he thought. Their minds were already made up. "Don't worry, Mr. Stoneworth. I ain't gonna lose."

"We'll just see about that!" Chastity huffed.

She stretched her fingers, then made a tight fist, repeating the motions to ease the tension in her hands. She was quite good with a bow, or at least she had been a few years back. There had been an old Washoe Indian named Joe who'd taken quite a shine to the bullheaded little girl with "hair like the summer moon." In one of the rare moments when he had not been deeply engrossed in a poker game, Joe had given her a fine bow and she had given him a few pieces of Deborah's jewelry. At the time it had seemed like a fair exchange. For the next few months the bow had hardly left Chastity's hands. With a few vague pointers here and there, and hours upon hours of practice, she had finally worked up enough strength in her arms to keep the bow stretched taut, allowing a clean shot. After that, she seldom if ever missed whatever it was she aimed at. But that had been a long time ago. She nervously hoped it would all come back to her when she lifted a bow. It did.

Jonathon made a fair showing in the men's competition, capturing third prize. After several lengthy rounds in the women's contest, the field narrowed to six contestants. This number included both Chastity and Maureen Murphy, who turned a shining pair of cow eyes on Jonathon before and after every shot. If it hadn't been for Chastity's asking him first, he would probably have come with her today, not to mention to the social last week. Chastity saw at once that Maureen was more interested in Jonathon than she was in any contest. But she had won this competition for three years running, and she had to be taken seriously.

The shooting line was moved back to a distance of sixty-five feet from the target. The first two women took their shots, and both missed the target entirely. Chastity stepped to the line, lifted her bow and drew back the bow-string, and let fly a perfect shot. The crowd went wild, Jonathon's jaw dropped in amazement, but when she turned her gloating smile toward them, Joey was nowhere to be seen. Well, there would be plenty of time for him later, she thought, and besides, the contest wasn't over yet.

With her work cut out for her, Maureen assumed her place at the line and concentrated on making the next shot. Her arrow pierced the target on the line between the gold center and the red first outer ring, and once again the crowd broke into applause. This was shaping into quite a contest and attracting even more spectators than usual.

The field then narrowed to two contestants, and the shooting line was again moved, to a distance of seventy-five feet. The crowd murmured with expectancy as Chastity prepared her next shot. She assumed perfect posture, lifted the bow, and once again pierced the target almost dead center. The spectators roared their approval.

Maureen stepped confidently to the shooting line the minute Chastity had finished. She had never shot an arrow that distance before, but if Chastity Morrow could do it, so could she! She twisted her neck to flash Jonathon a wide smile (which he hoped no one else noticed), then bit her lip while setting up the shot and let the arrow fly. It missed the target by a mile. In a single instant her face contorted with shock, anger, disbelief, and frustration. For a moment Jonathon was actually afraid that she might turn the weapon on the victor of the contest. But instead she tossed it to the ground and stomped off in a fury, "forgetting" to offer congratulations to the winner.

Chastity hardly noticed. She smiled widely for those who cheered and applauded her victory, flying high on a newfound sense of accomplishment. She had been forced to work hard for the win, and she was all the more gratified that it had been a close contest. She returned the bow to the gentleman from whom she had borrowed it, thanking him for the favor and feeling better than she had in weeks.

She made her way slowly back to the red and white check-ered cloth, graciously accepting congratulations from peo-ple all along the way.

When she finally reached their picnic area, she sat down near the basket and frowned. Neither Joey nor Jonathon was anywhere in sight. She let out a sigh of disenchant-ment as she noticed that her fingers had been cut and scraped by the bowstring, and at about that same time she became aware of a ferocious ache in her arm muscles after the strenuous workout. Still the winning had been worth it all, and she felt wonderfully alive. When she saw Jona-thon walking toward her she flashed him a warm smile. "Where's Joey?"

He frowned and quickly glanced around. "I don't know. I haven't seen him since the start of the contest."

"Is Maureen going to recover?" she asked innocently.

Jonathon didn't answer, but he lifted his head as he caught sight of Joey making his way quickly through the crowd back to their picnic spot. He was struggling to carry something, something he obviously didn't trust to keep in his much-mended pants pockets. By the time he reached the edge of the cloth, Joey was in deep trouble. There was no doubt at all what he was carrying—it was money; about five dollars, Jonathon guessed, and he certainly hadn't had it when they'd arrived.

"We had an agreement, Joey. There was to be no steal-ing."

"I didn't steal nothin'!"

"Then where did all the money come from?"

"I won it."

"You won it?" Jonathon repeated doubtfully. "How?"

"We-e-e-ell . . ." He sighed and waited a good half min-ute before he finally blurted it out. "I bet on Miss Morrow in the archery contest."

"You what?" It was difficult to tell who was more sur-prised, Jonathon or Chastity. Both were absolutely wide-eyed with astonishment.

He scowled as if their reactions were ridiculous. "I bet on Miss Morrow. It was almost a sure thing, after all," he explained logically. "Considerin' how bad she wanted t' see me lose."

Jonathon shook himself calm and tried to look at the situation objectively. It was possible, but . . . "You've got a lot of money there, Joey."

"Four dollars and thirty-six cents," he interjected happily. "Mike Simmons still owes me fourteen cents."

"But where in the world did you get enough money to cover all those bets?" he demanded.

The pleased smile left Joey's face as he fingered his money and considered how to answer.

"Joey . . ."

"I, uh—"

"The truth."

"I—" He shrugged his shoulders and spilled the beans. "I tol' em ya was coverin' all bets, Mr. Stoneworth. An' I even gave 'em odds." He smiled proudly at that. "They all thought they was robbin' me, since that Murphy dame wins every year. Then Miss Morrow picked up that bow . . ." He raised his hands to mimic her stance. ". . . and *pow!*"

For a split second Chastity thought she might kill him. But suddenly she started laughing, and she laughed until she was absolutely weak with laughter. Joey had gotten the best of her, yes, but also Jonathon, and the First Ward kids, and who knew who else—all in a single fell swoop! She thought back to her own childhood, and her memories of treachery seemed tame in comparison. Deborah wouldn't have lasted a month if she'd been forced to contend with Joey Bates! She reached out and rumpled his shock of red hair with something that resembled affection. He wrinkled his nose in distaste and pulled away from her.

"Good afternoon, Miss Morrow, Mr. Stoneworth." Regan's eyes flicked over the boy without acknowledging him. "It seems I've just missed something very amusing."

Chastity's smile shriveled into a look of utter mortification. She felt her cheeks burning with what she knew must be a deep scarlet blush. Regan Spencer! She had been so certain that he wasn't here. She mumbled a greeting as Jonathon rose to shake his hand and—horror of all horrors!—introduced Joey Bates. Chastity prayed that Regan would forget he'd seen Joey with her before he heard the stories about the town's worst troublemaker.

"I'm happy that your stepmother decided to let you come to the picnic," Regan remarked sarcastically. "It would have been a shame to miss all this." He tossed a glance at the red-haired boy, who was busily counting a considerable number of nickles and dimes.

She managed a kind of a weak smile. "Yes."

He nodded, then looked Chastity deliberately in the eye as he bid them all a pleasant good-day. She watched him amble across the lovely green lawn toward the house and wanted to cry. Today had been a total failure. Worse than a total failure, if that were possible. She sighed and her face showed all the disappointment she was feeling. She just couldn't help it.

"Don't worry. He'll be back."

She snapped to attention. "What did you say?"

"I said, he'll be back," Jonathon repeated.

"I'm sure I don't know what you're talking about."

"And I'm sure you do."

Her jaw squared ominously but she kept her silence, tossing a meaningful glance at Joey, who had stopped figeting with his money and was all ears. They would finish this discussion later, or not at all.

The day dragged on despite Chastity's burning desire to see it over and done with. There were games of croquet, a brief tour of the beautiful mansion, and a rather improper wade in one of the swimming pools, which finally managed to coax a smile from Chastity, if only a tiny one. It was a long day, a tiring day, a day of memories made from broken plans. It was very late evening when they returned on the train to Virginia City, and Joey's eyelids barely remained open for the carriage ride home. Chastity almost smiled as he nodded off, then jerked and shook himself awake for the fourth time. Somewhere between there and Washoe, an unspoken truce had been declared between them. She opened her hand to stare at the coins he had insisted she accept—exactly two dollars. It was a fortune to a boy like Joey, and Chastity fully appreciated their value. She was forced to admit that he had added something almost pleasant to this day, a child's enthusiasm over simple, unnoticed pleasures. Of course, it hadn't begun to make up for her ruined plans, but there would be other days, other gowns, other picnics.

The carriage eased to a stop at the north end of G Street and Joey hopped off, called a sleepy good-night, and traced a wobbly path toward the small white house where he lived. Chastity watched him for a moment, then sighed and settled her head back against the seat.

"It was a nice day, wasn't it?"

She eyed Jonathon, then looked away without answering the question.

"Joey's really a good boy at heart. Intelligent, too."

Chastity didn't want to appear agreeable at this point, so she stared in silence at the houses passing by.

"You worry too much about what he thinks."

She scowled and shot him an angry glare. "I don't care in the least what Joey thinks."

Jonathon grinned. "I'm not talking about Joey."

She lifted her chin indignantly. "Then I don't know what you're talking about."

"Oh, yes you do," he tossed back knowingly. "You're transparent as glass, Chastity Morrow. I didn't know at first why you wanted me to accompany you to this picnic, but I'm not blind. You came in the hopes of seeing Regan Spencer, of making an impression on him. What I still don't understand is why you didn't just go with him in the first place." His eyes narrowed thoughtfully. "Or didn't he ask you?"

"Of course he asked me!"

Jonathon raised a skeptical brow.

"He did ask me," she insisted, "but . . . but . . ."

"Yes?"

She bit her lip and sighed in utter frustration. She might as well go ahead and tell him the whole story. "But I didn't want to appear too eager, so I told him perhaps."

"And?"

She swallowed hard and felt her cheeks burning. "And so he withdrew his invitation."

In spite of himself, Jonathon laughed, a loud hearty laugh that made Chastity absolutely furious. "I don't see what's so funny!"

"You wouldn't. Chastity Morrow, I'm afraid you've met your match in Mr. Spencer. Don't you see? He baited you. And you fell for it—hook, line, and sinker."

She snorted and turned away in a huff. "You don't understand anything."

He smiled and shook his head. "'I'm afraid you're the one who doesn't understand anything, Chastity. Games like the one you're playing are dangerous. Love is a lot more than smiles and pretty dresses and—"

"Yes, I know," she interrupted tartly, vowing never again to tell him anything. "Deborah's told me all about it."

"It's feeling and growing and giving," he continued, ignoring her interruption, "and a great deal of effort."

How romantic! she thought sarcastically.

"And if I were your father—" He stopped short.

She perked up immediately. "If you were my father, what?"

He scowled and muttered something under his breath, which gave Chastity no small degree of satisfaction. "If you asked me, Jonathon, I'd say you're too straight-laced and prudish for your own good," she told him bluntly.

He lifted an amused brow. "Is that right?"

"And furthermore," she went on curtly, "there is nothing wrong with flirting. In fact, it's a very amusing pastime." She flashed him a disdainful glare. "But I suppose you've never once trifled with a woman."

His lips curved the slightest bit upward before he turned his attention to the passing houses, completely ignoring the question. Chastity frowned, her eyes narrowing thoughtfully. "I'll wager there've been quite a few women who've trifled with you, though."

He said nothing and his continued silence caused her

mouth to twist into a quick, mischievous grin. She stifled that grin and quickly slipped from the seat opposite to take a seat beside him. "Tell me about them, Jonathon," she crooned softly, letting her gloved fingers play in his hair.

He turned his head in annoyance, and his eyes measured her carefully for a long moment. "Why would you want to know?"

She fixed a wide, innocent look to her eyes. "I want to know *everything* about you, Jonathon," she insisted sweetly, tilting her head just so. For once he might even slip and give her the upper hand, she thought excitedly.

"Well . . . actually," Jonathon began softly, his voice much lower and huskier than it had been a moment before, "there was only one woman . . ." His eyes moved deliberately from Chastity's eyes to her lips, while at the same time a hand slipped behind her neck, kneading the downy softness there with lean, expertly gentle fingers. "She was very, very pretty . . . ," he went on, his eyes drifting lower still until they lingered on her breasts, until he saw a hot flush pour into her cheeks. "Blond . . . dark blue eyes . . . and she was constantly . . ." His voice was a whisper now, and his lips had found the curve of her neck. He felt her shiver. ". . . pushing me . . ." His mouth moved slowly upward, toward her ear. She backed away to the far side of the carriage. He pursued. ". . . to the very limits . . ." The tip of his tongue touched her earlobe. ". . . of my endurance."

Chastity gasped aloud as her back met firmly with the corner of the leather seat. She stiffened as Jonathon moved closer still. He was nearly on top of her. His hands found her shoulders and her eyes widened with dismay. She was certain that he was going to do something absolutely scandalous to her, though she wasn't sure exactly what. "Jonathon . . . ," she pleaded earnestly.

His eyes were so serious, so intent on holding hers that for a long moment she held her breath. Then to her complete amazement he abruptly released her and sat up straight. "Have I made my point, Miss Morrow?" he inquired calmly, with an infuriatingly casual lift of a single brow.

For a long moment she could do nothing more than stare at him. She could not even catch her breath. But a moment later she moved as far away as she possibly could, drawing herself up haughtily in the corner of the carriage where he had trapped her a few minutes before.

"If you play with fire . . . ," he taunted as she smoothed her skirts and pointedly avoided his eyes.

She ground her teeth in utter frustration. He was odious! she thought indignantly. She flashed him an accusing glare. "I suppose no one ever flirts where you come from," she retorted.

"Never," he returned matter-of-factly.

Her eyes narrowed to angry slits. "Where *did* you come from?"

"Boston, Massachusetts," he returned with a proud inflection to his voice. "Home of the finest and fastest racing schooners in all the world."

In spite of herself, Chastity's frown softened a bit as she glanced at his face. "Did you race?"

"Certainly."

Her eyes widened with sudden interest, albeit begrudging. "Really?"

He nodded. "Every summer we went up to the North Shore to our summer house in Manchester, my grandfather and I. He used to say in jest that the *Laddy*—that was my boat—that the *Laddy* was launched in June and didn't dock again until September."

She smiled dreamily, caught up in the enthusiasm she had heard in his voice, her anger suddenly forgotten. "I think I'd like to try sailing, but I've never had the opportunity." She sighed, then studied his face. "Don't you miss it?"

"Terribly."

"Then whatever made you leave Boston?"

His smile faded slowly and another kind of look softened his eyes. After the war he'd gone back to Boston, but only long enough to learn that his grandfather had died, that the only remnant of the powerful and wealthy

Nathaniel Stoneworth was an impressive marble monument which bore his name. The fine house on Beacon Hill had been sold to strangers, the lesser partners in Nathaniel's law firm had quickly deleted his name from their door, and the Stoneworth fortune had been dispersed to charities and educational institutions according to the instructions of Nathaniel's will. Jonathon remembered standing in silence high above the sea on Copp's Hill, staring at the perfect block letters chipped in cold marble and picturing his grandfather's stern features, feeling the warmth of those long summer days he'd spent with him on the North Shore, hearing the crackle of a warm fire in his grandfather's library on winter nights when he'd studied till dawn. But there were other memories too, of letters written from nameless battlefields, letters that had never been answered and probably never read. "I suppose," he admitted softly, after a long moment, "that I just woke up one morning and found that I didn't belong there."

She smiled, her eyes intently watching him now as she wondered at his mood. "And do you belong here?" she asked him quietly.

The carriage jolted to a stop before he had a chance to answer. He swung open the door and agilely swung to the ground before he turned to offer her assistance. She slid into his arms and paused, her eyes searching his face. "You didn't answer my question."

His eyes held hers for a long moment before his mouth curved into a smile. "I suppose I belong here . . . for now." His expression faded a bit. "At least until your father recovers."

She turned slowly and began to climb the steps. He was at her side. "You've been very good for my father," she admitted softly, as much to herself as to him. "I—I'm glad you were here when he needed you." She tossed a quick glance at his face before she looked away.

"Your father has been good for me too," he said with a warm smile.

She bit her lip at the affection in his tone. She was still a little bit jealous of the relationship he had with her father.

She couldn't help it. She turned to face him as they reached the porch. "Thank you for a nice day," she mouthed quickly. She forced a smile before she turned away from him then and hurried into the house.

Chapter 9

The mild warmth of spring disappeared beneath a white-hot summer sun, and great clouds of dust churned about Virginia City streets with the relentless movement of horses and carts and wagons and people. The longer, hotter days passed slowly for Regan Spencer as he waited longer and longer for news of the bonanza in the Consolidated Virginia Mine to break. Stock in the Con Virginia was almost impossible to buy now, and it seemed obvious to Regan that the owners of the mine and other persons aware of the as yet unannounced bonanza were buying up shares as soon as they were put on the market. But there had been no public declaration as yet, only an end to assessments on the stock, and Regan had been forced to sit tight and wait. The waiting did not come easily to him, especially here in Virginia City, where the clattering, roaring, whistling cacophony of round-the-clock mining operations disturbed his already restless sleep. With each passing day it became more apparent that he had made a mistake investing nearly all his money in mining stocks. The stock market was a crazy, unpredictable seesaw which fluctuated daily on the strength of rumor alone. News of a bonanza might cause stock market prices to soar to ridiculous heights, while a whisper in the wrong ear could cause a panic that would mean financial ruin for hundreds of investors. A few months ago Regan had been like everyone else, caught up in the possibility of instant fortune, certain that he would be one of the lucky winners

121

in the game. But the longer he waited, the more uncertain
he became. For every man who boasted happily that he
had come out millions ahead, there were thousands of
others who had lost their life savings and were desperately buying stocks on the margin in an attempt to win
them back. The odds were risky, too risky for a professional gambler like Regan even to consider, and he saw no
chance of stacking the deck—not unless one owned and op-
erated a mine all by himself.

Regan had been lucky thus far, winning enough here
and there at faro and poker to afford assessments on his
stocks when they were due, and most of the ones he'd purchased were on a gradual rise due to the new bonanza at
the Crown Point and rumors of other bonanzas to come.
But Regan no longer believed that stock certificates would
bring him the kind of wealth he desired.

As he walked past shops and businesses lining C
Street on a dazzling morning in mid-July, he was preoccupied with his present situation and the scores of possible
solutions to his dilemma. His silver-blue eyes scanned the
dozens of gleaming plate glass windows, each proudly
displaying an unbelievable selection of some of the finest
goods in the world. Jewelry stores, restaurants, clothing
stores, bathhouses—all steeped in luxury, all jammed with
customers anxious to spend their coin. There had to be a
surer way of getting one's hands on a share of the
Comstock's silver, but it would mean channeling one's efforts into something safer and more secure than a stock of
paper certificates. A plan of action was forming in his
mind, a plan that had begun to take shape when he won a
piece of property in a poker game the night before. It was a
large lot on the north end of C Street, a prime location
though the building on it was worthless, gutted by fire a
few months back. Regan paused before reaching the Morrow Mining Company office and bit off the end of an expensive cigar, shaking his head at the man who brushed
brusquely past him hurrying toward the exchange. A
Spencer ought to have no trouble making his fortune in a
town like this, where everyone had money and seemed
eager to spend it. But any kind of enterprise he decided

upon would require capital, and that would take a bit of thoughtful planning, too. He lit the cigar and drew on it thoughtfully.

It was time to make his move with Chastity, there was no doubt about it. But that Stoneworth fellow she'd been with at the ball, and again at the Bowers Mansion picnic, bothered Regan. He'd heard quite a bit about Stoneworth these past few weeks, and what he had learned didn't calm his worries. Apparently Stoneworth was Samuel Morrow's confidant as well as his lawyer, and a close friend of the Morrow family. Regan had taken an immediate dislike to Jonathon, and he had the distinct feeling that Stoneworth wasn't very fond of him, either. Worst of all, Stoneworth was a handsome fellow, pursued by a good many ladies about town and a few women who were not ladies at all. Even Patsy Justice, an acquaintance of Regan's who claimed to have bedded more gentlemen west of the Mississippi than any woman, white, black, or Oriental, was attracted to Jonathon, ". . . but he just ain't the payin' type," she had told Regan frankly. It stood to reason that Chastity would be taken with Jonathon as well. And Regan didn't like the idea of competing for Chastity's favors with a man like that, particularly when his entire future might hinge on the use of her father's fortune. But he didn't have much of a choice at this point. He sighed deeply as he took up walking again, deciding that a luncheon engagement at the International Hotel would be as good a place as anywhere else in this town to begin a courtship. At least he was confident that Chastity wouldn't have to ask her stepmother's permission this time before accepting his request.

Chastity flitted happily about the office, performing her usual tasks with a wide smile dimpling her cheeks while Jonathon crumpled yet another sheet of paper in his hands and sent it flying into the waste receptacle to land atop at least a half-dozen others. It should not have bothered him so much to learn that Regan Spencer had finally requested the honor of Chastity's company for lunch at the International. It had been obvious the evening of the char-

ity social, and even more obvious at the Bowers Mansion
picnic, that Spencer had an interest in her, that he intended to become more than just a nodding acquaintance.
But maybe it wasn't Spencer who bothered him at all.
Maybe it was Chastity herself. Jonathon didn't like the
triumphant gleam in her eyes or the confident smile she'd
worn all morning long. She was too infatuated with Spencer for her own good, too intent on making him her latest
conquest. She was heading for trouble with this man; Jonathon could feel it. Regan Spencer wasn't the type to make
a fool of himself over a woman. He was too self-centered
and ambitious and proud, though Chastity saw none of
that in his dashing, handsome smile. She only saw something she wanted and intended to have. And there was no
one in the world who could tell her otherwise.

Jonathon rose to offer his hand as well as an appropriate
greeting to Spencer when he entered the office. Then he
busied himself with a stack of urgent correspondence
Chastity had just placed on his desk. But his mind was not
on his work as the door of the office closed behind them,
nor did it return to his work for a long, long while after
they had gone.

Chastity turned her brightest smile on Regan as soon as
he had taken his seat across the table. "The heat's been
unbearable this past week, hasn't it?" She lightly fingered
the white lacy flounce at the end of her mint green half
sleeves, confident that the color of her gown gave her a
cool appearance in spite of the heat.

"I suppose," he responded without raising his eyes from
the menu card, which had just been handed to him.

"Spring flies by so quickly," she sighed, "but summer
seems to linger on and on."

He said nothing. A moment later he lifted a pair of distant blue-gray eyes to meet her expectant smile. "I'm having the lamb with mint sauce. Have you made up your
mind yet?"

Chastity's smile faded quite a bit at his question. Trying
very hard to hide her disappointment, she lifted the menu
and chose the roast ham with champagne sauce.

"I didn't see you at the opera house last week," she remarked several moments later, after he had ordered.

He met her eyes for a moment. "The opera house?"

"At the benefit for Mrs. Bowers."

"I wasn't there," he returned flatly, his eyes leaving hers to wander about the dining room.

Chastity frowned, following his eyes, wondering what on earth he found so interesting in walls and ceilings and floors and woodwork. She had thought to find him much more receptive to her charms after waiting such a long time to court her. She had considered this invitation to luncheon a giant step in the right direction. But he was ignoring her again, just as he had before, and she couldn't for the life of her figure out why.

"There's a charity bazaar for the hospital next week," she hinted with a pretty tilt of her chin. "I've been reading about it in the *Enterprise.*"

"I think I saw something about that . . . ," he mumbled, his eyes narrowly observing the patrons of the dining room now, moving from one table to the next. Chastity let out a sigh of frustration as her eyes once again attempted to follow his. She felt a pang of jealousy as she saw couples smiling at one another, engaging in intimate conversation. Regan seemed to have no desire to converse with her. Her meal was placed before her and she stared at it without interest. Regan's mind was otherwise occupied as well. She looked up, meeting the eyes of a young gentleman at an adjacent table. He was dressed in a twill tailcoat and bright red brocade vest, and he was smiling at her with obvious admiration. She colored a bit, her confidence bolstered just enough to try again. She turned her attention back to Regan, her brow furrowing lightly in thought. If he had ignored her pretty new dress and flighty feminine prattle, then perhaps he would respond to conversation along a more serious vein.

"The new pump at the mine broke down yesterday," she remarked suddenly. "And it will be at least a week before it can be repaired. Everything's at a standstill until the parts on order arrive from England. That means a much smaller payroll for us to work on this week."

For the first time since their arrival Regan's eyes met hers with a spark of interest. He lifted a casually curious brow. "Us?"

"Jonathon Stoneworth and I work on it together," she told him matter-of-factly, holding back the coquettish smile that came to her quite out of habit.

"I see." His gaze was fixed on her now as she daintily sipped at her coffee.

"I read in the *Enterprise* that the Carson City Mint has been stamping valuations on every bar of silver they assay and process. It's utterly ridiculous, if you ask me," she went on convincingly, repeating almost verbatim what her father had told Jonathon earlier that morning. "Government regulations will ruin the silver market. Silver prices ought to be determined by supply and demand, not arbitrary figures from the government." (She'd heard that from her father a dozen times over.) She could feel Regan's eyes measuring her all the while she added a bit more sugar to her coffee.

"What do you think of this place?"

Her blue eyes lifted immediately. "This place?" she repeated with a blank expression.

"Yes. This place. The International. What do you think of it?"

Her eyes still mirrored puzzlement, but she responded with unmistakable pride. "Why, it's the finest hotel in the whole state."

Regan's eyes brightened and his lips curved upward ever so slightly. "And what if there were an even grander hotel here in Virginia City?"

Chastity frowned at him, thinking that totally impossible. The International rose to a grand height of four stories and covered almost an entire city block. The exterior ironwork alone had cost thousands and thousands of dollars, and there were over a hundred hotel rooms, not to mention several resident businesses. She glanced about the dining room, which was at least forty feet long and forty feet wide, at the elegant high ceilings, at the lovely glow given off by scores of soft gaslights. And the menu at the International dining room included lobster, truffles, and the finest imported wines. It was impossible to think that another hotel would ever match this one.

"What do you suppose would happen if there were a grander hotel in this town?" Regan said again.

"Why, everyone would go there, of course," she answered curtly.

He smiled. Of course everyone would go there. Comstockers naturally sought out the finest, the most luxurious, the most expensive. A hotel, Regan thought with a smile. An extraordinarily beautiful hotel set here in this crazy town on the mountainside. The more he considered it, the more the idea appealed to him. The lot he'd acquired a few days ago would be a perfect location for the place, set in the very heart of this town. And the building would have to be at least five, maybe six stories tall so that it would tower gloriously over every other building in town. But it would take capital. Quite a bit of capital . . .

Regan smiled warmly into Chastity's frown of confusion and it quickly disappeared. When she returned his smile and coyly dipped her eyes, he felt more confident in his future than he had in weeks. "Did I hear you mention something about a bazaar next week . . . ?"

Chapter 10

The longest, hottest days of summer descended on Virginia City in late July, and the dry, dusty breezes stirring the air did little to alleviate the discomfort of living under a brilliant, scorching sun. For Regan the summer days passed quickly in spite of his distaste for this dry, desolate mountain town. Now that he had made up his mind to build a hotel here, he had made himself a very busy man. He spent many hours studying the International and the way it was run, spoke in general terms with several knowledgeable men about construction methods and costs, and even made a special trip to San Francisco to have a look at the spectacular beginnings of the Palace, a hotel being built by William Ralston, who controlled the Bank of California. Of course, Regan realized he could only raise a fraction of the funds available to Mr. Ralston, and that his hotel in Virginia City would not begin to duplicate the Palace. But his visit to San Francisco made him all the more confident of success in this venture. There were a dozen luxurious, expensive hotels in San Francisco, and only one in Virginia City. He planned to change all that very soon.

As the days of July flowed into August, Regan stepped up his efforts to court Chastity in the hopes of securing a generous loan from her father before summer's end. He made it a point to see her three or four times each week, even if their meetings were sometimes limited to a brief stroll from the Morrow Mining office to the C Street ex-

change. One morning in mid-August Regan left his boardinghouse room and went to rent a buggy at the livery
stable nearby, planning to spend the entire afternoon with
Chastity and hoping to arrange a meeting with her father. As he hoisted himself into the seat and took up the
reins, he once again contemplated his plans, in which
Chastity played an integral part. It was very important
that he maintain a firm hold on her so that there wouldn't
be any question when he approached her father about a
loan. He turned the buggy west, in the direction of Howard
Street, and slowed the horse from an eager canter to a
sluggish walk. He always made it a habit to arrive late to
remind Chastity that she was not the only thing on his
mind. He never allowed himself to forget that he was
pursuing her for strictly monetary reasons, even though
he had taken a fancy to her and had come to enjoy her company. He certainly had no intention of letting his feelings
get in the way of what he really wanted from her: money.
He smiled confidently as the familiar house came into
view, secure in the knowledge that Chastity was counting
the minutes until his arrival.

Chastity paced her room petulantly, inspecting her
frilly pale blue gown each and every time she passed the
looking glass. Why, oh why was he always so late? she
ranted silently at her reflection. She stamped her foot and
marched to the window, resolving for the twentieth time
not to descend the stairs until he arrived. He was a half
hour late for their picnic already, so it wouldn't do to have
him know that she'd been ready for over an hour. Not
since Regan always kept her waiting. She sighed her annoyance as her eyes scanned the street for some sign of
him, and a moment later she caught sight of the buggy
slowly approaching the house. She stifled a smile in spite
of her anger. There was such an air of mystery to Regan
Spencer; there was so much hidden by that dark, handsome face. She knew now that she would marry him the
moment he asked her, and she was certain that he would
ask her very soon. She made a childish face at the buggy
and laughed to herself. She felt giddy just thinking about
being married to Regan, and finally being absolutely cer-

tain that he loved her. Regan was by far the most handsome man in Virginia City, and she always noticed the way other women gawked at him when they paraded down the boardwalk to the stock exchange, or whirled about the room at a social, or rode slowly down C Street in a rented buggy. They made an eye-catching couple—Regan with his dark, dramatic coloring and crisp black suit, and Chastity with her fair, silver blondness, dressed in softest pastels. The contrasts between them only served to accentuate his chiseled handsomeness, her deceptive fragile beauty. She tossed her head and grinned as she took one last appraising look in the mirror. How fortunate she was to have found a man like Regan! She would never be caught in the trap of a boring, day-after-day existence, because Regan was different from other men. There would always be that mysterious part of him, the part of himself he held aloof. And there would always be the excitement of the challenge to hold him.

Regan slowed the buggy to a halt in front of the painted mansion and leisurely mounted the steps to the main entrance. Sarah had scarcely opened the door before Chastity appeared at the top of the staircase carrying a large straw bonnet with a light blue sash. She flounced down the winding stairs, pausing with a pretty pout to tie the sash under her chin. "You're late again."

He raised a careless brow. "Am I?"

"Yes, you are. And what's more, you know perfectly well you are." She descended the last few steps and peered up at him from beneath the floppy brim of her bonnet. "Why is it that you're always trying to make me angry?"

His eyes lit with amusement at her annoyance. "Do I do that?"

She sighed her exasperation. "Yes, you do!"

The next moment he caught her wrists and pulled them behind her back, drawing her slowly forward until she was flush against his chest. "It must be because you're so beautiful when you're angry," he said huskily, his eyes lingering hungrily on her mouth. She felt a shiver of pure delight run up her spine as his fingers tightened about her wrists, as he deliberately lowered his mouth to hers.

"Good afternoon, Mr. Spencer." There was a slight tremor of discomfort in Deborah's voice as she mouthed the greeting which interrupted them. They immediately withdrew to a more proper distance. Deborah felt herself tensing as she met her stepdaughter's indignant glare. "I thought you'd already gone, Chastity," she said in that soft, patient voice which grated on Chastity's nerves. "You will be back before sunset, won't you?" Her tired blue eyes moved to question Regan.

"Have no fear, Mrs. Morrow," he responded in a blatantly patronizing tone of voice. "I intend to return your stepdaughter safe and sound and at a most proper hour."

Deborah bristled inwardly at the arrogant way his eyes dismissed her, at his condescending manner. She didn't like Regan Spencer at all, and she didn't approve of all the time he was spending with Chastity. But she had the distinct impression that her disapproval only reinforced Chastity's feelings for the man, feelings that were far too obvious to Deborah already, so she said nothing more. "Have a nice time, Chastity . . . Mr. Spencer."

"Thank you, Mrs. Morrow. I shall do my best to see that she does." Without another word, Regan took hold of Chastity's arm, gathered up the picnic basket Sarah had brought from the kitchen, and led her out of the house.

They left Howard Street and eagerly made their way to a favorite picnicking spot a good distance up the side of Mount Davidson. The roads proceeded up the mountains just so far before running dead, but here were several well-worn footpaths, and Chastity knew them all. From high above the view was breathtaking. Rocky hills and mountains rose infinitely in the distance, each reflecting the sun's light with a different shade of color. From the silver-purple peaks to the glistening white desert sands, all of Nevada seemed sprawled gloriously below.

Chastity raced with Regan up the path the last hundred yards or so, and when they had reached their goal they dropped breathlessly to the ground, laughing. As her breathing slowed and her laughter faded, she stared at the awesome beauty displayed before her and her heart filled with pride.

"There's not a view in the whole world to compare with this one." She raised her eyes to Regan, smiling, glad that he was there beside her to share this moment. She watched his blue-gray eyes roam thoughtfully over the miles and miles of hills and mountains.

"Not a single tree or patch of green to be seen," he remarked in wonder.

"It doesn't need any green," she returned defensively. "This place is far more beautiful than any tended garden or manicured lawn."

He sighed and shrugged, moving closer to her side. Chastity was blindly loyal to her birthplace, and he wasn't about to begin an argument with her. His eyes lingered on the pretty flush in her cheeks; the incredible dark blue color of her eyes; the sweep of long, sooty lashes; the soft yellow, almost white tendrils of hair that fluttered about her face. She met his eyes again and smiled, not the practiced, coquettish smile she usually employed, but a warm, passionate smile that made him want to take her into his arms. He took her chin between his thumb and forefinger and tilted her face so that her mouth was only inches from his own. He intended the same kind of brief, proper kiss he'd shared with her several times before. It began that way. She closed her eyes and felt the light touch of his lips against her mouth. She felt so strange, as she had before when he'd kissed her, as if there were some kind of war going on in the deepest, most secret part of her. His lips lingered on hers for a moment before he instinctively began to explore the smooth, full lines of her mouth, playing, teasing, tasting the velvety texture as he pulled ever so gently at her lips. And then suddenly his purpose changed. He opened his mouth and hungrily sought to know more of her than ever before. She felt his tongue, warm and insistent against her teeth, and she gasped and pulled back slightly but offered no resistance when a hand at the back of her head prevented her full retreat. She felt her heart race, her stomach fill with butterflies, her breath come in short, almost painful gasps, as if she'd run a mile. Her whole being tingled with a rush of hot, dizzying sensations, and all at once she was welcoming the intrusion, the sweet, deep thrusting into her mouth. Regan ran his fingers along her jawline toward her chin in a light caress, coaxing her to respond. And then she was matching the movements of his tongue, eagerly exploring his mouth, tasting the sweetness of their kiss to the fullest measure. The crazy, delightful shiver racing through her was stronger than ever before, triumphing completely over any thoughts about rational or proper behavior. Chastity had sensed from the first that Regan was different from other men, but this magical moment held more promise than she'd ever dared to imagine.

She would have kissed him forever, but suddenly Regan pulled away from her, halting a rush of exhilarating, freeing sensations he had not expected at all. He wanted her, not as he had wanted other women, to satisfy a passing physical need. The wanting went deeper, to a part of himself he had thought no longer existed, to a part of him he had thought destroyed by the war and all that came afterward. For a long time he searched Chastity's face, wondering why he was suddenly remembering the boy he had been so many years before, running over the grassy hills of home, feeling alive and free, so utterly free. She smiled at him, a shy kind of smile, as she let her hand slide affectionately over his cheek. "Tell me what you're thinking," she whispered, feeling closer to him than she could ever remember feeling to anyone.

He returned her smile and his eyes lit with a soft, distant gleam. "I was thinking of home," he said softly.

She moved to settle her head against his chest, to listen to the quiet rhythm of his heart. "Tell me about your home."

He let out a lengthy breath and a strange mixture of regret and pride touched his voice. "It was called *Regalia*," he began slowly, "and it was one of the finest plantations in all the South." He paused, his eyes slipping over the mountains and distant hills while his mind saw a very different picture. "I remember those endless, neat rows of tobacco and cotton, the deep brown color of the freshly plowed earth, the slaves in calico and brightly colored clothing, the dark green grass bordering the fields . . . the cool, welcome shade of magnolias and willows and dog-woods . . . and the hills, so soft and thick with green grass . . ." He sighed and closed his eyes. "I remember company comin' up the long drive . . . ," he said with a little smile, "Mammy bustlin' in and out of the house, relayin' orders from Mama . . ." He sighed again, and his voice was touched with tenderness. "And Mama in her wide hoop skirt, sitting there on the veranda in a white wicker chair—" He stopped short, his eyes suddenly hard-ened. The peaceful life of such grace and beauty was gone forever now, a forgotten part of his youth. The father who had taught him everything about pride and honor and duty had fallen on some forsaken battlefield. And Mama, who had held him so tightly and told him not to cry the day the soldiers burned *Regalia*, had died only a few weeks af-ter she had learned of her husband's death. She had lost her will to go on.

Chastity frowned and lifted her head, aware of the sud-den change in him, and wondering what had brought it about. She placed her hand tenderly on his cheek and forced him to meet her gaze. "It hurts you to remember. I know. Sometimes when I remember back as far as I can, to the time when my mama and papa and I lived all together, it hurts me to think that those times are gone, that they'll never come again, that all I really have left is the memory . . . and the pain." Her eyes misted with tears and she had to struggle to force a smile. "But we have today. We have now." Her eyes scanned the hills and the city that lay at her feet, and her chin lifted with unmistakable pride. "We have this," she whispered. She turned back to face him and lifted his hand, entwined in her fingers. "And this . . ." She smiled tenderly at him again and laid his hand against her cheek. "For me that is enough."

Regan sighed and looked away, not wanting her to sense that for him this would never be enough. Someday he would rebuild the life he had known before the war. And he would marry a woman who would make his life a peace-ful, wonderfully tranquil existence, who would fill his home with grace and beauty just as his mother had done for his father. Chastity, with her stubborn will and driv-

ing determination, could never be that woman. Her plebe-
ian background was all too apparent in everything she
said and did. He shook off any stray emotion that had
clouded his oneness of purpose and changed the subject to
business. "How is your father these days?"

Chastity dropped his hand reluctantly and turned to
search the picnic basket for something to eat. She had
skipped breakfast, planning on an early lunch, and Regan's tardy arrival had given her ample time to work up
an appetite. "He's doing exceptionally well. Dr. Perkins
says he may even be able to return to the office in the fall.
Only for a short time each day, of course," she added.
"And probably because Papa's pestered the poor man so
these past few weeks." She found a fat, ripe apple and eagerly bit into it. "But that's much sooner than any of us
had expected, so we're all very hopeful."

"I'd like very much to meet him as soon as he's well
enough," Regan said offhandedly as he took the basket
and found something more to his liking than an apple.

Chastity's eyes flew to his face and she nearly choked on
a piece of apple. "You would?"

He flashed her a smile as he took a bite of cold roast beef
sandwich. "Yes . . . although he probably won't have time
to meet all of your admirers before he returns to work," he
teased.

"Probably not," she mumbled dumbly, still staring at
his face in amazement. "I mean, I'm certain he would
make time to meet you," she amended hurriedly. "What
about Sunday afternoon?" she blurted out, wondering if
she could even endure waiting that long. He wanted to
meet her father! And though he hadn't yet mentioned
marriage, of course this meant that he would declare his
intentions. Chastity's heart soared higher still with the
memory of the kiss they had just shared. And now he
wanted to meet with her father!

"Are you sure he'll be up to having a visitor then?" Regan asked with a rather surprised arch of his brow.

"I'll see that he is," she grinned. "Honestly, he's getting
very tired of seeing nothing but four walls and three
women." She sighed, knowing how difficult it had been for

her father to refrain from any physical exertion, including taking the stairs. If it hadn't been for Jonathon's company, she was fairly certain he'd have been much more difficult about things. She looked up at Regan and pictured him keeping her father company, just as Jonathon did. "Perhaps he won't be so bored after Sunday," she said brightly, "because then he'll have a new friend to keep him company, won't he?"

Chapter 11

"I'll just leave you two alone for a little while," Chastity said just moments after she had introduced Regan to her father. "But remember, dinner will be ready in half an hour." She flashed them a brief but wide smile before she made her exit from the men's smoking parlor.

Things were going splendidly, much better than she'd even dared to hope. When she told her father that Regan planned a visit for Sunday afternoon, she hadn't expected him to insist on meeting the young man downstairs in the smoking parlor, nor had she expected Deborah to insist on Regan's staying to Sunday supper. This was to be a special dinner, too, celebrating the first time Samuel would join them for a meal in the dining room since Chastity's return home. She sighed happily as she paused to finger an arrangement of bright silk flowers on a small table in the hall. Everything was going so perfectly! Her blue eyes were aglow with confidence as she turned her head to stare at the closed door of the parlor, imagining what was being said at that very moment. If only she could hear!

"I've heard quite a few things about you too," Samuel returned with a hearty handshake before he offered Regan a glass of wine and took a seat himself in his favorite chair. He settled himself comfortably and smiled contentedly as he took a sip of wine. "You've been spending a lot of time with my daughter these past few weeks, Mr. Spencer. She seems quite taken with you."

Regan gave a slight shrug. "I'm rather taken with her as well, Mr. Morrow."

"Samuel, please."

Regan nodded but made no move to insist on the same familiarity. "I'm glad to hear that, Mr. Spencer," the older man went on after a slight pause. "I won't pretend I don't want to see Chastity married and settled in life before I meet my Maker."

Regan took a sip of his wine and let a moment pass before he responded to that. "I'm not very settled in life myself, Samuel. But I have been thinking very seriously about settling down, about embarking on a major business venture here in town." He hesitated. "Several months ago I was told that the Comstock gives up enough silver to change a hundred paupers into millionaires each and every month. And I believe it, too. The wealth of this place astounds me. But I think that too many people put their faith in paper stock certificates, and very few are going to become wealthy that way. A business that would cater to the lucky ones who have already become wealthy would prove a much safer and surer investment, to my way of thinking."

"A walk down C Street will tell you you're right, Mr. Spencer," Sam agreed, surprised at the obvious change in topic, but he was curious to hear Spencer's ideas. "Virginia City's businesses flourish in direct proportion to the mines. But just about every type of shop and service you could imagine is already here," he added quickly. "And it would be difficult to match the fine merchandise you'll find in any of our shops, much less outdo them."

"True," Regan conceded. "What I had in mind, however, was not a shop. I was thinking of building a hotel . . . something so great and grand that it would totally outshine the International."

A slow smile spread over Samuel's face. He liked the idea very much. He remembered the days when the International had first opened as a rough-hewn building with only ten or so sleeping rooms, and he also remembered the way it had grown and been improved over the years. Mr. Spencer was right. A flashy new hotel in town would surely attract attention . . . and customers. "It sounds like an interesting endeavor, Mr. Spencer."

Regan evenly met the animated blue eyes before he spoke, a silken smooth edge to his voice. "It could be a most profitable endeavor, Samuel," he mouthed slowly, "for you as well as for me." Sam's smile faded as Regan went on. "I have acquired a lot on C Street that affords a perfect location for the building. But I will need financial backing before I can begin construction on anything. I thought you might be interested in giving me that capital—as a partner in the venture, of course."

Of course, Sam thought as he gulped down the last of his wine. He felt a bitter taste in his mouth, which had nothing to do with the fine vintage. Spencer's message was very clear. He wanted to borrow money, a lot of money, so that he could build his hotel. And though he hadn't said it in so many words, he obviously hoped to become financially independent before he considered marriage to Chastity. Samuel frowned and turned his back on Regan as he got up to pour himself another glass of wine. He saw now that Spencer was no nail-biting young lad blindly in love with his daughter and intent on marrying her no matter what. Regan Spencer was a clever, calculating man who intended to make a fortune before he even thought about taking a wife. It bothered Samuel to know that Regan was not so much infatuated with Chastity as he was with his own success. The realization dashed the mountain of high hopes he'd been building ever since Chastity had first told him Regan Spencer wanted to speak with him. Suddenly he felt very old and very tired. "It's possible that something might be worked out," he mumbled as he dropped wearily into his chair. "But you will need to speak with Jonathon Stoneworth about it. Jonathon has taken charge of all my affairs since my illness."

Regan barely kept his face from revealing his disappointment. He forced a halfhearted smile. "But you're looking so well. Chastity told me you're making a wonderful recovery. She tells me you're even talking about returning to the office sometime in the—"

"I've talked about it, yes," Sam interrupted. He sighed

deeply and stared distantly at his empty glass. "But I'm not ready for it yet. I'm tired and I'm old and I . . ." He stopped himself suddenly and drew a deep breath before he raised his eyes to meet Regan's. "Jonathon handles everything for me these days, and you'll have to speak with him about this business venture of yours. I'll discuss it with him myself, of course, and have him set up a meeting with you."

Regan narrowed his eyes on the old man's face and calmly sipped at his wine. He was angry, really angry. Samuel Morrow was obviously well enough to make his own decisions, but he was refusing to do so. Regan had been so certain that the old man would be accommodating, particularly after the reception he'd received when he arrived at the house and the invitation to stay to Sunday supper. He finished off his wine and set the glass on the table nearby. He hadn't lost yet, he reminded himself. Samuel was promising to speak with Stoneworth about the loan, and promising to set up a meeting for him, so he was not really being turned down. He swallowed the anger he felt at the change in plans and resolved to make a fine show of gentleman's manners at dinner. A good gambler never gave up a strong hand while there was still a chance at winning the pot.

Chapter 12

Regan drained the glass of the last drop of Kentucky bourbon and tersely nodded to the bartender for a refill. It irritated him that Stoneworth was late for their meeting, and for that matter, that he was forced to deal with the man at all. Just four days after his meeting with Samuel Morrow, Stoneworth had made arrangements to meet him here, at one of the quieter, better saloons on B Street. But he was late for the ten o'clock appointment and Regan was growing angrier by the minute. He didn't like the idea of asking for a loan in the first place, and he disliked dealing with a hireling even more. Particularly a man like Stoneworth, who wore his integrity like a badge of honor, reminding Regan almost pointedly that he had sacrificed that same virtue for the sake of ambition. He drained his glass again just as Jonathon entered the saloon and moved to take the open spot next to him at the bar.

Jonathon apologized for his tardy arrival, though in truth it had been a calculated maneuver meant to give him a slight advantage over Regan at the outset. The annoyance he saw now in Spencer's eyes told him he had won that advantage. He suggested that a table might be a more suitable place for them to conduct their business and led the way to a dimly lit corner. They both ordered whiskey and waited until they had been served to begin serious conversation, each man sizing up the other as they exchanged trivial comments about nothing in particular.

Jonathon felt all the more confident as he recognized Re-

141

gan's continued irritation despite the other's leisurely smile and comfortable position in his chair. He silently observed as Spencer lit an expensive cigar and drew on it thoughtfully, sending a thick cloud of aromatic smoke rising to the ceiling. Jonathon sipped at his bourbon and allowed the smooth warmth to settle his nerves before he got down to business. "I understand you wanted to speak with me about financing a business venture."

Regan puffed on his cigar and met Jonathon's level gaze. "Actually, I wanted to speak with Mr. Morrow about it. *He* wanted me to speak with you."

Jonathon's smile did not reach his eyes. "Regardless, I'm here to consider your request. Did you have an amount in mind?"

Regan carelessly flicked an ash to the floor and took a sip of his whiskey. "Forty thousand dollars." He was fairly certain that the bank would match the sum once things were under way. And besides, investors would come to him eagerly enough if word got out that the Morrow fortune was behind his plan.

"That's quite a bit of money, Mr. Spencer."

"I have collateral for part of it. And it isn't a gift by any means. Mr. Morrow would be a full partner in my venture . . . until I could buy out his interests."

"Your collateral . . . it wouldn't be mining stocks, would it?" Regan considered lying, then reconsidered and gave a slight nod. "All bought on the margin, I assume."

"Some of them were, yes."

"You must be aware that stocks are not really adequate collateral for a loan, Mr. Spencer. Any bank in town would tell you—"

"The stocks could be sold. I would have almost ten thousand dollars cash if I sold them."

Jonathon frowned and toyed with his bourbon as if he were carefully considering what Regan had said. "I'm sorry, Mr. Spencer, but I cannot, in good judgment, make you such a large loan for the purpose of a purely speculative venture, which is what you are asking."

For an instant Regan's eyes burned cold with hatred. He had lowered himself to ask for a loan from this hireling of

Morrow's and had just been turned down without any real consideration at all. But a heartbeat later a glint of something besides contempt glowed in his blue-gray eyes, and he lifted his drink to his lips in triumph. "There is another collateral I hold, Mr. Stoneworth, which I will use only if I am forced into it."

Jonathon lifted a mildly curious brow, waiting for him to explain himself.

"As I said, I would rather not use it, but as you seem to have rejected my initial proposal, I am forced to lay all my cards on the table." His lips curved slightly as he ran his fingers over the rim of his glass. "I think you are aware that Mr. Morrow has a daughter."

Regan swiftly raised his eyes, hoping to have caught Jonathon off guard. But if Jonathon was surprised by the mention of Chastity, he certainly didn't show it. He sat there with the same wordless expectancy as before, forcing Regan to be even more blunt. "If I do not get the money I need using my stocks as collateral, I am considering marrying Chastity a bit quicker than is considered proper by the nicer folks here in town. Then perhaps my bride's family will offer to help me get started in business. . . ."

Jonathon drew a sip of whiskey and gave a small sigh. "That, Mr. Spencer, would be an unfortunate mistake."

"Unfortunate for whom, Mr. Stoneworth?" Regan's brow puckered in feigned thoughtfulness before he smiled. "It *would* put Chastity even further out of your reach, wouldn't it?" He noticed that a tiny muscle had begun jumping in Jonathon's jaw.

Jonathon drew a lengthy breath and squarely faced him. "The mistake would be yours, Mr. Spencer, if you expect to collect that kind of money immediately after marrying Miss Morrow." He hesitated and then went on slowly, carefully. "I am not in the habit of divulging any information concerning the Morrow financial situation, but in this case I must make an exception. As little as six months ago, forty thousand dollars might have been easily drawn on Mr. Morrow's private account at the bank. But as you know, Samuel is not a well man. So, in the interest of protecting his wife and daughter from the terrible pain of losing all financial security should he pass on, to insure that they will never suffer the horror that poor Eilley Bowers is enduring at this very moment, he asked me to set up a trust that would include all of his holdings except the Morrow Mining stock itself, which I have done. If something happens to Samuel, both Deborah and Chastity will be able to live comfortably on an income from the trust. But an amount as large as the one you mention would take a considerable amount of time to accumulate—even for Samuel himself. These past few months he has been living on the income from it himself, the same money that would go to Deborah and Chastity if something were to happen to him." Jonathon paused and finished his drink. "Unfortunately, the way it was written up, the trust is irrevocable."

Regan stared at him coldly, sensing that he was not telling the whole truth. "Are you trying to tell me that Samuel Morrow can't even touch his own money?"

Jonathon folded his hands and rested them comfortably on the table, his face a perfect blank. "That's correct."

Regan snorted and shook his head.

"I can assure you that what I'm telling you is true," Jonathon went on smoothly. "If you would care to consult with a bank or another lawyer concerning the terms of an irrevocable trust, they will tell you exactly what I have told you."

"But there must be some way to dissolve such a thing!"

"There is," Jonathon admitted, thoughtfully fingering the brim of his Stetson, which lay to the side of the table. "But it would require litigation, and that takes time and money, Mr. Spencer, and I'm afraid you're short on both those commodities."

Regan narrowed hard blue-gray eyes on Jonathon's cool brown ones. He was a professional when it came to reading faces, but Stoneworth's gave nothing away. There had only been that slight twitch in his jaw when Regan had accused him of wanting Chastity for himself. "You're refusing me the loan, then?"

"I really don't feel as if I've much of a choice," Jonathon replied with an apologetic shrug.

"Well then," Regan said with a malicious smile, "if I don't find another investor, it seems I'll have to content myself with a 'comfortable income' from that trust, won't I?"

The words hit home, and for an instant Jonathon's face was ablaze with indignation. But he said nothing as he reached for his hat and tossed a coin on the table, and he even nodded a polite farewell as he left Regan alone at the table.

Regan settled himself leisurely in his chair and ordered another drink, pleased at momentarily holding the upper hand. He had been bluffing about considering marriage, of course. He sighed and pondered over what his next move ought to be. An irrevocable trust—damn! This ruined all his plans. He had been so certain of getting that loan. Why hadn't that old man told him that it was impossible in the first place? If Stoneworth weren't so disgustingly honest, he wouldn't have believed that story he'd just been handed. But everyone in town knew about Stoneworth, and Chastity had told him more than once that he was honest to a fault. Surely he wouldn't risk that spotless reputation of his with a lie that could be so easily uncovered. No. Regan couldn't afford to make an issue of wanting Chastity's money at this point, not unless he were certain that Stoneworth was lying. He would simply have to find another source of money, and he would probably have to go to San Francisco to do that. But he wasn't going to let Stoneworth know that he had won so easily in the matter of Samuel's daughter. For a while at least, Regan intended to play out his bluff. He lifted another cigar from his pocket and ran it thoughtfully under his nose. In a way, that might prove quite a pleasure.

It was after dinner the following evening at the Morrow house when Jonathon first had a chance to speak with Samuel alone. The two were in the parlor; Sam had just finished scanning the papers Jonathon had given him. He insisted now on being kept up-to-date on everything being

done in the office, since he hoped to return to work part
time within the next few weeks. He felt a rush of enthusiasm as he read the initial reports from the assayer,
reinforcing what Michael Murphy had told him a few days
before. They were close to something. Another rich vein of
silver lay buried in the rock just beyond their grasp. He
leaned back in his chair and let out a hearty sigh. He
opened his mouth to remark on the recent trouble with the
water pump at the mine, then reconsidered as he took a
moment to study Jonathon's face. The brown eyes were
distant and troubled and he was pacing the room nervously, carrying an untouched snifter of brandy in his
hand. There was also the barest touch of anxiety in his
expression—only a touch, but enough to worry Samuel.
Jonathon's face so rarely showed anything but a perfect
calm. Sam cleared his throat loudly and shuffled his papers, and Jonathon's expression immediately changed.

"It will do my heart a world of good to get back to the office after all these months," Samuel said. "I know it's been
a great strain on you, handling everything like this."

"The only strain I've felt has been the worry about your
health. And I'm still not convinced that you should be up
and about so much, Sam."

Samuel's mouth twisted with annoyance and his shaggy
brows drew together. "Humph! You and Deborah both!
Why, Dr. Perkins said I could go back to the office in a few
weeks—"

"I know very well what the doctor said," Jonathon
broke in, his tone reproving. "He said that if you were too
damned stubborn to give up that mining business of yours
once and for all, he couldn't keep you chained to this house
forever. I'd hardly call that a clean bill of health, Sam."

The older man scowled and motioned Jonathon to lower
his voice. Deborah might have guessed as much, but she
didn't know for certain that her husband had bullied the
doctor into giving permission for his return to work. And
she wasn't going to find out. "I need to get back to it, Jonathon. I can't bear the thought of existing like this, a
useless old man penned up in this house with Deborah trying so hard to keep my spirits up. And it's not as if I'll be

overexerting myself or doing anything like what I did before. But I do have to get back to the business of living, and that mine's a part of me. You can understand that, can't you, Jonathon?" His eyes were suddenly pleading, searching for understanding.

Jonathon gave him a reluctant smile. Of course he understood. Samuel *was* the Morrow Mining Company. His sweat and determination and defiant dreaming had single-handedly transformed a crudely marked claim on the side of a barren mountain into a highly successful business on which hundreds of people depended for their livelihood. To take all responsibility for the mine away from Samuel now would be to take away his pride, his sense of accomplishment, his sense of worth. And those were things that Sam, like his daughter, thrived upon.

Samuel smiled as he folded the papers and handed them back to Jonathon. "Don't worry. I feel better than I have in years. Fit as a fiddle." Jonathon accepted the papers with a skeptical lift of his brow, and Samuel, anxious to sidestep any further discussion of his health, quickly sought about for another topic of conversation. "Have you set up a meeting with Mr. Spencer yet?"

For the barest instant Sam was certain he saw that same look of anxiety in Jonathon's eyes that he had seen a few moments before. But it was gone so quickly that he almost dismissed it.

"Oh, I'm sorry, Sam. I forgot to tell you. I met with him just last evening." He turned away to slip the papers into his briefcase. "Our meeting wasn't very productive, I'm afraid." He flashed his employer a perturbed look. "Why didn't you tell me that Spencer had several other investors interested in his project?"

Samuel's face reflected his surprise. "Because I had no idea! Are you sure, Jonathon? When he spoke with me, he said nothing about anyone else showing interest. Only that he needed capital."

"Well, perhaps it's just been in the past few days that these other gentlemen have come forth," Jonathon inserted casually. He shook his head. "Regardless, Sam, when he told me about them and then explained what

kind of terms you'd have to match to become a partner in
this little venture of his, I took the liberty of telling him
you weren't interested."

Jonathon spoke the words so nonchalantly that Samuel
was tempted to let the matter slide. He had made so many
decisions on his own in the past months, and he had always shown such excellent judgment. But Mr. Spencer's
request had not been a business matter, and Jonathon had
been very aware of that. Sam was willing to lend Spencer
money strictly for Chastity's sake, and he thought he had
made that perfectly clear to Jonathon when he asked the
younger man to handle the particulars. Samuel's blue
eyes held Jonathon's for a moment, seeing no sign of the
tension and uneasiness in the younger man, but he sensed
it all the same.

"Is something wrong, Sam?"

Samuel forced a smile. "No, nothing really. It's just that
Chastity seems to be very serious about this young man."

"That hardly makes him a good credit risk," Jonathon
returned in a slightly patronizing tone, smiling himself
now.

"No . . . but I believe he has a good idea, Jonathon. Virginia City could use another fine hotel."

Jonathon's smile faded and he let out a lengthy sigh. "If
you're that enthusiastic about this project, Sam, I can contact him again and make him a loan. But I hardly think
it's a wise investment for a man who's so recently put all
his affairs in order. There's just too much risk involved.
After all, what do you really know about Regan Spencer—
beyond the fact that he'd use his relationship with a
woman to get money?"

Samuel lowered his eyes, considering Jonathon's words.
In spite of his indifferent air, he had revealed quite a bit
with his last question. His feelings for Spencer ran deep
and bitter. And suddenly Samuel realized why.

"I suppose you're right, Jonathon. And if he has other
investors willing to give him the money he needs—" Samuel hesitated for a moment, wondering now if there were
any other investors or if Jonathon's feelings for Chastity
were strong enough to have forced him to lie about that. It

mattered very little at this point. Samuel's decision had already been made. He was going to gamble that if Jonathon cared enough to prevent Regan Spencer from using Chastity in this matter, he would also care enough to protect her from whatever happened in the future. It was the one thing Samuel wanted more than anything else, to have a man like Jonathon love his daughter. He let out a weary sigh and shook his head. "You're right, of course, Jonathon. We'll let it go."

Chastity called a cheery good-night over her shoulder to Jonathon as she linked her arm in Regan's and left the office. She let out a sigh of elation as they made their way leisurely down C Street, very much aware of the people who paused to stare at them. For the fourth day in a row Regan had appeared at the office just in time to escort her home. And he had taken her to luncheon every day in the last week as well. Chastity could not have been happier at the sudden burst of attention he was paying her, especially after the disappointment she had felt two weeks back after the meeting he'd had with her father. She had been so certain he would ask for her hand in marriage, but she knew from her father's evasive remarks that Regan had not even broached that subject. And he had shown absolutely no interest in meeting with her father again, in spite of her suggestions that he do so. That worried her.

"Can you stay to supper tonight?" she asked hopefully, flashing him her brightest smile. "I know Deborah wouldn't mind at all, and Papa—"

"Not tonight," he cut in. "I've made other plans."

"Oh . . ." Chastity did her best to conceal her disappointment. "Tomorrow night, then? Sarah could make something extra special."

"I'm leaving for San Francisco tomorrow," he said curtly.

"You are?" She stopped walking and turned to face him, feeling a sudden panic at the thought of his leaving.

His eyes lit with amusement. Her feelings were as transparent as glass. She was afraid he was leaving for good, and for some reason her reaction pleased him. She would miss him while he was away. "I'll only be gone a couple of weeks."

He saw the relief in her eyes immediately. "Is it business, then?" she blurted out, realizing almost at once that she had made a mistake by asking. She held her breath, wondering if she could survive the humiliation if he said no.

"As a matter of fact it is," he admitted finally, the amusement still bright in his eyes.

"What kind of business?" They reached the B Street steps and began to climb them slowly.

He hesitated a long moment before he answered. "I am going there to speak with possible investors about building a hotel here in town."

Chastity's expression lit up immediately. He had talked about building a hotel here earlier, she remembered now. And if he built it, then of course he would be staying. "Why do you need to go to San Francisco, Regan? There are men here in town who might be interested. Why, my papa—"

"I'll handle my business matters on my own, if you don't mind," he interrupted sharply. His eyes were suddenly so cold that Chastity felt a shiver go up her spine.

She swallowed hard. "I—I'm sorry. It was only an idea." She glanced up at his face, wondering why he was so moody of late, wondering if she would ever understand the hard, impenetrable side of him that frightened her almost as much as it attracted her.

"Well, I don't like women interfering in matters that don't concern them. The quickest way for a man to get into trouble is by listening to a woman's ideas."

Chastity's pride stung at that remark, just as it had several times before when Regan had told her that he didn't approve of her working in the mining office. He hadn't understood when she'd tried to explain it to him, and he had rolled his eyes doubtfully when she'd defensively repeated what Jonathon had told her. "He said that I accomplish as much as any man could," she had stated proudly.

"Well, I really don't blame him for humoring you," Regan had remarked sarcastically. "After all, you are the boss's daughter. And a lot prettier than any man he could have hired."

Chastity still bristled inwardly whenever she remembered that. But she shrugged off her disappointment and forced herself to smile at him again. He was leaving town, after all. She could not afford to have a disagreement with him now. And he was probably just tense about the trip to San Francisco. That had to be it, since he had been so attentive these past days. "Will I see you again before you leave?" she asked hopefully.

"That depends. Are you free for lunch tomorrow?" he inquired easily, knowing full well that he would be leaving town before the noon meal. He had baited Stoneworth enough in the past week, and now it was time to end the game.

"Of course I'm free," she smiled, feeling relief at the invitation. As soon as Regan got himself on firm financial footing with this business venture of his, everything would change, she told herself. All that she needed to do was to have patience and to be careful what she said, and to wait a little while longer. And though she had never been a patient woman, she was very willing to wait for Regan Spencer, even if it took forever.

Chapter 13

Regan finished off his drink and drew a final puff on his cigar before he followed John Rahling down the stairs and out of the Pacific Club. Rahling was a tall, slender man who dressed exceptionally well for an immigrant. Though a longtime resident of California, Rahling still spoke with a distinct German accent, and Regan guessed him at about sixty years of age, though the keen alertness in his eyes was that of a much younger man. Rahling had capitalized on the boom of gold rush days two decades before and had subsequently invested in the railroad to become a very wealthy man. This was the third time Regan had met with Rahling this month, after being introduced to him at a friendly card game the very day he arrived in San Francisco.

From the moment of introduction there seemed to be a mutual understanding between the two men. Regan respected the older man for his wealth and his cunning, and Rahling immediately recognized Regan's ambition and ability. Though Regan had spoken with dozens of other possible investors in the past four weeks, he felt from the start that Mr. Rahling would ultimately become his business partner. But getting John Rahling's financial backing for his hotel might prove a disappointment as well as a victory for Regan. The man was extremely cautious with his money and anxious to know where each and every dime went. At their last meeting Regan had refused to accept the twenty thousand dollars Rahling had offered him after he'd asked for fifty, and a miffed Mr. Rahling had promptly departed his company, leaving Regan to wonder if he'd made a mistake holding out for more money. But this morning's note from Rahling told Regan that he had made all the right moves. Rahling believed in Regan's idea, and he was anxious to be a part of it.

Regan kept abreast of the older gentleman, matching his long-legged, deliberate strides as they traced a southward path toward Market Street. He said nothing as the older man paused before the Grand Hotel, which had opened for business just a few years before. At a cost of a million dollars, the Grand boasted four hundred rooms and was the finest hotel in San Francisco. But not for long. Rahling sighed thoughtfully as his eyes scanned the structure from top to bottom. Then he did an abrupt about-face and began walking again the short distance to the Palace.

It was an awe-inspiring sight even now, with all the confusion and clatter of construction clinging about its noble foundations. The seven-story building would enclose two and one-half acres and would be tiered around a grand courtyard into which carriages could drive, entering directly from Montgomery Street, where they stood now.

"You see zis, vat is happenink here?" Mr. Rahling said at length to Regan. "Ze buildinks are bigger and bigger, und grander und grander." He smiled indulgently and lifted his hand, gesturing toward the building. "You see zis? Mr. Ralston is buildink his Palace. Und for whom? I ask you, for whom?" Regan was silent, and Rahling sighed. "I do not zink zere are enough kings in San Francisco to pay for zis Palace of his. No. I do not zink so." He stared at the building for a long time, his eyes narrowed in contemplation. "I have been to your Virginia City, Mr. Spencer. Und I believe zat you vould be right to build a fine hotel zere. But to me, ze investment is not made for ze pleasure of making ze fine buildink. Ze investment is made for ze prospect of return. I vill not invest my money in somezing vich vill not in turn make me more money."

"I have never suggested that the Crown Point be built without any regard to cost," Regan insisted soberly. "But if too many corners are cut for lack of funds, then it will never be able to compete with the International for business. And it must surpass the International from the very beginning, Mr. Rahling, or it will never attract the clientele capable of paying back the initial investment."

Rahling drew a deep breath and thoughtfully studied his cuticles. "Twenty five zousand dollars. Zat is my final offer."

"Thirty, and you have yourself a deal," Regan countered smoothly.

A pair of indignant blue eyes flew to meet Regan's even gaze. A long moment passed. Then Rahling smiled a slow, cunning smile. "I have far more confidence in you, Mr. Spencer, zan in anyzing you might build." He offered Regan his hand. "Tirty it is."

Regan hesitated barely a second before he took it firmly in his own. It was less money than he had planned on, but he was sure that once things were under way . . .

"Very vell, zen. It is settled. I vill have my attorney draw up ze papers in ze mornink. Und zen you can return to your Virginia City und get to vork."

Chapter 14

Regan sighed deeply and gave a slight smile of anticipation as the train hissed and slowed, then pulled to a stop in Virginia City Station. He had enough money to begin construction on his hotel, and that was certainly a step in the right direction. But he knew he'd never see the place completed with the thirty thousand dollars he had in his pocket. It was only a start. It would have been a lot easier if the place had been backed by the Morrow name and fortune, but perhaps his failure to get that backing made him more determined to see the place built than ever before.

Regan intended to see that the Hotel Crown Point (named in honor of the mine presently in bonanza on the lode) was opened. The citizens of Virginia City would clamor at its doors, anxious to be served exotic dishes unknown even at the International, waiting to be housed in sumptuous splendor that the decade-old establishment could not hope to match. And all would pay outrageously for the privilege, boasting happily their success to all the world. Regan thought of the scraggly assortment of nouveaux riches who daily pranced down to the stock exchange, showing off their latest fashions. To a Southern gentleman born to a world of refinement and elegance, Virginia City's finery was nothing more than a farce. Intelligent, farsighted men made their fortunes here, then moved elsewhere, away from the madness of the Comstock. It was a place to be plundered, then left behind and forgotten. And Regan intended to do exactly that.

He left the train carrying both of his leather cases and began the long uphill climb to his boardinghouse on B Street. It was barely noon and a harried, bustling crowd clogged the boardwalks and businesses all along the way. Regan stopped short as he neared C Street, catching a glimpse of a light blond head somewhere in the congestion. He frowned as he lost sight of it and began walking once more, angry that he had paused at all, wondering why she had been on his mind so often in the past two weeks. He had sensed that she would bring him trouble from the very beginning, and he had done his best to avoid her entirely. But then he had been forced to pursue her in the hopes of getting a loan from her father. Well, he wasn't going to get that loan, and he ought to have stopped seeing her the moment he found out she couldn't help him financially. But instead he had made it a point to see her nearly every day before he left for San Francisco, knowing that Stoneworth would be fit to be tied. Somehow just knowing that another man wanted her made Regan want to hold on to her that much longer. It was difficult to explain away the jealousy he felt when he thought of giving her up to another man. After all, she was headstrong and opinionated and far too stubborn for him to ever consider taking for a wife. The woman he married would be serene and gracious and charming, as Spencer women had always been. She would be flawlessly educated in the arts and feminine graces, a woman who could be placed on a pedestal the moment she assumed the Spencer name. Chastity Morrow could never fill such a role. Her pride, her determination might have earned her a certain fascination, but that could never change what she was. She was a fighter, in many ways very much like Regan himself. And if she had relinquished a part of herself for the sake of survival, then so had he. In one sense, Chastity was a bitter reminder to Regan of the man he had become. He drew a lengthy breath and scowled as he took the steps up to B Street, not liking the way that beautiful face was so firmly rooted in his mind. It was unthinkable that he should take her so seriously, but it was becoming almost impossible for him not to. What he needed was another woman, he told himself, to take his mind off this one. And he would see to that this very evening and forget about Chastity beginning now. He paused in front of his boardinghouse and stared at its stark, ugly lines. He was not looking forward to returning to that tiny, uncomfortable room of his or to greeting Mrs. McCormick, his gossipy landlady, or to sharing the noon meal with a table full of common men. Someday he would be above all this, someday very soon. And as for today—well, he'd had a fairly successful trip and could afford an extravagant luncheon at the International just this once. He heaved a sigh as he lifted his bags, then mounted the steps to the boardinghouse.

"I have the hardest time believing that the Savage won't hit a bonanza," Samuel grumbled. "I've made a fortune holding on, and I guess it's just habit by now."

"That stock's cost you a fortune too, Sam," Jonathon reminded him. "A fortune in assessments over the years, and all they've ever had is *borrasca.*"

"Well then, we'll just wait until the price climbs a bit," Sam countered.

"It's about as high as it'll ever go on a mine that's never made a penny for you or any of its stockholders."

"But with new bonanzas coming in the other mines, that stock is sure to rise in sympathy." It was the argument Sam always used, and Jonathon could never debate with that. He sighed in exasperation and tossed the papers on Sam's desk. "Okay. So we'll pay the assessments and hold on a little while longer."

At a small kneehole desk, which had been positioned just to one side of her father's, Chastity sat smiling in silent understanding, her mind on her father and Jonathon's conversation even as her hand moved to formally pen the notes her father had hastily scrawled on a scrap of paper. Samuel's handwriting had never been easily deciphered, but it seemed to have deteriorated even more during the months of his illness. Chastity completed one letter and carefully addressed an envelope before she lifted her eyes and met Jonathon's look of reluctant resignation. His eyes brightened and warmed, as they met hers, and he easily returned her smile. She looked away, biting her lip to restrain a wider smile. There were times when she felt so close to Jonathon, particularly when she saw the way he dealt with her father, when she saw the respect and the affection that was between them. But there were other times when Jonathon's eyes made her uncomfortable, though she didn't really know why. Perhaps it was simply because he never responded to her the way other men did, because he so easily saw through her every time she tried to pour on the charm. She wondered for a moment if he saw through other women as easily, and if that was why he had never married. She glanced up at him again, studying his face and wondering if he'd ever been made a fool of, and if that was why he recognized flirtation for what it was. Or perhaps he didn't need a woman to make his life complete; perhaps he was content with what he had now. Her brow furrowed and she wondered just what it would take to make him want something more, to make him want marriage. She bit her lip and looked away, suddenly thinking of another man who was every bit as hard to figure out. She pondered for the hundredth time why Regan had not come to take her to luncheon that day, four weeks ago, as he had promised. She wondered just what she had done or said to make him angry or make him change his mind. She wanted to scream her frustration sometimes, and just as often she simply wanted to cry.

"Well, it appears to be lunchtime," Samuel announced, examining the heavy gold watch he had just pulled from his vest pocket. He wore a suit to the office these days rather than the denims he had worn before his illness, when he'd often spent the better part of each day with Michael Murphy working in the mine itself.

Jonathon's eyes lifted quickly with a puzzled expression. Samuel had agreed to working a half day, and only two days a week, returning home for his midday meal. But since his very first day back he had made a habit of ignoring the time and stretching the morning well into afternoon, so that Chastity or Deborah usually had to coax him out of the office. Yet here it was, just barely noon, and Samuel was already clearing off his desk.

"I was thinking of taking Chastity to the International for luncheon today," he went on matter-of-factly, "and we thought you might like to come along, Jonathon."

"Now?" He glanced forlornly at the morning's paperwork, which had scarcely been touched.

Samuel nodded, then tossed his daughter a "help me" sort of look. "I'll be happy to stay late this afternoon and help with the paperwork, Jonathon," Chastity offered. "But come with us. It will be nice for a change."

He looked from one face to the other, sensing there was more to it than he was being told. "Is there any special reason?"

Chastity shook her head vigorously, while Samuel looked away and mouthed, "Not really," in a less than convincing tone.

"Well . . . it does sound like a nice idea . . . ," he said cautiously.

"Good. Then let's be about it. Deborah is going to meet us there promptly at noon," Sam said gruffly, flattening his hat on his head.

They made a rather noisy threesome, walking along the planked sidewalk toward the International Hotel. "Washoe zephyrs" were blowing crazy gusts in every direction at once, stirring up dust and dirt and reminding them that autumn was just around the corner. They bent low and made allowances in their steps to counteract the wind, laughing as one or another of them was pulled this way or that. Spirits were high in spite of the difficulty walking, and Chastity's giggling blended easily with her father's booming protests to Jonathon's tongue-in-cheek legal advice. The banter reflected a warmth and camaraderie that drew all happily together in spirit and made their steps light and easy.

Deborah was waiting for them at the main entrance to the International on B Street and immediately led them into the dining room, where a table had been reserved for their group. They were promptly served and their meal was nearly finished before Regan stepped into the room and saw them. None of the four noticed him standing there, even after he dismissed the maitre d' who had offered to seat him. He approached the table slowly, feeling anger for having been ignored by Chastity, though her slight was certainly not intentional. She was the first to see him, and the moment her eyes met his she rose from the table and all but ran to his side, just barely restraining an urge to fling her arms about his neck. "Regan! When did you get back?"

"Just this morning." His tone reflected none of the warm excitement she was feeling.

She leaned forward to lay a hand on his arm, her blue eyes wide as they searched his face. "Did everything go well?" she asked hopefully, confused and troubled by the anger she saw in his eyes.

"Well enough." His gaze moved pointedly toward the others, and Chastity instinctively stepped back at the reminder. She forced a smile as she reintroduced him to her father, Deborah, and Jonathon, then turned her full attention to him again, wishing very much he would give her some sign that he was happy to see her too, that he had missed her as much as she had missed him. But there was still only that unexplained anger.

"Can you join us, Regan?" she pleaded. "We'd love to hear all about your trip."

His lips curved a little at that, though she didn't have the slightest notion why. "I wouldn't want to intrude . . ." He glanced about the table.

"Nonsense!" she insisted. "You aren't intruding at all. Is he, Jonathon?"

There was a slight pause. "You are obviously welcome here," Jonathon said slowly.

The eyes of the two men met in perfect understanding, and for a long moment an unsettling silence fell about the table. Regan moved a chair between Chastity and Jonathon and took a seat at the table, caring little that their meal was finished since he had suddenly lost his appetite.

"Tell us about your trip," Chastity began, feeling the un-

easiness as much as anyone else. "You said it was successful. Does that mean you'll be building your hotel?"

Samuel shifted uncomfortably in his seat and took a
long swallow of his coffee. His blue eyes instinctively settled on Jonathon, who showed not the slightest trace of
anxiety.

"Not now, Chastity," Regan said after a moment, his
eyes locking with Jonathon's.

"But you said—"

He took hold of her hand and gave it a pat, his voice
sounding every bit as patronizing as his gesture. "I don't
want to bore everyone with the details now, Chastity. Suf-
fice to say that the trip was a profitable one."

Samuel's eyes clearly reflected his relief at Regan's silence. "Well, we all wish you the best of luck with your
project, Mr. Spencer," he said in earnest, his eyes once
again straying to Jonathon even as he spoke.

"Yes, of course we do," Deborah chimed in, anxious to
change the subject. She was keenly aware of the tension
all about her, and particularly Samuel's nervousness,
though she could not begin to guess the source of either.

Regan's smile was cold. "I'm sure you all do."

As soon as the table had been cleared of its dishes and coffee cups replenished, the maitre d' returned supporting a
large, grandly decorated layer cake bedecked with thirty
tiny, glowing candles. Nearly everyone in the crowded
dining room turned to stare as it was gingerly positioned
before Jonathon, whose expression momentarily reflected
embarrassment and surprise. A moment later his eyes
flung accusations at Sam, Deborah, and finally Chastity,
who laughed aloud at his reaction, eagerly breaking the
tension. "Well, well. We really did catch you off guard,"
she teased. "And to think all it took was lunch, a cake, and
a few candles."

"I—I don't know what to say."

"That's fairly obvious," Sam chuckled.

"All right, so I'm speechless." Jonathan eyed the suspects
once more, narrowly this time but with a gleam of amusement in his eyes. "Who was responsible for this—this conspir-

acy? And how in the world did you find out it was my birthday?"

"That was your fault," Chastity confessed. "You left some of your personal papers floating around the office, and that stunning bit of information was included on one of them. As for the party . . ." She hesitated, exchanging a guilty glance with her father. "I'm afraid we were all willing accomplices."

Sam's eyes twinkled mischievously. "Don't feel left out, counselor. If you blow out the candles you can be an accessory after the fact."

Deborah smiled at him. "You'd better be about it, Jonathon. Everyone in the dining room is waiting for something." It was true. Nearly everyone in the room was staring, waiting for him to blow out the candles.

Feeling very childish, Jonathon obediently took a deep breath and easily extinguished the candles to what seemed to him a tremendous outbreak of applause and cheering. A few moments later the diners returned their attention to their meals and some of the embarrassment finally began to wear off. "I hope you remembered to make a wish," Deborah reminded him.

"Oh, I did! I wished that by next year, everyone forgets my birthday."

"Not a chance!" Chastity assured him.

"Just you wait!" Sam chimed in with a wink. "The whole town will know next year. I was thinking about a banner draped from one side of C Street to the other. Or perhaps I could convince Dan at the *Enterprise* to do a feature." The table broke into laughter at that, and Jonathon shook his head in despair.

When the waiter returned to the table to serve the cake, he paused uncertainly before Regan and asked if he would be ordering lunch. He declined, but remained seated, knowing full well that he didn't belong there yet drawing some perverse satisfaction from the barriers he had placed between himself and the others. His face fully reflected his disinterest as Sam told several long-winded tales about the Comstock in earlier days when Virginia City had boasted tents, silver, whiskey, and little else. And his boredom with talk about family friends and Sam's relations in St. Louis was even more apparent, as was his lack of appreciation for the subtle, dry comments Jonathon inserted, which sent the others into fits of laughter. But only Chastity seemed to take note of his mood, her laughter dying away long before the others, her repeated attempts at drawing him into the conversation meeting with no success.

It was well after two when Deborah finally rose from her seat and insisted that Samuel return home for his rest. He followed reluctantly, grumbling all the while about who was boss in the Morrow household these days. Chastity gave a small smile as she watched her father leave, then turned her attention to emptying one last cup of coffee. It was apparent in the next few moments, however, that the high spirits had departed with Samuel and Deborah, and Chastity's attempts to keep a light conversation going with such an undercurrent of hostility between Jonathon and Regan only resulted in a biting sarcasm beneath the casual flow of words.

"I'm so glad you came back in time to help us celebrate today," Chastity said fervently, wanting more than anything to change Regan's strange, distant moodiness. "Jonathon always says, the more the merrier." She flashed Jonathon a forced smile, which he returned halfheartedly.

"I had no idea Mr. Stoneworth was so generous," Regan said with a sarcastic lift of his brow.

Chastity frowned nervously and quickly returned her attention to finishing her coffee. With a calculated look at Jonathon, Regan casually removed a cigar from his breast pocket and lit it slowly, pointedly, without so much as a questioning glance at Chastity. Jonathon frowned his disapproval, but when he met Regan's cool eyes, he instantly recognized the unspoken challenge he was posing. Chastity should not allow a gentleman, any gentleman, such an obvious breach of conduct in her presence. Yet Regan was certain that she would overlook it, and his smile told Jonathon as much. Jonathon drained the last of his coffee and rose from his seat. "I have to be getting back to the office," he said nonchalantly, though he knew very well he was asserting a threat to Regan's position. "Are you ready to go?"

Chastity glanced up at his expectant smile, then at Regan's indolent, self-assured grin. She knew instinctively that Regan expected her to stay, that he would be very angry if she did not. But this was Jonathon's birthday and she had offered to help him with the payroll for the mine this afternoon. She bit her lip and avoided his eyes, feeling guilty about refusing him what she'd already promised, but more afraid of risking Regan's anger. He was so unpredictable; he had lost his temper with her a half-dozen times just before he left for San Francisco. And she just couldn't take the chance of losing him, even if it meant disappointing Jonathon. "I—I—"

"Never mind," Jonathon interrupted before she could even mouth a feeble excuse. "It's late and perhaps it would be best if you called it a day. I'll finish up what has to be done at the office . . . and what's left will just have to wait until tomorrow." Chastity's eyes met his with gratitude, then quickly lowered with remorse. Jonathon did not miss the gleam in Regan's eye as he retreated, however, as if the situation amused him greatly. But he forced himself to smile anyway, swallowing his pride and his anger for Chastity's sake. "Thank you for the trouble you went to today. It was a very kind gesture, and I shall always treasure the memory." He gave a brief nod then and left the dining room, somehow managing to dissolve a large part of Regan's victory.

Regan leaned back thoughtfully in his chair and watched Chastity's face as he departed. "He plays the part of Sir Galahad so well," he remarked snidely.

"What?"

"Stoneworth. Paragon of virtue. Purity personified."

"Don't talk about him like that," she returned defensively. "He's a good man, Regan."

"Yes, he is. Too good, if you ask me."

"What's that supposed to mean?"

He grinned recklessly, knowing that he held the upper hand and anxious to make the most of it. "It means, my dear, that we are all human, and we all have faults. Some of us just hide them better than others . . . under the guise of total honesty."

"Are you trying to tell me that Jonathon is hiding something?" He gave a casual nod. "What?"

He drew a long puff on his cigar and sent an aromatic cloud of smoke swirling about his head. Then he smiled, a slow, cunning smile. "He wants you, Chastity. And not in any pure, saintly way, either. He wants you . . . and badly."

She glared at him with all the skepticism she could muster. But for all her anger at his suggestion, she couldn't help but remember certain times when Jonathon had looked at her with something more than friendship, or that one kiss the evening of the Bowers picnic. It made her feel uneasy now, but she shook off the feeling, remembering the many times she had deliberately flirted with him, remembering the numerous opportunities he'd had to declare his desires, if indeed they existed. He had not done so.

"You don't like Jonathon," she said after a long silence, "and you don't understand the way he is."

He chuckled softly. "I understand him better than you do." He stamped out his cigar and covered her hand with his. "I'm only warning you. Don't forget that Stoneworth is a man. He cannot help what he wants."

For a long moment she searched his face, trying hard to find some sign of affection in the chiseled, handsome features. "And you are also a man," she said quietly. "What is it that you want, Regan?"

His smile faded as he stared at her face, then at her soft, warm lips alone. He lifted her hand and let his longer, darker fingers play on its fine slender lines. "I want a great many things."

Chastity's heart fell, and she quickly lowered her eyes to keep from showing her disappointment. Not long ago, she had thought it an exciting challenge to extract a proposal of marriage from a man. But with Regan it had become a bitter struggle, a game where the stakes had been carried so high that she couldn't bear the thought of losing. It was beginning to hurt. And it was beginning to frighten her. In all their time together, Regan had never declared his affection, never even mentioned marriage. She had been so certain several weeks ago when he had talked with her father, but nothing had ever come of it. Then too, she knew that Regan kept company with other women, and not the right kind of women, either. And he had broken their last engagement, just before he left for San Francisco, for no reason at all; he had not even bothered to make up a plausible excuse.

Yet Chastity was almost certain that he loved her; she knew that she loved him. There were times when he kissed her and held her and made her feel so alive, so bursting with emotions no other man could begin to arouse. She needed him, and all she really wanted to know was that he needed her, too, and wanted to be with her always as she wanted to be with him. And how she ached to hear him say that he loved her! She would have done just about anything to hear those words. But she had played this game by the rules, had bitten back her own words of love while she waited for him to speak first. Even so she had given so much of her pride, so much of her heart, that she was left feeling afraid and aching and wondering if she had made a very serious mistake. He lifted her hand to his mouth and kissed each one of her fingers, holding her eyes in his own. She felt herself tremble, felt the skin at the back of her neck tingle with the pleasure of his touch. What was this game he was playing, she wondered, and what would he win by playing it?

His lips touched the pulsepoint at her wrist and he smiled as he felt it race wildly. A hot flush poured into her cheeks. He was glad that he had come here this afternoon. But there was no point in toying further with something that was clearly off limits. "I have to go," he said abruptly. "I have some business to attend to this afternoon and I wanted to stop by the exchange . . ."

"I'll go with you."

He studied her face, feeling all the more reassured by her eagerness. He enjoyed holding the upper hand. And there had been enough satisfaction in today's encounter with Stoneworth that Regan decided to trifle with Chastity a little while longer. He laughed, as if he had suddenly thought of something very amusing. "Judging from that guilty expression on your face, you ought to go back to the office and help Sir Galahad. After all, it's his birthday."

Chastity's blue eyes lowered in hurt confusion. But Regan seemed not to notice. Without another word he assisted her with her chair and her wrap, then walked her down C Street, placing a discreet kiss to her hand before he left her in front of her father's office. Chastity drew a long, calming breath and forced the helpless look of defeat from her eyes before she entered the office. For some reason, she couldn't bear the thought of anyone, particularly Jonathon, knowing how she felt.

Chapter 15

Ground was broken on the site of the Crown Point in mid-September, soon after Regan had purchased an adjacent lot and contracted to have all buildings on the premises demolished and removed. The excavation and foundation work was completed by late October, so that when the bonanza in the Consolidated Virginia Mine was finally made public, the iron framework for the structure was just being positioned.

The Consolidated Virginia bonanza of 1873 was the biggest silver find in the history of the Comstock Lode. The news broke on the front page of the *Territorial Enterprise* in a feature by Dan De Quille, the most respected reporter on the *Enterprise* staff. De Quille had been chosen by Mackay and Fair, owners of the Consolidated Virginia, to "see for himself," and he had done exactly that. After a visit to the depths of the mine, which had been closed for months to all visitors, Dan's story burst with the news: An estimated one hundred and sixteen million dollars of silver ore in sight, just waiting to be mined!

In the weeks following the announcement, De Quille's estimate was doubled and tripled by self-proclaimed experts in the field, and Con Virginia stock jumped skyward on the exchange, pulling all other Comstock stocks higher in sympathy. Virginia City was a town reborn. All the mines on the lode began drilling and blasting as if there were no tomorrow. Adolph Sutro stepped

up work on his tunnel through the base of Mount Davidson to drain and ventilate the mines from below, and
many, many speculators turned millionaires overnight.

For Regan Spencer, the soaring market and new bonanza meant much more than thousands of dollars
made on his mining stocks. As soon as the story broke,
he received an urgent telegram from John Rahling dou-
bling the man's initial investment in the hotel and asking Regan to return to San Francisco during the winter
months, as soon as construction was halted, so that final
details for the completion of the Crown Point could be
discussed.

Weather held fair during November, as Regan had
hoped it would, and the construction of the Crown Point
proceeded at a frenzied pace, allowing the basic structure to be completed and huge boilers to be put in place
before the first snows. Even some of the final touches
were put to the exterior of the building, rows of false columns and arched doorways, which would be painted
white and accented with ornate ironwork next spring. It
was an eye-catching structure already, and soon the
great glistening panes of French plate glass and polished marble sills would rise grandly above the other
buildings on C Street—a full, proud six stories. With the
news of the break in the Con Virginia, Regan adopted a
no-holds-barred plan of elegance and opulence, opting to
install all kinds of modern contraptions in the Crown
Point: A steam-powered rising room (the only one west
of the Mississippi, except in San Francisco), a system of
electric request bells, hot and cold water in every suite
of rooms, and speaking tubes to allow each room constant vocal access to the front desk. He had yet to place
the final order for carpeting and furnishings, but he
intended to do that as soon as he reached San Francisco, duplicating many of the ideas being used at Mr.
Ralston's Palace. Regan's work was cut out for him, and
he was thriving on the challenge, elated with the luck
that seemed to be with him every step of the way. Everything he had dreamed of and worked so long to achieve
seemed finally within his reach.

Winter took firm hold of Virginia City by the second week of December, and bitter winds whipped mercilessly across the face of the mountainside, bringing the threat of snow. Nevertheless, Piper's Opera House was filled with an enthusiastic audience that delighted in the talented Miss Cathcart's dramatic portrayal of *The Lady in Red.* The night of the play's very last performance in town was also the eve of Regan's departure for San Francisco, so after a quiet dinner with him at the International and a visit to the opera house afterward, Chastity was still reluctant to say her good-night. Regan planned to be away at least two and a half months, possibly longer, and the thought of existing without him for so long a time was something Chastity didn't want to face. She had not so much as smiled at another man since she had fallen in love with him, and every time he touched her she knew that he was the only man she would ever love.

She took her time fastening her heavy woolen cape and gathering up her things, and the opera house was all but empty before she and Regan made their exit. She was silent as he lifted her into the buggy and took a seat beside her. She maintained that silence as she tucked a warm lap robe beneath her knees, and even as the horse struggled up the steep stretch of road toward Howard Street. She noticed that the first hesitant flakes of snow were swirling and dancing about in the breeze, and she closed her eyes and sighed, picturing the sparkling beauty of Virginia City under a freshly fallen blanket of snow. The picture, coupled with a rush of bitter cold air on her cheeks, brought to mind memories of Christmases past, of building snowmen and waging childish wars with snowballs, of slipping and sliding down the treacherous, ice-covered streets. But she resisted the urge to slip into the past and instead opened her eyes and smiled at the sight of the man beside her. He was silent also, alone in his thoughts. The lack of conversation no longer vexed her. She had grown accustomed to his pensive, brooding moods and had come to treasure every moment she spent with him even if very few words passed between them. And though it saddened her to think of his leaving tomorrow, she forced herself to savor the present and not to look ahead. She slipped her fingers from the warmth of a fur-lined muff and placed them gently on the large gloved hand that had guided the buggy to a smooth stop before her home.

As if the light touch of her hand jarred him from his daydreams, Regan's eyes immediately lowered to stare at the soft, white fingers, then rose to meet her eyes. For a long moment their gazes were locked. Then his blue-gray eyes softened and a warm smile of affection touched his lips. There was such unguarded innocence in Chastity's face, such vulnerability. He sighed and lifted her hand to his mouth, brushing her cold fingers softly against his cheek. But the quiet tenderness of the gesture did not satisfy him, and the next moment he was tilting her chin and his mouth began to search hungrily. He felt her fingertips playing with the fringe of his hair, felt the gentle yet impudent thrust of her tongue against his own as he tasted the sweet warmth of her mouth. He could hear the quickening of her breath as she drew herself more tightly against him, and he could easily sense the trembling of her body despite her heavy clothing. His own breath came shallow and rapid at the feel of her, and from somewhere deep within himself a strong, hot wave of wanting flooded his consciousness. All at once he was consumed by a burning hunger such as he had never known. A thousand emotions churned inside him, awakening feelings and desires from the deepest recesses of his spirit, making him feel weak and irrational. His body, his heart, and even his soul screamed with the need to possess her, to be one with her. For a moment his arms closed so tightly about her that he feared he might crush her. Then suddenly, he grasped her by the shoulders and held her, gasping, at arm's length. He swallowed hard and struggled to gain his composure. It was not the first time he had wanted to take her. But the need in him had never been so strong before. For weeks now he had attempted to rationalize his feelings, telling himself that it was only natural to desire a woman as beautiful as Chastity, that every other male in Virginia City with eyes in his head desired her as well. But he could no longer rationalize the disappointment he felt lately when he bedded other women, nor could he explain away his unconscious habit of comparing every other woman he met to her. And now, as her confused, passion-filled eyes met his, as his eyes lingered on her sweet, trembling lips, he realized just what a fool he had been.

Without another word he released her and got out of the buggy, politely yet rather coldly helping her to alight. Chastity sensed the change in him, and reluctantly she climbed the steps beside him in silence, turning to face him only when they reached the landing. Regan kept his distance, hunching his shoulders and wrapping his arms about himself to keep the gusty air from tearing at his clothing.

"You're probably happy to be getting away from this cold," she said as lightly as she could manage. She forced herself to smile, but her lips quivered with the effort it took to hold that smile in place.

"I never have been partial to cold weather." He sighed, matching her halfhearted smile. "Well, I'd best be saying my good-byes or I'll freeze to death before I ever have a chance to leave this town." His tone carried the same forced levity as hers.

He inclined his head slightly and made to place a brief, brotherly kiss on her forehead. But she flung her arms around his neck and pressed velvet-soft lips against his face, not realizing what temptation she was placing before him. She did not understand when he disentangled her arms with a distant, determined look in his eyes, even as she urgently whispered his name. Just before, he had responded so differently!

"Good-bye, Chastity," he mouthed softly, then turned quickly away and hurried down the steps. Chastity stood silent in the bitter cold, watching his eager departure, assuring herself that he loved her and desired her, that he intended to marry her someday, but that he simply was not the type of man to subject himself to a tearful farewell scene. She shivered as a blast of wind howled angrily about her, wishing she could banish the doubts that clouded her mind. Then she sighed wearily and turned away to open the door to her house.

As soon as he had returned the buggy to the livery stable, Regan hurried up the stairs to his room, briskly rubbing his hands together in an attempt to ward off the chill. It was going to be difficult to forget her, he knew, after spending so much time with her. He hadn't meant to do that in the beginning. She was so damned like him in so many ways—proud, selfish, determined, and beautiful—and for a time she had filled a void in his life. But it had to end. He had never seriously considered her a candidate for marriage, and a woman like Chastity wouldn't fit into the perfect life he intended after the Crown Point made him rich. All this time he had been fair with her. He hadn't pushed her to do more than a proper woman usually did with a gentleman—not much more, anyway. He had taken his physical needs elsewhere even though it had become increasingly difficult to do that. But if he continued to see her . . .

He frowned and sighed as he opened his leather suitcase and began packing for his trip. It had all begun as a game, he reminded himself. And that was still all it really was. But he couldn't deny that he had played longer than he'd ever intended, or that it was very, very difficult to walk away from the table. Yet, as a gambler who knew well the folly of risking all with a weak hand, he had little choice but to turn his back on her and walk away.

"Oh, Jonathon! It's lovely!" Chastity cried as her fingers smoothed the deep blue velvet fur-lined cape and lifted it from the torn wrappings of the package. She flashed him a warm smile as he attempted to shrug off her gratitude, then watched him as he rose to refill his cup with the wassail punch Sarah had been fussing over all afternoon. She remembered the morning a few weeks earlier when she had admired this very same garment as they had passed by a C Street dress shop. She hadn't thought he'd noticed then. She smiled as Deborah and Sarah examined the gift and gave their enthusiastic approval; then she impulsively rose from her chair and came to slip a single arm about his neck, to place a brief kiss to his cheek. She was surprised when he caught her hand in his own, his brown eyes holding hers for a long moment until both of their smiles faded, until she nervously looked away. "Thank you for the gift, Jonathon," she mouthed softly, turning quickly to resume her seat.

She lifted her cup of punch from a nearby table and drew a thoughtful sip from it, thinking how different things might have been had Regan stayed in town just a week or two longer. It would have meant everything to her to receive a gift like this from him; it would have meant everything to her to spend Christmas Day with the man she loved. Of course she knew that he was a very busy man these days, that his business in San Francisco was urgent and that the construction of the Crown Point necessarily took precedence over all else. But knowing all that didn't make her feel any less lonely or any less empty inside. She set her cup on the edge of the serving table and watched as the others opened their gifts, her eyes drifting distantly from her father's beaming countenance to Deborah's warm smile. She was jealous of the love they shared, of the intimacy so apparent when they looked at one another. She had always been jealous, but it cut her even more deeply now because she felt so alone. She rose from her chair to wander about the parlor, feeling somehow separated from the spirited conversation, from the Christmas joy and hope on everyone's face. She paused at the window, where the air was chilled with the brisk winter winds which churned and thrashed angrily about the house. The window glass was thick with frost and the lower corners of each pane were filled with curved slivers of silver-white snow. Chastity closed her eyes and sighed, running a finger over the frosted glass and feeling very much like the little girl who had waited through so many winter storms for her father to come home. She opened her eyes and searched out her father's face, remembering how lost she had felt not knowing if he would ever come back to her. But he had come back. And someday very soon, Regan would come back too. She sighed again and stared at the countless blurred specks of light that glowed in the city below. They were barely visible through the iced windowpanes. But they were there, in the distance. Someday, she thought.

Jonathon grinned as Sarah refilled his glass of punch and thanked him for the twentieth time for her pretty new pink bonnet. But his smile faded as his eyes strayed to Chastity, standing alone at the window now, deep in her own thoughts. He took a sip of punch and tried to pull his eyes away. He knew exactly who was on her mind. He set his cup on the table and managed to smile at Samuel, hoping that a smile was an appropriate response to whatever it was he had said. But his feelings for Chastity were becoming more and more difficult for him to deal with and almost impossible for him to hide. There were times when she would simply smile at him, or innocently lean very close to study something on his desk, or unintentionally rest her hand on top of his as they worked on an oversized graph projecting assessments for the mine. Jonathon dreaded those moments every bit as much as he longed for them to happen again. He wanted her. More than anything else in his life, he wanted her.

He lifted his cup to drain the last bit of punch, wondering at the emotions that raged inside him whenever he looked at her. She was still a child in many ways, he thought, a child with arms so heavily laden with toys that it was impossible to hold any more. And yet she stood there at the window, staring at the night and mourning the single toy she couldn't have. He scowled, reminding himself that his arms were also full, that he also mourned the one toy that was denied him. But that was not exactly true. Because to him, Chastity was anything but a toy. She was a treasure whose worth could never be measured . . . a treasure that unfortunately belonged to someone else.

Chapter 16

The arrival of spring brought drier, milder air to Virginia City and a much welcome end to the bitter cold of winter, mingling a faint, pungent hint of sagebrush with odors of smoke and dust. The unceasing clatter of horses on the graded streets, whistles sounding round-the-clock shift changes in the mines, and intermittent muffled blasts from shafts cut deep inside Mount Davidson were all constant reminders of the new prosperity. The traffic was heavy, and C Street clogged with people and vehicles from sunup to sundown. The stock exchange rocked with its usual excitement, and every man and woman seemed caught up in the high-strung restlessness, the mesmerizing thought of millions of dollars of silver lying beneath their feet. Miners' boots fell deliberately on the wooden boardwalks; Piute women carrying their infants in willow baskets on their backs scrounged patiently about in piles of rubbish; Chinese vendors hawked their various wares in strange-sounding singsong chants. Below the packed streets of the center of town lay the Divide, a rise of land that had once separated Virginia City from neighboring Gold Hill. The Divide was now covered with houses and the two towns had been fused into one.

It was a lovely spring morning when Chastity woke. She sighed as she rose from her bed, her eyes lifting instinctively to the rocky peaks in the distance, which mirrored every shade of pink, blue, and gold in the early-morning sun. It was a fantastic sight, a perfect backdrop for a city

perched so high above the canyon, a city on whose wealth
the fortunes of thousands depended. The sky was clear and
a deep brilliant blue, much like the color of Chastity's
eyes. The sights and smells and sounds of home had never
before failed to raise her spirits. She belonged here, and
the wild excitement of boom days ought to have been her
excitement too. She was doubtful, as Regan had once accused her of being, that Sun Peak would ever be completely emptied of its silver. But for the first time in her
life she was beginning to doubt things she had always believed in, things she had always taken for granted. She
gnawed at her lip as she stared at the morose reflection
that met her eyes in the looking glass. It was a face much
different from the one she had known only a year ago, a
face that had reflected such certainty and confidence. She
shook her head and forced the furrows from her brow,
pulling her mouth into a pleasant line. Regan would be
back soon. He'd already been gone weeks longer than he'd
planned, but that could easily be attributed to any number
of things. Financing a building, a major structure on C
Street, was no small matter, and with new bonanzas on
the lode he would be anxious to see that the hotel opened
in the spring. So he had a great deal of work to do, a great
many things on his mind. That was why he hadn't written,
not a single word. There was too much work for him to do.

But she didn't really have the time to stand here pondering all this now, she reminded herself as she turned
away from her reflection and chose a simple cotton dress.
A special stockholders' meeting had been called in San
Francisco, a meeting her father had insisted on attending
with Jonathon in spite of his doctor's objections. The trip
to San Francisco took little more than twelve hours, Samuel had argued, and the Morrow Mining Company's private car was every bit as comfortable as home, and quite a
bit more luxurious. And since he would be doing nothing
more strenuous than attending a meeting . . . Chastity let
out a sigh, recalling the way Jonathon and Deborah and
even she had argued with him until he had actually
threatened to travel to San Francisco all by himself,
paying regular fare. He was so tied to his work these days,

she thought, that it was impossible for him to let go, even if it endangered his health. Frowning again, she slipped out of her nightgown and began to dress. There would be plenty to keep her occupied at the office this morning.

Chastity had just finished sorting the day's mail when the door to the office opened and Mrs. Bates casually strolled in. For a moment Chastity's face showed her surprise. She hadn't seen the woman in almost a year, not since the day she had thrown herself at Jonathon last spring. With the memory came a flash of indignation, and Chastity's eyes narrowed with annoyance. "Can I help you with something?" she offered with exaggerated politeness.

Mrs. Bates sighed as she toyed with the worn strips of a small pouch-type purse. "I s'ppose Jon—Mr. Stoneworth ain't in."

"No, he isn't." Chastity abruptly abandoned the mail and took a seat at her desk. She made a show of picking up a pen and jotting down a few notes for herself, a silent but clear act of dismissal.

"I guess he's still in San Francisco," Rhonda sighed, ignoring the hint and running her hand regretfully over the edge of his desk.

"I guess he is," Chastity returned without raising her eyes.

"Seems like all the men go runnin' off t' San Francisco for one reason or 'nother these days."

Chastity's brow darkened but she held her tongue, busying herself with a list of things she wanted to be sure to discuss with Jonathon as soon as he returned. She was unaware that Rhonda was glaring at her with contempt. Mrs. Bates had never liked Miss Morrow, and she was insanely jealous of the way Jonathon looked at her, and the way she led him around whenever that Spencer gentleman was too busy. Well, Miss High-and-Mighty had it coming to her, she thought smugly, and today she was going to get it.

"Did ya see how close the Crown Point is t' bein' finished?" She paused, but Chastity continued to ignore her.

She smiled. "That Mr. Spencer bought all kinds of fine things t' furnish the place when he was in San Francisco," she dropped casually, noting with satisfaction that Chastity was all ears at the mention of Regan's name. "A friend o' mine, Miss Patsy Justice, he tol' her all about it . . ." She sighed. "Got back from San Francisco a week an' a half ago, an' already he's talkin' 'bout openin' the place the end o' May . . ." It was difficult to keep from giggling at Chastity's reaction to the news. So Patsy had been right, after all. She hadn't known he was back in town.

With all the composure she could muster, Chastity forced her eyes back to her notes and hoped that Mrs. Bates had missed her initial reaction to the news. Regan had been back for over a week! And she hadn't heard from him, not a single word! The thought of it made her go all cold inside, and she could feel the color draining from her face.

"Jonathon ought to be back by the end of the week," she managed in a distant voice. It took every ounce of strength she had to mouth the words. "He'll be sorry he missed you."

Rhonda's mouth curved into a catty smile. "Oh, I'll be back," she called over her shoulder. She whirled about to make her exit and closed the door carefully behind herself. Then she made her way down C Street, happily twirling her purse.

It was late afternoon when Chastity left the office for the night, having spent most of the day trying in vain to concentrate on her work. She nodded mechanically to several acquaintances as she made her way to B Street, to Mrs. McCormick's boardinghouse. She was feeling nauseous and light-headed, but she had to know if it was true. If he was here, if he had come back, then she would face him squarely and ask why he hadn't seen her. There had to be a reason, a simple explanation, and she desperately needed to know what it was.

Mrs. McCormick was a notorious gossip whose sharp blue eyes never wavered from Chastity's flushed face as she listened to a hurriedly concocted story about a pocket watch Regan had inadvertently left at Mr. Morrow's office. It was a very expensive watch, and Chastity had come across it this afternoon, and she was here to return it to him if he was home. When she had finished the tale, she felt her cheeks getting hotter as the woman stood there silently gaping at her, considering. "You can't give it to him now."

"But why not?"

"Because he doesn't live here anymore." She frowned thoughtfully and let her eyes appraise Chastity from head to toe. "You're Deborah Morrow's daughter, aren't you?"

Chastity winced at that and almost retorted that Deborah was her *stepmother* and no blood relation at all. But she was far too desperate for information to do anything more than brush off the question. "Yes. I'm Deborah's daughter. Do you mean that he's moved out?"

"That's exactly what I mean. And he didn't give notice, either. Just came and got his things last week and left without so much as a howdy-do. Could have had another gentleman in his room by now if he'd have given notice."

"Do you know where he's living now?" Chastity interrupted impatiently.

The older woman's eyes narrowed in suspicion and her mouth tightened stubbornly. "I don't know where he went and I don't care where he went. Humph! Probably to that fancy hotel he's building down on C Street," she muttered as an afterthought. She shook a warning finger in front of Chastity's nose. "If I were you, I'd let him worry about getting back his own pocket watch. A decent young woman wouldn't ask so many questions about a man like Regan Spencer. And her mother might just be interested in hearing . . ."

Before she could finish, Chastity drew herself up proudly and showed the woman her back. She didn't care at all what Mrs. McCormick told Deborah. She didn't care about anything except finding out why Regan had done this. What had she said? What had she done to make him angry? It was beyond all reason that he should be avoiding her. But Mrs. Bates had told the truth, she thought as she blinked back a tear. He had been in the city for over a

week without making a single attempt to see her. She
swallowed hard against the stab of painful emotions
welling up inside her. She felt as if the deepest part of her
were being torn to shreds, as if her pride had been
scourged and flung without a thought to the ground. It
was only habit that made her lift her chin as she hurried
along the steps, forcing her way through a group of people
headed in the opposite direction. It was at that very moment that she saw him. Just a half block away, walking
nearer and nearer. He met her eyes for a split second, and
Chastity almost ran to him. But then he deliberately
looked away from her and wrapped his arm around a
flashy blond woman who was walking beside him wearing
a sly, self-satisfied grin.

Patsy Justice . . . the name finally rang a bell in Chastity's mind. Miss Justice had achieved notoriety about town
for her flourishing business in a small D Street cottage,
and no decent man would ever have been seen in broad
daylight with a woman like that.

Chastity did an about-face and almost frantically
pushed her way along the crowded sidewalk, no longer
able to hold back her tears. She would rather walk a thousand miles than confront the man she loved with that—
that woman. With her eyes fixed to the boardwalk, she
walked and walked and walked, her feet falling quickly,
thoughtlessly, one in front of the other. When she finally
slowed her pace she realized that she was in the lower part
of town, almost at the edge of the Chinese section. The acrid smells of smoked fish and strange, pungent spices
filled her nostrils. She glanced about, trying to get her
bearings, her eyes scanning the crooked, flimsy shacks of
the Chinese, then the slightly more habitable residences
of the less fortunate white residents, and finally her eyes
met with the familiar buildings above in the center of
town. They riveted on the Crown Point rising gloriously
above her, hiding the last rays of the sun behind its massive six stories.

Chastity bit her lip hard and wiped a tear from her
cheek. There was no chance of Regan leaving Virginia
City for a while at least. His hotel would tie him to this

place indefinitely. That gave her time to think, to plan, to act, and she intended to do exactly that. She straightened her spine and lifted her chin. She had never been one to accept defeat, and as she turned away from C Street's newest building and headed in the direction of home, she was preparing to fight with every bit of her strength to get what she wanted.

Chapter 17

It was a gloomy spring for Chastity, for it seemed that every warm, bright day was pervaded with the feelings of loneliness and hurt. She forced herself to attend a few parties and affairs with Jonathon, but only to remain properly social. She could bear Jonathon's company only because he was a friend; but with other men it was different. She couldn't help but compare them to Regan, and in doing so she only became more painfully aware of what she had lost. Regan had been avoiding her for weeks, and the few times their paths did chance to cross, he did little more than tip his hat and bid her a good day. But the first week of May, when the announcement of the Crown Point's opening appeared in the *Enterprise* and the *Gold Hill News,* she resolved that she would not allow him to ignore her any longer. If it took every trick in the book and every ounce of her pride, she would find out why he had broken things off with her, and once the misunderstanding had been cleared up they would begin again. And this time she would see that things worked out perfectly.

The Hotel Crown Point was completed by the first week of June, less than one year after its construction had begun. During the entire month of May, scores of wagons were unloaded before its grand, false-columned entrance until the interior of the structure gleamed with brass, silver, and polished wood and marble. Draperies of heavy gold velvet fell in perfect folds from floor to ceiling, framing the fantastic view of city and mountains from the upper floors. Accommodations were plush and spacious, and a rising room stood ready to whisk patrons to the sixth floor in a matter of seconds. The cost was prohibitive for all but the very wealthy, but Virginia City was filled with wealthy these days who were anxious to be guests of the finest hotel in the state. Regan had been fortunate in finding an excellent chef on such short notice, a man unhappy with his position in a fine San Francisco restaurant and willing to take charge of the kitchens at the Crown Point. He had hired besides over a hundred waiters, busboys, valets, and errand boys, many of them Chinese, all of them well versed in their duties after three weeks of vigorous training. Finally all stood in readiness for a glorious day of celebration, and everyone who was anyone planned to make an appearance at its opening.

The foyer of the Hotel Crown Point was nothing less than breathtaking. A great marble staircase with carved mahogany balustrade curved upward to an elegant balcony where floor-to-ceiling windows provided a spectacular view. The great crystal chandelier suspended from the ceiling was fully seven feet in diameter, and hundreds of smaller gaslights were reflected to infinite numbers in the gilded mirrors and the fixtures of polished silver and brass. The dining room was filled to capacity, strains of orchestra music flowed from adjacent rooms, and dancers crowded an impressive muraled ballroom. Scores of neat, uniformed men hurried about in the crowd filling glasses, clearing tables, and serving the whims of the Crown Point's guests.

Once inside the building, Chastity and Jonathon were assailed by dozens of people inquiring whether her father and Deborah would be making an appearance later in the evening. Chastity explained at least a hundred times over that while her father had returned to work for a short period each day and had even managed a brief trip to San Francisco, he was still under strict doctor's order to curtail his activities and get adequate rest. She didn't mention that Samuel had put up quite an argument before finally giving in to Deborah's pleas that he stay at home and retire early as he had promised the doctor he would every night.

As she mechanically answered all of the questions from her father's well-meaning friends, Chastity could not keep her attention from straying about the foyer from one corner to the next until they fell on the man she sought. Dressed in an elegant suit, he stood on the staircase casually gesturing with a long, thin cigar as he spoke to a pair of gentlemen and an elderly lady Chastity didn't recognize. He gave a polite nod and moved on, greeting his other guests with that mixture of aplomb and arrogance that had captivated her from the first moment she saw him. He gave the appearance of a monarch in the midst of a crowd of people, at ease with them yet never one of them, possessed of a superiority and cynicism that set him apart from the nabobs of Virginia City. He believed himself better, and he subtly managed to project that belief in his stance, his stride, his every gesture.

Only when it was well into evening and a good many guests had departed was Chastity finally ready to admit that her schemes for the Crown Point's opening celebration had come to total failure. She was tired and heartsick; her pride and her determination had been bit by bit torn to shreds. She had spent every moment struggling to remain within his range of vision, smiling, conversing, mingling, waiting . . . waiting . . . waiting . . . But something had gone wrong. Time and time again, Regan had looked the other way. She had waited, and she had failed. She glanced down at the blue-gray evening gown so simple and elegant of line and cut, reproaching herself as she allowed Jonathon to lead her onto the dance floor. She had chosen it with such care, certain that it created just the right image to attract Regan's eyes. And if he had shown even the slightest interest, she might have played any one of a hundred games she'd rehearsed in her head during the past few weeks. But he had not, and he had left her only one thing to do. She smiled prettily at Jonathon and playfully squeezed his hand, pretending that she was utterly enchanted with the beauty of this place, the magic of the night, the charm of the gentleman who whirled her about in his arms. No one would ever guess that her heart was being cut so deeply even as her laughter spilled about the room. At least she still had that much pride. As the dance ended she brushed an imaginary fleck of lint from the starched lapel of Jonathon's coat, smiling into his eyes. No one must ever guess.

Regan forced a smile as he shook the hand of a gentleman just about to leave, listening politely as the man lingered to expound on the wonders of the Crown Point. But even as the man spoke, Regan couldn't keep his eyes from wandering about the room . . . until they rested on Chastity. He had been conscious of her from the moment she had walked through the door wearing a gown of blue-gray silk trimmed in delicate lace, simpler and much less revealing than her usual formal attire. Its understated elegance gave her an air of coolness, of maturity, which Regan had never noticed before. He felt certain that she had chosen it in the hopes of catching his eye, and she had succeeded in doing exactly that. But it was the casual intimacy she shared with Stoneworth that had kept him from dismissing her as he had these past few weeks. He had observed them all evening, the private jokes, the unconscious cues they tossed to one another, the easy way she smiled at him and became a part of a handsome, admired pair. Stoneworth, always Stoneworth. The first man Regan had ever encountered who made him question his own superiority. Relinquishing his claim on Chastity to such a man was almost like admitting defeat. And Regan would never, never admit that someone had gotten the better of him. But what claim did he have on Chastity, really? He was infatuated, nothing more. A Spencer would never allow himself to love a common woman, even if she *was* wealthy. Regan drained his glass of whiskey and set it aside, trying to explain the emotions taking hold of him. But as he watched her being whisked about the Crown Point's ballroom in the arms of Jonathon Stoneworth, saw the way she looked at him and heard her sweet, musical laughter, it suddenly didn't matter who or what she was. Regan wanted her. And he meant to have her.

The dance had hardly ended before he was beside her,

requesting the honor of the next. She nodded slightly and kept her eyes averted, hoping that her shock was hidden beneath a semblance of composure. Her heart was thumping like a drum in her ears and her hand was trembling as he took it in his own. The music began and she tried to think of something to say. But the witty, intriguing comments she had had on the tip of her tongue all evening had suddenly disappeared in a wave of panic. Her mind was a complete blank. Her feet managed to follow the steps, her expression remained unreadable, but she couldn't begin to raise her eyes. It took everything she had to keep from betraying the turmoil inside her, and she didn't know how long she could remain in his arms without letting it show.

"You are more beautiful than ever tonight, Chastity." He said it only after an eternity of silence.

She continued to stare at the crowd, avoiding his eyes. Her response was mechanical. "Thank you. I didn't think you noticed."

He hesitated, and she felt his fingers tense against her hand, her waist. Finally he replied in a low, longing tone. "I noticed."

Her eyes flew to his in surprise, then quickly looked away. What did he expect her to say? "Your—your hotel is beautiful. I—I'm sure it will be very successful."

"If you like it, then it already is a success."

His voice was so husky and filled with desire that again she glanced up at him in astonishment. But this time he caught her eyes and held them, wordlessly telling her everything she desperately wanted to hear until she felt her calm demeanor melting beneath his expectant gaze. It seemed like an endless moment in a world of only two, a moment of honesty, of revelation. He loved her. It was there, in his eyes; without a doubt she saw it. An all-encompassing feeling of joy and triumph filled her heart. Regan loved her! He loved her! But suddenly the music ended. The spell was broken just as quickly as it had been cast. Her eyes darted nervously about the room and she felt her cheeks burning hot as she wondered if the intimacy of their dance had been obvious to any of the others. She turned away in embarrassment, but Regan caught her arm before she had taken a single step. And then she was being led from the ballroom, through the foyer, to a private office in the rear of the building. The room was quite small, but she did not notice. She stood in silence as he closed the door behind them; she was still somewhat dazed by all that had happened in the space of a few moments.

Regan went immediately to pour himself a glass of straight whiskey from a crystal decanter. Chastity shook her head at his questioning glance. He quickly returned to stand before her, silently contemplating her as he sipped at his drink. It drove her to near madness to stand there enduring his eyes as they wandered over every inch of her. Yet she sensed that for the moment she held the upper hand. He didn't know that she'd thought of him day and night for months on end; he didn't know that she was longing to fly into his arms, that she wanted to scream and cry about all the hurt he had caused her, that she wanted more than anything to hear him say that he loved her and had missed her, too. And as long as he wondered, she had a distinct advantage—her pride. So she waited.

Her patience was rewarded when he set his glass aside and pulled her into his arms. "I missed you," he murmured huskily against her cheek. "God knows how much I missed you!" He kissed her long and hard, almost violently. With her last bit of courage Chastity held herself rigid, refusing to respond, coldly forcing him to meet her gaze. He scowled and released her abruptly, then took a long swallow of his drink, failing to recognize the weakness of her position. "What game are we playing now, Miss Morrow?" he demanded with a sarcastic smile.

"That's something you will have to tell me, Regan." She spoke as calmly as she could, but she heard the slight tremor in her usually assertive voice and suddenly noticed the hot flush in her cheeks, the quiver of her bottom lip. So she had been affected by his kiss, after all.

"You're right," he conceded. "It was I who threw in the cards before the hand was played."

She turned away from him and took a few steps. Her fingers ran over a neat row of brass tacks on the back of a

large leather chair as she carefully contemplated her next
words. "To me . . . it was not a game, Regan," she admitted quietly, no longer caring whether or not she lost her
advantage. "And . . . and I thought it meant something
more to you than just—"

"It did."

She whirled about to face him. "Then why did you end
it?" she cried out, her control finally breaking. "How
could you forget? Everything? And act like none of it ever
happened?"

Regan finished the last of his drink and set his glass on
the desk, wondering what he could say to explain his behavior. But Chastity would never understand the truth—
she had far too much pride to understand that she was not
the kind of woman Regan could marry. She was crying
openly now, and tears raced down her cheeks one after another.

"I waited for you to come home!" she choked out. "I—I
waited—and I trusted you. I—I thought you loved—"

"I do love you, Chastity," he whispered, taking her into
his arms. He was astonished that the words came so easily
to him and was somehow relieved that he had finally said
them.

"Then why, Regan? How could you ignore me like you
have? Forget all about me and . . . and take up with that
Justice woman? There must be a reason!"

He sighed and stared at her lovely face, which was free
of everything but real emotion. She touched him deeply as
countless other women had failed to do; he knew that she
truly loved him. And the knowledge lit a flame of passion
deep inside him, a flame that had been too long denied. He
lifted her chin and his mouth sought hers with a desperate
longing, but she struggled with all her strength to resist
his advances.

"No! It won't work, Regan! How can you hold me like
this after you've acted as if you don't care for all this time?
What can I expect tomorrow? Will another woman be in
your arms?" She squeezed her eyes tightly shut, trying to
block out the image of Regan and Patsy Justice. How
many nights had she cried alone, unable to get that same

picture out of her mind? "I have to know why you're doing this, Regan."

In anger and frustration, Regan thrust her away. He was not accustomed to being refused. He had said that he loved her, and now she was demanding more. "You want to know why?" he threw back at her. "Then I'll tell you why! Because I got tired of keeping company with a little girl who plays at being a woman!"

She stiffened and raised her trembling chin. "Plays at—?"

"You heard what I said. A man has needs and desires, and if one woman can't or won't fulfill them, then it's easy to find another who will."

She stared at him wide-eyed, in numb disbelief. A moment ago he had said that he loved her, but now he was saying that it didn't matter, that if she refused him, he would simply find someone else. "But . . . what about marriage?" she whispered weakly.

He poured himself another drink. "What of it?"

"I—I want to be your wife, Regan. Men don't marry women who aren't"—she swallowed hard—"pure."

She cringed when he laughed at her. Then he came toward her, sipping at his drink, circling about her with a cruel, taunting smile. "You believe everything those old hags tell you, don't you? Well, let me tell you something now. Most women keep their purity because they're afraid of what losing it entails. And they're even more afraid that they won't be able to please a man once they're in bed with one." He stopped before her and boldly traced a finger along her neck, then lower, until it grazed the thin blue fabric that curved naturally to the swell of her breast. For a moment Chastity thought she was going to faint. "Is that what you're afraid of, Chastity? Don't you think you're woman enough to please me?"

Her mouth had gone completely dry, but she tried to swallow and straighten her spine. Her breath was coming in short, painful gasps, and her nerves were tingling with tension and utter confusion. She had to think, but she couldn't think. He was standing so close to her that she could almost feel the strength of his desire. "I—I can't, Regan," she blurted out. "There just isn't time. Jonathon is waiting to take me home." She faced him squarely then, wondering if he guessed what relief she was feeling at her momentary reprieve. But Regan's face remained smooth and intent, his eyes piercing with oneness of purpose.

"There's nothing to keep you from coming back here after he's taken you home . . . unless, of course, you're afraid."

She hesitated, forcing her mind to function though her senses were weak with doubt and uncertainty. She had been a perfect lady up to this point, and where had it gotten her? Perhaps Regan was right about most women and their purity. Judging from the bits and pieces of overheard conversation, Chastity knew that many women thought their husband's bed a duty, on a par with mending his clothes and putting dinner on the table. She had never once heard a lady admit to feeling what she felt whenever Regan kissed her. Perhaps she was different . . . perhaps—

"Sir Galahad is waiting."

She drew a deep breath and made her decision, slipping her hands about his neck and pressing her lips hard against his. "Wait for me . . ."

Chapter 18

Regan's suite at the Crown Point was decorated in blue and gold with the same extravagant, luxurious appointments that graced the elegant foyer. He retired to his room immediately after Chastity left him, and spent the next two hours attempting to counterbalance a troublesome conscience with a good deal of whiskey. He had told her that he loved her and maybe it was true, after all. He would soon find out. If it was simply that her games had captured his fancy, then he would lose interest after tonight was over and this would be the end of something that had mistakenly gotten out of hand. And if he felt the same after this, if he still wanted her . . . Regan paced the floor, having no answer for that. But the chances of its happening were slim anyway, he told himself. Odds were, tonight would mark the end of the affair.

And Chastity would recover. He smiled in spite of himself. If there was one quality she was possessed of, that quality was resilience. Another man, possibly several, would quickly step in to ease the heartache she might suffer if this didn't work out. His smile faded abruptly as he thought of Stoneworth taking his place—but enough! She would be here soon, willing and ready to lose her virginity. He felt himself tense with anxious longing. He had never wanted a woman the way he wanted this one, had never spent so many long nights dreaming of a woman's smooth ivory skin against his own. How many times had he closed his eyes and imagined those incredible dark blue eyes ablaze with passion? He poured himself another drink.

The carriage ride home with Jonathon seemed to last an eternity, though in truth it took less than a quarter of an hour. Chastity tried to conceal her nervousness, but she found it impossible to keep her mind on anything Jonathon said. After a few moments he was silent and she was grateful, though his eyes upon her made her all the more aware of the seriousness of her decision. If only she could retain her courage for a little while longer, if only she could force herself to go through with this tonight, then everything would be right again, she told herself.

When the carriage finally reached the house, she allowed Jonathon to assist her from her seat and mounted the steps with agonizing slowness. She smiled up at him then and rose on tiptoe to press a quick kiss to his cheek.

"Chastity?" He called her name just as she was about to turn away.

She stiffened and faced him again with a timorous smile. "Yes?"

He searched her face for a long moment. She swallowed hard and when she could endure no more, lowered her eyes uneasily. "Is everything all right?" he asked quietly, his fingers gently smoothing her hair.

"Yes, of course," she managed lightly. "But I am tired, Jonathon." She let out her breath as she turned away from him and made to open the door. He knew her far too well for her to risk any more conversation, and she couldn't bear to meet his eyes again, not tonight. She entered the house and closed the door behind herself. Turning low the lamp that had been left to burn in the hallway, she listened to Jonathon exchange a few words with the liveryman and wondered all the while how long she would have to wait before leaving the house again and returning to the Crown Point. The sounds of conversation faded and suddenly all was quiet. Thank goodness it was late, she thought, and no one had waited up. She could not have borne a confrontation with Deborah at this point. Even alone, each moment of waiting was pure agony!

She bit her lip and forced herself to wait a few moments longer, then quietly slipped from the house and with a brief, cautious glance about to see that no one was in sight, she hurried down the steps to the street. She actually ran along the familiar boardwalks and steps, her heart soaring magically at the thought of what was about to happen. The loneliness, the terrible emptiness she had lived with for so long had finally gone. Tonight she would become a woman by giving herself to the only man she had ever really loved. And she had no doubt that by doing so she would win his heart forever.

A short, grinning Chinese valet was waiting at the door of the hotel, and he immediately gave a bow and led her up the stairs to Regan's suite. He bowed one last time and left her at the door, where she stood for a moment trying to catch her breath.

Regan paced the floor nervously and checked his watch for the third time in as many minutes. Perhaps she had decided against coming, perhaps at the last minute . . . He spun about as the door opened and Chastity, breathless with excitement, eyes shining with anticipation, stepped into the room and closed the door.

At the sight of him she froze and swallowed hard, the impact of her hasty decision suddenly hitting her full force. He had discarded his formal jacket and tie, and his shirt was unbuttoned, revealing a good deal of curly black hair on his chest. It was quite enough of a man's anatomy to bring a blush to the cheeks of any proper young lady. Chastity gulped and retreated a step, startled by the burning intensity in those cold blue-gray eyes.

Without a word he deposited his drink on the bureau and walked toward her, his eyes lingering on her mouth, then her breasts, somehow claiming possession even without touching her. When he stopped only inches away from her trembling body, his bare chest almost touching her, she lowered her eyes in confusion. She did not know what was expected of her and had little notion what losing her purity would entail. Before she could settle the doubts that had begun to loom before her, he had drawn her into his arms and kissed her hard, sending the familiar giddiness swirling in her head and limbs. No other man had ever made her feel this way, and yet the power of his kiss made her all the more uncertain. She suddenly realized that she was gambling for the highest stakes, wagering all on a single night with this man. She would never regret it if in turn she won his love. But if Regan did not marry her, if he chose to cast her aside—

He unfastened her wrap and dropped it carelessly to the floor, then immediately set about undoing the buttons at the back of her gown. She drew a sharp breath and tried to pull away. "No!"

"There's nothing to be afraid of, Chastity," he whispered, kissing her lightly.

"I—I'm not afraid," she breathed in a tiny voice. She squeezed her eyes tightly shut.

He felt her go rigid when his tongue touched her ear. "You're stiff as a board!" He chuckled softly. "I'm not going to hurt you. . . ." He sighed and gave up struggling with her buttons, reminding himself that she had never done anything like this before, that she was different from any of the other women he had known, that he was her first man. He smiled at the thought and gently began playing with her hair, one at a time pulling out the dozens of pins that held the lovely silver curls in place, until long strands of white gold toppled in soft waves about her shoulders. His fingers toyed in the silken masses, coiling each strand about his hand, while his mouth drifted over the curve of her cheek, her eyes, her forehead, her temple. She let out a deep breath and relaxed in his arms, giving herself up to the warmth of his sleek, masculine body, foundering past the bounds of rational thinking.

Regan immediately sensed his advantage and drew her head back to kiss her more assertively, letting his tongue slip over her lips, between them, and over them again, tasting, toying, making her long for more. "I love you, Chastity," he murmured as his mouth wandered quickly down her throat, over the velvet skin which pulsed wildly with her heartbeat. "I want you so very much . . ."

Her arms tightened about his neck as his mouth returned to claim hers, his tongue thrusting deeply, possessively in her mouth. Slowly, timidly, her tongue responded, moving against his, and her heart soared with the knowledge that she had given him pleasure too. Flames of desire leapt magically inside her, sending hot, fiery sparks of desire coursing through her veins, a strange sort of trembling through her entire body. She did not protest this time when he began to unfasten her gown. Indeed, she was relieved to feel his fingers touch her bare shoulders, to feel him loosening her petticoats and unlacing her corset, and she anxiously shrugged to be rid of the barriers between them. For a glorious moment she reveled in the feel of his arms around her, her flesh against his flesh, her mouth against his mouth, her tongue moving in an erotic kind of game against his tongue. The manly scents of spiced cologne and tobacco and bourbon rose to fill her nostrils, while the very heat of his darkened skin burned like a searing brand through the thin fabric of her chemise. Chastity moaned with pleasure as his calloused fingers eased the straps of the garment from her shoulders, causing the last vestige of her modesty to slip silently to the floor. Regan drew back then to gaze at her, and his breath caught sharply in his throat. Chastity was lovelier than he'd ever imagined even in his wildest dreams. Thick silver-gold hair shone splendidly in the soft glow of the gaslight, falling in disarray over full, rounded breasts and gleaming satin shoulders. Her body tapered naturally to a tiny waist, then curved to a luscious line of smooth, firm hips and limbs long and as flawlessly sculpted as a work of art. Yet all was warm, gold, and silken beneath the touch of his fingers; all of Chastity was alive and responsive, all of her burning with a desire to match his own. The sweet, heady fragrance of rain and flowers drifted softly to his nostrils, and he finally found her eyes . . . those same dark blue passion-filled eyes he had seen time and again in his dreams. A tiny spark of confusion and uncertainty appeared in those eyes as Re-

gan hastily stripped the clothes from his body. She
watched him from beneath discreetly lowered lashes, fas-
cinated yet fearful of the sight of his nakedness. But
scarcely a moment later he was pulling her against himself once more, his mouth fiercely seeking out her softest
flesh, playing, pulling on her breasts until the tips became
hard and erect. The touch of his tongue made her shudder
and cry out his name in ecstasy and wiped out all but a
single, overpowering desire to press ever closer, to feel his
hard, unyielding flesh against her. She heard him whispering strange-sounding, indistinct words of longing, felt
his fingers roaming everywhere about her, drifting knowl-
edgeably over her hips, pulling her so close that his fully
aroused shaft nested intimately between her thighs. Her
breath was jerked from her body as she strained against
him, bursting with a powerful need to have more, to feel
more, to reach out with all her strength for something . . .
something . . .

He swept her into his arms and laid her on his bed, his
darker body stretched full length above her. All the
while she clung to him, welcoming his touch, gasping,
shivering with the pulsing fire his manhood had kindled between her thighs. She pulled his dark handsome
head toward her opened mouth as she writhed in hunger, scarcely breathing at all for the heat that was
exploding everywhere in her, even to the tips of her
fingers and toes. He raised himself above her and forced
her thighs apart, shuddering violently with restraint
as he lowered himself between them.

Chastity let out a startled cry as he drove deep, tearing
unmercifully at her flesh. He covered her mouth with a
kiss that demanded submission, muffling her cries and
driving deeper still until she felt she was being torn apart
by the sharp, burning pain. Tears spilled onto her cheeks
and she struggled to free herself, but it was too late, and
he was too strong. With all her strength she tried to stop
his violation of her flesh, arching her back in a futile attempt to avoid his advances. But then, in the very midst of
all her straining and fighting, the burning pain retreated
and her woman's body took firm command. Each of Re-

gan's thrusts became a sweetness as well as a torment, and within moments she was caught up in a mindless battle for her own fulfillment, arching against him with a different purpose, faster and faster and faster, wanting more and ever more. Suddenly she seemed to break free of everything, and she felt as if she'd been flung toward the sky by some magical force. The fire was exploding all around her and in her, and she felt a magnificent tensing of every fiber of body and soul, a completely and totally triumphant feeling, which went beyond anything she'd ever imagined. She cried out with the fierceness of its release and clung to Regan desperately as he fell, limp and trembling, against her.

It was over so swiftly that within moments the night was silent and peaceful, broken only by the sounds of two heartbeats and whispery sighs of contentment. Chastity lay in Regan's arms, her eyes closed tightly, her head turned away, so full with emotions she had never known before that tears slipped silently down her cheeks. Regan bent his head to kiss her, to smooth away her tears. "I'm sorry I hurt you," he whispered. "The next time, I—" He stopped for an instant, realizing that there would indeed be a next time. "The next time, I won't hurt you. I promise." He smiled at her with a tenderness that reached his heart, a heart that had long been buried beneath years of bitter memories and driving ambition.

"I—I love you, Regan." She held him tightly, feeling even closer to him now than before. There was nothing to separate them now, no part of herself that she had withheld from him. "I think I've always loved you, from the first moment I saw you."

He grinned and quirked a doubtful brow. "Even when you threw that shoe at me?"

"I didn't hit you with it," she argued sheepishly. She sighed and looked away. "And besides, you were going to leave me there all alone."

He wiped an errant tear from her cheek and chuckled at the irony. "I've been trying to turn my back on you ever since I met you. Somehow I just haven't been able to do it."

"I hope you're ready to stop trying now. . . ." She searched his face with wide, hopeful eyes.

He kissed the tip of her nose. "I'd say I'm about ready to throw in the cards."

She laughed and threw her arms about his neck. "Oh, Regan!" She drew back just enough to smile up at him. "Does that mean we'll be married?"

"I thought I was the one who was supposed to ask that question."

She giggled. "Then ask it. And hurry. I've waited long enough."

Regan's eyes suddenly lost all trace of amusement, and Chastity immediately sensed that their playful banter had come to an end. She waited, trying desperately to hold on to her smile yet knowing all the while that in a single fleeting moment everything had changed. Something had come between them when she mentioned marriage, even though his arms still held her close and his heart still beat comfortably against her breast. He said nothing.

Regan closed his eyes and sighed, all at once confused by the elation and serenity that had taken hold of him, temporarily distorting reality when he'd made love to her. It was something that had never happened to him before. He was in love with Chastity. There was no longer any doubt in his mind. But she would never be a proper bride for him, a Spencer. And to marry her, knowing who and what she was, would be to give up a dream, to admit that he would never be the man he had been born to be. He wasn't about to do that, not even for the sake of the pleasure he had just shared with her. "I cannot marry anyone now, Chastity. I intend to wait until this hotel shows a profit."

"Which shouldn't be too long," she interjected hopefully, latching on to the explanation as a drowning man latches on to a piece of driftwood. "The hotel is a tremendous success!"

He gave a short laugh. "One night will hardly pay back the construction costs, my dear." He sighed and released her, got out of bed, and pulled on his black trousers. He made his way across the room and poured himself a drink, then stood sipping it at the window, staring distantly at the city spangled with lights below. Her eyes followed him in bewildered confusion and she was filled with despair at the change in him. He was sullen and silent as he had been before, and he had retreated into that same mysterious part of himself that he'd always refused to share.

"Regan?"

He whirled about quickly as if awakened suddenly from a dream. He sighed and relaxed then, and with his drink returned to the bed to take up a seat beside her. He smiled at her as she sat up, hesitantly clutching a sheet to her breasts. Just the sight of her bare flesh made him desire her again, and he leaned over to kiss her. But Chastity's mind was far too troubled by other matters to enjoy his affectionate gesture. "Regan . . . if you don't want to marry now strictly for financial reasons, then perhaps my father could . . ."

His eyes narrowed instantly and he stiffened with anger. "Your father is a very busy man these days, Chastity," he said bitterly.

"I know. But I am his only daughter, and if we were to be married, I'm sure that he—" She stopped short as he rose to his feet, trembling with a rage that frightened her. He took a long swallow of whiskey before he faced her again, running a hand tersely through his hair.

"I will make my own way financially." His voice was cold and as sharp as a well-honed blade as he hissed the words. "I don't need your father or you or anybody else to help me. Do you understand that?"

She nodded uncertainly, wondering why the mere suggestion had angered him so intensely and wishing that she had said nothing at all. It was so hard for her to remember that he was an extremely proud man, that a poorly phrased comment or thoughtless action, however innocent, could send his temper flying. It was something she constantly dreaded.

He drew a deep breath and made his way to the bureau again to pour himself a fresh glass of bourbon. He finished it off with amazing speed as she watched him in silence, praying that his mood would change. Finally he set the glass aside, gathered up her clothing, and returned to toss it on the bed. "It's late. You'll be missed if you don't hurry back."

Carefully avoiding his eyes, she took the proffered pile of clothing and dressed quickly, retaining as much of her modesty as she was able to under the circumstances but feeling soiled and uncomfortable in the atmosphere of his anger. He came to aid her with the fastenings of her gown, but it was obvious to her that he was still provoked and his touch was lacking in tenderness. She turned to face him when he had finished, searching his face for the reassurance she needed. She did not find it. "I love you, Regan," she choked out finally, with tears pricking her eyes.

He seemed to lose his anger when she spoke the words, and he held her for a time before he drew back to kiss the tips of each of her fingers. He smiled at her then, and she could not help but return that smile. Then he turned to take her home.

The low, piercing whistle sounded once, twice, three times to announce the change of shift at the Morrow Mine. Two o'clock in the morning. Jonathon banged his fist into his pillow and rolled over, sighing his frustration as a comfortable position eluded him. He rose and lit the gaslight, deciding that a sleepless night would be much better spent in walking than in tossing and turning in bed. Tonight had already been too long a night.

If only he hadn't taken Chastity to the Crown Point's opening! But she would have gone with someone else if he had not. He must try to remember that with Chastity there would always be someone else. She was too beautiful, too wealthy, too desirable to not have other men eager for her attention. He jerked on his trousers and pulled on his shirt, scowling at the thought of her in another's arms. He had never loved a woman as deeply as he loved Chastity. It was almost as if a little part of him died whenever he thought of not having her, of never holding her close in his arms.

He ran a hand roughly through his hair as he hurried out of his room at the B Street boardinghouse, anxious to be out in the cool night air. He took the steps two at a time up to A Street, unconsciously heading along the familiar path to the Morrow home. He slowed to a walk as the silhouette of the tall, gaudy house rose faintly against a night blue sky. His eyes swept the street, all dark and quiet at this late hour, with only the sounds of distant ribaldry and tinny music echoing from the streets below. He stood in the shadows, staring at the door where he had left Chastity just a few hours before. Even now he could picture her in that gown of swirling bluish gray, dancing with Regan Spencer, looking up at him with such love in her eyes. He pressed his fingers to his temples and shut his eyes, but the vision was not so easily banished from his mind. So she still loved him. And judging from the look on Spencer's face, he loved her, too. If he was capable of love at all, Jonathon thought bitterly. He jammed his hands into his pockets and began walking away, muttering phrases long forgotten, kicking angrily at the dirt with every step he took.

A moment later he paused. Frowning, he cocked his head at the sound of approaching footsteps. It was late, shift changes were over, and the nearest saloon was three blocks in the opposite direction. Instinctively he retreated and waited for his curiosity to be satisfied.

A man and a woman, walking arm in arm, whispering and laughing quietly. As they passed a gaslight, the pair of faces were fully illuminated in the darkness. But Jonathon had recognized that crisp black suit and arrogant stride long before the face was visible, and he knew even more certainly the identity of the woman beside him. He took a single step toward them, then stopped short as Chastity threw her arms about Regan's neck and kissed him. It was a deep, passionate kiss, one that left no doubt as to why she was with him at this late hour. A moment later she broke away from the embrace and hurried up the steps and around to the rear of the house. Jonathon did not see her whirl about to blow one last kiss to Regan before she was engulfed in the shadows. Long before then, he had turned and walked away.

Chapter 19

Chastity opened her eyes and smiled, stretching contentedly on her bed as the sounds of fireworks and band music rose from the streets below. Independence Day, 1874. Virginia City's celebration was already in full swing. Chastity kicked off her blanket and giggled, feeling as young and alive as the warm summer morning. How wonderful life is when one is in love, she thought happily, choosing a bright yellow gown from her wardrobe. She hugged the soft muslin to her breast as she spun about the room, imagining Regan's arms around her, imagining his handsome smile as he danced with her while dozens of women gazed on in envy. She was still swaying and humming softly when Sarah gave one short knock and entered her room, carrying a tray of steaming breakfast. The older woman's face reflected her surprise at finding Chastity awake and about, for in the past several weeks she had taken to sleeping well into morning. Sarah frowned as Chastity bid her a too-cheerful good morning, eyeing the breakfast tray all the while.

"You been doin' a lot o' singin' an' dancin' lately, Miss Chastity," she said, her small brown eyes narrowing suspiciously. Chastity ignored the remark as she took the tray from Sarah and set it on the vanity to examine its contents. Sarah sighed. "It seems t' me that I ought t' see a ring on that finger by this time."

Chastity's dreamy smile vanished and her eyes flashed with anger. Sarah had never approved of Regan Spencer,

and during the past few weeks, when he had begun to see
Chastity nearly every day, taking her to dinner, to Piper's
Opera House, to every possible social engagement in town,
Sarah had managed to make her feelings perfectly clear.

"Regan and I have an understanding," Chastity
snapped coldly, "and anyway, it's none of your business."

"Understanding, is it?" Sarah snorted and shook her
head. "There's only one thing that's understood between a
gentleman an' a lady, an' that thing has t' do with a
preacher an' a ring."

Chastity lifted her nose in the air with obvious indifference, but she was far more anxious than she let on.
"There's plenty of time for that in the future," she told
Sarah flippantly. "For now, Regan is too involved with the
success of the Crown Point to think of marriage." She
turned away from breakfast, suddenly finding herself
without an appetite. "Stop shaking your head and help me
with this," she ordered tersely, jerking the muslin gown
from the bed where she had dropped it a moment before.
Sarah obeyed without another word, but she continually
shot disapproving glances at Chastity in the mirror while
she was fastening the back of her gown. Chastity avoided
her eyes, making herself busy adjusting the collar of the
dress and turning from one side to the other to survey her
figure. She cocked her head and frowned, suddenly unhappy with the cut of the dress, the color of her hair, and
even the shape of her nose. Before Regan, she had never
even thought to worry whether a man would find her attractive, but lately she saw every minute flaw in herself
and imagined quite a few that weren't there at all. She
was obsessed with looking her absolute best and even then
she was never really satisfied.

"You look as fine as a lady ought t' look," Sarah commented as if she had been asked for her opinion. "An' the
mornin's half over anyway." Her eyes met Chastity's in
the mirror and fastened an accusing stare on her already
troubled face. "You seem t' be keepin' peculiar hours the
last fortnight or so . . ."

Chastity scowled and shrugged her shoulders in a show
of indifference, but she could not keep a deep scarlet blush

from flooding into her cheeks. It was difficult to hide anything from Sarah, and the fact that she often went to the
Crown Point rather than the opera house, and returned
home later than anyone ever suspected, would not go
unnoticed forever. She was running out of excuses for
sleeping late, and she was thankful that neither her father nor Jonathon had ever so much as mentioned her
tardy arrivals at the office, once or twice barely before
noon. But then, a new find at the Morrow Mine had caused
a flurry of excitement, quite enough to keep Jonathon and
her father preoccupied with other matters. As usual, rumors of a healthy strike, particularly on the heels of the
great discovery in the Consolidated Virginia, had brought
a flood of counterclaims against the mine, sending Jonathon to the Storey County Courthouse for several hours
each day. And Samuel, who was still a simple miner at
heart, had taken to wearing his coarse denims to the office
again so that he could "drop by" the workings, talk with
Murphy, and see any progress firsthand.

But today the office would be closed, everyone would be
celebrating, and Chastity meant to enjoy every minute of
it. Far too much time of late had been spent in useless
worry, in wrestling with a guilty conscience over the lies
she'd had to tell. The Crown Point had been an instant
success, and though Regan had not mentioned marriage
since their first night together, she was sure that he would
very, very soon.

It was after ten when Regan arrived at the Morrow
home to accompany Chastity to the day's festivities. Vir-
ginians certainly knew how to celebrate their nation's
birthday—with parades, fireworks, and more than the
usual revelry clogging the streets, particularly near the
most popular saloons. Lawmen patrolled the streets, temporarily relieving scores of the more belligerent drunkards of their firearms in order to protect the law-abiding
citizenry.

When the sun moved center sky, there was quite a crowd
that left the city, heading for the racetrack a few miles
north. There, under a huge canvas canopy erected to pro-

vide shade, Chastity and Regan enjoyed a box lunch and did some friendly wagering with Samuel and Deborah over a much-publicized race between two champion-blooded California racehorses. Then it was back to town for the final rounds of the citywide spelling bee, a pitting of the best young scholars representing every ward, to be held on a special podium in the center of town.

It was already late afternoon by the time the podium had been cleared of youngsters and a tall, skinny girl with long dark braids and thick glasses had walked off with the highest honors. Then the platform became a vehicle for political candidates, all anxious to take the opportunity to conjure up support for the upcoming election. It was at this late hour that Jonathon finally joined the holiday celebration, having spent the entire day in his room preparing a brief for the next day in court. As he approached the crowd that had gathered at the podium, his neck was stiff with tension, his temples pounding from the extended mental effort he'd put into his work and the stifling heat of his tiny room at the boardinghouse. The physical discomfort only compounded with all his mental preoccupations of late, bringing his normally even temper very close to its breaking point.

Jonathon was becoming bored with the continual litigation, which kept him busy with technicalities, robbing him of much of the satisfaction he had once known working for Samuel. And he was worried, knowing that Samuel had resumed so many of his old responsibilities contrary to his doctor's advice. Why just last week, Jonathon had found him at the mine, stripped to the waist and sweating freely, braving the hellish temperatures with the other miners as he and Murphy turned a drift to trace a tiny thread of silver, sniffing out the rich ore like well-trained bloodhounds. He was taking his life in his hands by exerting himself that way, Jonathon knew. But Samuel was no child. If he chose to ignore the doctor's warnings, then there was nothing more anyone could do. "You can't save a person from himself," Jonathon remembered his revered grandfather telling him. In this particular instance, Grandfather was right.

And, Jonathon thought as he took a place toward the rear of the crowd, eyeing a flash of silver-blond hair much closer to the podium, like father like daughter. His eyes turned cold as he saw Regan Spencer leaning close to hear whatever secrets she was whispering to him. Jonathon braced himself and clenched his fists when he saw her smile up at him. Regan was only using her, taking advantage of what she felt for him. And the speculation, the inevitable whispered rumors about their extended courtship had already begun. It was no wonder, the way she looked at him. It would not be long before some long-winded gossip got hold of a substantial piece of evidence and ruined Chastity's reputation for good. And there was nothing Jonathon could do about it but stand by and watch it happen. He ground his teeth as the frustration churned inside him, scarcely even managing a polite nod when Maureen Murphy smiled and waved at him. He turned to leave, then stopped himself and firmed his footing. His eyes riveted on Bill Sharon, the first speaker to ascend the podium, and he forced himself to concentrate on the impeccably dressed, pompous man as he spoke. Damn if Jonathon Stoneworth intended to run away.

Chastity felt Regan's fingers tug at her sleeve when the political speeches were about to begin, but she shook her head and begged to stay just a little while longer. Her daily exposure to the discussions between Jonathon and her father had kindled her interest in politics, and she was no longer bored by something she didn't understand. She cocked her head and narrowed her eyes as William Sharon began his speech. Sharon had freely wielded the funds of the Bank of California to build the Virginia & Truckee Railroad, and had once controlled most of the major producing mines on the lode, as well as the stamping mills. Chastity's father had never approved of Bill Sharon's tactics, though he begrudgingly admitted that Jonathon was right—the railroad had rescued the Comstock from depression ten years earlier by cutting transportation costs and making a lower grade ore profitable to mine. In effect, Sharon had saved the mines of Virginia City, but he had charged a pretty penny to do it. Quite a few of Samuel's

friends had lost their mines when the bank refused to re-
new loans and promptly foreclosed. Chastity frowned as
she listened to Sharon's harangue, deciding with her father. She did not like this man who wore an obviously expensive suit and smiled a bit too much. But Sharon had
spent thousands of dollars already on his campaign and
was certain to be elected, according to what she'd heard.
He'd even purchased the *Enterprise* to insure his victory.

The next man to mount the podium was small of stature
but so dynamic that he drew an immediate burst of applause from the crowd. Adolph Sutro was a short, balding
man with a full, silver-threaded mustache meeting generous sideburns at his cheeks. A former cigar salesman who
was now a leading citizen of the city, Sutro spoke with the
enthusiasm of a man totally commited to a single dream: a
tunnel four miles long to be bored into the base of Mount
Davidson for the purpose of draining and ventilating the
mines. Sutro believed the tunnel would be well worth
the cost, for it would solve the problems of working in the
depths and, most important, provide an emergency exit for
miners in case of a fire in the mines. Mine owners were
generally against the project, which would cost them two
dollars for every ton of ore removed through the tunnel;
but the miners, who remembered the tragic fire at the Yellow Jacket and several smaller fires since, generally fa-
vored the plan. Sutro was challenging Sharon's bid for the
Senate seat, but he was not really expected to threaten
Sharon's chances. He simply hadn't the funds to launch
the kind of campaign his opponent had.

Still, Chastity was impressed by Sutro's speech and by
the man himself, as she had been the first time she'd met
him. She joined the miners in a spirited round of applause
as he left the podium.

Daylight was waning, the crowd was thinning, families
with small children were departing the scene for the evening meal. Then yet another speaker ascended to the platform, this one not a familiar face in Virginia City and
certainly not a candidate for the Senate. Chastity and
those who still remained all lifted their chins with mild curiosity as the woman, tall, slender, and proudly erect,

cleared her throat and began to speak. She was not a beautiful woman, but Chastity immediately thought her so because of the determination in her features, the animation in her eyes. While thick, unruly red hair blew stubbornly about her face, she addressed her audience with poise and apparent ease, handling herself with the same dignity and aplomb as the distinguished speakers who had preceded her. She spoke of the first Independence Day, and of the courage of the men and women who had fought to free themselves from the bonds of tyranny. She spoke of the war that had torn the country apart, with the central issue of slavery. And finally she spoke of the present, of a fight for freedom that had barely begun.

"The time is now!" she proclaimed with a raise of her fist. "America is the land of the free, and it is our duty to fight for freedom—for *all!*" There was an uncertain scattering of applause about the crowd, and a good deal more suspicious mumbling. "We hold these truths to be self-evident . . . that all men *and women* are created equal!"

A chorus of boos and hissing rose from the crowd, but the speaker continued undaunted. Chastity tensed and glanced anxiously about her, fearing for the woman but admiring her courage in the face of such obvious hostility.

"Women, too, have rights that will no longer be denied them—God-given, natural rights protected by the Constitution. And the time has come for women to demand what is rightfully theirs to claim."

As Chastity resisted Regan's attempts to pull her away, she noticed that most of the conservative-minded husbands in the crowd were forcing their wives to leave. A few of the rougher elements were beginning to shout insults and make obscene gestures, which thinned the crowd out even more. The troublemakers, all obviously inebriated, were yelling comments unfit for a lady's ear as they clustered together and muscled their way to the foot of the podium, looking to have a little fun at the expense of the speaker.

"Women have the right to demand the vote—"

"Shut up, ya ol' witch!"

"Find a man! He'll give ya what's comin' to ya!"

"I'll give ya what's comin' to ya!" another volunteered to the delight of the others. He eyed the speaker with a lewd grin and moistened his lips.

The woman on the podium drew a deep breath and raised her chin, ignoring the insults and addressing what few listeners remained, by this time less than a dozen. Chastity smiled in admiration at her courage.

On realizing that his threat had been ineffectual, the man who had offered his services a moment before was thrown into a fit of temper. He hurled his half-empty bottle of whiskey at the woman's head, and only by ducking did she escape serious injury. She let out a shaky breath as the bottle shattered against the building to the rear of the podium, and though she was visibly shaken, she rose nonetheless and cleared her throat. "Women have the right—"

The sound of splintering glass only made the man who had thrown the bottle more angry for having wasted his brew. "I said, shut up!" he barked at her, swooping down to take up a handful of dust from the street to hurl at the woman.

Chastity instinctively lurched forward to stop him, but Regan quickly moved to stop her and forced her to turn away. She fought with him for a moment until she realized that his patience was wearing thin. Then she immediately gave in. Nothing was worth making Regan really angry. As she dutifully followed him down the street, away from the trouble, she could not help twisting about to see what was happening. Only about ten men remained in the street, some of them anxious to start a ruckus, others hopeful spectators to some kind of fight. The very last thing Chastity saw was Jonathon taking hold of the man who had thrown his bottle a moment before, and whirling him about to face a tightly doubled fist. For an instant her step faltered and she held her breath, but she hadn't even the chance to see the impact of Jonathon's blow before Regan led her around the corner. She lowered her head and followed him in silence then, all the while mouthing a prayer that Jonathon would make it out of the fight in one piece.

It was only after Jonathon's fist had made contact with that cocky, unshaven face of the lead heckler that he finally realized just how angry he was. As the first man went down, a second flew at Jonathon head on, striking him just below the rib cage and sending him sprawling backward in the street. Two other men were quick to follow, hoping to capitalize on Jonathon's prone position. Though he had been knocked breathless by his fall, Jonathon recovered in time to lift his arms and feet and catapult the first of the two over his head, sending him skidding for a good, painful distance over the loose gravel of the street.

Jonathon rolled to avoid his next attacker's boot while at the same time groping for a fistful of dirt to hurl at his face. The dust and gravel met its target, and the man staggered about coughing and sputtering and wiping gingerly at his temporarily sightless eyes. By then Jonathon was again on his feet, braced in readiness as he made a quick survey of the various men who had joined in the fighting, all holding their own in their private bouts with one or two of the hecklers.

The last and largest of the drunkards had remained on the sidelines until now, smiling a silly, guileless grin and sipping sloppily at his half-empty bottle of whiskey. But when he saw that Jonathon had put so many of his friends out of commission, he narrowed his eyes with newly born hostility and took one last swig of whiskey from his bottle. He stepped toward Jonathon, whom he towered over by at least six inches and a good fifty pounds. He began circling about him, smiling a confident, bloodthirsty smile and licking his generous lips. He drew a deep breath and held it as he lashed out with all his might, whirling and stumbling when his fist met no target. Jonathon had ducked the blow. The man who had been blinded a moment before had recovered enough by this time to grab Jonathon from behind, but a swift backward kick made him loosen that hold, and an elbow thrust deep in his abdomen made him grunt and double over in unbearable pain. Gasping for breath now, Jonathon raised his arms in readiness as he pivoted on a single foot. But he was totally unprepared for the mammoth fist of solid rock which crashed abruptly into his jaw. His vision blurred and an explosion of hot, white pain shot like lightning through the entire right side of his face. He reeled unsteadily, seeing double and hearing a strange buzzing sound in his ears. He was powerless as his opponent took hold of his shirtfront and jerked him to attention, but the sight of that giant fist of steel coming at his face again made something click in his mind. Pure instinct mingled with years of street fighting in his youth took over, and he fell forward against the man, completely limp. Then, without any warning, he braced himself and jerked his knee with all his might upward to meet the giant's groin. The man's mouth fell open and a terrible shriek was heard for blocks. The tables had turned. Though still unsteady on his feet, Jonathon took hold of the giant's collar and closed his gaping mouth with a solid blow, then quickly followed it up with a second before he let the larger man drop to his knees.

He spun about with renewed caution, his muscles flexing in readiness, his breath so short that his chest ached with the exertion. He fully expected to encounter any one of the others, but after his victory over the giant of the group, he encountered only shocked faces and embarrassed frowns.

He met each pair of eyes with a question before he dropped his guard, but he knew that the fighting was over. He drew a deep breath and calmed himself as he dabbed gingerly at his lip with his sleeve. Then he went to retrieve his hat from the dust while the drunkards floundered off, much the worse for wear, in search of a friendly saloon.

As Jonathon made a quick examination of his torn, dirty clothing, he noticed that scarcely four men had remained to hear the rest of the red-haired woman's speech, and each of the others looked in even worse shape than he. He sighed and glanced up apologetically at the woman, who still stood on the podium, gaping at him in speechless amazement. He felt badly that all the women, who might have benefited from the progressive ideas the speaker had put forth, had been forced to leave before she had finished her talk. He shrugged his shoulders and attempted a reassuring smile, but he only got so far with it before an excruciating pain flared from his jawline to his temple. She stared at him a moment longer, then gave a sigh of resignation, shuffled her papers, and began her speech again at exactly the point where it had been interrupted. Her voice was clear and firm, and every bit as deliberate as before, but Jonathon noticed the way her fingers were trembling and he knew the effort it took for her to continue, to hold her chin so high. He was reminded of another woman, far lovelier but no less determined, no less driven to get what she wanted.

". . . and the right to vote for all!"

There was a tiny burst of applause as she finished and made her descent from the platform, but she seemed oblivious to the remaining listeners as she folded her notes and tucked them under her arm. Jonathon approached her and politely offered to see her back to her place of residence, to which she curtly replied that she needed no assistance from a ruffian, thank you. He nodded and touched a forefinger to the brim of his hat, silently admitting that about this time he probably looked to be exactly that. She had a perfect right to be angry about her reception in this town, he thought as he turned toward home. But then, most women's rights advocates spoke on specially scheduled lecture tours, not impromptu before a group primarily of miners . . . miners who had been drinking, at that. He had taken several steps in the opposite direction when she stopped him.

"Mr. . . . Mr. . . . ?"

He spun about and removed his hat. "Stoneworth, Jonathon Stoneworth."

The woman moistened her lips and timidly approached him. "Anna May Taylor, Mr. Stoneworth," she said with a nod of her head. She paused and lowered her eyes nervously. "I—I'm sorry, Mr. Stoneworth. I know that it wasn't your fault. I suppose . . . I suppose I'm just disappointed with the way things happened, that's all." She frowned and peered up at him appraisingly. "You might have been arrested for starting that fight, you know. You might have been put in jail!"

He gave her a half smile, wincing slightly with the pain. "I know a good lawyer," he told her. "He would have gotten me out somehow."

"I'm quite serious, Mr. Stoneworth," she insisted soberly. "I've spent a few nights in jail myself." She paused to study his cool, totally confident brown eyes, noting as well the rather amazed lift of his brow. She nodded and went on knowingly. "Most lawmen don't like to be hard on women, but they think a woman who demands her rights ought to be taught a lesson."

He seemed amused as well as skeptical. "You obviously haven't learned that lesson."

She lifted her chin and narrowed her eyes, finding herself attracted to this "ruffian's" rakish sort of half smile. "Oh, I'm a very, very slow learner, Mr. Stoneworth. Especially since I know I'm right. They'll have to do a lot more than arrest me to keep me quiet!"

"I'll wager they will at that, Miss Taylor."

He smiled at her then, and she found herself melting a little at the rich, masculine sound of his voice. "Have you had dinner yet?" he asked her. She shook her head. "Neither have I. Would you consider it terribly forward of me to invite you to join me?"

She raised a thin reddish brow, her eyes lingering on that handsome, flashing smile. "I was just about to ask you the very same question." She grinned at the shock that registered on his face. "Are you certain you can eat after the beating you just took?" She eyed his torn and tattered clothing. "Your face looks a bit worse for wear as well."

He raised his fingers to the large knot that had risen along his jawline. "You have a point there, Miss Taylor," he conceded thoughtfully, "but regardless, I could certainly use a drink." He caught himself and eyed her with renewed caution. "Are you a temperance leaguer too?"

"Heavens no!" she told him quickly. "One cause is enough for any woman." She removed her papers from beneath her arm and linked it in Jonathon's with a friendly smile. "My room's at the International. And I might even join you for that drink. . . ."

The room was private, the appointments elegant, the food superb. Yet Chastity could do no more than stare at her glass of wine and toy with the fine cuisine prepared especially for her by the Crown Point's celebrated chef. Regan hurriedly emptied his plate, but only from habit. He had been watching Chastity carefully ever since he'd brought her here, and he was more than a little anxious to make love to her. But she was quiet and brooding, and he hadn't even told her yet that he was leaving Virginia City tomorrow morning.

The Hotel Crown Point had proven a gold mine. In just a few short weeks it had taken in far more than Regan's optimistic projections, and soon, very soon, every dime he'd invested would be returned to him with interest. But Regan was still a skeptic. The mines might produce for another year or another decade, and then again they might not. Some day the silver would run out. And the money would be gone. And the people would be gone. The Hotel Crown Point was a sound investment for the moment, but there was no denying that it would go the way of the Comstock, and Regan didn't want his financial future to depend on the uncertain treasures buried in the solid rock of Mount Davidson. He wanted out.

So, figures in hand, he planned to return to San Francisco, sell out his interest in the hotel to Mr. Rahling or any one of a dozen other men who had now voiced a desire to be a partner in the venture, and invest in a large tract of virgin California soil. There were many parts of California that reminded him of home, where the winters had been mild, the summers long and green . . . everything had been green. His eyes were distant as he finished his wine. Land. It was the one measure of wealth that endured, that always brought with it power. And to Regan it seemed fitting that he should root himself in soil a continent away from where his forefathers had laid claim to *Regalia* seven generations before. A continent away; a lifetime away. How different he was from the boy who had ridden proudly beside his father through the fertile fields! But Regan intended to rebuild that life, to make a home for himself as much like the life he had lost as it was possible for him to make. His residence would have the same fluted Corinthian columns gracing tall, stately lines; lush, perfectly landscaped grounds for entertaining all the proper people; and land, stretching in every direction to meet the sky. Land that belonged to him.

He lifted his empty goblet and stared thoughtfully at Chastity's face, blurred and slightly distorted through the fine cut crystal. Everything in his life had fallen neatly into place . . . except this. Chastity was the one part of today that constantly intruded on Regan's plans for tomorrow.

But he didn't want to think about that now. He only wanted to hold her, to feel her responding beneath his touch, to wipe away whatever foolish preoccupation furrowed her lovely brow. "Is something wrong with the food?"

"Hm? Oh. Oh, no. Nothing's wrong." She cut a small piece of beef and lifted it to her mouth. "It's delicious," she said with a forced half smile. She swallowed it and took a sip of wine, staring forlornly at the remainder of her dinner. At the moment it seemed like enough food to feed an army. "I guess I'm not very hungry."

"So I noticed." He smiled and leaned forward to study her face. "What in the world are you thinking about? You haven't said a word in over an hour."

"I'm sorry. I have been poor company, haven't I?" She sighed, not knowing whether or not to explain her troubled thoughts. She didn't want to anger Regan, but he seemed to want to know. "It—it's just that I'm worried about that fight. Jonathon was alone, and the other men were drunk—"

"Stoneworth can take care of himself," Regan interrupted sharply.

Chastity sighed again and made herself smile as she reached for his hand. His moods worried her, and she hated to argue with him. And the mention of Jonathon's name always seemed to start an argument. So short a time ago she had thought to solve everything by giving up her virginity, by becoming one with him in every way. But it had changed things so very little between them, and she realized now that it had left her totally vulnerable. She had already played her final trump card, and now there was nothing more for her to give. And a part of her knew that she had not really won his heart, that her hold on him was tenuous at best. But the very thought of losing him was agonizing, terrifying, and it made her feel as if she were walking on a tightrope, as if one wrong step would break that tenuous hold, as if one wrong word would cause her to lose him forever. She had to be very, very careful not to take that single wrong step. "Did you hear what that woman said?" she asked as brightly as she could manage. "About women having the right to vote?"

"I heard, all right."

"And you don't think they should?"

He snorted and rolled his eyes skyward. "Women ought to concern themselves with having babies and keeping their menfolk happy. They know nothing about politics, and they wouldn't be able to understand if a man tried to explain things to them."

"But you're wrong, Regan," she insisted with a lift of her chin. "I probably know more about the upcoming election just from listening and reading about it than most of the miners who'll be voting in it."

He raised a disapproving brow and evenly met her gaze. "That doesn't prove anything, Chastity."

"It does to me. I've always wanted to know what goes on behind closed doors when the gentlemen retire to the parlor for their cigars. Men have such secrets!"

He laughed. "Women have secrets too."

"Humph! Only gossip and fashion and the trials of childbirth! Why do men think that women aren't interested in important things?"

He scowled, silently admitting that the woman beside him was probably capable of understanding far too many things. She had the intelligence and drive of a man, but her body and her emotions were all woman. He tossed his napkin on the table and took hold of her hand, standing and drawing her into his arms. "Any woman as beautiful as you ought not to concern herself with politics. Her head should be full of fluff and nonsense," he murmured as he kissed her forehead, "and her heart should be full . . . with only one man . . ." His mouth drifted over her face and he smiled as her blue eyes darkened in response.

"My heart is full," she whispered urgently, slipping her arms about his neck and slowly drawing his head toward her trembling mouth.

She sighed contentedly as he touched her hair and his lips traced over the smooth column of her throat. Perhaps Regan was right, she thought distantly. Perhaps after they were married her mind would be satisfied with "fluff and nonsense" and caring for Regan and his children. Certainly at this moment her heart was full to bursting with love for this one man.

Anna May Taylor's face wore a comfortable smile as she left the dining room of the International Hotel with Jonathon at her side, seeing her safely to her door. She had never met anyone quite like him, and in the short time they had spent lingering over dinner she had forgotten her normally defensive attitude in dealing with men and found herself totally at ease and enjoying herself completely. He was handsome, devastatingly handsome and utterly masculine, with his smooth, vibrant voice and his quick-witted, flashing white smile. But he seemed unaware of the women who stared at him, as if his confidence came from something within rather than anyone else's approval. She found herself wanting to study him, wanting to take in every tiny line that crinkled at the corners of his eyes when he smiled. For Anna, the dinner they shared had passed much too quickly. She turned to him and smiled as they reached her room, very aware now of the broad, muscular chest and shoulders that towered over her, of the intriguing magnetism in his deep brown eyes. She had never deceived herself about her own appearance.

She knew well enough that her face was at best average and her bright red hair was her worst and most memorable feature. And the gown she was wearing—a tan poplin with pagoda sleeves and a gored skirt—did little to draw attention to her womanly assets. But Jonathon made her feel beautiful, interesting, and special as no man had made her feel in a very long time. And she wasn't about to let him slip out of her life as quickly as he'd just slipped into it.

"Can you come in for a few minutes? I have some brandy that I indulge in . . . on special occasions."

"And do you consider me a special occasion?" he asked with an amused arch of his brow.

"I most certainly do." Her eyes softened and her voice was low and serious. "Please stay. I'd enjoy the company far more than the brandy."

He hesitated, then gave a nod. It took a very strong, unique individual to be committed, as Anna was, to an oftentimes unpopular cause. She probably spent far too many evenings alone, Jonathon thought.

The room was a far cry from the opulence of the Crown Point's luxurious suites, and not even the best the International had to offer. Anna lit the gaslight and swept her arm toward a chair, which Jonathon declined to take, strolling instead to a window to view the ever-growing rowdyism along C Street.

Anna opened a battered leather valise and quickly found a small glass flask of brandy she always traveled with but never used. She glanced about the room, frowning as she took one water glass, filled it about a quarter full, and offered it to Jonathon with an apologetic shrug. "Not hand-cut crystal, but it'll serve the same purpose."

He smiled and raised the glass as if to make a toast. "Where's your glass?"

She timidly raised the flask with a pained expression. "There doesn't seem to be another glass. Will it shock you if I drink from the bottle?"

He grinned and obligingly touched his glass to her flask with a pleasant clink. "To women's rights."

"And to the men who support them," she added.

She eagerly took a swig of brandy, then immediately wished she had remembered herself. The liquid was much stronger than she'd expected and it seemed to scald her mouth and throat. She gasped for air as the burning sensation intensified and spread lower. She dropped the flask and doubled over in a fit of coughing while her face turned a shade of red even darker than her hair. Jonathon set his glass aside and pounded anxiously on her back. "I—I guess I'm—not much of a drinker," she choked out, trying desperately to hide her embarrassment.

"I guess not," he agreed quickly. Anna stole a glance at him and found his dark eyes dancing with amusement despite his mouth's refusal to smile.

"It's not funny, you know," she scolded him sternly.

"I know." His lips lost a bit of their tightness and curved slightly upward.

"Here I am, doing my utmost to impress you with my independence and sophistication—"

"Is *that* what you were trying to do?"

Her eyes flew open in surprise. "You mean you didn't guess?"

He shook his head and Anna hid her face in her hands. "Oh . . . I've managed to do it again."

"Do what?"

She spread her fingers apart and peeked out at him through them. "Make a perfect mess of things." She sighed and stooped to pick up a few of the larger pieces of glass where the flask had shattered. "I'm not just talking about this mess, either," she confessed as she busied herself with the task. "My personal life has never been anything like I wanted it to be . . ." She forced a small nervous laugh. "I'm sorry. I didn't mean to burden you with any of that."

Jonathon retrieved a towel from the washstand and stooped to help her. "Don't be sorry. You're not burdening me at all."

She lifted her eyes and found his face very close to hers. She felt a tremor go through her as she quickly moved away. He was stirring emotions in her that had long been dormant, and she wasn't sure she trusted herself with those feelings now. She made herself busy mopping up the liquid and tiny splinters of glass with the towel. "It's a very long story."

"And it's going to be a very long night," he countered. He put a finger beneath her chin and forced her to meet his smile. "I've been told I'm a very good listener."

At the sight of that smile, Anna melted. "And I've been told I'm a good talker." It seemed easy after that to confide in Jonathon. She took a seat on the edge of the bed while he sat close by in the room's only chair and she briefly confessed her entire life's story.

Anna was the third of three daughters born to a wife of a strict, overbearing Philadelphia schoolmaster. To her father's disappointment, she was neither scholarly and brilliant like her oldest sister nor beautiful and talented like the second. She was plain and ordinary and no matter how she tried she seemed destined to stay that way. At the age of sixteen she ran off with Andrew Taylor, a member of a troupe of traveling actors. Andy was the first and only man Anna had known up till that point who was interested in her even after he met her sisters. She was happy with him, though there was never enough money to allow her the comforts she had been raised to expect—like regular meals and a decent place to sleep. Anna found the situation challenging, however, and soon found ways to supplement her husband's income, doing laundry and mending and even attempting an acting career herself. But she was never able to win over an audience the way her husband could, and any ambition for the theater was cut short with the arrival of her first child.

From the moment of his birth, Paul Taylor was a frail and sickly child prone to colic and colds. Anna, who loved him as fiercely as mothers usually love their firstborn, insisted that her husband give up acting so that they could end their traveling and settle down. She had become an accomplished seamstress, she told him, and could support them all until he could find some other kind of work. Andy seemed agreeable to the idea . . . until Anna woke up one morning and found him gone.

Anna was left alone in San Francisco desperately seeking out enough work to feed herself and her child, barely managing to keep a roof over their heads and food in their stomachs for the first few months. During the first winter her baby contracted a serious chest cold which quickly went into pneumonia, and in spite of a doctor's care and everything she could do, the baby died. It seemed unfair and bitterly ironic that the money came so much more easily after Anna was left alone to grieve the loss of her child. There had been so little for her to live for at first. But then, quite by chance, she had attended a lecture given by Elizabeth Cady Stanton, and that lecture had changed her life. Anna now worked as a seamstress for several months out of every year, and then used her savings to travel and work in support of women's suffrage for a good deal of the summer. "Susan Anthony spoke right here in Virginia City a few years back," she concluded proudly. "And I decided to do the same—to follow in her footsteps, as it were."

"But I believe Miss Anthony spoke in a hall, and her audience was considerably more sympathetic than a group of hardened miners celebrating the Fourth of July."

"But it's my right as a citizen to speak out, even if it is a hostile group I'm speaking to! Especially on the Fourth of July!" She stopped herself and smiled. Her defenses were up again, but she really didn't want to argue with Jonathon. She had enjoyed talking out so many of her memories, had found a real peace sharing them with him. She sighed. "You're right. You are a good listener. But so am I. Tell me all about yourself, Jonathon Stoneworth."

He smiled at her and gave a shrug. "There isn't really much to tell."

"You're being far too modest," she returned with a roll of her eyes. She smiled and appraised his long, lean body, her eyes lingering on his hands, warm, strong, gentle. "But you know that, don't you? Just the fact that you bother to consider the possibility of a woman's equality makes you a very unique kind of man. Somewhere in your life there must have been a very special woman." She paused and narrowed her eyes in thought. "Were you ever married?"

"Not that I recall," he returned with a grin.

"In love?"

He gave an uncomfortable, halfhearted shrug.

"Hmmm . . . must have been your mother, then. What was she like?"

"My mother?" he repeated doubtfully. He gnawed at his lip for a moment, recalling her smooth features, her quick, warm smile. "Yes . . . I suppose my mother was an exceptional woman. My father's equal as well as his complement. Of course, he never thought of her that way . . ."

"Men never do," Anna inserted with regret.

"But neither do women," Jonathon returned. "And that's not what's really important, Anna."

"Then what is important?" she demanded.

"A strong bond of affection, and trust, and respect," he said slowly. His voice softened. "And love . . . To my father, my mother was the sun and the moon and the stars. Everything that was bright and warm and beautiful. And my mother felt the same way about him."

Anna stared at his eyes, which had grown distant and sad, and she lifted her hand to touch his swollen cheek. "So . . . you didn't learn how to fight like that at home."

The distant look disappeared from his eyes as he laid his larger hand atop hers. "Not exactly." He bent forward to kiss her, slowly, until his lips just barely touched hers. The gentleness of the gesture made Anna's heart stop. But suddenly he drew back and turned away as if to leave.

"Jonathon . . . ," she said urgently, jumping up from the edge of the bed. He paused for a moment. She stood looking up at him with wide, pleading eyes, then frowned and looked away in confusion. She had never offered herself to a man before and would probably hate herself later

for this moment of madness, but she simply couldn't let
him go. The silence became uncomfortable until Jonathon took her chin between his thumb and forefinger and
kissed her again. This time she slipped her arms around
his neck and returned the kiss, their lips meeting lightly,
inquiringly, then deliberately. She could feel the lean,
hard muscles of his chest and arms and thighs tensing,
and she knew that he was beginning to desire her by the
way he held her, by the subtle advances made ever so
cleverly as his mouth moved upon hers. But all at once
he put his hands on her shoulders and firmly held her at
a distance. "I'm sorry."

"Sorry?" she repeated in disbelief. "Jonathon, I was
married for five years. I know what I'm doing."

"No. You don't." His voice was very low and strained,
and Anna felt tears stinging her eyes as she saw that same
distant, hurting look return to his expression. And then
she understood. There was someone else.

"I'm not asking for any promises, Jonathon," she told
him quietly. "I'm only asking for tonight."

He closed his eyes and sighed, his mind wrestling with
the temptation that lay before him. Even as he did so, he
saw the moonlight hair and dark blue eyes that haunted
him no matter what he did. "You are a very, very special
lady, Anna May Taylor. I admire you and I respect what
you're doing and I like you very much, but—" He sighed
again and shook his head. "I suppose that's just the problem. I like you too much to use you."

Anna swallowed hard and blinked back a tear of disappointment, trying to make it easier for him to do what he
felt he had to do. "All right. Then I guess we'll have to say
good night and part company as friends."

He smiled at her and lifted her hand to his lips, and she
felt herself aching again for the feel of his kiss. "You're a
remarkable woman, Anna," he said softly, with a great
deal of tenderness, "and don't you ever forget I told you
so."

Anna forced herself to smile as he left the room and
made his way down the long hallway toward the stairs.

Forget? she thought as he disappeared from her sight. Never. She sighed and closed the door slowly behind her. Feelings change in time, she consoled herself, and someday she would see Jonathon Stoneworth again. She intended to make certain that she did.

Chapter 20

Chastity raised her eyes from her work to stare at the hurry-hurry, nonstop movement of traffic along C Street, a sight which hardly ever failed to light a flame of optimism within her. But this morning her mind was a million miles away, and the throngs of nameless people shuffling past the office door only heightened her wistful mood. Three weeks, twenty-one endless days, since Regan had left for California. For Chastity, the time without him had been more difficult than ever before because he had been so much more a part of her life just before he'd left. She sighed and gnawed at her fingertip, reminding herself that he had spoken of buying land in California, land on which to build a grand home, a showplace rivaling the splendor of the Spencer plantation destroyed in the war. And once he had bought his land and built his fine home, it would be perfectly logical for him to take a wife to share that home with him, to give him children to carry on the proud Spencer name. Why then had Regan failed to mention such a logical conclusion to his plans? Her brows drew together in a nervous frown. She had to admit that she was anxious about becoming his wife and worried about his avoidance of the subject. Yet he loved her—she was almost certain of that. Everything was so perfect between them . . . except this.

She hurriedly returned her attention to her work as Jonathon swung open the door and marched into the office, letting it slam behind him with a bang. She timidly glanced up as he threw his briefcase on his desk and watched him glare at the thing, nostrils flaring, arms folded across his chest. "Bad day at the courthouse?"

He closed his eyes and let out a lengthy breath through clenched teeth. "No worse than usual."

She frowned at him, noticing the taut set of his mouth and the furrow at his brow. They had become all too common to his expression of late, and just yesterday she had even heard him speak crossly with Joey Bates. Good-natured, even-tempered Jonathon was prone to fits of depression for some strange reason these days, and Chastity wondered at the change in him. "Papa's gone down to the mine already, but he's left a whole day's worth of work on his desk. I've started on the payroll . . ."

Jonathon was leaning over her desk, checking the work she had done, when the door of the office flew open and a breathless, red-faced miner gasped out the news. "A fire! There's a fire at the mine!"

Chastity and Jonathon exchanged an instantaneous, panic-stricken glance before scrambling out of the office and heading for the mine. Twelve blocks they ran, to the main works at the far southern end of C Street, only to have their worst fears confirmed. A thin cloud of smoke and gas puffed erratically as the ventilation system forced air into the main shaft.

A small crowd had already gathered when the cage, crowded with six men, all coughing and dizzy from their hasty ascension, rose to the surface level. They were hurriedly removed and the cage was at once lowered into the mine. Twice, three, four times the cage was dropped to the twelve-hundred-foot level where the fire had apparently begun in a winze, a connecting passage, near the new find. Time and again the crowd waited, tense and silent, for the signal to raise it again.

Chastity's face reflected her fear as the miners continued to evacuate the mine. There was still no sign of her father. And each time the cage rose to the surface, the men seemed more affected by the smoke and gas being emitted by the fire. She forced her way through an ever-growing

crowd toward a group of miners who had been brought up
several moments before. They stood in a circle of sorts, recounting the situation below and assuring one another
that the mine was in good hands, that the fire would be
stopped before it spread to the main shaft.

"Is my father still down there?" she interrupted one
man.

He nodded quickly, recognizing her at once as Samuel's daughter. "Mr. Murphy an' Mr. Morrow both is still
in th' mine, Miss," he affirmed. "They tryin' t' get th'
winze blocked off—it's either that or lose th' whole
shaft."

"He an' Murphy knows what t' do," another told her,
trying to offer something in the way of comfort.

"An' Shaunessy's a better man wi' explosives than any
on the lode!" another added with pride. "He be able t' do it,
sure."

In an unobserved moment, Jonathon motioned one of
the miners aside, turning away from Chastity to speak in
a lowered voice. "How bad is it down there, Danny?"

The young miner's eyes reflected an anxiety he had hidden from Chastity. "It's bad, Johnny. Real bad. Hard as
hell t' breathe an' hot as th' dickens. Th' boss should ha'
come up wi' th' rest of us."

Jonathon gave him a reluctant nod, turning swiftly as
the cage surfaced again. Chastity's face lifted with renewed hope as she pushed toward the front of the crowd.
But it fell immediately when she did not recognize any of
the three men being removed. Three men—and the hoist
had a capacity of six. Why hadn't he come up? Why? Her
eyes flooded with tears of frustration and she glanced
about for Jonathon, meeting his eyes with a look of utter
helplessness. It was that look, coupled with his own rising
fear for Samuel's survival, that made Jonathon jump
aboard the cage along with a fireman who was going below
to check the progression of the fire. Before he had a moment to reconsider his decision, the cage was being lowered into the mine.

The light vanished in a frightening instant and the

air became thick, cool, moist. For Jonathon, the descent into a mine was always like being swallowed up by a huge predatory animal, or sealed in a tomb of earth and timber. His heart stopped for a moment, until his eyes slowly adjusted to the fireman's lantern. By then the cool air was gone and the temperature was rising quickly. Deeper and deeper they descended, until the air that whipped about them was like the exhaust from a blast furnace. Jonathon tore at his tie, drew off his suit coat and tossed it aside. But he was still drenched in sweat before the cage reached the thousand-foot level.

He was aware of the fireman's eyes upon him and sensed the older man's displeasure. The fireman had seen too many fires in the mines to like the idea of having a civilian along, particularly a fancy-clothed lawyer. He was sure that Jonathon would wind up being in the way at best or another body to be brought up at worst. "You shouldn't have come down here, mister. If you want to be a hero, there's lots easier ways."

Jonathon wiped the sweat from his brow with his sleeve and shook his head. "I'm not trying to be a hero," he returned softly, the putrid odors of gas and smoke already making it difficult to breathe. "I just want to make sure everyone makes it up."

"Then follow orders," the fireman said tersely, checking his lantern. "We get the rest of the men out to the cage and send them up. Use force if necessary. If Shaunessy hasn't set the explosives yet, then everybody but him and me go up."

Jonathon nodded, his nostrils stinging as he breathed the smoke-filled air. He felt a strange tightness in his chest.

"And be sure you're conscious on the hoist so you can keep all the bodies on. I guess you know what happens if there's a slip."

Again Jonathon nodded, remembering all too vividly the man who had fainted and fallen into the shaft a few months back. All that remained of the body had been bits and pieces of limbs caught here and there against the supporting timbers, and a hunk of flesh at the bottom which vaguely resembled a human torso. Not a single bone had escaped being shattered. Jonathon had learned quickly that such accidents were not uncommon on the lode.

The hoisting line finally tightened, pulling the cage to a stop at the twelve-hundred-foot level. The fireman turned and motioned Jonathon down as soon as they were out of the cage, and the two began to crawl along the bottom of the tunnel off the shaft, where comparatively clear air had stratified below the rising smoke and heat. Jonathon followed closely, his eyes unable to adjust to the pitch-blackness, nothing visible but a dim, flickering spot in the smoke-filled air that was the fireman's lantern. They rounded a turn and saw them, two almost nonexistent lights glowing weakly from a perch in the rock near a ventilation pipe. Huddled in a single shadow nearby were two men, one gasping visibly at the meager source of oxygen. That same man made a lurch at them when he saw their lantern. "Shaunessy's settin'—the explosives," he choked out. He broke off in a fit of coughing and the fireman motioned him toward the cage.

"Get the hell out of here!"

Murphy gave a vigorous shake of his head. "Sam's—fainted." He directed their attention toward the unconscious man, and Jonathon immediately groped his way to Sam's side.

He took hold of the older man's shirtfront and shook him hard. "Samuel?" He grasped his shoulders and shook him again. "Sam?" Jonathon's voice broke with emotion, but still there was no reply.

He lifted the limp body to his shoulders and made to carry him, his muscles trembling as he drew a deep breath of burning, gas-filled air. He began to crawl toward the cage, but the fireman stopped him with a hand on his arm. "Wait at the cage. We'll all go up together."

Jonathon nodded, then hurried off toward the cage, following after the small light Murphy raised before him. His body was soaking wet; his skin felt as if it were being melted to his bones. But the physical stress was nothing in comparison with the mental agony he was suffering, the fear of slipping, the fear of an explosion, the fear that Sam's body might remain limp and lifeless even if they made it to the surface. They managed to find their way back to the cage and had just gotten aboard when the fireman and a thickly built, sturdy-looking man appeared from a dense cloud of smoke, each coughing and stumbling onto the hoist. Shaunessy hurriedly gave the three pulls on the line, and for a split second that seemed an eternity, all stood motionless, gasping, waiting. Then miraculously the line pulled taut and they were rising from the depths of hell faster and faster and faster, returning to a world of light and air and living.

Jonathon felt a sudden wave of nausea and dizziness as the air cooled around his damp skin and clothing. With all his resolve he struggled with the lifeless body, holding it tightly against himself. He felt himself shaking as his fingers roamed over the older man's throat, then frantically moved about his chest, searching, hoping against hope . . . There was no pulse.

"If you stay awake another minute or so," the fireman said, taking hold of his shoulder and shaking him alert, "you might just be a hero after all."

Jonathon tightened his grip on Sam's body and shuddered, forcing himself to hold on as the earth shook with the force of the explosion set deep in the mine. In the dim light he saw the faces of the other three men as they knowingly nodded to one another and smiled. The fire would be stopped before it got to the main shaft.

Jonathon squinted against the blinding light as the hoist reached the surface, and several pairs of hands aided him from the cage. As Sam was pulled hurriedly from his arms, a massive cheer was rising from the crowd. "Everybody's up! They all made it!"

Breathless and dizzy from the change in temperature, coughing and shaking off those who reached for his hand or patted him heartily on the back, Jonathon followed unsteadily after the men who carried Samuel. They all expected Samuel to live. They expected him to be revived, as had hundreds of other miners who had dropped from asphyxia and come back to life within minutes of reaching the surface. But none of them had held that lifeless body all the way up from the bottom of that mine, feeling the coldness of it, the intangible lack of something that made Jonathon shiver even now, when sweat dripped from his forehead and chin and beaded along his upper lip. It was sheer willpower that kept him from fainting, that forced him to follow the men to the place where they laid Sam down for the doctor to examine him. Chastity was there, kneeling beside her father, holding his pale, cold hand against her cheek. Her eyes were wide and frightened like a lost child's as she stared down at that pallid face, already knowing, yet hoping, desperately hoping . . .

The doctor drew a deep breath and stroked his mustache nervously before he glanced up at Chastity and shook his head. An odd silence fell upon the those who had seen the gesture and it quickly spread through the crowd. They had expected a miracle, but now whispers and murmurs of sympathy took the place of the cries of elation and euphoria. The main shaft of the Morrow Mine had been saved, but it had cost the life of Samuel Morrow.

Chastity's eyes were pressed tightly shut and tears were running quickly down her cheeks as Jonathon knelt beside her to gently disentangle her father's hand from her own. She opened her eyes and stared at him helplessly. "He—he's gone, isn't he, Jonathon? He's gone—" Her voice broke off as he nodded, swallowing hard to keep from crying himself.

With reverent silence he folded Samuel's hands on his chest, took a coat someone offered from the crowd, and slowly covered the dead man's face. He raised his eyes to scan the crowd until he found Murphy, who gave a brief nod. Then he helped Chastity to her feet and led her away, past the men who still worked furiously pumping the winze with steam, past crowds of people who stared at her with understanding or curiosity, past the familiar buildings of C Street . . . home.

Chapter 21

For Chastity, the days immediately following the tragedy at the mine passed by in a strange blur. It was Jonathon who made the decisions that had to be made, helping Deborah to choose Samuel's best brown suit for burial and making arrangements for services and a final resting place, and Jonathon who stood for hours beside Chastity and Deborah, sharing their grief and offering his much-needed strength.

It was impossible for Chastity to accept the finality of her father's death, and by living a detached, playacting kind of existence, she instinctively put off facing the truth . . . and the hurt. She was barely conscious of an endless stream of people who came to the house to pay their respects and offer their condolences, and only vaguely aware of her father's absence and what it all meant. For long, exhausting hours she stood beside Jonathon and Deborah and went through the motions of greeting her father's friends, of listening to the same useless words of sympathy over and over and over again without really hearing them at all. Even when she stood at the gravesite under a scorching hot summer sun, staring numbly at the elaborate bronze coffin being lowered into the ground, she was totally removed from what was happening. During all that time she was aware of only one thing—that she needed Regan beside her and he was not there.

It was several days after Samuel's body had been interred that Jonathon returned to the house in answer to a note from Deborah. He found her in the parlor, thoughtfully pacing and staring about as if she were seeing everything there for the first time. "Deborah?"

She started and spun about, then relaxed and smiled at Jonathon, her somber black taffeta rustling as she came forward to take his hand. "I didn't expect you for another hour or so, Jonathon. Please come in and sit down. Would you care for tea? Some brandy, perhaps . . ."

Jonathon shook his head and took a seat while Deborah seated herself comfortably nearby and poured herself tea. He eyed her cautiously, wondering at her momentary composure. She noticed his expression and gave him a sad half smile. "No, I haven't gone completely daft, Jonathon. I just— I guess I'm just cried out, if that's possible. I've done my share of public grieving these past few days and now I want to get on with 'the business of living,' as he would have called it." She bit her lip and struggled to remain calm as she recalled Sam's voice gruffly mouthing those very same words. "That's why I asked you to come here today, Jonathon. I need to get away from this place . . . this house . . . I've spent so much time in this house in the past year, caring for him, nursing him, trying to convince him to take better care of himself . . ." Her voice trailed off and she let out a weary sigh. "Everywhere I look are memories, and I'm just not strong enough to face them all now. Maybe I never will be."

"But you have friends here, Deborah—"

"Not my friends, Jonathon. His friends, our friends, but I have never really had a life of my own here in this city. And I never felt . . ." She hesitated and stared down at her hands. "I never really felt as if I belonged here. I don't belong here without Sam." She raised her eyes immediately, ready for his arguments. "No, don't argue with me, Jonathon. My mind is made up. I'm going back to San Francisco as soon as the proper arrangements can be made."

He drew a lengthy breath and went to pour himself the brandy he'd declined a few moments earlier. He took a sip and let it warm his throat before he spoke in a calm, professional manner. "It might take a little while to come up with enough cash to purchase a house for you there. At the last two stockholders' meetings I spoke with two or three men who were interested in purchasing a large block of Morrow stock, but there was nothing definite, and with the fire and Samuel's death . . ." He sipped at his brandy and tossed her a sidelong glance. "You realize, of course, that I could not simply throw the shares on the open market. The stock would plummet and—"

"I understand all that. But don't try to maneuver me into staying in Virginia City any longer than I have to, Jonathon. My mind's made up."

"All right. There's been a special meeting called for the end of this week to decide on who will be running the mine office now that Samuel's gone. There's talk of moving the bulk of the paperwork to San Francisco, of letting Mr. Murphy maintain a small office here. Someone made a motion to that effect at the last meeting, and if Samuel hadn't been there himself to argue against it, it might have happened then. Regardless, I shall have to attend that meeting, and while I'm there I'll make inquiries for you."

She lifted her chin and her eyes met his squarely. "I'm sorry, Jonathon. That's not good enough. I intend to leave by the end of this week. We can travel together." She held up her hand to stop his protests. "Yes, I can be packed and ready to go in that short a time. And I don't expect to buy a grand house, or any house right away. I have friends in San Francisco with whom I can stay indefinitely, or I could stay at a hotel until we can work something out."

Jonathon frowned and took another sip of his brandy, thoughtfully studying its warm amber color. "And Chastity?"

Deborah sighed and avoided his eyes as she placed her cup on the serving table and folded her hands primly in her lap. She had expected him to ask about her. "I shall ask Chastity to come with me, of course. But she will not leave here." She made herself smile, but her face began to show the strain of the last few days. "She may even laugh at me when I ask her to come along." She bit her lip and blinked several times while Jonathon remained silent, wishing he knew what to say. But he had never under-

stood that part of Chastity, the part that refused to give
Deborah a chance, the part that refused to be anything
more than polite.

Deborah smiled tremulously. "Did you know that when
Samuel and I were first married, I tried to be a mother to
her? The very first time I saw her, she was such a tiny
thing! And she had cut off all that beautiful silver-blond
hair when she learned that we were married, so that all I
really remember were those two enormous blue eyes." She
laughed as the memory became clearer in her mind. "She
was always doing things like that—cutting off her nose to
spite her face, I believe is the expression. She was so willful and stubborn and . . ." Deborah's smile faded quickly.
"And angry. So much anger in that tiny blond head!" She
sighed and her eyes showed the hurt which remained,
even after all these years. "How she hated me! She tried
everything to get me to leave this house, to drive a wedge
between Samuel and me." She swallowed hard and braced
herself against the pain of remembering. "But I never
hated her, Jonathon. I tried so hard to love her, to care for
her. She simply wouldn't let me. I couldn't even get close
to her." She blinked as a tear slipped over her cheek. "It's
the only thing I really regret about the years I spent with
Samuel, that I failed to reach his child, that I failed to
have children of my own."

Jonathon handed her a handkerchief and placed his
hand on her shoulder. "It's not too late, Deborah. Chastity
needs someone now more than ever." He thought of the
way Chastity had stood beside him as they laid her father
in the ground, ramrod-straight, dry-eyed. But he knew
that Chastity did need someone to care for her, though she
acted so aloof, so independent.

Deborah dabbed at her eyes and shook her head. "No,
Jonathon. If she couldn't accept me in all these years, then
she'll never accept me now. And besides, I haven't the
strength to begin all over again with her." She lifted her
tired blue eyes to meet his. "I'm an old woman now, Jonathon. And I just haven't got the strength."

His brow drew together in an understanding frown, and
he knew that she spoke the truth. She looked so tired and

pale in her somber black dress, and as much as he thought Chastity needed her, he couldn't bring himself to make her feel guilty about leaving. She had tried all these years; now she had a right to live a life for herself.

"I am not blind, Jonathon. I know how difficult this has been for her," Deborah said, putting his thoughts into words. "She loved her father so very much! She hasn't eaten for days, she spends hours at a time alone in her room . . ." She sighed. "She has no one to turn to now, except that young man of hers, that Regan Spencer." She scowled as she spoke the name. "And where is he when she needs him beside her? Off to California on business of some sort! Why, she hasn't even heard from him in weeks! And I know for a fact that she's written him a dozen times over."

Deborah closed her eyes and her anger gave way to sympathy. "I can only guess what she went through these past few days, waiting for him to come back. I could see the disappointment on her face every time someone else stopped by to pay his respects. She was so certain that he would come back. . . ." Her voice trailed off and she hesitated before continuing thoughtfully, unaware of the effect of her words on Jonathon. "I never understood what she saw in that man, really. He's pompous and arrogant, and he acts as if he is so much better than the rest of us. Of course, Chastity acts that way at times, too. But she's changed over the past year, come around some, if you know what I mean. I remember the way she helped plan your birthday party . . ." She started to smile, but suddenly bit her lip and reached out for Jonathon's hand. "Oh, Jonathon! I don't want to desert her, but I don't know how to help her. She's so like her father with all that pride. I'm so afraid that man will hurt her—" She finally lost control of her emotions and began sobbing into her hands. "Just a—a few months back, when—I spoke with—with Samuel about Chastity," she choked out brokenly, "he told me not to worry. He told me that you would care for her after—after—" She grasped tightly at his hand and lifted a tear-stained face. "You—you do care for her, don't you, Jonathon?"

He stiffened and withdrew his hand. So Sam had known. He reproached himself for being so transparent with his feelings, and couldn't help but wonder if Chastity had guessed the truth as well. He felt like a fool. "I promised Sam that Chastity would be comfortable financially for as long as she lives," he answered flatly, moving quickly to help himself to another glass of brandy.

Deborah wiped her tears from her cheeks and crumpled the handkerchief in her fist. "And you will look after *her?* Not just her money?"

Jonathon sighed and finished the second brandy without turning to face her. It was ironic, almost humorous, for her to ask him such a question. "I'll do what I can." There was a long pause. "But I don't think my concern will be at all appreciated if Chastity chooses to marry Regan Spencer."

She gave a rueful smile which Jonathon didn't see. "If that indeed happens, Jonathon, then I think that Mr. Spencer will have done the choosing."

Chapter 22

Stuart Baston's coal black eyes never wavered from Regan's face as he drew a long, thoughtful draught from his glass of imported wine. He set the glass aside and his eyes narrowed as he took in the proud, erect posture of the man clad impeccably in black broadcloth. He wore it well, even in this stifling heat, Baston mused with admiration. And it was no wonder. He claimed to be a Spencer, of the Carolina Spencers, one of the South's finest families . . . before the war, of course. Baston vaguely recalled a rumor that the last of the Spencers had been killed in the war. He knew for a fact that the family's great plantation had been destroyed to the last timber. Stuart's gnarled fingers closed tightly around his carved lion's-head walking stick, and he struggled to his feet. He pulled his left leg stiffly along as he approached the younger man and circled about him in wordless appraisal. A Spencer, he called himself. Yes. It was very possible that he spoke the truth.

Regan gave no sign of the annoyance he felt at having to endure such close scrutiny. He kept his silence until some moments later when the older man once again met his gaze. "Do you understand, sir? I am requesting the hand of your daughter in marriage."

"I understand what you said, Mr. Spencer. But I'm afraid you've caught me quite by surprise. You've known Charlene for less than a month—"

"Three weeks and five days, to be exact," Regan interrupted. "But the devotion and sincere regard I feel for your daughter could never be measured in time." He paused. "I realize that all this may seem sudden, but I am not an inexperienced youth, unaware of the seriousness of my request. I am fully aware of what marriage entails, which is why I never considered it until now." He drew a deep breath and tried to discern what impact his words of explanation were having on Mr. Baston. "You probably know that I have purchased the Rancho Verde, that I am planning to build a home there. It will be a fine house, I can assure you. Charlene will be proud to be mistress there."

The older man's eyes began to twinkle and his lips bore the barest trace of a smile. He raised his cane and shook it with feigned belligerence at Regan. "So you're going to deny me the pleasure of lecturing you on the importance of such a decision, are you? Well . . . you seem to have a head on your shoulders, I'll say that for you." His eyes lost their sparkle and he struck his cane sharply on the floor before he hobbled back to his chair. "I reckon you had to, to survive all that's happened." He grunted and let out his breath as he settled heavily in his seat. "Sit down, sit down," he ordered brusquely with a careless wave of his hand.

Regan obliged him, taking a seat opposite. "We're alike, you and I," the older man said as Regan nodded his thanks for the glass of wine offered him. "We were the best of the Old South, and we have lived to prove it." He sighed and finished his drink in a single gulp. So many memories crowded together in his mind . . . Louisiana; the family's sugar plantation, which had prospered on the banks of the Red River for five generations. So different from this California land where a new and different life had been won with blood and sweat and pure determination.

"We've done more than simply survive," Regan added softly, also lost in his memories of home. "We've prospered, in spite of all that the war cost us. And we will continue to prosper." He drained his glass of wine and set it aside, assuming a more businesslike tone. "Which is why I want to make Charlene my wife."

"I assume you've spoken with her."

Regan smiled and nodded, picturing Charlene's tiny, delicate face framed perfectly by waving coal black hair. Her skin was lily white—she never allowed it to be darkened by the sun—and she moved with the grace of a dancer and spoke with the slow, unaffected inflection of a properly bred Southern gentlewoman. She was the woman Regan had always dreamed of taking for a wife, a woman he could immediately place on a pedestal, a woman who would fit perfectly into his new life, a life he had struggled and sacrificed so much to rebuild. She was so different from Chastity, purer, shier, far less passionate— He scowled and shook off the comparisons, which always came to his mind. Chastity was part of the past, and he was relieved to leave her and all the memories behind him, to give himself totally to his new life with a woman of breeding and honor.

Stuart bent forward to pour more wine, then raised his glass until it clinked against that of his future son-in-law. "To your new life with Charlene. May you both find total happiness."

"To Charlene and total happiness," Regan repeated heartily. And for the first time since the war, he believed that total happiness was well within his grasp.

Chapter 23

Jonathon waited patiently until the train had all but emptied of passengers before gathering up his belongings and heading for the exit. He paused on the platform, his eyes automatically scanning the sea of unfamiliar faces. It was strange to arrive here at the station and not be in a hurry to report to Sam about the happenings at the stockholders' meeting. Jonathon's usually brisk stride was slow and thoughtful as he left the depot and approached the ever-thickening traffic in the center of town. His feet carried him on to the office, an office that would be closed as soon as he could sort out Sam's personal effects from the files and turn over the mining company paperwork to Michael Murphy. Jonathon entered the office and closed the door behind his back without bothering to lift the shade to admit the day's light. Time . . . how quickly it passed, how relentlessly it continued on as it had before. Jonathon had heard it said that time healed all wounds; it was something he did not believe. Time merely forced a person to go on, placing a comforting distance between the pain of the past and the present. But there were moments when past memories hopelessly entangled themselves in the present, and this was one of those. He could not enter this office without remembering the first time he had done so. Nor could he shake off the emptiness he felt standing here all alone, knowing that Sam's booming laughter would never again fill this room. And Chasti-

ty—well, she was a part of it too. It had been well over a
week since he'd seen her, and he had hoped to find her
here. He had asked her to sort the mail and record the
assessments that had been paid while he was gone, if
she felt up to it. But she had probably decided never to
come back to this place after what had happened. From
the looks of things, she hadn't been here once since Jonathon had left town. He closed his eyes and sighed as he
leaned his back wearily against the closed door. Regan
Spencer must have returned by this time. Perhaps he
was the reason for Chastity's not being here. Regan
would be happily surprised when he found out how
much money Samuel had left his only daughter, and
how little of it really was tied up in an irrevocable trust.
Chastity would most likely become Mrs. Regan Spencer
in a matter of days. And though it infuriated Jonathon
to lose her that way, to a man who would marry her
strictly for her money, he had to admit that he would be
relieved to see it over and done with. After all, only his
lie had kept Regan from marrying her a year ago, and
had indirectly forced her into her present situation. As
much as Jonathon would have liked to blame Regan totally for Chastity's unhappiness, he could not forget
that he had also had a hand in it. He had lied to Regan
about her father's money and had even refused to give
the loan Samuel had instructed him to extend. At the
time it had been easy to rationalize a gallant motive for
his dishonesty, but now he realized that his actions had
been purely selfish. He hated Regan Spencer, and he
was in love with Chastity himself. So he had done the
type of thing his grandfather would have done, and
made a decision that had not been his to make.

But there was nothing to be done about that now, he
thought as he tossed his briefcase on the desk and
turned to raise the blinds. There were pressing matters
of business to be taken care of, contracts to be drawn up,
signed, and posted to conclude the sale of stock he'd
worked on while in San Francisco, attending the meeting and seeing Deborah settled in her new home. There
were also records to be checked at the courthouse, and

an office full of paperwork to be sorted out before it was
handed over to Michael Murphy, who would take care of
sending it on to San Francisco. And later, much later,
he would make a call to the Morrow home and have
a long talk with Chastity. After that, it would be up
to her whether or not he continued to handle her affairs.

Jonathon leaned back in his chair and ran a hand over
his eyes, trying to relieve the strain of several long hours
of paperwork. He got up and lit the gaslight nearest his
desk, noticing that the shadows were already falling heavily on Virginia City. Autumn was approaching, though
there were no brightly clothed trees to herald its coming,
only the early passing of the sun and a cool, sharp edge to
the evening air. He returned to his chair, picked up one of
several letters and let his eyes scan the words, but his
mind refused to grasp the meaning. Twice, three times he
mouthed the meaningless jumble before heaving a sigh of
resignation.

He began to clear off his desk, gathering up the papers
he had prepared for Chastity to sign and hoping that Regan Spencer would not be there when he called. He
slipped on his suit coat and buttoned his shirt, then ran
a reluctant hand over a day's growth of beard. Perhaps
he should stop by his boardinghouse room on the way,
he thought as he extinguished the lamp. He was certainly in need of something to improve his sagging spirits. Perhaps a shave and a change of clothing would
help. He was locking the office door when a familiar
voice hailed him from across the street. He whirled
about to face the grinning nine-year-old countenance
framed by unruly bright red hair.

"Hiya, Mr. Stoneworth!" Joey gasped out breathlessly.
"Ya been—gone fer—a long time, ain't ya?"

"Almost two weeks," he answered with a distant half
smile. It seemed so much longer.

Joey gave a nod. "Thought so, cause I ain't seen ya
around." He chewed thoughtfully at his lower lip, then
narrowed his eyes in serious thought. "I was just think-

in' . . ." He waited until he had Jonathon's full attention before he went on. " 'Bout all the fun we had las' year at the picnic."

Jonathon's smile brightened a little at that. "It was fun, wasn't it?"

"Sure was! 'Bout the most fun I ever had in my life!" He paused again and pressed his lips together in concentration. "I was thinkin' that since we had so much fun that day, ya jus' might wanna' take me to the circus?" His boyish blue eyes were suddenly wide and hopeful.

Jonathon raised a brow. "Is there a circus in town?"

"Not yet. But I heard one o' th' rich kids say his pop was gonna' take him in a couple o' days. It was in th' paper an' all." He sighed in dreamy anticipation. "Sure would like t' go . . . with a real ticket an' all, I mean. I went before but I never got t' see th' whole show without gettin' chased out."

"I can't think of anything I'd rather do than take you to the circus, Joey. . . . Under one condition."

Joey's toothless grin faded to a scowl of annoyance. "There's always a condition."

"The condition is that we wait our turn in line to buy the tickets and take our seats." Joey's scowl darkened and he jammed his hands deep in his pockets until Jonathon added, "If we get there early enough, we'll get good seats."

"Then let's get there real early!" Joey cried. "I wanna sit in th' front row. I want ever'body t' see me!"

Jonathon rumpled his hair. "It's a deal." He glanced at the dusky sky. "Aren't you going to be late for dinner? Your mother—"

"Oh, my gosh! She said if I was late jus' one more time this week—!"

Jonathon let out a laugh as Joey took off running, weaving in and out of the people who clogged the crowded boardwalk. And suddenly it felt good to be home!

"Oh, Johnny! It's more than happy I am t' see you!" Sarah's full face beamed with pleasure as she gave him a quick hug, then backed away in embarrassment. "Thank heavens you've come home!"

"If I'd known this warm reception awaited me, I'd have come directly from the station," he teased her.

She blushed and lowered her eyes for a moment, but her smile remained every bit as warm. "Are you hungry after your trip? O' course you are! Come in an' have a bite t' eat. Is Miss Deborah settled in now? Did she find a nice house?"

As Sarah led the way through the hall to the dining room, Jonathon patiently answered all her questions about Deborah's new home, its size, the help she had hired, and so on. Candles burned brightly on the table and the gaslights were lit, but the table was not set nor was there any sign of someone's having taken dinner recently. "Chastity hasn't eaten yet?" he asked hopefully, interrupting Sarah's prattle.

The smile on Sarah's face suddenly froze, and her eyes lowered uneasily. She closed her mouth and bit her lip hard. "Miss Chastity hasn't come down from her room in nearly a week, Johnny. Not since . . ." Her voice trailed off and her face reflected her pain.

"Not since what?" he demanded anxiously.

She closed her eyes and sighed before she met his eyes. "Not since she read 'bout Mr. Spencer's weddin' in the papers."

Jonathon's brown eyes searched her face in utter disbelief. "Regan Spencer is married?" he whispered. "To someone else?"

Sarah gave a curt nod and a bitter frown darkened her brow. "She wouldn't believe what they said at first. But they all carried the story. Mr. Spencer's a rich, important man nowadays. Didn't know his wife long before he married her, accordin' t' the papers. But she's a beauty, they say, an' she comes from money . . ." Sarah went on for several moments, repeating every word of gossip she'd heard in the past week. All the while Jonathon stood there speechless, unable to believe that Regan had actually married another woman when he might have had Chastity.

"She read it in the papers, you say? He didn't even write or—?"

"Hmph!" Sarah snorted in obvious disgust. "She went through the mail like she was huntin' fer buried treasure, an' nary a word did she hear from the scoundrel!" She clucked her tongue and shook her head. "I never agreed wi' the way she chased after him, mind you. But then, Miss Chastity's always been that way. Once she gets an idea in her head, there's no gettin' it out. Stubborn as a mule, she is, an' has been ever since I've known her." She sighed and her face softened with obvious concern. "I thought it would be better for everyone if he never came back here. But now I just don't know . . ." She raised her eyes helplessly to Jonathon's. "She's hurtin' real bad, Johnny. Ain't had a bite t' eat since Lord knows when. Just sits there in her room an' stares an' stares . . ." She sniffed and blinked back a tear. "An' . . . an' when she goes t' visit her papa's grave, she won't let anyone go with her. She goes there every morning . . . all alone . . . all alone . . ."

Jonathon placed his hands on Sarah's trembling shoulders and gave them a reassuring squeeze. "It's all right, Sarah. I'll talk with her."

"She won't talk t' you, Johnny. She won't talk t' anyone."

"She'll talk to me," he told her with a confidence he was far from feeling. He squared his shoulders and retraced his steps to the front stairs, doing his best to proceed slowly, to remain calm, to keep his mind clear so that he would do and say all the right things. But in spite of his good intentions, his feet hurried up the stairs and his mind flooded with emotions he couldn't control. His hand was shaking when he raised it to knock on her door. She did not answer. He knocked again and waited for what seemed like a long time. He called her name. Silence. Fear took hold of him then, and he promptly cast aside propriety. He tried the door. It was unlocked. He opened it and found the room in total darkness. He groped about in the shadows until he felt a lamp. He lit it and slowly closed the door behind himself.

She was curled up in a chair at the far side of the room, staring at him as he fumbled with the lamp, then swiftly avoiding its light. Her hair fell in careless tangles about her shoulders, and the long, sleepless days and nights had left their mark on her face. She was noticeably thinner, and her eyes had lost their brightness, their warmth; they were glazed and distant. The very sight of her filled him with pain and with anger for the man who had done this to her.

"Chastity?" His voice was very soft, little more than a whisper.

She gave no sign that she had heard him at first. Then she began to nervously finger the front of her wrapper, drawing it more tightly about herself. Her eyes remained fixed on the pattern of the wallpaper on the nearest wall.

Jonathon brought another chair across the room and placed it next to hers. He took a seat facing her, sitting very close to her. "I want to talk with you."

He leaned forward and reached for her hands but she shrank away from him. "No."

He sighed and sat back in his chair. "I only want to talk."

Her eyes hardened as she stubbornly kept her face averted. "Then talk to yourself. I'm not interested in what you have to say."

His brow darkened with frustration. But at least she was angry—that was something. Perhaps if she were more angry . . . "Listen to me, Chastity. I don't intend to kowtow before you each and every time I need your signature on a contract. If your manners don't improve, I might just be tempted to dump all this useless paperwork right in your lap!"

"I don't care what you do," she told him sullenly. "Just leave me alone."

Jonathon drew a long, calming breath and rose from his chair to pace the floor. His hands were tight fists and his mind was racing furiously. Think, Jonathon, think.

There must be some way to jar her from this apathetic cocoon.

"You can't go on like this, you know," he tossed at her from across the room. "You just aren't enough of a coward to stay up here feeling sorry for yourself until you die."

"Don't tell me how brave I am!" she flung back bitterly. She met his eyes for the barest moment, then hugged her arms tightly about her chest. "You don't know anything about me, Jonathon Stoneworth."

He stopped his pacing abruptly and came to place an arm on either side of her chair. "I know a hell of a lot more than you give me credit for."

She snorted skeptically and glared at him. "What do you know?"

"I know—" He hesitated a moment before his eyes softened and his voice came low and husky, without a trace of the anger she'd heard a moment before. "I know that I love you . . . and that I want you more than I've ever wanted a woman before in my life."

Her eyes widened in panic and she wondered if she was going mad. It was the one thing she had never expected him to say—he hadn't really expected it himself. She swallowed hard. "Damn you, Jonathon! Damn you for joking—"

He took hold of her shoulders. "I'm not joking."

"No! Don't touch me!" She squeezed her eyes shut and squirmed out of his grasp, hurrying all the way across the room before she whirled to face him. "I don't want your pity!" she cried. "Do you hear me?" Her voice was shrill and on the verge of breaking. "I don't want any part of that Christian charity you squander on every poor soul you meet!"

"Who the devil said anything about Christian charity?" he growled back at her, his temper becoming harder by the minute to control. He muttered something she didn't understand and quickly closed the distance between them. But she continued to struggle with him, violently shaking her head as if to negate his words.

"I want you, Chastity Morrow. I desire you, as a man desires a woman . . . and I love you." He took her chin between his thumb and forefinger to keep her from shaking her head. "Yes! Look at me, dammit! I've waited a long time to say what I'm saying and you're going to listen to me whether you like it or not!"

Tears were streaming down her cheeks when she reluctantly opened her eyes to face him. "I love you," he repeated softly. "To me, you are the sun and the moon and the stars . . . everything that is bright and warm and beautiful." His fingertips gently brushed a tear from her cheek. "I want you for my wife, Chastity."

She stared up at him, seeing the honesty of every word so clearly written on his face. Jonathon loved her! Jonathon, who had always been at her side when she needed him, who had loved her father and suffered his loss almost as deeply as she. She couldn't help but feel a fondness for him. And he was offering her an alternative to the terrible loneliness she'd suffered these past few weeks, to the fear she felt about facing everyone who guessed about her and Regan, the fear of being pitied or ridiculed for being a fool.

But a sickening kind of feeling struck her even before she began to feel relief. Jonathon did not know everything. He was a religious man, a strict Catholic. He would not want to marry her if he knew the truth. She shook her head and struggled to be free of his arms. "I can't marry you, Jonathon."

"Can't?" he repeated doubtfully. "Then you'd better have a damned good reason why not." He waited. She said nothing. "Well?"

"I—I'm not Catholic."

"Father Manogue will be happy to convert you."

"No, he won't. I mean . . . he can't."

"And why not?"

"Because . . . because . . ." She turned away from him in shame. "I am not pure."

They were tortured words, but all the same Jonathon almost smiled. He hadn't really expected her to be so honest with him. He turned her and pulled her into his arms.

"Chastity," he whispered gently. "I didn't ask if you were."

Her tear-filled eyes rose to meet his in surprise. "Do—do you mean you—you still want me?"

"I love you, Chastity," he told her, placing a hand to the side of her head and coaxing it to rest against him. She offered no resistance this time. "That means that no matter what, I'll always want you . . . always." He sighed as his fingers smoothed her tangled hair. "I can make you happy if you'll let me try, Chastity. Please let me try."

She felt his mouth fall softly upon hers, barely touching her lips at all before he pulled away. She did not know what such restraint cost him, she only knew that it was very different from the savage passion she had shared with Regan. It would take some getting used to; perhaps she would never get used to it. But at least Jonathon's touch was tender and not unbearably clumsy, like that of some men who had kissed her. And at least, she told herself as her head lay comfortably against his broad shoulder, at least she would not be alone.

A feeling of peace settled in her as she gave herself up to his strong arms, allowing him to lift the burdens of guilt and shame she had borne in such loneliness. And if the volatile excitement of first love was absent, then so was the fear. She had always been so frightened by the power Regan held over her; she had been forced to swallow so much of her pride to prove her love for him. Then, in spite of everything, she had lost him.

She felt tears stinging her eyes and she forced the memories from her mind. Now there was Jonathon. Dependable as the morning, her father had said. There was something reassuring in the feel of a man's arms around her, a kind of pride derived from knowing that Jonathon loved her and wanted her, not for a single moment of pleasure but for a lifetime.

She would never have chosen to be Jonathon's wife, but

Regan was married to someone else. It was time to pick up the pieces and begin again. And she knew that she just couldn't do that all alone. She closed her eyes and nodded. "Yes, Jonathon. I will marry you."

Chapter 24

Virginia City rarely saw rain at the end of the summer, but on Chastity's wedding day clouds clung tenaciously to the mountainside, and the day was broken by intermittent showers. Chastity wore an elegant gown of white French lace with a high, delicate collar that accentuated the smooth, slender line of her throat, a fitted bodice with melon puff sleeves, and a snug skirt drawn back to an elaborate drape of lacy flounces and a small train at the rear. Her silver-blond hair was pulled into a high chignon with a few wispy curls falling softly about her pale face and a single layer of white veiling fastened to her crown with white silk flowers. Her bouquet blended baby's breath with red roses and dark green ferns, but Chastity felt no pleasure as she grasped it tightly and fixed her eyes firmly on the flowers in an effort to appear calm. The private, informal ceremony held in Father Manogue's parlor was a far cry from the grand church wedding long in Chastity's dreams, and afterwards, rather than hosting a large celebration, she and Jonathon made a brief visit to her father's grave where she laid a single rose from her bridal bouquet.

It was a long, silent ride in the rain back to the house. Chastity found herself engulfed in memories and she could not help what she was feeling—the aching sadness, the knowledge of all that would never be, the terrible feeling of loss. She stared numbly at her bouquet, at her new white lace gown, at the gold band circling the third finger

of her left hand. She was a married woman now, Mrs. Jonathon Stoneworth. She raised her eyes timidly to Jonathon's, then quickly lowered them again. He reached for
her hand, saying nothing. She was grateful for the silence.
She hoped he would never know how unhappy she was,
how foolish she felt for having hastily agreed to this marriage.

The carriage halted in front of the house and Jonathon
alighted and turned to aid his bride. She forced herself to
smile up at him as she slid into his arms, then abruptly
turned away and ran up the steps. When he caught up
with her and swung open the front door, neither was prepared for the crowd of people who jammed the foyer, par-
lors, and dining room.

Deborah was the first to come forward and greet them,
giving each of them an enthusiastic embrace. Chastity's
eyes darted all about her in bewilderment. "Who—how did
you know?"

"Sarah wired me as soon as the plans were finalized.
And I came the moment I heard." She beamed at Jonathon
and hugged him again while Chastity's eyes ran over
scores of faces, most of them friends of her father's and
Deborah's, faces smiling and expectant and curious as
they watched her and Jonathon. Her eyes stopped short
when they fell on a cluster of scowling women gathered at
the foot of the stairs, all staring at her with narrowed eyes
and whispering to one another. She didn't need to guess
about what.

". . . and Samuel would have been so pleased! We're all
just ecstatic!"

Chastity distantly fingered the flowers in her bouquet
and tried to smile. But she was remembering that Deborah had never liked Regan, that few of the people here
had even known him. She watched as Michael Murphy,
looking quite uncomfortable in his crisp Sunday suit,
slapped Jonathon on the back and laughingly called
him a "sly ol' fox." She swallowed hard and looked
away. It was then that she met a pair of light brown
eyes, narrowed so with jealousy that Chastity felt as if
she'd been slapped. Maureen's eyes drifted pointedly

over Chastity's white lace gown, then lifted in an accusing, self-righteous glare. Chastity could feel her cheeks
flush hotly as she, too, stole a glance at her gown, half-
expecting to see a scarlet letter branded across the flawless lace.

". . . I said, why don't you make your way into the dining room and cut the cake?" Deborah repeated into Chastity's blank stare.

"What cake?"

Deborah heaved a patient sigh and met Jonathon's eyes
with a brief smile. "Your wedding cake. The one Sarah
stayed up all night preparing." She gave Jonathon a
knowing grin. "The bride looks as if she needs a glass of
champagne, don't you think?"

Somehow Chastity drifted through the next few
hours, smiling as much as she could manage, dancing
with several friends of her father's and Jonathon's
when they insisted, and drinking toasts to a long life
and happiness. Every moment was a struggle, every
smile an ironic act of pride, when she truly felt she had
no pride left at all.

It was after four when the guests finally began to depart, and another hour passed before the last of them left
the house, many obviously feeling the effects of huge
amounts of champagne. At Jonathon's insistence, Deborah shared dinner with the newlyweds before leaving to
catch a late train for San Francisco, so that it was well into
evening before he and Chastity were actually alone. He returned to the dining room after seeing Deborah to the carriage, sat down beside Chastity, and poured himself a
fresh cup of coffee.

"Well. It's been a long day. Much longer than I'd
planned on, to be sure."

He sounded as if he expected an answering smile, but
the one that resulted was weak and almost sickly. He
immediately put a stop to his trivial conversation. It
was obvious to him that Chastity was tired and emotionally drained, and that really wasn't surprising. A
single afternoon of celebrating could not begin to erase
the pain that had accumulated over the past few weeks.

And face it, it was too soon for her to have forgotten Regan Spencer. Perhaps he was a fool to think she would ever forget him. He sipped at his coffee and studied her face, so lovely, so filled with torment. He wished that he could read her mind, that he could ease the worry that showed itself so plainly in her eyes. But only time could cushion the hurt she was feeling, and only love would allow her to grow close to him, to trust him. All in time . . .

Chastity glanced up at Jonathon's serious expression and realized at once that her grace period had ended. He was silent as he rose and held the chair for her, and even as he mounted the stairs close behind her, though her mind was in such a turmoil that she probably wouldn't have understood anything he might have said. It was something she had not allowed herself to dwell upon, this first night with Jonathon, beyond firmly resolving to endure it no matter how much it cost her. Jonathon deserved that much for accepting a tainted bride. But she couldn't help dreading what was going to happen, or fearing the worst.

She hesitated a little as she walked past her bedroom door and continued down the hall, toward the room her father had once shared with Deborah. All her things were there now. She had watched Sarah move the last of them in this morning. Jonathon reached in front of her to open the door and followed her into the bedroom, closing it behind him. Alone. Jonathon lit the lamp and she took a seat before what had been Deborah's vanity, avoiding the bottle of iced champagne and two goblets placed discreetly on its edge. She drew off her veil and began brushing out her hair, feeling like a foolish child playing a grown-up game, wishing more than anything that she could end it. Her nerves were frayed, her control very near its breaking point. She stared at her reflection and saw her fingers trembling, her face pale and drawn, like that of a stranger.

Jonathon sighed as he loosened his tie, removed his jacket, and unbuttoned his shirt. He sat down and took off his shoes, then glanced up at Chastity's wide-eyed, almost terrified reflection in the mirror. She immediately took up brushing again, this time at such a frenzied pace that Jonathon almost laughed. He walked across the room and touched her shoulder, his reflection capturing her gaze momentarily in the mirror before she hurriedly lowered her eyes. She swallowed a painful lump in her throat and slowly placed the brush on the vanity.

"Chastity?" His voice was soft, his fingers gentle as they rested on her shoulder. She slowly lifted her eyes and turned her head to face him. "Are you frightened?"

She wanted to cry. She wanted to run away to her own room and leave all of this foolish charade behind her. But it was too late for that. It was too late for everything. She bit her lip hard and forced a timid nod.

"What are you afraid of?" His tone was patient, his eyes warm and understanding. He waited.

After a moment she covered her face with her hands and felt her eyes fill up with tears. Oh, God, how had she ever thought to pretend with him? He was not a fool, and she couldn't begin to tell him the truth—that the thought of making love with anyone besides Regan repelled her. She felt his arms go around her with tenderness and care, and then she was sobbing against his bare chest.

"Don't cry, Chas. I know what you're feeling. I know that it will take time." It will take forever, she thought. A woman has only one heart, and hers had been broken. Oh, why had she married him? Why had she ever let him think that she might be able to love another man?

Jonathon sighed and waited a long time until she had quieted before he spoke again in the same soothing whisper. "You needn't worry that I will demand my 'rights' before you're ready for that part of marriage."

She lifted her tearstained face to stare at him. "But—but, Jonathon, we—"

"Yes, we. I as much as you. I vowed today to honor you as my wife. A man does a woman no honor by forcing her to submit to him." He smiled and let his fingertips brush the moist, smooth skin of her cheeks. "You're my wife, Chas, not my slave. I didn't buy you. I married you. From now on, we are partners. We make decisions together." He sighed again with relief, noticing that she had calmed somewhat. "You're tired, aren't you? So am I." He smiled. "I think we'd both do well with a good night's sleep." He hesitated as his eyes flicked over the bed. "I will spend the night elsewhere if—"

"No!" She almost screamed the word, and seemed on the verge of hysteria again for a moment. The idea of even more speculation about their marriage—she couldn't bear to consider the possibility. She closed her eyes and drew a long, calming breath, then leaned forward and pressed her cheek to his chest. "No, Jonathon," she told him quietly. "You belong here. I—I want you here." Strangely enough it was the truth. And not only because she feared more gossip.

"Well, then, you'd better be getting ready for bed," he said lightly. He felt her tense and quickly added, "I'll turn out the light."

He left her standing there and went to the lamp, where he waited until she had gathered up her nightgown in her hands. Then he extinguished the light, shed the rest of his clothing, and settled himself in bed.

The room was in total darkness for some time before Chastity nervously struggled with the fastenings of her dress, then carelessly stepped out of it and tossed it aside. She fumbled hurriedly with her underclothing while her eyes darted about the room, picking out familiar shadows in the moonless night. Once in her nightgown, she approached the bed timidly, one step at a time, almost as if she were walking to her death. She cautiously lifted the bedcovers and eased herself in beside Jonathon. For a long time she lay there rigid, hardly daring to breathe. Every muscle in her body was taut with apprehension. Then there came a vague awareness of slow, hushed breathing beside her. Jonathon was asleep. The dreaded transformation from friend to demanding husband had not occurred. Gradually the tensions of the last few hours took their toll and she drifted off into a deep, exhausted sleep.

* * *

Chastity stirred as a deafening crack of thunder shook the house, then sighed and settled her head more comfortably against Jonathon's shoulder. She had not awakened during one of the most violent storms in Jonathon's memory, and he hoped she would continue to sleep straight through till morning. She badly needed the rest. He touched her shoulder and lightly fingered her hair. How strange the feelings crowding his mind, so new and different to him, though he had loved her for such a very long time. A fierce possessiveness, an overwhelming desire to shelter and protect, a need to share so many parts of himself he had never shared before with anyone. He stared down with warm affection at his wife, whose face was soft and childlike in the sporadic light. In so many ways still a child, he thought with a sigh. But with enough love to guide her, she would soon become a woman.

Another bright flash of light cut a jagged path across the sky, and the thunder that followed sent a tremor echoing through the whole of Mount Davidson. Chastity started awake with a gasp, clinging fiercely to Jonathon until the frightening numbness of a deep sleep faded away. She realized gradually where she was and who was with her. Now and again the room was lit by quick bursts of lightning, allowing her to see Jonathon's face. He was wide awake.

"It sounds like a bad storm," she said softly.

"You've slept through the worst of it," he told her.

She glanced at the window, then closed her eyes and tried to go back to sleep. But she was unused to the idea of sharing a bed with anyone, and even though Jonathon refrained from touching her intimately, she was very conscious of the fact that he was wide awake, and was becoming more and more aware of the feel of his body through the thin cotton nightgown which separated them. He was so warm! She could feel the heat of his thigh against her leg, and it made her very uncomfortable. She did her best to move away without being obvious about trying to avoid contact with him, but it seemed that every way she turned she met with lean, hard muscle. And as she struggled to find a slightly less compromising position, she was becoming unintentionally acquainted with the crisp black hair on his chest, the unyielding hardness of his arms, his legs, the round, sinewy feel of his muscular body. After several minutes of rustling about and making intimate contact with every move, she restlessly sighed her frustration and abruptly sat up in bed.

"Is something wrong?" he inquired with a trace of amusement in his tone. He knew exactly what the problem was.

She folded her arms across her chest. "I can't sleep."

"Well, just lie down and try for a little while longer," he told her as he pretended to stifle a yawn. "You'll go back to sleep eventually."

It annoyed her that he sounded so cool, so nonchalant about her discomfort. She shook her head. "It won't work, Jonathon," she insisted irritably. "I can't possibly sleep with—" She stopped short as a flash of lightning glinted brightly on the silver bucket on Deborah's vanity. Her face brightened considerably when she realized that it held a full bottle of champagne! Without a moment's hesitation, she went to light the lamp and retrieve the prize, wrapping a towel about the bottle and bringing it back to Jonathon to open, totally unaware of the picture she presented in her diaphanous gown. Jonathon's eyes lingered for a long moment on the silhouette of full, high breasts, rounded hips and long, tapering limbs so distinctly outlined through her nightgown as she stood before the lamp. With a reluctant sigh of resignation, he pulled his eyes away and set himself to the task at hand, needing a drink of something strong now every bit as much as his wife did.

With a pop that seemed at least as loud as the thunder, the cork flew across the room and bounced off the wall, landing with amazing accuracy in the washbasin. Chastity giggled and applauded as Jonathon poured two glasses, then handed her one and patted a spot beside himself on the bed. She obediently took up a perch there for all of two minutes, in which time she managed to drain her glass of its contents. She promptly rose and refilled it to the brim. It tasted wonderful! And she felt much better already.

"I think we're supposed to drink toasts, my love," he remarked with a reproving arch of his brow as she gulped down her second glass, then filled it a third time.

"What? Oh. Yes. All right, then. To . . ." Her voice trailed off aimlessly and she gave a shrug of her shoulders. "To Papa. May he be as happy about our marriage as everyone says he is." She lifted her glass to touch Jonathon's, then downed number three and mechanically filled it again. She stared at her glass for a moment, trying to think of something else to toast. Finally she stood up and said broadly, as if to a crowd at the foot of the bed, "To Deborah . . . who couldn't wait to remind me that she was right about Regan."

Jonathon's brow darkened at the words. "That's not fair, Chastity. Deborah didn't come here to gloat. She came here because she cares about you very deeply."

"Cares!" Chastity repeated in disbelief. She gave a short, sarcastic laugh. "Oh, yes! She cares, all right." She finished off another glass of champagne as her eyes narrowed angrily on Jonathon's face. "I suppose you're just naive enough to think that all those good people 'care' about me. Well, let me tell you something, Jonathon. The only thing they care about is gossip, and I happen to be one of the more interesting scandals around Virginia City these days. There wasn't a one of those good Christian ladies thinking that you married me for any reason but to save my reputation, and probably as a favor to my dear departed father. Maureen Murphy stared at me so hard I was beginning to think I was marked with a bright red letter A." She paused just long enough to refill her glass and gulp down its contents. "And every single one of those good, caring people expects you to claim paternity of a black-haired brat before a half year's over," she added bitterly.

"And will I?" Jonathon inquired calmly, hiding the revulsion he felt at the idea.

Chastity bit her lip and averted her eyes. It had been the one thing that might have bonded her to Regan forever. "No."

She reached quickly for the bottle and drained another glass of champagne almost as fast as she had filled it. Then she repeated her actions, while Jonathon took a thoughtful sip of his original glass and wondered just how much his bride intended to drink this evening. But she was talking to him, at least, and not holding it all inside herself the way she had a few hours ago. Perhaps it would be just as well if she did drink herself senseless for once. A few moments later he did a double take when she turned the bottle upside down and shook it ruefully above her glass. She had downed the entire bottle in less than half an hour!

"This marriage will never work, you know," she announced suddenly.

"It won't?"

She shook her head vigorously and had to grasp the bed-post for support. All of a sudden she was beginning to feel dizzy. "It was d-doomed from the start."

"Well, we'll give it another hour or two," he agreed amenably, "and then if it doesn't work out . . ."

She threw back her head to let the last drop of champagne flow into her mouth. Then she sighed forlornly and made to set the glass on the night table. But she misjudged the distance, and the glass shattered into a thousand pieces when she banged it against the marble top of the table. In an instant he was beside her, examining her hand with real concern in spite of her protests. It was only a scratch, but he dabbed at it gingerly with the towel until she insistently shook him off. "You—*hic*—you aren't listening t-to me."

He smiled pleasantly. "That's because you're drunk."

"I know. You—you see? H-husbands are s'pposed t-t' get drunk on th' wedding night. B-but I'm th' one who's drunk. Me." She pointed a thumb at her chest and nearly lost her balance and fell to the floor. "I'm the sinner. An' you're the saint. You d-didn't even—" She frowned and gulped, glancing pointedly at the bed. "You know, much

less get d-drunk . . ." She shrugged her shoulders. "But I
d-don't suppose that s-*hic*-saints go in for that sort of thing.
I r-really don't know."

Jonathon scowled and straightened indignantly at the
suggestion. Was it possible that after all the months
he'd waited, never even daring to touch her for fear of
ruining whatever slight chances he did have of winning
her love; after the hundreds of nights he'd spent
dreaming of holding her in his arms, of making love to
her, of despairing that none of it would ever come to be,
was it possible that she truly thought he did not desire
her? Was it possible that she believed him above the
normal, healthy drives of a man? He stared at her, suddenly anxious to prove to her that she was very, very
wrong.

She closed her eyes and sighed. "This'll never work,
Jonathon."

His brown eyes lit with anger as she mouthed the
words. She thought it wouldn't work, did she? Well, she
was going to find out just how wrong she was! He pulled
her into his arms and began to kiss her, letting his lips
tug gently at the full curves of her pliant mouth, and his
tongue dart playfully between her lips. He withdrew a
bit, just enough to plant scores of brief, teasing kisses
all over her face. All the while his hunger mounted, and
when at last his lips returned to claim hers, his kiss was
deep and probing, and there was no longer any question
as to his purpose. He fully expected some show of resistance; he did not get it. Quite the contrary. His eyes
opened wide in surprise and he let out his breath with
considerable elation before he proceeded onward. He
had waited long enough.

Chastity did not know exactly why or how it happened, but suddenly Jonathon was kissing her, and in a
way he'd never kissed her before, in a way she'd never
expected him to kiss her. It was such a titillating, pleasurable sensation that she found herself wanting it to go
on and on. She felt his tongue slipping cleverly between
her lips, gentle yet teasing, expectant, arousing. Her
head was spinning faster and faster as she closed her

eyes and gave herself up to what was happening, responding without reservation, instinctively returning the light thrusts of his tongue, until all at once she was breathless and madly anxious to have more. She slipped her arms eagerly about his neck and leaned full against him as her knees weakened under the assault. As she did so, her soft, pliant flesh met with the firm, unyielding chest, the trim, solid waist, the rock-hard muscles of his thighs. Something far in the back of her mind recalled a very different man, who had held her and touched her in a very different fashion, and she knew a fleeting moment of uncertainty. Jonathon was not Regan, and she should not be in his arms, should not allow him to kiss her this way . . . but suddenly, she simply didn't care.

Jonathon disentangled her arms from about his neck and slowly, gently slipped the nightgown from her shoulders, so that she hardly even knew it was gone. He froze at the sight of her, amazed at the perfection of her breasts, the flawless ivory skin and soft pink nipples rising and falling in anxious excitement, the full, lush line of hips that tapered to long, slender limbs. Long before his eyes had their fill of this vision, she reached out for his shoulders and drew him against herself, only vaguely realizing what she was doing. Nothing was really registering in her brain, and she didn't want to think at all. She only wanted him to kiss her and hold her and . . .

She sighed contentedly as his mouth returned to hers, as his lips moved eagerly to possess her mouth before slipping on to trace the column of her throat. He murmured soft, strange-sounding words she didn't understand as his lips moved to explore ever more of her flesh, meeting the tips of her breasts with quick, light thrusts of his tongue until she moaned and entwined her fingers tightly in his hair, drawing him closer. And then they were falling on the bed, rolling about in a jumble of bed linens as their mouths met again and again and their kisses became deeper and mindless and erotic. He manuevered himself beneath her, allowing her to take

the lead, urging her to a wild abandon that unleashed
her passions to unquenchable heights. She was above
him, crouching like a lioness, tempting him with the
touch of her breasts, the soft fullness of her woman's
body as she pressed against him and withdrew, again
and again. Flames of desire soared violently through
her, and as she shuddered and pressed brutally against
him, he knew that she was very close to being satisfied,
and that she wanted him. But he resisted a natural im-
pulse to hurry, pulling her beneath himself and kissing
her softly, lingeringly, deeply, then heaving a ragged
sigh as his fingers brushed lightly at a lock of hair,
which had fallen across her forehead. The mere sight of
her nakedness was so arousing, so pleasurable, that for
a long moment he let his eyes wander, drinking their
fill. Chastity opened her eyes in utter confusion and felt
her cheeks flush hotly as he looked at her. Her lips
parted and trembled with longing as his fingers moved
to stroke her breasts, softly, easily, until the satiny rose
crests darkened and grew taut, stretching and straining
toward his touch. His hand slid lower, gliding over her
stomach and slipping familiarly between her thighs. He
touched her, fondled her, drove her to near madness, until she gasped and held her breath, squeezing her eyes
tightly shut. "Is something wrong?" he asked innocently, his voice a husky whisper. "Don't you like
that?"

"Oh, yes!" she burst out fervently. Then she blushed furiously and turned her head away. "I mean . . . you aren't
s-supposed to talk, Jonathon!"

His eyes widened in surprise; then he grinned at her
and let his fingers run deliberately over her stomach
once more, drifting lower, and lower, until she gasped
with pleasure. Oh, why was he taking so much time
with everything? With Regan it had always been a hurried, frenzied rush to find release, but Jonathon acted as
if he wanted to spend a lifetime finding every sensitive
spot on her body and arousing each one to its fullest excitement.

"Why aren't I supposed to talk?"

"Because . . ." she gulped, "because . . . it just isn't d-decent." Oh, she wished he would stop! But she prayed he would never stop!

He smiled and let his hands cover her breasts, then played with the points of her shoulders and gently kneaded the muscles of her upper arms. "You, my darling, have a lot to learn." He let one hand slip lower, toward the silken skin of her inner thigh, caressing with that same slow, erotic movement. She held her breath until she was certain she would faint. "And I intend to teach you . . ."

Unable to stand it a moment longer, Chastity's hand moved boldly to take hold of him and her body arched high to meet his. She was more than a little eager to have this thing over and done with—she was not sure just how much more she could bear. The pleasure of one kiss had blossomed into desire, and desire had exploded into need, a mad, feverish, animal sort of need. She had not thought herself capable of wanting a man's body as badly as she wanted Jonathon now. But with every passing moment it grew fiercer and stronger and ever more frantic until the delicious ache to feel him inside her actually made her cry out. "Jonathon!" She was bursting with wanting him, pulsing, panting, gasping with frustration.

Finally he joined with her, taking up her struggle with a need of his own, becoming her lover, her husband, her mate, pleasuring her with one after another deep, impatient thrusts, which she arched to match with every ounce of her strength. The whole world burst with the explosion of heat and joy that ended their struggle, an explosion of such intensity that she fell into a deep, velvet sleep in his arms. The barest moment later, he joined her in slumber, feeling light and free as a feather in a windstorm, and more totally fulfilled than at any other moment in his life. For so very, very long this had all been a dream. Now it was real . . . and more beautiful than he'd ever dreamed of it being.

* * *

The sunlight cast a golden glow on everything as it streamed through the windows of the bedroom. It was early morning. Very early. Chastity rolled over and pulled a cover over her face to prevent the daylight from disturbing her slumber. But she could not stop the constant flow of unfamiliar noises carrying from the far side of the room. She reluctantly peeked out to discover the source of her irritation. "Good morning," Jonathon called cheerily as he rinsed his razor in the washbasin.

She winced and pulled her pillow tightly over her ears.

He smiled expectantly at her reflection in the mirror as he once again rinsed his razor. "I said, good morning, Mrs. Stoneworth. Do you intend to stay in bed all day?" He paused, giving her more than ample time to respond. She pretended to be asleep. "If you do, then I might just join you there. . . ."

With that, she sat up slowly, pressing her hand to her head and clutching the sheet to her naked breasts. "I never talk to anyone until I've had my coffee," she mumbled as sort of an explanation.

He wiped the remains of shaving soap from his chin and slung the towel over his shoulder. He was smiling brightly as he came to take a seat beside her on the bed, and she winced with pain at the slight jarring as he did so. "Offhand, I'd say you had a little too much champagne last night, wouldn't you?"

"No, I wouldn't," she grunted back with an indignant scowl. "I told you, I never talk to anyone until I've had a cup of coffee . . . sometimes two." She yawned and ran a hand over her face, finding it strangely numb. "I think this morning it'll be two."

"Shall I get it for you?"

"What?"

"Your coffee."

She blinked at him in surprise, then cocked her head and frowned as a flow of strange, disjointed thoughts ran through her mind. She did remember drinking champagne last night, and then . . . and then . . . She blushed hotly and stared at him in amazement. No! It wasn't possible. Naive, straightlaced Jonathon could not possibly have been such an ardent, passionate lover, and she couldn't possibly have done— No. She must have dreamed the entire thing. She must have— Her thoughts scattered as he leaned close and kissed her, the same kind of playful, tantalizing kiss she had recalled a moment before. And as his fingers rested lightly on her bare shoulder, she realized that she had indeed lost her nightgown at some time during the night. She gasped and pulled away from him as his fingers drifted deliberately up her arm. "Are you always like this in the morning?" she demanded in horror.

"Like what?"

"Like this!" she snapped back at him. "Happy and . . . and helpful . . . and . . . and . . ." She hid her face in her hands. "Oh, no, Jonathon, I don't know if I can stand it."

He raised a brow and gave his head a shake as if to clear it. "Do you want me to get you your coffee or not?"

She drew a long breath and bravely lowered her hands. "Definitely not."

"All right, then. I'll leave you to get dressed. But I'll expect you at the table in . . ." He paused to check the time on the small porcelain clock above the fireplace. ". . . fifteen minutes?"

Chastity fell back on her pillow and pulled the sheet up to her chin. "Thirty. Don't put me on a schedule, Jonathon. It's been tried before and it just doesn't work."

He laughed and rose to finish dressing himself before he returned to the bed and bent to kiss her lightly on the forehead. Then he left her and went downstairs to breakfast.

"I want your opinion on something, so as soon as you've had enough coffee to discuss it with me, just let me know." He eyed her doubtfully as she finished off the last of a gigantic platter of eggs and ham he would have wagered a fortune she could never consume. She glared at him, then reached for a second sweet roll. He raised a disbelieving brow. "Do you always eat like this in the morning?"

"Like what?" she returned innocently as she liberally buttered the roll.

"Never mind. I take it you're ready to talk now."

She nodded.

Jonathon drew a long, important-sounding breath and fixed his eyes on her mildly expectant face. "I think it would be a good idea if we went away for a while."

Chastity stared at him, immediately setting aside her roll. She had suddenly lost her appetite, and she had to struggle to swallow what remained in her mouth. The idea of going away with Jonathon disturbed her, partly because she hated the idea of running away from the gossip and speculation surrounding their marriage, which she would have to face sometime and she would rather not put off, and partly because in spite of a haze of memories from the night before, Jonathon was not Regan Spencer and she was not in love with him. It seemed a betrayal of everything she felt and all that had happened to take up with Jonathon this way. It made her feel soiled, as if she had been passed from one man to the next. Last night had been different. She had drunk much too much champagne to know what she was doing. But the next time he wanted her . . . She swallowed hard. She was Jonathon's wife now, and she really had very little choice. She forced her face to remain totally blank, but she couldn't help but lower her eyes. She knew well enough that the truth could not be hidden if she met his too-perceptive brown eyes.

Jonathon frowned and reached for her hand. "We don't have to go anywhere if you don't want to, Chas. I just thought that—"

"We'll go. When should I be ready?"

He met the determined eyes she lifted to meet his and held them for a long moment. She was trying very hard to hide her reluctance, but he could see it all too clearly. "The train leaves in about an hour. Do you think you could throw a few things together in time?"

"Of course. Sarah will help me." She rose from the table, chin high, back straightened, and made to leave the dining room. She was at the doorway before Jonathon stopped her.

"Chastity?"

She turned inquiringly.

"Don't you want to know where we're going?"

A blush crept into her cheeks and her determined posture drooped somewhat when she realized how transparent her feelings were to Jonathon, in spite of all her efforts. "Yes," she said, forcing a smile that did not reach her eyes. "Where are we going?"

"To the Glenbrook . . . if you're certain you want to go."

Her face brightened the slightest bit when he told her that. The Glenbrook was a popular hotel on the southeastern shore of Tahoe, a deep blue, crystalline lake embraced on all sides by alpine mountains. It was accessible by a short trip on the V&T to Carson City, then a ride to the lake via Benton Stage Lines. Chastity had always thought it the most beautiful place in all the world, a place full of peace and natural serenity, a corner of heaven which had been left here on earth by God's generous hand. "How long will we stay?"

"A few days, perhaps a week. If we manage to catch the train, that is."

She spun about and raced up the stairs, calling for Sarah to help her pack.

For some time after she disappeard from view, Jonathon remained at the table, thoughtfully fingering a heavy silver spoon marked on the stem with an ornate letter *M*. Last night, with the help of a bottle of vintage champagne, he had broken through Chastity's defensive facade and embraced a loving, passionate woman. It had been his kiss that had aroused her, his touch that had left her trembling, his body that had brought her to shuddering fulfillment. But this morning, she still ached for Regan Spencer. Perhaps she had even thought of him while they were making love. Jonathon slammed the spoon on the table and angrily turned away. What ironic justice it would be if she never forgot her lover, if her husband had to face her brave little acts of loving submission every day for the rest of his life. He walked over to the window and slid open the olivewood shutters, shaking off that thought. This was no time to dwell on the possibility of failure. The sun was shining brightly as it always did here in Virginia City, and this was a place where impossible dreams came true every day. He sighed, lifted his chin, and went to pack himself.

Chapter 25

Chastity maintained a distant silence during their trip to Tahoe, forcing a timorous smile now and again at Jonathon's light comments but otherwise keeping her blue eyes fastened carefully to the passing mountains and hills. Their room at the Glenbrook House was small, but light and homey and comfortable. After the owner had left them alone, Chastity wandered nervously about, checking the view from each window twice and acquainting herself with the furnishings: two large chests of drawers; a square, wood-frame mirror hung above a washstand; a sturdy, heavily padded chair covered with a drab brown homespun material; and a simple four-poster bed made up tidily with a colorful patchwork quilt. (She didn't take very long inspecting that.) She swallowed uncomfortably and turned away to find that Jonathon was already unpacking his things. She stared at him for a moment, feeling trapped and awkward, like a child caught in the act of telling a lie. She thought that if he would only offer to spend the night elsewhere, this time she would gratefully accept his offer. Then she bit her lip hard and lowered her head, feeling guilty for ever thinking such a thing. Jonathon was her husband, she reminded herself, and she was his wife. She lifted her chin and began to unpack her things, dutifully following his lead. She had barely even begun the task when he stopped and shook his head. "Let's leave all this for the time being."

Her head jerked up in surprise, and she felt a rush of dread, cold and gripping, in her stomach.

"I want to see the sunset tonight, don't you?" He acted as if that were a perfectly logical question to ask, and she watched dumbly as he crossed the room to the window and cocked his head to view the nearest ridge. "I noticed a path to the top of that ridge . . . ," he said thoughtfully, "and if we left right this minute, we could make it to the top in plenty of time." He turned to face her with an inquiring lift of his brow. "Well, what do you say? Feel like working up an appetite?"

Though she could not have been less interested in working up an appetite, Chastity felt obligated to do what Jonathon wanted to do; and so, after a lengthy climb up a well-worn path, she stood obediently beside him, viewing a splendorous descent of the red-gold sun upon the placid deep blues and greens of Tahoe. The sight was so glorious, so breathtaking, that Chastity was happy she had come. She was also happy that Jonathon was silent, and even happier that he did not touch her, except in a purely pragmatic fashion when she carelessly slipped and lost her footing during their descent.

She was momentarily relieved when they returned to the Glenbrook, and the moment the delightful aroma of roast capon and herb-flavored creamed vegetables reached her nostrils, she realized that she had indeed worked up an appetite. She ate with relish and enjoyed the meal immensely, remarking more than once that she had never tasted such marvelous food. It was only after her stomach was satisfied and she sat slowly sipping at a glass of wine that the smile of contentment faded from her face, and she felt the same sickening feelings clutching at her insides. She lowered her eyes uneasily.

"There's a full moon tonight."

Chastity lifted her eyes and tried not to wriggle in her chair. She knew her discomfort was already too apparent.

"I was thinking about taking a walk, exploring the shoreline."

Her eyes widened and her brows shot upward. "Tonight?" Not only had they risen at daybreak, but they had done all their packing, traveled, and just finished an exhausting hike up a mountain before supper!

"There's going to be a full moon," he repeated, as if that explained everything.

She tried not to stare at him as if he were mad. "Oh."

Though Chastity was already feeling the effects of a very long day, she found herself plodding stoically beside him, tracing a stretch of nearby shoreline, pausing again and again to gaze in wonder at the perfect reflection of a silver moon on the clear, dark blue water. All the while, Jonathon did nothing more threatening than hold her hand.

The initial awkwardness she felt at the thought of sharing a room with him was greatly diminished by her total physical exhaustion that first night. By the time she finally undressed and fell into bed, she was simply too tired to worry about what her new husband did or didn't intend to do. When she woke the next morning, Jonathon was already up and dressed and had even made arrangements to take a boat out on the lake for the day. After spending so many days and nights doing nothing but thinking, brooding, and regretting, Chastity was suddenly restless and full of energy, and her drive and determination returned as she struggled to keep up with Jonathon. He rode, walked, raced, climbed, and swam, and she staunchly forced herself to match him step for step.

The mindless physical exertion coupled with the beauty and serenity of Tahoe somehow managed to strip away the anxieties that had trampled Chastity's spirit. During the entire first week at the Glenbrook Jonathon silently challenged her, while allowing her time to adjust to the idea of marriage by making no demands on her. He sensed that she was uncomfortable when he touched her, or even when he smiled at her in that warm, intimate way that clearly communicated his desire. One morning, when she woke to find him staring at her, his brown eyes sparked with a hunger she recognized too well, he knew at once what she was feeling.

"I don't expect you to pretend with me, Chas," he told

her quietly after he kissed her. It was the first time he had kissed her since their arrival at the Glenbrook.

Her eyes, which she had squeezed tightly shut the moment he touched her, flew open in surprise, and she suddenly realized how tense and unyielding she held herself in his arms. She drew a deep breath and her guilty countenance timidly met his gaze. He smiled at her and playfully planted a kiss on her nose. "Do you still imagine I'll be transformed into an ogre? And flog you unmercifully if you refuse me my rights?"

She wanted very much to laugh at that, but for some reason she could not.

Jonathon sighed and let his forefinger drift, light as a moth's wings, over her trembling lips. "Chastity . . . Chastity," he reproved in a whisper. "It will be right between us. It will take time, but it will all be right."

She swallowed hard and nodded, but at the same time he saw a tear glistening in her lashes. "I love you, Chastity," he added quietly.

He made to turn away then, and was truly surprised when she drew him closer and strained to press her lips to his. She meant it as a simple, affectionate gesture of gratitude, but it swiftly became something else as Jonathon seized the lead, letting his tongue probe lingeringly into the warmth and sweetness of her mouth. She felt a small stab of uncertainty as his embrace drew her firmly against the length of him, and she drew a sharp breath as his fingers tugged insistently at the straps of her nightgown. But all doubts and insecurities were swiftly flung aside as his mouth continued to claim possession, his tongue teasing and coaxing her to meet his thrusts, his hands gently caressing her breasts, her hips, her thighs, until her body burned with a frantic need to be fulfilled.

When it was over and she lay quietly with her head pressed against the rhythmic beating of his heart, Chastity felt as if she had been set free. Somehow the wonderful, full days she had shared with him, hidden away from sly whispers and accusing, self-righteous stares, and his constant, often silent reassurances of his love for her, had made this joining with Jonathon right . . . and good.

A week at the Glenbrook spilled over into two, and even then Chastity was reluctant to leave the place that had imparted such peace to her troubled soul. The thought of returning to Virginia City and all those memories frightened her now more than leaving with Jonathon ever had. But it was an inevitable step, and she knew it could not be put off forever. And so, after the carefully nurtured seeds of their new life together had finally taken root, Chastity and Jonathon departed for home.

Chapter 26

Chastity made a face as her forefinger traced Jonathon's initials on the dusty stack of leather-bound volumes in the corner of the room. "Are you going to take all of these with you, too?" she asked him, blowing at them so that a cloud of dust danced in the air. She coughed and waved a hand in front of her face. "These don't seem to have occupied much of your time lately."

"Those are my law books!" he replied indignantly, rushing to rescue one of the volumes from her hands. He laid it reverently atop the others. "I'd sooner leave every stitch of clothing I own behind than leave them."

Chastity rolled her eyes toward the ceiling. "Maureen Murphy would just love that!"

He caught her eye and flashed her a stern glance. "If I haven't spent much time with these books lately, perhaps it's because something else has kept me extremely well occupied."

"Something?" she returned with a playful lift of her brow.

"Someone," he amended, taking her into his arms. His head bent to kiss her, but she slyly dodged his mouth and slipped out of his arms. They had already made love earlier this morning, and now was not the time or the place . . . though neither time nor place ever seemed a very legitimate deterrent to Jonathon's desires. He never forced her to do anything she didn't want to do, but she had found out very quickly that if she allowed things to proceed for a minute or two, there just weren't many things she didn't want to do. And Jonathon wasn't like Regan, moody and unpredictable. She could tease him out of a bad mood quite easily, and arouse him with the slightest effort. Of course, he could do the same with her, so it wasn't as if she held complete control of their relationship. Instead, it was very much as Jonathon had told her it would be. They were partners. And she was beginning to feel confident and sure of herself in this relationship with him, winning back some of the pride she had lost in the past months . . . as long as she didn't look back.

She wandered curiously about the boardinghouse room, staring at the clutter of Jonathon's worldly possessions and wondering where to begin with the packing. He did not appear to keep things as organized here as at the office, she thought wryly as she paused to pick up a sock, which had been revealed when her foot disturbed an old newspaper, fallen from the nightstand. She held it up by the toe with a pained expression.

"I wondered where that went," Jonathon admitted candidly.

She closed her eyes and shook her head. Until this moment, she hadn't realized that Jonathon had needed a wife. The thought made her smile in spite of herself.

"What's so funny?"

She opened her eyes. "You."

"Oh, you think so, do you?" He came and snatched the sock from her hand. Then he squared his shoulders and planted hands on hips, towering over her with a threatening expression.

"Yes, I do," she returned, undaunted. She slipped her arms around his neck and toyed with his shirt collar. "You are also kind . . ." She kissed him lightly. ". . . generous . . ." She kissed him again. ". . . sweet, loving, handsome, affectionate . . ."

"You forgot intelligent."

Her lips obligingly touched his. "Intelligent . . ."

"Tidy."

She burst out laughing. "Honestly, Jonathon, how did you ever find anything in all this clutter?"

"What clutter?" he returned with an innocent glance about.

"Seriously! How did you ever survive bachelorhood?"

"I survived quite well, thank you," he assured her with an arrogant lift of his chin.

She sighed her exasperation. "Well, now that you've tricked me into helping you pack up all this trash—"

"Trash!" he exclaimed indignantly. "Some of these things are priceless! And you insisted on helping me pack, if I recall—"

"And you said that you still had a 'few things' here, if I recall," she countered. "Well, no matter. I'm here, so we might as well get to work."

It took most of the morning to dust, sort, pack, and label the contents of Jonathon's room, though he fumed that he could have accomplished the task in half the time without Chastity's painstaking methods. They had finished except for a desk, which Chastity had expected to find empty or nearly so, since most of Jonathon's things had found a place in a room that had been her father's study, near their bedroom. She sighed as she opened the top drawer of the desk and made to close it again, thinking it empty. But as she pushed it closed, a small picture in a rounded frame of gilded wood slid forward. Chastity frowned, opening the drawer again and lifting the picture into her hand. It was a badly faded photograph of a young woman, creased and worn long before it had been placed beneath the protective glass of the frame. She studied it for a long moment, noting the smoothly sculptured line of nose and chin, the full mouth which hinted at a smile, the almost defiant arch of dark brows over dark, expressive eyes. There was laughter in those eyes, and a youthful confidence Chastity had once seen in her own. She lifted her eyes until they found Jonathon's broad back, watching for a moment as his hard muscles rippled beneath the thin cotton shirt he wore. Her eyes returned to the portrait she held in her hand. She frowned a little, feeling a sudden pang of jealousy. "Jonathon . . ."

He turned to face her, his eyes expectant. She glanced down at the picture. "Who is she?"

He hesitated for a moment, then came to stand beside her, his fingers covering hers as she held the small gilded frame. "She was my mother."

She met his eyes and held them before she glanced at the photograph again. She saw the resemblance now and felt silly for having been jealous. "She was very beautiful," she said with a smile.

"Yes," he agreed, his voice touched with affection.

"And your father?" she asked. "Do you have a picture of him too?"

"No," he said quietly. "There's nothing left of him . . ."

She frowned a little at that, and looked at the picture again. "I'll wager he was handsome, though," she said with a dreamy sigh. "A wealthy, gallant gentleman with a quick wit and a smooth tongue who swept your mother quite off her feet." She grinned up at him only to find that the light in his eyes had died.

"My father," he admitted softly, all the while holding her eyes, "was a poor, uneducated immigrant."

Her smile faded as she searched his face. His words had been difficult, from the heart, and his eyes bore nothing akin to levity. But what he had said did not fit with what little she already knew of his background, of his fine education, of his ease with luxury and wealth. She frowned as she looked again at the woman in the picture, noting the dark curls, which fell in a meticulously arranged coiffure about her lovely face, and the gown, which fit her perfectly with fine, expensive details of lace ruching about the collar and bodice.

"My mother was a lady," he replied to the questions in Chastity's eyes. "She was the only child of one of Boston's most famous lawyers. But she turned her back on the life her father had arranged for her to marry the man she loved. My grandfather never forgave her for that."

"The same grandfather who took you sailing?" she asked, a frown flitting across her brow.

"The same grandfather who saw to my education and made a fine gentleman out of me after both of my parents died," he told her. His eyes were distant as he gazed at the photograph and he almost smiled. "My grandfather was everything I wanted to be—powerful, wealthy, successful . . ." He gave a short laugh. "All I'd ever known were foolish dreamers, like my father. Men who worked themselves into their graves, all the while believing in their stupid dreams."

He met Chastity's eyes. "He was a tailor, you know. A good one, too. He might have made something of his life if he hadn't married my mother. But he did marry her, and because of it my grandfather saw to it he lost the job it had taken him years to get. And my father spent the rest of his life making promises to her that he could never hope to keep." There was a sudden bitterness to his tone, and he turned away so that she could no longer see his eyes. "I—I hated him for that," he said after a long moment. "I hated him even more because he was a failure. I remember the look on his face when I called him that," he went on softly, the words coming slower now and much harder. "I'd been caught stealing an old crippled man's watch, and I remember the way he looked at me, the way he spoke of right and wrong and God and justice . . ." He paused, his fingers kneading briefly at the back of his neck. "I remember laughing in his face and calling him a liar and a fool. But more than anything, I remember the look in his eyes when I called him a failure, like a part of him was dying . . . and I remember that I was glad—" His voice faltered and broke as Chastity's arms quickly slipped about his waist, her cheek pressing affectionately against his broad back.

"Everyone makes mistakes, Jonathon," she said in a whisper, remembering the countless demands she had made on her own father. "Sometimes I think that if only

I could live a part of my life over again, I would do everything so differently!" She blinked back a tear and shook
her head. "But I can't go back. None of us can. We're left
here with our memories"—she swallowed hard—"and a
chance to do everything different today." She let out a
ragged breath, feeling a tear slip over her cheek. "But
you're wrong about one thing, Jonathon," she told him
in a small voice. "You said that there was nothing left
of your father. But a part of him is in you."

He took hold of her hand and drew her into his arms,
pressing his lips to the softness of her hair. She lifted her
eyes to meet his, dark eyes, still full of the pain of remembering. "I think he would have been proud," she told him
softly.

He smiled a little as she spoke the words, his fingers
moving to caress her cheek, to drift hesitantly over her
full, soft mouth. He felt the slight tremor of her lips at
his touch, saw the welcoming brightness in her eyes. He
kissed her gently, deliberately, seeking the reassurance
of her love, aching for the freeing peace he always
seemed to find in her arms. In the next moment both forgot where they were and what they were supposed to be
doing. And as Chastity held him, touched him, gave herself fully to him, Jonathon was very sure that she was
beginning to love him in the same way he had come to
love her.

It was always a special time after they made love, a
time for savoring the quiet peace of fulfillment, for
sharing the private joy they had known in one another.
Jonathon's arms held Chastity close for a long time,
until her heart slowed to a monotonous rhythm and
her breath fell softly against his chest. Only a month,
only four short weeks of marriage, he thought silently,
and already they had come this far. There were still
times when he saw the pain in her eyes, when someone mentioned Regan's name or told a story about this
event or that held at the Crown Point. But yesterday

was past and gone. There were many more tomorrows that promised to dawn bright and new. And there was today, with its dream of happiness already being fulfilled.

Chapter 27

The mild, golden days of September flitted by, and the last remnants of summer were tersely swept aside by the brisk winds of October. With the passing of each day, Chastity felt more settled in her new role as Jonathon's wife, and though there were still moments when she reflected on her first love and what might have been, she allowed herself very little time to waste on regrets. She kept busy managing the household (as Deborah had once done), and spent a part of every day at the C Street office working beside her husband, who was busy organizing his own law firm now that the mining office had closed. When evening arrived, there always seemed to be something Jonathon had promised to do, like visiting the home of a recently injured miner, or attending a meeting of some sort, or taking Joey Bates to the circus. More often than not, Chastity was coerced into tagging along by Jonathon's persuasive prodding, and for all her initial reluctance, the outings usually gave her a feeling of accomplishment and satisfaction. Only occasionally, when she was simply too weary to keep up with him, or not up to facing an encounter with Maureen Murphy, did she inform Jonathon in no uncertain terms that she intended to spend a quiet evening at home, period. And generally, on those occasions, Jonathon managed to slip away from his commitments earlier than usual and return home long before Chastity retired.

On one particular evening in late October, however,

Jonathon came home from a citizens' meeting on taxation reform several hours after Chastity had gone to bed. The next morning at the breakfast table she managed to convey her annoyance with him by nibbling at a piece of toast and skimming the *Enterprise* all the while he gave an account of the goings-on at the meeting. But suddenly one of his remarks penetrated her guise of disinterest, and she lowered the paper and blinked at him in amazement. "Mr. Murphy said *what?*"

"That I'm being considered for appointment as city attorney," he repeated in the same bland tone. He took a sip of coffee, winced, and added more cream. "Are you finished with any of that yet?" he inquired politely, nodding at the newspaper. "I'd like the front page if—"

"Jonathon!" she cried in exasperation. "You're acting as if nothing at all has happened! This is an honor! Aren't you excited at all?"

He cocked his head in a thoughtful pose. "Yes," he admitted cautiously. "But the appointment won't be made for months yet—not until late next spring. And there are several other men being considered—"

"But none as well qualified as you!" she stated confidently.

He was amused by her impromptu show of allegience, but he did not let it show. Instead he sighed and took hold of her hand. "Don't get your hopes up, Chas," he warned soberly. "Appointments like this are not always filled by the 'best' man for the job. Oftentimes they turn into personality contests. And there are quite a few men who have lived in town longer than I, and had a lot more time to make names for themselves here."

"But everyone knows you, Jonathon," she insisted, "and everyone likes you."

He smiled and shook his head. "There are two or three aldermen who probably wouldn't even recognize my name."

She lifted her chin and squared her shoulders, and a strange kind of gleam lit her deep blue eyes. "Well, that's certainly a situation that can be rectified," she said with finality. Without another word, she rose from the table

and went to find Sarah. If Chastity had her way, everyone
who was anyone in Virginia City would soon recognize the
name Stoneworth.

With a series of small, elegant dinner parties, Chastity
set about wooing the present Board of Aldermen, the su-
perintendents of all the major mines, the elected officers of
the miners' union, and of course, all their wives. For once
she found herself wishing that Deborah had remained in
town to help, for she had known most of these people intimately, while Chastity was only beginning to win their
friendship. It was proving a battle every step of the way,
both because she had taken no time with them before and
they felt slighted by her previous cold indifference, and because she was still the object of some speculation by the
town gossips, even months after her marriage to Jonathon.

For Chastity, the most difficult part of entertaining always occurred when the women retired to the front parlor
for tea, and the men to the smoking parlor for cigars and
brandy. Because she had always been confident in her
dealings with men, she usually managed to converse quite
well at the dinner table, but when the women were left to
themselves, Chastity felt at a loss. Some of the wives were
witty, charming, and friendly, but others were conniving
gossips or dull creatures whose entire lives revolved
around only one or two narrow personal interests, and a
few seemed to have a personal vendetta against Chastity's
ever taking a place in Virginia City's proper society.
These women had a way of making things extremely difficult for her.

The first of the dinner parties was not as difficult as
Chastity had envisioned, however, and she managed to
find something in common with most of her guests. Sometimes she would simply smile and pretend to agree with
something someone said rather than express her true feelings, and this seemed to win them over. But after some
four successful evenings of entertaining, Chastity encountered a group of women that was different. She felt it the
moment they all were seated in the dining room, though
conversation was trivial and light and flowed as evenly as

during the other dinners. On this particular occasion Maureen Murphy MacRae, freshly returned from her honeymoon, was in attendance, staring at Chastity with a hatred and hostility brighter and more vengeful than ever before. Maureen had managed to snare herself a husband just last month, an important man about town, though Ralph MacRae was not young or handsome, nor was he as well liked as Jonathon. It was a mystery to Chastity why Ralph had ever married her, and with the looks Maureen flashed Jonathon all during the dinner, it was clear that she was hungry for a lot more than food . . . or Ralph.

Maureen's mother, Eileen Murphy, was the one bright point of Chastity's evening. She was a short, heavy-set woman who carried herself proudly, and had soft dark eyes whose warm good humor quite naturally made Chastity want to smile. Eileen was the perfect match for the hard-working, gruff-talking man who was her husband, Morrow Mine's superintendent Michael Murphy. In public she doted on his every word so that everyone thought him undisputed ruler of the Murphy household. But it was actually Eileen who ruled the roost, cleverly plotting her husband's moves without his ever realizing it. Eileen had been a close friend of Deborah's and over the years the two had socialized and worked together on just about every charitable function in Virginia City. Chastity had known Eileen for many years, but just in the past few months had a real bond of friendship formed. It began when Eileen stopped by after Deborah's departure to visit Chastity herself, and it was reinforced when Eileen was the first to invite Chastity and Jonathon to dinner after their marriage. Eileen and Chastity came to know and like one another in spite of Maureen's bitter jealousy, but those feelings made things difficult for both women, and kept the two from becoming really close.

Besides Eileen and Maureen were Mrs. Nathan, a harmless, fat little woman who spoke only when there was a lull in the conversation, and never about anything of interest to anyone else; Mrs. Gracely, a notorious gossip who prided herself on what she knew about everything; and

Mrs. Grogan, a tiny, unassuming woman who usually came and went without saying a single word.

They had been seated in the parlor for a few minutes, long enough for Chastity to serve tea all around, when Mrs. Gracely took a deep breath. Chastity braced herself and concentrated on sipping her tea very slowly. If it took every bit of gumption she had, she was going to bite her tongue and listen to what the woman had to say.

". . . and did you know that Colleen McDonald just had a baby boy? And her married to Dennis only last April!"

Chastity never missed the sidelong glances flashed her way whenever such a subject was mentioned. Nor did she fail to notice the way Maureen managed to work Regan's name into the conversation every chance she got, several times at the dinner table alone. She was turning the talk in that direction right now, and eyeing Chastity like a hungry cat ready to pounce on a canary.

". . . and Mr. Thomas, a friend of Father's from San Francisco, bought twenty percent of the Crown Point Hotel last month. He says it's a gold mine, and a lot safer investment than stocks." She paused to smile at Chastity, a smile completely lacking in warmth. "Of course, Mr. Spencer must think so too, since he still owns about ten percent of the Crown Point himself . . . according to Mr. Thomas."

Chastity evenly met her stare without any sign of interest. "Really."

All eyes turned to Maureen for a reply, but she suddenly became interested in her tea. "So Mr. Thomas says."

There was a momentary silence, and Chastity, fueled by anger and nervousness, made up her mind to fill it with anything rather than listen to another long, drawn-out story about Mrs. Nathan's dyspepsia. "I think Mr. Sharon will win the Senate race next week," she announced just as Mrs. Nathan opened her mouth. There was a space of utter silence.

"Yes," Eileen Murphy agreed, after what seemed an eternity. "Mr. Murphy says he's sure to be elected. He's spent so much that he's bought himself the office, that's what Mr. Murphy says."

"And what do you think of that?" Chastity asked her.

Eileen's warm, smiling face went completely blank. "What do I think of what?"

"Do you think he'll make a good senator? Do you think it unfair that money buys votes here in Nevada?"

Eileen was shocked by the question. "Why, I don't know. It really makes little difference to me."

"But you're wrong, Mrs. Murphy! It does make a difference to you . . . to all of us." Every eye in the parlor riveted on Chastity as she continued. "The laws made in the United States Senate affect women as well as men. When you hear your husbands discussing the unfair rates charged by the V&T, don't you realize that it eventually translates to the food on your tables, the roof over your heads?" She had their undivided attention now, and a surge of strength rose inside her. Her words had reached them. Perhaps they weren't such dull old girls after all. Perhaps they'd never been given the chance to see beyond their narrow roles of wives and mothers. Thank goodness Jonathon realized that she had a brain and expected her to use it.

"Government has the right to reach into our pockets because it holds the power to control and limit commerce. It seems to me that Mr. Sharon's interests in the railroad will conflict with the people's interests when he is given his seat in the Senate."

Maureen was the first to interrupt with a haughty rise of a single brow. "I thought *Mr.* Stoneworth was the aspiring politician in this house."

"He is," Chastity returned without flinching. "But that doesn't mean that his wife is ignorant of politics." A quick glance at the faces of the other ladies about the room told her that they were on the fence, unwilling to agree with Chastity, yet slow to admit their ignorance about the subject at hand. "Some women feel that they ought to concern themselves with their husbands and children and nothing else. But if we aren't deaf, dumb, and blind, our interests naturally branch out . . . to church, to schools our children attend, to the community in which we live . . ."

"That's very true," Eileen agreed.

"But it isn't feminine to speak about such things as politics!" insisted Mrs. Gracely. "Why, Mr. Gracely would keel over if I ever questioned him about a—a Senate race! And frankly, no matter what I think about Mr. Sharon and his railroad, I can't do anything about it, so what difference does it make?"

"Are you saying that your husband doesn't respect your opinion, Mrs. Gracely?" Chastity drew startled gasps from each of the other women with that question.

"Certainly not! I am merely saying that I can't vote, so Sharon's or Sutro's or Jones's election is none of my affair."

"She's right, Mrs. Stoneworth," Mrs. Nathan joined in. "Women have no place in politics. It's men's business."

"It's not men's business in Wyoming," Chastity returned with a quiet precision she had learned from Jonathon. "Women have had the right to vote there for years."

"Well, Wyoming won't be admitted to the Union until it's been taken away," Maureen told her, twisting her mouth into a condescending smirk. "But if you like the idea so much, why don't you just move there?" She took a sip of tea and sighed with an imperious lift of her chin. "Really, Mrs. Stoneworth. One would think you were advocating women's suffrage for the state of Nevada!"

"I certainly am!" Chastity surprised herself as much as anyone by saying that. Though she had felt for a long time that she was as intelligent as most men, she had never publicly admitted to being in favor of women's suffrage. In doing so, she took a radical stand.

"Mrs. Stoneworth!" That came from Mrs. Grogan. It was the first word she had spoken the entire evening.

"Come now! You aren't actually admitting that you're a member of the 'shrieking sisterhood'!" Maureen's eyes glittered with malicious amusement.

"I am only admitting that I have a mind of my own. I do

not want to be led about or owned or put on a chain by any man, even if he professes to love me. I want to walk by his side and be his equal." As she spoke the words, she realized almost for the first time that it was her marriage to Jonathon, so different from the marriage she had dreamed of, that had strengthened her feelings of her own worth so that she truly felt equal to any man, or woman.

"And I suppose you agree with that Anthony woman's ludicrous attempt to vote a few years back? In spite of the fact that she was breaking the law?"

Chastity frowned. "To be perfectly honest, I don't recall the incident."

"Well, I certainly do!" Mrs. Gracely chimed in quickly. "It was all a dreadful scandal! Miss Anthony went to the polls and demanded to vote—and vote she did! She and about twenty other women she brought with her. But she was arrested later and thrown in jail, and fined heavily, too."

"How dreadful!"

"Well, it serves her right," Maureen interjected. "A woman like that does nothing but give decent women a bad name."

"What's so indecent about demanding what we deserve?" Chastity tossed back at her.

"Women ought to remember themselves!" Mrs. Nathan insisted.

"And that means acting with dignity and restraint," Mrs. Gracely agreed. "No real lady would ever demand what the law prevents her from having."

"And what if the law is wrong? Not very long ago a war was fought because Negroes were denied their rights. Obviously, the law is not infallible."

Battle lines had been drawn and tempers were steadily rising as the parlor talk digressed into a heated argument. When the men emerged from the smoking parlor, they arrived unnoticed on the threshold of the main parlor and stood watching in silent amazement as their womenfolk engaged in a verbal battle far more animated than anything in recent memory. Even small, soft-spoken Mrs. Grogan was tossing in a word here and there. One by one, each man caught the eye of his spouse and the room fell quiet in a matter of minutes. Then, in an embarrassed absence of further conversation, the guests made various excuses to depart for home. Only Mrs. Murphy managed to stay a moment longer, drawing Chastity to the side and admitting with some degree of pride that she had actually heard Miss Anthony speak a few years back, but that Mr. Murphy knew nothing of it and would surely be shocked if he ever were informed of the fact.

Jonathon smiled and nodded good night to the Murphys, then warmly shook the Mister's hand before he closed the door behind them. They were the last to leave.

His smile faded instantly as he turned to face Chastity, and was replaced by a perturbed frown of accusation. "I don't suppose you had anything to do with the argument going on when we joined you ladies in the parlor this evening?"

"It was a discussion, Jonathon," she said innocently. She turned away and began clearing the cups from the parlor. "But yes . . . I suppose I did initiate the subject of the discussion. Women's suffrage."

He caught her arm and whirled her about until she faced him in some surprise. "I thought you wanted me to get this appointment."

"I do."

"Then why did you deliberately upset those women? Do you think their husbands will stand behind me if you try and turn their wives into suffragettes?"

Her face fell with bitter disappointment. "But you support women's suffrage! You said that you do!"

"I said that I think it will come in time."

"But you won't do anything to help it along, is that it? Whether it's right or wrong doesn't really matter to you, as long as you get your appointment!"

"Chastity . . ."

She was almost in tears as she shook off his hold on her. "And I thought you were so dedicated to what you believe in."

"Calm down, Chastity. You're upsetting yourself over nothing. I have a chance to be city attorney, not governor or president, and what I feel about suffrage isn't really an issue here at all."

"Well, I'm glad it's an appointment, Jonathon," she flung into his calm, rational statement. "Because I wouldn't vote for you even if I could!" With that she turned and ran crying from the room.

It was impossible for Jonathon to sleep with Chastity lying rigidly beside him, sniffling every now and then as a fresh onslaught of tears began. He sighed and punched his pillow, unable to endure it a moment longer. "I'm sorry, Chas. You were right."

If he expected her to fly into his arms at the apology, he was sorely disappointed. She remained with her back toward him, crying softly. "I said I was sorry," he repeated earnestly. "I don't really know why I was so concerned with that appointment all of the sudden, but you were right. If I can't keep my integrity, then I've lost everything." Even as he said the words, he recalled another occasion when he had lied to get what he wanted, and how much pain he had caused the people involved with that lie.

She turned to face him, her tear stained face barely visible in the moonlight. "I—I do want you to get that appointment, Jonathon. I—I know how important it is to you."

He gathered her onto his arms and drew a long, calming breath as she lay her head against his chest. "You are much more important to me than any political office, Chastity. You know that, don't you? That you're really the most important thing in my life?"

She blinked back more tears as she looked up at him, straining to see his face in the meager light. How she had needed to hear him say that! "And would a child be important to you, Jonathon?" she whispered.

"What?"

"I asked you if a child would be important in your life, too." She smiled at his absolutely dumb-struck expression and nodded. "I am with child, Jonathon." Her smile widened as she felt the excitement tensing his muscles beneath her hands.

A father! He was going to be a father! "I—I can't believe—you are certain? When? When will it be? Are you feeling well enough to entertain like you've been doing?"

"I feel wonderful!" she assured him happily. "After all the stories I've heard, I expected to spend every morning with my face in the washbasin. But I feel very well, really. Only a little tired every once in a while."

For the first time since she told him, he smiled too, and even in the darkness there was no mistaking the joy abounding in his voice. "When?"

"The spring."

"Spring," he repeated, grinning from ear to ear. "The perfect time for a baby to be born!" He bit his lip and sighed as he squeezed Chastity close against himself. "I'll build him a cradle myself—"

"It might be a girl," she reminded him.

"Well, then, I'll paint it pink and white and you can load it with frills."

"Jonathon, we can buy a cradle. We can order it made—"

"Not for my baby! I'm going to make it with my bare hands so the love's built in even before we put him in it for the first time. And I'm going to buy him a set of law books . . ." He noticed her frown. "Or her—just as soon as he or she can read. And I'll teach him to sail . . . even if he's a girl. We can go to Boston for the summer, and I'll . . ."

Chastity grinned and sighed contentedly as he rambled on and on with his dreams. She could already picture him carrying a tiny bundle all over the city, everywhere he went, lamenting the trouble the poor little thing had endured cutting his first tooth, or boasting the child's latest precocious accomplishment. Jonathon was so full of love, so eager to give of himself, that she knew he would make a wonderful father. And she was full of joy and excitement too, and totally awed by the miracle taking place inside her own body. A baby . . . a tiny, helpless creature who would need her and love her as no one had ever needed and loved her before.

How perfect life seemed at this moment! She smiled as she lay close against her husband's heart, pondering the fact of a new life growing inside her at this very moment. It seemed to Chastity that the birth of their child would bring all the pieces of her life together, that she would finally be completely fulfilled as a woman. She closed her eyes and drifted off to sleep, while Jonathon's hand rested protectively on her belly.

Chapter 28

Jonathon slid open the olivewood shutters and allowed the strong morning sun to dispel the shadows that enveloped the upstairs hallway. The day was dawning clear and brilliant and full with the promise of spring. It was an encouraging sight, the lighting of countless hills and distant mountains, one at a time, as daylight spilled its full glory over Nevada with pinks and purples and golds. Jonathon sighed and rubbed his eyes with his fingertips, drawing strength from the beauty spread before him in every direction. Night had finally ended.

He left the window and began pacing the hallway, which ran the length of the house, tracing the same monotonous path over the thick Brussels carpet he had for nearly twelve straight hours. He reminded himself that worry didn't accomplish anything, but still he felt the tension gripping at his forehead. He had never had to endure anything quite like this before, had never felt so totally helpless. How long did it take for a baby to be born? he thought impatiently. And what was the father of the child supposed to do in the meanwhile, in between catching glimpses of the doctor and pestering Sarah for information as she shuffled in and out of the room? He paused restlessly before the closed door, watching, listening. Nothing. He had the distinct feeling that something was wrong, something more than the baby's early arrival.

Chastity had been quite upset when the pains had begun yesterday, a full month before she'd expected them. And the doctor had seemed anxious as well, though Dr. Perkins wasn't at all the type to set store on gossip. It would mean a smaller baby, he had tersely explained to Jonathon as he hurried up the stairs. That was the last time he had spoken with the doctor, who had disappeared into the bedroom and closed the door.

During the very late hours of the night, Jonathon had heard Chastity groaning, crying softly as the pains grew harder and closer together. There in the darkened hallway he had stood gripping the banister so hard that his fingers were still cramped, stood feeling the strength drain from him as his wife suffered the pain of childbirth without him. What seemed like hours later, the noises had ceased. An eerie silence had settled on the house. Some time later, when Sarah had gone to fetch clean linens, she would only say that the baby had not been born yet and that Jonathon ought to wait in the parlor with a bottle of brandy. He had tried to follow those instructions, knowing full well that his pacing accomplished no useful purpose, but whenever the door to the bedroom was opened, he couldn't help but make a frenzied dash up the stairs to find out what was happening. Now it seemed ridiculous to return to the parlor at all. He could scarcely endure the waiting right here, outside their bedroom door.

Why wouldn't they tell him something! Anything! The last time Sarah had gone downstairs for water, she had only shaken her head and gone about her business. Of course, she hadn't the time now to spend discussing the weather. But he didn't like the way she avoided his eyes, or the strained, pinched look about her usually smiling mouth. Even through his own mounting fatigue, he could tell that Sarah was worried. And that frightened him; it really frightened him!

Dammit! Something had to happen soon! This couldn't go on forever!

A sudden cry of pain split like lightning through the stillness of the house. Jonathon froze and felt the bile ris-

ing in his throat. Chastity gasped and screamed again and
again and again, until Jonathon's head was aching with
torment. Oh, God! Please let it be over quickly! Don't let
her suffer like this! Over and over he heard her cry out,
then groan and strain like a wounded animal caught in a
trap. Please, God, please!

And then it was over. Jonathon straightened and took a
hesitant breath, staring at the door. All was quiet for a
long, poignant moment.

"No! Oh, no! Please . . . please . . ." Chastity's voice
broke off in heavy sobbing and Jonathon felt as if someone
were tearing his heart out. He had never heard her cry
like that before, in a voice so full of anguish that he instantly began fighting with the lock on the door. He took
hold of the knob and shook the door so hard that it rattled
against the frame, but it would not give. He fell upon it,
shaking, gasping for breath.

He was deathly pale when Sarah finally unlocked the
door and ran from the room, crying into her hand as she
fled past him down the front stairs. He stared after her in
mute bewilderment, then spun about when Dr. Perkins
emerged from the room.

The doctor's face was tired and drawn, but he was in
complete control of himself. He took one look at Jonathon and knew that the words would come hard. He
clamped a hand firmly on the younger man's forearm.
"Do you have any whiskey, son? I think you could do
with a drink."

"I don't want a drink! What's happened, Doctor? Is
Chastity all right? Is the baby . . . ?"

Dr. Perkins was all too aware of the feverish brightness
in Jonathon's eyes, but the man had demanded the truth
and he would have to be told. He sighed and rubbed his
hand roughly over a day's growth of beard. "It was a long
and difficult birth. The baby was in a very bad position.
Your wife will recover, Mr. Stoneworth, but the baby . . ."
He swallowed hard and forced out the words. "The baby
was too small and too weak to survive. It happens often
when a baby comes too early." He squeezed Jonathon's

arm as if to give him the strength of acceptance. "I'm sorry."

The fear receded slowly from Jonathon's eyes as the truth sank into his consciousness. Chas was all right. But their child, their baby, the tiny being who had squirmed and kicked with such strength in Chastity's belly just hours ago, the child who had been the object of so many fine plans, the infant they had loved without ever seeing . . . Jonathon was unaware of the tears that were streaming down his cheeks. So many thoughts were running through his mind. The hours he had spent making a cradle, the time that had gone into decorating the nursery, the scores of books he'd hurriedly read to Chastity about caring for a baby, and the plans . . . all the plans they had made.

"Was it a boy?" he whispered.

The doctor shook his head. "A girl."

"A girl," he repeated to himself. He stared distantly at the doctor's face without really seeing him. "We were going to name her Ruth, after Chastity's mother." His eyes wandered until his vacant stare fell on the hallway below. "My little girl . . ." He said the words quietly, but with such deep tenderness that it managed to penetrate even the doctor's practiced facade of detachment.

Dr. Perkins adjusted his glasses and sniffed, but his voice remained calm and precise. He had been through this before. "Your wife is resting comfortably now. Sarah went for Father Manogue. He will want to baptize the baby, and arrangements will have to be made for burial." He paused and gnawed thoughtfully at his bottom lip. Jonathon was taking this hard; he wasn't even sure that the man had heard what he'd just said. "There will be other children, Mr. Stoneworth."

Jonathon's eyes flew to the doctor's face and he glared at him for a long moment, unable to believe what he had just said. Other children! The words echoed bitterly in his head. As if this baby were an interchangeable object, as if any other infant could replace her, one the same as another. And what was he to do with the love he had for this child? he wondered. For he did love this baby, created from the love he had shared with her mother. He wanted her, not words about some future replacement. He lifted his chin. "I want to see her." He said it in a strong, clear voice after the doctor had already started back to Chastity's room.

Dr. Perkins turned back to face him. "I'm sorry, Mr. Stoneworth. She's asleep. I gave her something to make her sleep. This was all very hard on her."

Jonathon shook his head. "I want to see my daughter."

Dr. Perkins frowned and bit his lip. He'd seen men on the verge of hysteria before, and sometimes they were never right once they lost control of themselves. "It would be better if you didn't."

"Please . . ." His voice was hoarse and strained; the composure of a moment before had vanished. "I just want to see her . . . just once . . . Please?" He was begging, almost in tears.

Against his better judgment, the doctor gave a brief nod and returned a few moments later carrying a tiny bundle. Jonathon's eyes filled when he saw it, wrapped in a special white blanket Chastity had made all by herself. His hands were trembling as he took it into the crook of his arm and folded back the blanket. For a split second he was gripped with a wild, unexplainable fear. But then his eyes fell on a tiny round head, two tight little fists, and two legs curled up just as they had been in the womb. She was beautiful! Her face was a perfect miniature of Chastity's, with a hint of a square, determined jawline, the soft arch of almost invisible brows, and a sparse crop of featherlight hair atop her head. He breathed a sigh of relief and awe at her incredible smallness. He had been afraid that the sight might repel him, but instead he was comforted by the sweet face, which held only innocence and peace. He was somehow reassured to count ten perfect fingers and ten perfect toes, to touch the soft, down-covered ears, the rounded cheeks, the tiny shoulders. He held her close then, tightly against his heart, and sighed. His daughter, his firstborn child.

Dr. Perkins reached for her, but Jonathon held her a moment longer. Just for a moment. It was all he would ever have. Once again he looked lovingly at her round little face, then pressed a gentle kiss to her tiny forehead. "My little Ruth . . ." It was hardly even a whisper, it trembled so with helplessness and shattered hope, but it echoed with a father's love for his child. Brusquely, without a word, the doctor took the baby from his arms and turned away. And Jonathon broke down and cried.

He didn't remember much about what occurred after Father Manogue's arrival, except that somehow he got a rein on his emotions and managed to make the necessary arrangements for his child's burial. He listened to the quiet words of comfort, of faith and hope in the future. And Jonathon, being a man of strong faith, found the strength to accept what had happened and to go on. But Chastity found no such comfort in the priest's words, or anyone else's. They were just words to her, and they made no difference to the pain she was enduring. She could not even share what she was feeling with Jonathon, for she felt that she had failed him by losing his child, felt that she was being punished for past sins, for the pleasure she had known with Regan Spencer. Night after night she lay awake remembering, reliving the horror. And sleep brought nightmares, terrible, hideous dreams that terrified her and allowed her no peace. The birth had weakened her body as well as her mind, and her breasts were sore and full of milk for a child she had never even been allowed to hold. And in all her fears, her guilts, her agonizing memories, she was alone.

Jonathon was as patient and kind to her as he had always been. He even moved to another room since she seemed to want to be alone, allowing her time to grieve in private in the hopes that she would afterward share her grief with him. Chastity never knew of the nights he also lay awake, remembering, thinking, hurting. It did not occur to her that he needed her now more than ever before. And in the first real crisis of their married life, she felt further away from him than she had on their wedding day.

Chapter 29

From the green velvet chaise near her bedroom window, Chastity stared at the gray beginnings of morning, which had begun to lighten the eastern sky. Once she had reveled in the beauty of a Mount Davidson sunrise, but now the dawn only marked the end to another sleepless night. She hugged her knees to her chest and sighed, shaking off the terrible thoughts that haunted her every waking hour. And the nightmares were even worse. She sat up straight and began chewing at her fingertip like a little girl. Oh, God, what was she going to do? She couldn't bear all the sympathy from the dozens of people who came by the house to "see how she was doing." And she hated Jonathon's endless patience with her, the way he always said, "I know," with that tortured look in his big brown eyes. How could he, or anyone, know what she was feeling?

She lifted her head as she heard him enter the room. He hadn't slept with her since the baby died, but he always checked on her during the night, sometimes more than once. She usually pretended to be asleep when he came in, but this time she couldn't do that, so she simply turned away and hoped that he would leave her to herself. Instead, he came to stand beside her, placing a warm hand on her shoulder. "Couldn't you sleep?"

She drew a long breath and continued to stare at the silvery light curving on the horizon, flinching as the warmth of his fingers penetrated her robe.

"I couldn't either," he said, bending low to press a kiss

to her neck. She went rigid for a moment, then pulled away from him and hurried to the opposite side of the room. She stood there breathless, wishing that he would leave her alone. She had never asked for anyone's pity, and she didn't want Jonathon's now. She fingered the items scattered on her vanity . . . a brush, a comb, several bottles of perfume . . .

"I have to go to the courthouse this morning," he said, reminding her that he would probably be appointed city attorney soon, a position that had once meant so much to her. "But I thought maybe this afternoon you could come to town—"

"No." She did not turn to face him, but her reply was cold and final, one that answered far more than his simple question. Chastity had shut him out. He closed his eyes and forced himself to remain calm. He had to be patient. He knew it would take time. But it had been two months since that night, two months to the day. And still it seemed like yesterday. The wounds had hardly even begun to heal.

"All this brooding isn't doing anyone any good, Chastity. Sooner or later you're going to have to pick up the pieces and start over."

She did not answer. He heaved an impatient sigh. His temper was wearing thin. "I know what you're feeling, Chas—"

She turned on him instantly, her blue eyes ablaze with bitterness. "Don't tell me you know what I'm feeling!" she exploded. "How could you possibly know! You're a man, Jonathon! You didn't feel a life growing inside you for months and months. You didn't feel the pain of giving birth, the hours and endless hours of pain! And all for nothing! You couldn't know what it's like to wake up from that nightmare with breasts hard and sore and full with milk for a baby that's already been laid in the ground!" Her eyes filled with tears when she said that, but she raised her chin and went on, sarcasm thinly disguising the agony in her heart. "But I'll have other children, Dr. Perkins tells me. As if I want to go through the same thing all over again just as soon as I possibly can!" Her voice faltered and rose until it cracked with pain. "As if I could survive it!"

Jonathon hurriedly closed the distance between them and tried to take her into his arms. But she twisted away from him and finally he lost his temper. "Dammit, Chastity! Do you think I've forgotten her already? Do you think I'll ever forget? . . . the hours I spent making that cradle, especially for her? Or the first time I ever felt her moving inside you?" He almost cried as he spoke the words. "She was mine, too, Chastity," he whispered, no longer able to hold back his tears.

She stared at his face, at the tears spilling freely down his cheeks, and her own face twisted with the hurt she had kept inside for so long. "They wouldn't let me hold her, Jonathon." She fell against him, sobbing.

He sighed deeply and tenderly stroked her hair. "I know . . . I know . . ."

"They—they took her away—so quickly," she choked out. "I—I never even got to see—" Her voice dissolved in a terrible, heart-wrenching sob.

Jonathon drew a long, shaky breath and rubbed his wet cheek against his sleeve. "She was beautiful, Chas," he whispered. "She looked exactly like you."

She stared up at him, searching his face. "You saw her?"

He nodded slowly and almost smiled. "I held her. She—she was very, very tiny . . . and perfect, from her head to her smallest toe."

Chastity closed her eyes and breathed a ragged sigh. It had been one of her worst nightmares, that her child had been a monster, that they had taken the baby away to prevent her from seeing something horrible. Now she knew. It was something, at least. Something that gave her some small measure of peace.

For a long time after that she was silent, drawing strength from the realization that her husband, who had shared in the miracle of creating that new life, had also suffered its loss. It was not pity she saw in those eyes. It was understanding, and a hurt that was as real as her own.

"I—I don't know if I ever want to have another baby, Jonathon," she said quietly.

He kissed her forehead with great tenderness. "I know. We'll give it time. And we'll pray about it."

Chastity closed her eyes and sighed, feeling no solace in the idea of prayer. She couldn't understand how Jonathon could be so strong in his faith, even after what had happened. It seemed to her that God had been unfair and cruel, and she could not trust in a God such as that.

"I—I feel so empty," she told him, "like there's a—a vast, empty place in my life . . . and I just don't see how it will ever be filled!" She clung to him fiercely, wishing that she were strong enough to accept this tragedy and go on as before. But she wasn't. And she needed to tell someone who would understand. "I just can't think about another baby right now. I'm so afraid, Jonathon! I never felt so afraid before!"

He took her face between his hands and forced her to meet his eyes. "You aren't alone, Chas. Remember that. I'm with you."

She bit her lip and forced a nod, leaning close to place her cheek against his hard muscled chest. Relief and comfort seemed to flow from the strong arms that held her close. Jonathon was with her always. And though he hadn't actually said the words, she could see in his eyes that he needed her, too. He had been deeply scarred by all that had happened, and wasn't quite so strong and unaffected as she had always imagined he was. And he still loved her, perhaps now more than ever. She had seen that in his eyes as well. Love as dependable as the morning, she thought with a sad smile, even when yesterday's dreams lay scattered and ruined all about them.

Chapter 30

It was nearing the hour of noon when Chastity descended the stairs, dressed for her first outing in well over two months. She hesitated as she reached the landing, smoothing the folds of her skirt and lamenting her considerable loss of weight these past weeks. Once she had wondered if she would ever be thin again, but now her clothing did nothing to complement what little shape was left to her figure. It seemed odd to her that she could have let so much time pass without taking an interest in the mirror. But she had been truly surprised this morning to find her body so altered, so weak from want of exercise and lack of proper nourishment. And her face had aged so much, it was so different from the face she was accustomed to seeing in the looking glass. The vitality and confidence that had always shone brightly in her dark blue eyes were lacking, and try as she might, she could not force a spark of real warmth into her smile. She had stared at that face for a long time . . . the face of a stranger.

And then, a queer thought occurred to her as her mind flitted quickly through a haze of memories, through everything that had happened to her in the past year. She wondered if Regan would still think her beautiful. She didn't really know why she thought of him then, for the first time in a very long time. Perhaps it was only that he was a part of the past, of the frivolous girlhood of just a few short months ago. How simple life had seemed then! Nothing had mattered more to her than the choice of a gown for the

Sisters of Charity social. Her lips curved slightly, sadly as she entered the dining room. Her father's laughter and Deborah's smooth, sweet voice still echoed here in her mind. She could remember one of Regan's few visits to this house, could picture him at this table with Samuel and Deborah, sipping at a glass of wine and adding nothing to the conversation. But then, Regan had found her eyes and with his own said more to her than words could ever have said . . .

She sighed and reluctantly pulled her thoughts to the present. The dining room was empty. The table was set for luncheon. Sarah was singing and bustling about happily in the kitchen, and Jonathon would be home from the courthouse any time now. Just last night he had held her and loved her so gently, tenderly taking her as he had never taken her before. It had been an act of selfless love, of healing, of beginning again, for both of them. And this afternoon she intended to go with him to town, though she really had little enthusiasm for visiting the exchange or shopping for new clothing or running into old acquaintances. It was a start, at least. A step in the right direction, a movement into the world of the living. For Jonathon's sake as well as her own, she was going to take that step.

Anna May Taylor tried to calm herself as she checked the address against the one the man at the depot had given her. The house was much larger and grander than she had expected it to be. She hadn't an inkling that Jonathon was a wealthy man, though he hadn't said much at all about his family. She mounted the stairs to the front porch—there were quite a few of them—and knocked at the door. Then she turned to view the spectacle of hills and mountains and desert, which filled her with awe and appreciation, and calmed her a bit as well. She was nervous about seeing Jonathon again, and giddy as a schoolgirl. It was very forward of her to come here like this, an unannounced visitor appearing on his doorstep. But she'd had no way of writing to him—she hadn't known his address till a few moments before, and she just couldn't pass through Virginia City without trying to see him, without talking with him, without knowing if he had changed his mind. Not after all the nights she'd spent thinking of him, remembering his eyes . . . She whirled about as the door of the house was opened by a pale, frail-looking young woman in a soft blue dress.

"Yes?"

"Is this the Stoneworth residence?" Anna inquired politely, trying to place the woman as Jonathon's sister, cousin, or niece. She was rather attractive, perhaps even beautiful in a sad sort of fragile way. And she was certainly no servant.

"It is."

"I would like to see Mr. Stoneworth if I may. Mr. Jonathon Stoneworth."

Chastity frowned slightly. She knew this woman from somewhere, but for the life of her she couldn't place her. "I'm sorry, but Jonathon isn't here. Is he expecting you?"

Anna colored a bit at the question and felt like blurting out some excuse, but she couldn't think of anything! "Uh . . . no. He isn't expecting me, but . . . well, that is— My name is Anna May Taylor, and I am only going to be in town for a few hours, and I was hoping to have a chance to speak with him . . ." All that in a single breath.

Chastity tried not to stare as she wracked her memory. Taylor . . . Taylor . . . where had she met this woman before? "Jonathon ought to be home any moment now. Would you care to wait for him in the parlor?"

Anna let out her breath as she nodded eagerly. The woman had looked at her so oddly that Anna had almost expected to be questioned at length as to the purpose of this visit. Anna would have died from humiliation if she had been. But now this woman seemed to accept her presence and was even going out of her way to be polite, which put Anna much more at ease. She followed her into the foyer, her eyes taking in the dozens of costly details that enhanced its elegant decor. Reluctantly she continued into the parlor, long before she had seen all she wanted to see. But the parlor was every bit as lovely as the foyer had been, and Anna stopped on the threshold and gaped. It was a spacious room with walls of hand-blocked gold leaf, and a fancy plaster ceiling which supported a great, polished brass chandelier. Three windows, which stretched almost floor to ceiling, flooded the room with sunlight, showing off the blue-gray upholstered walnut furniture and the three matching walnut tables with polished mother-of-pearl tops. A thick, dark blue Brussels carpet with a pattern of countless tiny flowers was in complete harmony with the blues and wood tones and the grays of the mother-of-pearl, and the entire room echoed with both elegance and warmth. Anna was almost afraid to sit down.

Chastity raised an arm to direct Miss Taylor to her seat, then frowned at herself and gave a frustrated sigh. "You must forgive me, Miss Taylor. I have totally forgotten my manners. I am Chastity Stoneworth." She extended her hand and Anna took it promptly with a friendly smile.

"I'm very happy to meet you, Miss Stoneworth."

"It's Mrs. Stoneworth. I'm Jonathon's wife."

Anna's smile drooped in utter amazement, and a queer stunned look appeared in her eyes. "I beg your pardon, Mrs. Stoneworth," she whispered weakly, feeling her cheeks grow hot with embarrassment.

Chastity seemed not to notice her guest's discomfort. "That's quite all right. Would you care for some tea, Miss Taylor? Or perhaps a cool drink? Summer seems upon us already, I'm afraid."

"Yes, please," Anna mumbled. Something! Anything!

Chastity rang for Sarah and ordered refreshments, while Anna did her best to recover from her shock. Married! Jonathon had lied to her!

Chastity rose from her seat and began to pace the parlor. "I know you probably think me a bit light in the head, Miss Taylor, but is it possible that we've met before? Your face seems so familiar to me . . ."

"I—I was in Virginia City once before," Anna admitted guiltily. "But only for a very short time. I was only here to give a speech for women's suffrage—"

"Of course!" Chastity's face brightened with recognition. "Now I remember. It was last Fourth of July. You were wonderful!"

Anna's eyes widened in horror. "You were there?"

"Oh, yes!" Chastity hurried over to the chair nearest
Anna's and perched on its edge. "I thought it was absolutely marvelous the way you handled yourself! And I'm
truly honored to meet you after all this time." She gave
Anna a warm smile, and Anna did her best to return it.
She had almost succeeded when Chastity innocently
asked the next question. "How do you know Jonathon?"

"I—uh—I don't know him. That is . . . not very well.
That is, we—I mean, *I* met him just last year. After he and
a few men who weren't acting like gentlemen got into a
fight." She stopped short and swallowed hard. Should she
have mentioned the fight? Of course, his wife would have
to know about that, but—

"Oh, yes. I remember now. There was quite a fight, if I
recall. I didn't stay to see the end of it, but I'm fairly certain I know what happened after I left." She laughed as if
at some private joke, and Anna felt as if she might be sick.

When the drinks were served a few minutes later, Anna
had already made up her mind to take one large swallow
and bid Mrs. Stoneworth good day. On top of everything
else, she didn't want to risk seeing Jonathon face-to-face.
She took hold of the glass and tried to keep from shaking
as she raised it to her lips. "I—I didn't see you in the
crowd, Mrs. Stoneworth," she murmured apologetically as
she set the glass aside. "And I'm certainly sorry Jonathon
didn't introduce you to me." Very sorry!

Chastity's face lost every trace of amusement at that
moment, and Anna almost expected her to burst into
tears. She didn't know if she could handle that. Oh, Lord,
what had she done?

"I wasn't with Jonathon that day," Chastity said distantly, after a long, heavy silence. She reluctantly remembered the last time she had been at Regan's side, the last
time they had . . .

Anna managed not to look too surprised at that. "Oh, I
see." She didn't really see at all. Unless . . .

"Jonathon and I have not yet been married a full year,"
Chastity continued quietly.

Aaaah! Now that explained everything! Well, almost

everything. Anna's eyes followed Chastity's thin form as she paced uneasily about the parlor. Jonathon's wife was beautiful, some would think extremely so. But Jonathon was not the type of man who would marry a woman for her beauty only. She looked about her, at the gorgeous mansion and all its fine appointments. Money? That was a possibility. But Anna couldn't bring herself to believe that Jonathon would marry for wealth, either. There must be something more to Chastity Stoneworth, something very special, for a man like Jonathon to love. The thought brought a burning pain to Anna's throat and the sting of unshed tears to her eyes. Jonathon loved someone else. She had known that all along, of course. But she had imagined that things would change, had allowed herself to dream about the next time she saw Jonathon, and the next and the next. For an instant she felt a sharp pang of jealousy for the woman pacing the parlor, the woman chosen by the man she loved. But that jealousy was quickly dissolved in the confusion Anna felt as she watched Chastity, for she instinctively knew that Chastity was not at peace with herself. Beauty, money, a perfect home, a perfect husband. Anna envied her all. Any woman would gladly have changed places with this one, yet unhappiness was written all over that pale, lovely face.

Chastity concentrated on walking the entire length of the parlor several times before she felt sure enough of herself to face Miss Taylor again. Independence Day a single year ago. That single year had been a lifetime.

She lifted her eyes to find that her guest was watching her intently. "I'm sorry," she said softly. "I'm afraid I've been less than the perfect hostess. And I do feel so fortunate that you have stopped by." She raised her chin and Anna saw a glint of determination shatter the deep sorrow that had been in those beautiful blue eyes a moment before. "I would be interested in learning all about the work you are doing for suffrage, Miss Taylor."

Anna's appraisal of Chastity jumped a few notches. "Are you interested in women's rights?"

Chastity returned to take the chair she had left a few moments earlier. "Of course. I feel I'm as qualified to vote

as any man. There are times when I truly feel I've been
cursed to have been born a woman. Men seem to have the
upper hand no matter what we do. And the worst of it is,
most women are afraid to challenge tradition, to demand
changes, even those they know in their hearts are right."

Anna smiled and leaned back in her chair. Chastity
Stoneworth had the makings of a true militant. Perhaps
Jonathon hadn't been blind after all.

Words flowed easily after that. Anna forgot her intentions to leave as she began to sketch a brief history of the
idea of women's suffrage, the giant strides made in recent
years, and the current work in which she herself was involved. Chastity was a bright, attentive listener and as
her questions about the various aspects of Anna's work
arose, the conversation drifted and touched on other matters. Anna found, to her surprise, that she had a great deal
in common with Chastity, and within an hour they were
chatting like a pair of schoolgirls, giggling over the outrageous things each had done in her childhood, feeling a natural kinship as they shared ideas and stories, many of
them trivial, some of them close to the heart. Chastity felt
completely at ease with Anna, perhaps because there was
no trace of sympathy in those soft brown eyes, only friendship and challenge. Chastity needed both at this moment
of her life. She had completely forgotten that Jonathon
was expected when he appeared at the parlor door, and she
had absolutely no idea that he was over an hour late for
luncheon.

Anna was busy relating a story about a statewide resolution for women's suffrage that had been narrowly defeated at the Carson City Statehouse just a few years
before, when she saw Chastity's eyes drift away from her
face toward the parlor doorway. She halted midsentence
and turned her head to follow Chastity's stare. Her cheeks
flooded instantly with a brilliant blush.

Jonathon's wide brown eyes met Anna's for a long moment before he recovered enough from his surprise to return his attention to his wife. But then he was even more
surprised by what he saw. It had been a long time since he
had seen Chastity in a day dress, with her hair pulled into

a becoming style. And her eyes, those incredibly beautiful blue eyes, had begun to sparkle, to mirror the determination and excitement he remembered from a long time ago. Something had happened in the few hours he'd been away, something he considered a minor miracle, an answer to all the prayers he'd begun to believe weren't being heard. Of the scores of well-meaning visitors who had come with flowers and sympathy, none had been able to give Chastity what she really needed. His eyes returned warmly to the woman who sat fidgeting on the edge of a blue velvet chair. A remarkable woman, he thought with a smile as he came forward to take her hand. "Miss Taylor. It's truly a pleasure to see you again."

Anna gave a rather stilted reply, and felt her face growing even hotter. She was relieved when Jonathon withdrew his hand and went to stand beside his wife. "Well . . . I really must be going," she stammered with as close to a casual inflection as she could manage. She rose from her chair, firmly refusing their invitations to stay to luncheon. "My train leaves for San Francisco in less than an hour, and I really must get back."

"Then I insist that we accompany you to the station," Chastity said every bit as firmly. She flashed Jonathon an insistent look, and when he seconded the motion, Anna had little choice but to concede.

The ride to the station was not terribly uncomfortable for Anna . . . as long as she avoided Jonathon's eyes. She continued to converse with Chastity, mostly about the current work being done for the suffrage movement. "If you are truly interested in the work that's going on, Mrs. Stoneworth," Anna told her just before the carriage rolled to a stop, "then you ought not to ask, What is being done? but rather, What can I do?"

Chastity straightened for a moment, considering the challenge being laid before her. Then her eyes brightened noticeably and she turned to Jonathon with a slightly raised brow. He smiled at her, and she suddenly felt a whole new world opening up for her.

For scarcely a moment, Jonathon's eyes met Anna's with a warmth that she swiftly sought to avoid. She did not know that it was gratitude she saw there; she would never really understand the part she had played in Chastity's life. But Jonathon knew. And for that, he would always be grateful.

Chapter 31

"Our guests are arriving, dear."

Regan paused to meet his wife's sweetly expectant smile before he finished off his glass of bourbon and set it on the nightstand. "Make them feel at home, Charlene. I'm busy."

"But—" Her smile trembled a little as she met his cold blue-gray eyes. "You know very well you must come downstairs with me now, darling. After all, you're the master of this house and everyone expects—"

"I know what everyone expects," he broke in sharply. He rose from the bed suddenly and watched as she quickly backed away. Master of this house, he thought bitterly. With a perfect, submissive wife who cringed and held her breath every time he touched her. His eyes raked her, remembering last night, remembering all the times in the past year when he had tried to get her with child. It had been like making love to a dead thing, to a lifeless being who could not be made to feel anything at all. And when he remembered what he had shared with Chastity . . .

Charlene's eyes followed him as he moved to take a suitcase from the armoire, opened it on the bed, and began to empty his drawers. "You—you're packing your things."

"That's right."

"But—but where are you going?" Her voice held a tremor of bewilderment.

He paused, then continued with folding a shirt and placing it in the leather suitcase. "I haven't decided that yet,"

he mouthed distantly, knowing exactly where he wanted
to go, but afraid that he might not be welcome there anymore. The charade that was his marriage had ruined
everything . . . everything!

Charlene was silent for a moment; then she suddenly let
out a girlish giggle. "You're joking, Regan," she said in
her soft voice, forcing a smile which showed off her dimples. "We're expecting dinner guests tonight, remember?
You couldn't really be serious."

His eyes narrowed with contempt as he stared at her.
She was smiling again, that empty-headed, useless smile
that he'd come to despise more with each passing day. "I
can assure you, my dear, I'm very serious."

He saw the smile vanish and a spark of fear in her eyes.
It made him glad. "But you can't leave now," she mewled
helplessly. "Mama's planning a grand party for us next
month—an anniversary party."

"Do give Mama my regrets," Regan mouthed sarcastically as he fastened the suitcase and lifted it from the bed.
He turned away from her, making his way toward the
stairs, hearing the laughter and muffled conversation that
rose from the dining room. There was nothing for him
here, nothing left of the dream he had once sacrificed so
much of himself to attain. He hated the guests who constantly arrived at this house, always gushing about how
lucky he was to have a woman like Charlene, the perfect
hostess, always sweet and charming and smiling that dis-
gusting, syrupy smile of hers that brought a feeling of nausea to Regan's stomach. What a useless, harebrained
creature she was, he thought as she followed him down the
hall. And how he hated her constant coddling, the way she
always smiled and said, "Now dear, you know you really
don't mean that . . ." the moment he opened his mouth.

It was over now. He was leaving her, and less than a
year after he had made her his wife. He would go to San
Francisco now, and take a room at a plush hotel under the
pretext of conducting business. But the only business he
had in mind was personal. He needed to be alone, to think.
To try to salvage enough of his pride to go on, or perhaps to
go to her.

"Regan!" Charlene clutched desperately at his sleeve. "You can't be leaving me like this! You can't! I—I'll do anything you say, but please, you must stay! We have guests . . ."

He stopped, staring down at the wide, pleading eyes for a long moment before he lifted a hand to touch her cheek. She flinched and instinctively backed away. He gave a brief, mirthless laugh. "Good-bye, Charlene," he mouthed softly. And without another backward glance he left the house.

It was less than a month after her brief visit that Anna May wrote to Chastity, inviting her to spend some time in California working for the cause of women's suffrage. After much soul-searching, Chastity made up her mind to go and left for San Francisco after the current board of aldermen voted to appoint Jonathon city attorney. Somehow, the excitement and elation she felt at Jonathon's position failed to subdue the depression she still felt at losing their child. She needed more than a successful husband; she needed a challenge. And Jonathon was the first one to recognize that need, and to encourage her to spend some time with Anna.

It was not really surprising that the summer of 1875 flew by more quickly than any in Chastity's memory. She was swiftly caught up in a flurry of activity, and spent every waking hour discussing, learning, planning strategies for the months ahead with Anna and other women like her, dedicated to changing the course of history. For six weeks she traveled the lecture circuit with Laura de Force Gordon, the woman who had spoken before the Nevada State Legislature just a few years before. On her return to San Francisco, in early August, she and Anna labored tirelessly printing and distributing a newsletter in an effort to keep women all over the state informed about the progress being made in the suffrage movement. There was so much work to be done! So many new faces in every crowd, so many minds to be opened up to the new ideas of equality and suffrage! For Chastity that was the most exciting part of all—the thrill of seeing the realization dawn in the eyes of countless women in a crowded lecture hall, the elation of seeing the fruits of her labors, of knowing that her work had made a difference. There was no time for dwelling on the past, for thinking of what might have been. The challenge of the present left no room for that. And if her eyes instinctively scanned each crowd in fearful anticipation of seeing Regan's face, then at least all thoughts of him were quickly pushed aside when she was certain he was not there.

She had gone to California to work for suffrage, to learn, to be fueled by the spirit of women like Anna and Mrs. Gordon. But the summer was also a time of personal growth, of change, of learning to accept the person she was. She gradually began to recognize the value of friendship with other women, and no longer viewed them as rivals in a lifelong struggle for male attention. And as she became less preoccupied with what others thought of her, she became more dedicated to sharing the ideas she believed in. It was a time for forming strong bonds with other women, for making firm commitments, for finally coming to terms with herself.

And in her time apart from Jonathon, she came to realize just how much he had to do with her maturing. He had stood beside her when she needed him, like a stake that supports a sapling when it is not strong enough to stand on its own. Now she was flowering, reaching out further than she'd ever thought possible. And as the month of August drew to a close, and September laced the night air with a bittersweet coolness ending summer, a Chastity very different from the woman who had left Virginia City a few months before was ready to go home.

As she made final arrangements for her departure from San Francisco, Chastity knew that she had put off visiting Deborah as long as she possibly could. Still dreading the thought of enduring the trite, overly sympathetic remarks Deborah was sure to toss at her about the baby she had lost, and dreading the idea of facing her stepmother at all, she made plans to stop by Deborah's home on her way to the train station so that Anna would be with her and their visit would be necessarily brief.

Deborah's house was much smaller than Chastity had envisioned, but very well kept, with a delightful assortment of flowers lining a carefully tended walk. Chastity reluctantly followed as Anna practically dragged her up the walk to the main entrance and eagerly knocked at the door. She was very curious about this woman Chastity had been so hesitant to discuss, and wondered what in the world it was about her that Chastity feared so. Her knock was answered by a stout older woman in a starched black dress with a crisp white apron and matching white cap, who directed them promptly to a small but comfortable parlor.

Chastity held her breath as she entered the parlor with Anna at her side, gripped by an irrational fear that just seeing Deborah would bring back all the feelings of inadequacy Chastity had felt from the moment Samuel had introduced her as his wife. But when Deborah rose from her seat and smiled, and quickly came forward to take Chastity's hand, somehow the familiar resentment and jealousy failed to take hold. Chastity introduced Anna, whom Deborah welcomed every bit as cordially as she did her stepdaughter, and the three settled themselves comfortably while Deborah served them a delightful cup of warm, spiced tea.

"Jonathon wrote me a letter several weeks back," Deborah began, "mentioning that you'd be in San Francisco, and that I could expect a visit." She paused to sip at her tea, and Chastity swallowed a large lump in her throat, knowing full well that she ought to have come weeks ago. She expected Deborah to say as much, but instead she smiled and went on. "He said very little about what you were working on here, however, and I'd like to hear more about it if I may."

Still feeling very guilty, Chastity mumbled something vague about women's rights, which prompted a scowl of disapproval from Anna. "What Chastity means to say, Mrs. Morrow," she corrected, "is that she has become a dedicated proponent of the women's suffrage movement."

"The suffrage movement," Deborah repeated, cocking her head thoughtfully. "Ahhh, yes. The idea has always intrigued me, I must admit . . . though I find it a little frightening, as well as . . . well, radical. But I shall never forget the night Mrs. Murphy and I slipped out to hear Miss Susan Anthony speak in Virginia City." Chastity's eyes nearly popped at that revelation, but Deborah seemed not to notice. "Such a dynamic, inspiring woman she was! I was almost ready to sew a banner across my chest and parade down C Street!" She smiled. "As it was, once the initial excitement wore off, her lecture had us whispering about things I'd never have dared mention to Samuel." Her smile faded when she spoke his name, and her blue eyes clearly bore her pain. She lowered her eyes and sipped at her tea, and for the first time Chastity realized what Deborah must have suffered when her father died. How blind she must have been not to have seen it before!

"That was a long time ago," Deborah went on quietly, after a moment's pause. She raised her eyes and her voice was clearer and stronger. "But I'm really very happy to hear you're doing something more constructive than just whispering about suffrage when Jonathon isn't around. And I want to hear more."

Chastity could hardly hide her surprise. Deborah was actually interested in her work! She looked at Anna, whose eyes were flashing with expectancy enough to jar her from her momentary speechlessness. For the next quarter hour, with hardly any help at all from Anna, Chastity spoke proudly of her trip with Mrs. Gordon, the lectures, the meetings, the newsletter. Only the pleasant chiming of the mantel timepiece reminded her that she hadn't allowed much time for this visit, that her train was due to leave in less than half an hour. She rose and said her apologies for cutting the visit short, and oddly enough, she was truly sorry to be leaving so abruptly.

"You must promise to come again," Deborah told her, after she had thanked her several times over for stopping by. "I do miss you and Jonathon so."

Deborah took hold of her hand to say good-bye, and for a long moment Chastity gripped that smooth, slender hand in her own, feeling a fondness and gratitude she had never felt before. "Be happy, Chastity," Deborah whispered, giving a small but very sincere smile. "I'm very proud of you, you know."

There was something in Deborah's eyes when she spoke the words that made Chastity suddenly embrace her. It was a brief, almost awkward embrace, which Chastity was swift to break away from, and in her confusion and bewilderment she did not see the tears of joy it brought to Deborah's eyes. Instead, caught in a devastating rush of new, unsettling emotions, Chastity hurried out the door. But those very emotions were what Chastity thought of as she rode silently on toward the train station with Anna.

"She seems like a very kind woman," Anna told Chastity as soon as the carriage had jolted forward, putting Deborah's house behind them. "Of course, she's too conservative and quiet to want to work with us, but she seemed a sweet, gentle soul, all the same."

"Yes," Chastity murmured distantly. She fixed her eyes on the passing houses as the carriage rolled down the street. Kind, Anna had said. And for the first time in all the years she had known her stepmother, Chastity had also seen the kindness in those tired blue eyes. For a long, thoughtful moment she was filled with regret. Was it possible that these feelings of fondness and warmth had been inside her all along? She sighed and glanced up at Anna, who also seemed pensive as her eyes surveyed a small row of shops they were passing. Anna was almost a sister to Chastity now, after all they had shared this summer. She had even lost a child a few years before, and her willingness to share her experience had helped Chastity to deal with many of the feelings still buried deep in her heart. She had even begun to think about having another child, someday . . .

"Stop the carriage!"

Chastity started in amazement and her thoughts scattered in every direction as Anna flung open the door of the carriage, hitched up her skirts, and jumped to the ground. Without a word of explanation she ran down the street, her bright green skirts flying behind her. As soon as she could gather her wits, Chastity gave the driver an apologetic shrug and alighted in a similar manner in hot pursuit. In and out of carriages and buggies and people, Chastity ran, following the flash of bright green and leaving many eyes staring after in curiosity as she forced her way through the clogged street. She was gasping for breath when she finally found Anna in the crowd, standing beside a bright blue and gold painted pony cart, staring at it with a queer, awed look on her face.

"Would you—like t-to tell me—what we ran all—this way to see?" Chastity gasped out breathlessly. Anna stood there staring, as if she hadn't heard Chastity at all. "Anna May Taylor, are you suffering from heatstroke or what?"

Anna blinked the dazed look from her eyes and faced Chastity with a guilty grin. "I suppose you think I've taken leave of my senses."

"I am beginning to wonder . . ."

"I'm sorry. I know you have to catch a train, but . . . well, look! Isn't it gorgeous?"

Chastity frowned as she glanced blankly about the street. She saw nothing gorgeous. Only this silly, overly elaborate pony cart.

"This!" Anna shouted in annoyance. "This pony cart!"

Chastity looked at it again, but for all its frills and brightly painted trimmings, it was still just a pony cart, a child's expensive toy. "It's a child's pony cart, Anna."

Anna sighed her exasperation. "I know that! But didn't you dream of having one of these when you were a little girl? Or just riding in one—just once?" She bit her lip and stretched her forefinger timidly out to trace one of the decorations along its side. "I remember that Betsy something-or-other, the richest girl in the whole country, had a pony cart exactly like this one . . . only hers was red and white. Oh, how I used to dream of being rich and beautiful and having my own pony cart, just like this one!"

Chastity frowned and looked about her nervously to

see if they were being observed before her eyes returned to Anna's face. She was normally such a rational person, but she was certainly acting crazy now. "Anna May . . . you're all grown up now." She didn't know what else to say.

Anna's eyes met Chastity's in surprise, but a moment later her expression became serious, and a sad, distant smile curved her lips. "I know." She sighed again and took one last, affectionate look at the pony cart. Then she linked her arm in Chastity's and worked her way through the crowd with her usual determined gait.

They were almost to the station before Anna broke the uneasy silence that had settled on the carriage since they had stopped. "Chastity . . . about that pony cart . . ." She drew a long, thoughtful breath and smiled. "I can't let you leave here believing that I'm not quite sane. You are a dear, dear friend, and I hope you will try to understand what I'm going to say, no matter how ridiculous it may sound." She hesitated and bit her lip, as if reluctant to begin with the explanation, as if she feared she might not say the right words. "I want that pony cart," she said finally. "I mean, I want it—now! I know I can't have it, and I don't even know what I'd do with it if I got it." She laughed out loud, but avoided Chastity's eyes. "Perhaps I am crazy, you know. It's just something in my past that I—I dreamed about so hard and for so long that I still want it. Even though I know very well that a pony cart would never make me happy." She turned back to face Chastity and earnestly took both her hands in her own. "You don't understand, do you?" She sighed. How could Chastity understand? Chastity had Jonathon. "It's all right. I think you will . . . someday."

Anna's eyes became soft and faraway, and her voice was very small. "Dreams are such cruel illusions. They take hold of you and they never let go. And it hurts so much when they tug at you . . . even after you've outgrown them . . . even after life has given you more than you could ever have hoped for."

Her eyes brightened then, and her mouth twisted into its usual impish grin. Chastity returned her smile, but she didn't really understand anything Anna had told her. Life had given Chastity more than she'd ever hoped for. But she didn't see how any silly child's toy could ever interfere with the mature woman Chastity Stoneworth had become.

Chapter 32

Regan Spencer stood before the main entrance of the Hotel Crown Point and surveyed the mad bustle of C Street. The wind was brisk and dusty and already touched with winter here in the mountains, even though it was barely October. He crossed his arms over his chest and drew himself up against the chill of the evening air, longing for the milder breezes of California. But he certainly had no desire to return there, to his fine mansion, or to his wife . . . Everyone who visited the house fell in love with Charlene; every man assured Regan that he was to be envied such a wife. He wanted to laugh at the irony of it all. In just one short year of marriage he had come to hate the woman far more deeply than he had ever loved her. And to think that he had once wanted a wife he could place on a pedestal, a woman of unquestioning submissiveness. Submissive she was, Regan thought bitterly, but colder than the winter winds that whipped through this town on the darkest December nights. Proud, handsome Regan Spencer, who had been welcomed into dozens of beds by eager ladies of every description, could find no welcome in his wife's. And after knowing the pleasure and triumph of being one with a very different kind of woman, a woman of pride and strength and passion, a woman who had loved him completely, Regan had all too quickly come to know what he had thrown away.

It had taken Regan only a little longer to realize that the rest of it had been a mistake as well. He did not like living the life of a country gentleman, apart from the city, a full day's ride from the theater and fine restaurants and friendly games of chance at the more respectable men's clubs. And he disliked the idea of guests who stayed at the house for days and days on end, though perhaps that was rooted in his failing marriage. It was impossible for him to vent his frustrations, his anger, or even to express himself freely before his guests without Charlene's sweet, smiling voice softening any impression he might have made. But he had left all that behind, and he had decided a few weeks ago that he was never going back.

It was strange to stand here, in the center of town, and find it all exactly as it had been a year before. His eyes drifted over the countless faces rushing blindly past him, all flushed with excitement, all hurrying in pursuit of their dreams. So short a time ago, he had been like them, straining and stretching and struggling like a child clutching at a sunbeam. And he had finally gotten hold of all he had desired. But now, like that same child, he had opened his hand and found it empty. It had taken many days and nights of thinking and remembering before Regan had decided to return to Virginia City. Mr. Rahling had made him a very fair offer for his remaining interest in the Crown Point, and it seemed as good an excuse as any to come back here, to see how the hotel was prospering, to make a final decision whether or not to sell. But business was just that—an excuse, a reason that hid the true reason for his coming back.

How in God's name had he ever thought to forget her? Had he really ever imagined that Charlene, or any other woman, could take her place? His face creased with despair as he continued to scan the crowd, searching for the soft blond hair and dark blue eyes which were always in his dreams. He strained against the waning light. But he did not find her. And no matter how many hours he spent standing here, he somehow knew that he would not see her by chance. His chance had been lost, a single year ago. And he would have to go a long way to win her back after all this time; she would not be his now with a simple turn of the cards. She was married now, he knew. And Stoneworth had become an important man in town, had been appointed to the post of city attorney some months back. But Chastity loved *him*, not Jonathon, and a love like they had shared could not die in a single year, or five years, or twenty-five years. They belonged together; Regan knew that now. And he needed her. How he needed her! He was truly sorry about the thoughtless way he had treated her, and even sorrier about the life he had built without her. He had thrown away everything while groping for that sunbeam, and now he realized that she was really the only thing that mattered to him. And if he could convince her of that, if he could somehow reach her with all the love he felt for her now, then they could begin a life somewhere far away from here, Europe perhaps, and he would never, never take her for granted again.

He sighed as the evening shadows from the mountain-top fell ever darker across the streets of town. He still hated this place, with its lifeless gray-brown landscape, its endless clatter and dust and congestion, its crude, obvious opulence. But Virginia City had given him the chance he'd always believed he'd have, had allowed him to act out his dreams before drawing him back to the only woman he had ever really loved. He lifted his head to watch a moment longer. Then he turned his back on the crowded street and made his way alone into the Crown Point's elegant foyer.

Chapter 33

It was already that time of year again. Chastity hurriedly knotted the thread and bit off its end before she paused to survey her work. Why, oh why had she waited until the last minute to work on this quilt for the Orphans' Fair? And why had she volunteered in the first place? she thought with a grimace as she ran her finger over the not-so-even line of stitches. She was certainly busy enough these days with other work, with keeping up with correspondence and making plans for attending lectures and conventions during the coming months. But she was Jonathon's wife first, and she had to do some things to maintain the position she'd struggled to achieve with all her entertaining the past year. And besides, when Sister Fredricka approached her and mentioned that Deborah had always donated her time in this fashion, Chastity had felt an obligation to do the same. She ground her teeth with determination as she unfastened a stack of neat patchwork squares, chose the correct colors, and began to sew. She gasped as her haste caused her to prick her finger with the very first stitch. She had never been particularly good with a needle, and had never really taken any interest in sewing . . . except once. She let her hands drop in her lap for a moment as the memory of a small, frilly white blanket flitted through her mind. It seemed so long ago, yet the magnitude of her loss struck her hard, even now. But only for a moment. And then she forced herself to smile. Life had been good to her. Its trials had strengthened her, as well as its joys. She supposed that Father Manogue was right about not fully knowing one without knowing the other. She raised her eyes as Jonathon entered the parlor, then swiftly busied herself with her work in a futile effort to avoid his scolding.

"You're never going to finish that by tomorrow afternoon," he said with a frown as he lifted the last two bundles of patches and playfully juggled them in the air.

"Not if you keep interrupting me."

"You shouldn't have waited till the last minute."

"I thank you for such timely advice," she shot back tartly, seeing the familiar spark of desire in his eyes and quickly avoiding it.

Jonathon sighed and tossed the bundles back on the chair. At this rate she would be working on the silly thing all night long. And he had very different ideas about how she was going to spend the night. He went to stand beside her chair and stared down at her for a long time, watching her struggle with needle and thread, pricking her finger with almost every stitch. He frowned and thoughtfully circled the chair, pausing behind it. He bent low to plant a kiss on the side of her neck. She went on working. He frowned and kissed her again, this time lingering until he saw the flesh on her arms prickle with pleasure. But she still concentrated fervently on her work. He placed his fingers on her shoulders, then slid them to the back of her neck and began to unfasten the gown's demure collar. That she couldn't pretend to ignore.

"You're not helping, Jonathon!" she cried in exasperation.

"Well, I would . . . if it were possible," he murmured as he ran his lips over the sensitive skin he had laid bare.

She held her breath and clenched her teeth for a moment, before her eyes suddenly brightened. She twisted her head to face him, to run her fingers slowly down his cheek. "Would you really, Jonathon? Honestly?"

"Would I what?" he mouthed against her lips, kissing her deeply the moment he had spoken the words.

"Would you help me with this if you could?" she whispered, toying with his hair.

"Of course . . ." He lowered his mouth to hers once more, but she only twisted free, jolting him abruptly from his romantic mood.

"Then here." She tossed a bundle of patches into his face. "There's an extra needle in my sewing box, over there . . ." She nodded her head toward the box on the serving table in the corner. Then she once again returned her attention to her work, battling hard to hold back a grin.

For a long moment he stood there holding the bundle of patches and staring at her. Her manner had changed so abruptly that he was almost dizzy with confusion. "Chastity!"

She lifted a pair of wide, innocent eyes, though she was still fighting hard against a grin. "Yes?"

"Do you really expect me to help you with this?" he demanded.

She managed to look properly offended. "You did offer, Jonathon. And I certainly could use the help."

"But I—"

"You offered, Jonathon!"

He let out a pained sigh and slowly shook his head. How could he argue with that perfectly lovely pair of blue eyes staring up at him that way? He reluctantly gathered up the necessary implements from the sewing box and stared at them dumbly for a long moment.

"I thought your father was a tailor," she teased, unable to resist. "Didn't he teach you anything?"

He scowled. "My father made clothing for wealthy, well-dressed gentlemen," he retorted. "He did not attend quilting bees!"

She bit her lip to restrain a giggle. "Come here, Jonathon. I'll show you what to do."

He obeyed her order begrudgingly, but his annoyed frown faded a little as he pulled a chair close enough to hers so that he could easily observe her work and she could easily instruct him. "If you dare to tell a single soul about this," he threatened her, "so help me, I'll—"

"I won't tell. Cross my heart. Now watch closely. You match up the edges of the squares and pin them and then you—*ouch!*" She had jabbed the needle directly into her thumb.

He lifted a single brow and his lips curved into a smile of feigned enlightenment. "So *that's* how it's done!"

Still sucking on her injured thumb, she narrowed her blue eyes and her face brightened. "This is not funny, Jonathon. Now watch what I'm doing."

"I'm watching, I'm watching." He observed in silence for several minutes as she neatly fixed the patchwork square to the others, which had already been sewn together.

"Now then. You're ready to try it yourself. No, Jonathon! You can't sew a red square to a red square!"

"And why not?" he demanded.

She let out a breath through clenched teeth. "Because if you do, I'll make you rip it out and do it over again."

He gave a thoughtful nod. "That's a pretty good reason."

He strained clumsily with knotting the thread and making the first few stitches, but when he'd finished entirely with his first patch, his mouth broke into a self-satisfied grin. There was no denying that his stitches were straighter and far more even than his wife's. "Am I doing this right?" he asked innocently.

Her face twisted with annoyance when she inspected his nearly perfect work. "I suppose that will have to do," she returned with an indifferent shrug. "But you could try speeding things up a bit. I don't want to be here all night."

"Neither do I," he returned huskily. He caught her eyes and held them until her cheeks flushed a deep pink.

She bit her lip and pulled her eyes away. A moment later, when she glanced up at him, she almost laughed aloud at the sight of her muscular, broad-shouldered husband concentrating so intently on a silly little patch of fabric and a needle. She wondered if he realized what a funny picture he made. She wisely restrained her laughter and returned her attention quickly to her work.

"I challenge you to a race," he announced suddenly, several squares later.

She met his eyes with a blank stare. "A what?"

"A race. I'm rather good at this, in case you haven't noticed," he said arrogantly. "Must have inherited a bit of my father's talent after all. Now you take this stack of patches, and I'll take the other one. The first one finished wins."

"And what does the winner get?" she inquired.

He seized her hand and pressed a lingering kiss to her wrist, letting the tip of his tongue taste her warm, pulsing skin. "The winner," he murmured huskily before he released her hand, "gets whatever he or she desires."

His smile was nothing less than seductive, and it was a long time before Chastity could pull her eyes away. She drew a long, calming breath and tried to concentrate on her work. "Well?" he pressed expectantly.

"I think you have yourself a deal," she mumbled uncertainly.

It was far into the wee hours of the morning when the laughter and playful banter in the parlor finally came to a halt. Chastity folded the finished patchwork quilt with utmost care and laid it on the settee with a sigh of accomplishment. Her eyes lit with a mischievous grin as she glanced up at her husband and stepped slowly forward until she was close enough to unbutton his shirt. "I believe you owe me something, Mr. Stoneworth."

"Oh, no, Mrs. Stoneworth," he returned with a shake of his head. *"You* owe *me* something." He began to pull at the pins which bound her hair, carelessly dropping them to the floor. "I'm the one who finished first—"

She spread his shirtfront and pressed her palms deliberately to the firm, muscular discs of his chest. "But you sewed a blue patch next to a blue patch," she reminded him.

He touched his lips to hers. "So?"

"So you're disqualified," she murmured against his mouth. She let out a sigh of pleasure. "I really should have made you rip it out, Jonathon."

He straightened indignantly. "Rip it out!" he cried, aghast.

She gave a shrug. "Mmmm . . ." She molded her body brazenly to his and rose on tiptoe to kiss him. The kiss was leisurely and totally erotic, and when he responded she drew back to eye him in a way that left no doubt as to what she was thinking.

"You really are a very bad loser, Mrs. Stoneworth," he whispered. He lifted her into his arms and abruptly headed for the stairs, while Chastity yielded eagerly to his searching mouth, putting an end to further argument.

Chapter 34

The *Territorial Enterprise* called the annual Orphans' Fair "very beautiful and dazzling, a scene of wonderful and confusing animation." An entire column of the newspaper went on to detail the main attractions of the fair, mentioning the many items of interest for sale there, as well as the names of the women in charge of the various tables where those items were to be sold. Inadvertently, this generous mention in support of the week-long fair gave Regan Spencer all the information necessary to plan his first confrontation with Chastity.

The first floor of the Root Building had been neatly organized into long rows of tables, all lavishly decorated with brightly colored ribbons, rosettes, and ornaments. Regan wandered about for some time, slowly making his way through the crowd of noisy browsers, all the while alert for the sight of spun silver-gold hair and deep blue eyes. Finally he saw her, haggling over the price of a lace-edged tablecloth with a pinched old woman who was giving her quite a time of it. She was even more beautiful than he remembered. His heart raced at the very sight of her.

"That's exactly what I want!" He boldly stepped forward to interrupt the heavy bargaining session, causing both Chastity and the prospective buyer to be taken aback. "I'll pay whatever price you're asking," he went on, removing his wallet from the breast pocket of his coat without ever taking his eyes from Chastity's. "I've been looking for it every-

338

where." His voice had softened noticeably, and his eyes carried a deeper and more personal message than his words.

"Now wait just a moment there!" The elderly woman jerked the tablecloth from Chastity's hands and hugged it possessively to her breast. The idea of losing out on a bargain at the very last moment, when she had just about convinced Mrs. Stoneworth to lower the price another two bits, made her instantly hostile. "This item is sold, sir. I was in the process of paying for it when you so rudely interrupted." She turned to Chastity with a self-righteous thrust of her chin. "Isn't that so, Mrs. Stoneworth?"

For a moment, Chastity was unable to utter a single sound. Regan Spencer! My God, it was Regan!

The pinched old woman flashed a cold glare at Regan, then suspiciously eyed Chastity, who hadn't responded to her question. "Mrs. Stoneworth? Isn't that so?" she repeated more forcefully.

With a great deal of difficulty, Chastity pulled her eyes from his face. How had she ever forgotten what a tremendous physical impact he'd always had on her? She felt her knees going weak, her stomach filling with butterflies. "Uh . . . yes. It is. I believe seven dollars was the price we decided on, Mrs. Mooney."

Chastity concentrated on refolding the cloth and wrapping it, hoping that her trembling fingers weren't terribly obvious as she fumbled with the brown paper and string. Mrs. Mooney scowled as she begrudgingly counted out the money, then took her package and brushed abruptly past the man who'd cost her an extra twenty-five cents. He nodded pleasantly as she passed by. "All for the sake of charity . . . ," he said under his breath as she disappeared into the crowd. He smiled. She had done him a favor by hurrying with her transaction. Now he and Chastity would have a moment alone.

He turned to face her, and found her busy folding and rearranging the items on her table. The task was completely unnecessary, and his face lit with amusement as he observed her. She was trying to avoid his eyes. But fortunately for him, her table was located in a remote corner of the hall, so there was little chance of her escaping unnoticed, or finding another customer who demanded her immediate attention.

Why was she shaking so inside? She was a happily married woman now. She hadn't even thought of him in months! But she wasn't prepared to see him again, either, not like this. She reached for a set of embroidered dinner napkins and gasped as he covered her hand with his own. A shudder went through her. She stared at his fingers, long, perfectly manicured, fingers capable of arousing her so easily . . . as they did now. Nothing had changed, she thought in sudden panic. Even after all this time, he still held the upper hand.

"Chastity." His voice caressed her name, softly, hoarsely.

She swallowed and raised her eyes slowly, almost fearfully to his. He was every bit as handsome as she remembered, his blue-gray eyes a striking contrast to his darkened skin and jet black hair. She stared at him long and hard. She had loved him so. She remembered the way she had felt the very first time he kissed her, the tender way he had held her in his arms after they made love, the very precious moments she had treasured in her heart . . . She wanted to cry over all the pain that face had caused her, over all the nights she had spent longing for him to come back to her. A year. One single year ago she had loved him more than she had ever loved anyone. And now, all those forgotten feelings came gushing back. Forgotten . . . but still so very real.

But she couldn't love him! Her mind screamed in outrage against what she was feeling. He had left her without a word, he had wed another woman after promising her marriage, and he had never really loved her, for all his empty words to the contrary. She swallowed hard and lifted her chin. "Good evening, Regan. We have several other lovely tablecloths, if you're interested in buying one for your wife." Her voice sounded almost level, until she said the word "wife." Somehow she could not will away the bitterness as she spoke the word.

Regan smiled in admiration. She had never been the type to give in easily, and obviously that had not changed. But he noticed that she had changed some in the time he had been gone. She was thinner, more reserved somehow, and there was a new depth to her dark blue eyes, a kind of mystery to them he didn't understand. The changes intrigued him. "I need to talk with you, Chastity."

She squeezed her eyes tightly shut and shook her head, hating herself for the things she was feeling, for the part of her that wanted to be with him as she had before.

"Please. I just want to talk."

"We have nothing to say to each other."

"Yes, we do." He lifted her hand, and she only barely managed to snatch it away before he could touch it to his lips.

"Regan!" she hissed helplessly. She glanced about to see if the gesture had been observed. She felt completely trapped, like an animal in a cage.

"Please." His voice was pleading, and she had never been able to refuse him anything.

She let out a long breath and shook her head. "I—I can't."

It was almost as if he sensed her uncertainty. "I'll wait for you. I'll walk you home."

"No."

"I'll be outside when you've finished."

"No! I—I can't—"

"I'll be waiting." He turned away from her then and was swallowed up by the crowd before she had a chance to refuse him again.

For a long time she stood there, staring dumbly after him, wondering what she was going to do. She hadn't asked for this to happen. But now that it had, there was a part of her that wanted desperately to see him again, to talk with him, to find out why he had left her—he must have had a reason! She stared at the hand he had touched and felt the blood rush to her cheeks. And to think that she had almost forgotten . . .

She snapped to attention when Jonathon came up behind her, took hold of her shoulders, and gave them a playful squeeze. "So . . . how are the table linens moving this evening, Mrs. Stoneworth?"

"Well," she responded as lightly as she could manage,

with her thoughts in a terrible flurry. "Fairly well, that is.
Mrs. Mooney just paid seven dollars for a lace-edged cloth."

"Mrs. Mooney? Not *the* miserly Mrs. Mooney!"

She nodded and tried to smile.

"Well, congratulations!" he said with an appreciative
grin. "This must be your night!"

"Yes," she said with a small voice, "this must be my
night." She gnawed at her lip and took a deep breath, bracing herself for what she was about to say. "Jonathon . . .
would you mind if I . . . if I had Eileen Murphy drop me at
the house this evening after the fair?" The lie tasted bitter
in her mouth, but she rushed on. She had made her decision. "I wanted to speak with her about organizing a special centennial celebration for next year, including a full
week of lectures on women's suffrage. She said she'd be
happy to see me home." She avoided his eyes and refolded
a set of napkins, which were already in perfect order.

"The centennial isn't till next summer, Chas."

"I know that. But you're always scolding me for waiting
till the last minute!" She said it more sharply than she
had intended, then closed her eyes and bit her lip. Why
was she doing this?

Jonathon frowned, putting his forefinger beneath her chin
and forcing her to meet his eyes. "Am I really?" She nodded,
unable to speak as she faced those trusting, childlike eyes of
his. He sighed. "Well, I'm sorry if I'm overbearing at times. I
hope you know it's only because I love you."

She felt her lip start to tremble when he smiled at her.
He had always been so kind; he had never, ever hurt her.
And yet she was lying to him, doing something that would
surely hurt him if he ever found out.

But she only wanted to talk with Regan, she rationalized. She had no plans to be technically unfaithful to Jonathon. Then again, she had to face the fact that she was
tempting fate by meeting Regan at all. And lying to Jonathon . . . oh, damn! There really wasn't any justification
for that. She drew a long breath and blinked back a tear.
This had all been a mistake, and there was no way around
it. If she chose to go through with it, she was choosing to
hurt Jonathon. Hurting him was something she could

never deliberately choose to do. "You're right, Jonathon," she heard herself say. "It's much too early to think about the centennial. I'll tell Eileen to come to tea some day next week instead." She forced herself to smile.

"No, you're the one who's right, Chas. There's no reason to miss this opportunity to talk with Mrs. Murphy." He held up a hand to stop her protests. "As a matter of fact, I have a stack of briefs I've been putting off attending to for the last week, so I have a busy evening ahead of me, regardless." He planted a kiss on her forehead, effectively ending the discussion. "I'm off to work, Mrs. Stoneworth. But I will be waiting up for you when you arrive home, and I'll expect to hear about every napkin and tablecloth you sell in the meantime." He left her then, just as two prospective customers arrived at her table. She stared after him, wondering what she had done. Now she really didn't have any choice.

Jonathon gingerly made his way through the thickening crowd, nodding and stopping for a brief chat with several ladies at the less busy tables along the way. He was hailed by Mrs. Murphy, and meant only to return her hand greeting, until he noticed that she stood at a table that displayed blankets, quilts, and comforters. It was a much larger table than Chastity's, presided over by three women instead of one, and the mass confusion of the blankets attested to the table's popularity.

"What can I do for you, Mr. Stoneworth?" Eileen asked him as soon as she had finished with another customer.

"I was interested in a patchwork quilt. The one Chastity and I—that is, the one Chastity made and donated to the fair."

Eileen frowned, her round face puckering with concentration as she did her best to bring some organization to the disheveled table. "Well, I wish I could recall that exact item, Mr. Stoneworth, but look . . ." She raised her hand, palm upturned, to indicate the vast display. "There are so many things. We still have a half-dozen or so patchwork quilts left here somewhere, but I'm afraid I've sold at least that number since early this evening. The first night is always the busiest, you know. And those are popular items."

She sighed. "Would you be able to recognize it if I did still have it?"

"Of course."

She blinked at him in amazement. "You would? Well, then, it's a simple matter of showing you what's left."

She scurried about behind the table, gathering the quilts scattered here and there in the disarray. "Here we are," she sighed as she let her bulky load plop atop the table. "Go ahead and look through them."

To Jonathon's surprise, he couldn't pick out their quilt as easily as he'd thought. He frowned and opened one after another, running his fingers over the stitches and trying hard to remember. While he was wracking his brain, a lady beside him reached underneath his hands and removed the quilt on the bottom of the pile, opening it for her own inspection. In that very instant, he recognized it. A blue patch sewn mistakenly next to another blue patch. "This is it!" he cried triumphantly, snatching it away from the woman beside him.

She held on for dear life. "I was just about to buy this," she informed him icily.

"There are plenty of others," Jonathon said with an amiable nod of his head. But something in the woman's eye made him retain his firm grip on the quilt.

"You are welcome to any one of them, sir."

"You don't understand," he told her calmly. "My wife made this quilt."

"And donated it, did she not?"

Mrs. Murphy's eyes widened in dismay as a tug-of-war ensued with every exchange of dialogue. In another moment there would be two half quilts instead of one whole. "Miss Collins. Mr. Stoneworth." The two hostile faces immediately met her eyes. "If you are both interested in buying the same item, then there's only one way to solve this dilemma. We'll—we'll auction it off to the highest bidder!" She didn't breathe for a moment, expecting one or the other to protest the idea. But neither did. "Our quilts usually sell for fifteen dollars each. Who will open the bidding at twenty?"

The bidding did indeed open at twenty dollars, then mushroomed into a lengthy, hot-winded session of bidding and arguing and more bidding and more arguing. "Are you out of your mind, sir? Fifty dollars is an outrageous sum!"

"So was forty-five!"

"Humph! For the sake of principle, I can't let you have it. Fifty-one."

Jonathon clenched his teeth and shook his head. "Fifty-two."

Miss Collins raised a haughty brow. "Fifty-three."

He heaved an exasperated sigh. This had gone on long enough. "Seventy-five dollars."

Miss Collins drew a lengthy breath and eyed him narrowly. "Sir, you are mad!" She stuck out her chin and did an arrogant about-face before she made her way through the crowd, muttering something about the ridiculous lengths to which some men will go to prove a point. Jonathon watched her for a moment, then lifted a suddenly pained expression to Mrs. Murphy. "I think I got carried away."

Eileen folded the quilt with utmost care and avoided looking him straight in the eye. "I would say that." She swallowed hard and cleared her throat. "That will be, uh, seven—seventy—sev—" She just couldn't bring herself to say the amount, it was such an absurd price to pay for a quilt! Any quilt, but this quilt in particular. It was riddled with mistakes, and an hour ago she would have wagered against its ever finding a buyer at fifteen dollars!

Jonathon let out a long, thoughtful breath and grinned at the fool he'd made of himself. But it had certainly been for a good cause. And the quilt was his now. "Seventy-five dollars, Mrs. Murphy. And worth every penny of it."

She began to wrap his package while he counted out part of the money and signed a note for the remainder of the amount. "How is Mrs. Stoneworth doing at her table way back there in the corner?"

"Oh, as well as can be expected. Believe it or not, she sold old Mrs. Mooney a tablecloth for seven dollars!"

"No!" Mrs. Murphy was properly impressed. "Now that's an accomplishment!"

"Well, she'll probably tell you all about it later tonight."

Eileen flashed him a puzzled frown as she knotted the string around his package. "Tonight?"

He nodded. "She's planning to take you up on the offer of a ride home. You'll be sure not to tell her about this quilt, won't you? It's sort of a surprise."

She frowned as she took his money and handed him the package. "That's something you needn't worry about, Mr. Stoneworth. I'm leaving the fair early this evening, just as soon as Mrs. Grogan arrives to relieve me, in fact. I thought I mentioned it to Chastity earlier."

"Oh . . ." He frowned and tossed a thoughtful glance over his shoulder, but it was impossible to see Chastity through the throng of people who clogged the hall. He forced a smile and lifted his bundle into his arms. "Then I must have misunderstood what she told me. Good night, Mrs. Murphy."

Jonathon pushed his way out of the crowded building, feeling suddenly that the walls were closing in on him. He couldn't bring himself to believe that Chastity had deliberately lied to him. But when he thought back to their brief conversation, he immediately realized that something was amiss. Why hadn't he been paying more attention? And what did she intend to do tonight after the fair if she was not going home with Mrs. Murphy? Something was very wrong. He knew it instinctively.

Outside the night air was cold and brisk and it sobered him considerably after the mad confusion of the fair. Chastity had made a mistake. It was that simple. She'd forgotten about Mrs. Murphy's plans to leave the fair early, and come eleven o'clock, Chastity would have no way home except her own two feet. And by that time it would be very chilly, an uncomfortable time for her to be walking home all alone.

Somewhat reassured, Jonathon turned his steps toward Howard Street with every intention of returning for his wife promptly at eleven o'clock. After all those hours on her feet, she certainly would be happy to see him waiting for her with the buggy. He would come to the rescue and they would share a good laugh over her absentmindedness.

And then he would try to find out what it was that was really troubling her.

Chapter 35

The Orphans' Fair closed its doors promptly at ten o'clock to allow for last-minute purchases and an accurate accounting of the night's receipts from the various tables. Chastity straightened her merchandise, counted her money, and turned it over to Sister Fredricka long before most of the other women had even gotten their tables in order. She hurried out of the building, pausing as the crisp autumn air whipped about her. She had done quite a bit of thinking after Jonathon had left her this evening, and she had made up her mind that this would be the last lie she ever told him. This thing with Regan was over. It had ended a long time ago. And she intended to make that perfectly clear to him tonight, no matter what it cost her. She stepped forward into the light and glanced about in nervous anticipation. "Chastity."

She whirled about and saw him, waiting there in the shadows, scarcely visible at all until her eyes adjusted to the light. For a long moment she stared at him without moving a muscle, completely unaware of another man who waited patiently for her in front of the building, a single man whose buggy was parked amid a dozen other similar vehicles. She was oblivious to the deep brown eyes that followed her every step as she hurried toward Regan. She could not help the excitement she felt, the expectation. But there was also that heavy feeling of guilt, which clung to her heart even as it fluttered like a moth nearing a flame. It was almost as it had been before, that crazy sort

347

of joyous confusion . . . but she had to remember that it
was not.

She pointedly avoided his eyes and began walking along
the boardwalk in the direction of Howard Street and
home, remembering the nights not so long ago when she
had walked with him, her body aglow with the pleasure of
their love. But there had also been that emptiness when
he left her at her door, the constant anxiety of never being
certain of his feelings. She walked quickly, purposefully,
so that the arm that lightly guided her along never tightened or rested possessively on her waist. Neither spoke.

The chill of the evening air penetrated her clothing and
made her hurry all the more. They had reached the corner
of A and Sutton streets when Regan caught her by the arm
and swung her about to face him. She was short of breath
and her cheeks were flushed with the cold. He had never
seen her look more beautiful. "We must talk, Chastity."

"Jonathon is expecting me. I don't want to be late
getting home." She tried to turn away.

"Chastity, please. There are things which must be said.
If you'll just listen to me . . ." He sighed as she glared at
him, and relaxed his hold on her forearm somewhat, but
he did not release her. "I will talk while we're walking, if
you insist."

She met his eyes for a moment and gave a reluctant nod.
They began to walk again, slowly this time, while Regan
took a long, difficult breath and hesitantly began to speak.
The words came hard at first, then easier as his heart
drifted into the past, to a time and place he had loved more
than he could ever tell her. He spoke of the war, of what it
had destroyed, of his home, his family, of the life he had
been forced to lead for so many long years afterward. Only
a dream had forced him to survive those years, a dream of
building a new life in the likeness of the old, a life of grace
and peace and beauty like the life he had lost so long ago.
Regan paused then and turned to Chastity, not knowing
how to explain that she had not fit into that dream. He
sighed deeply and lifted his hand to touch her hair. "Once
I left you to pursue a dream. Now I've left that dream and

come back to you." He swallowed hard. "I was such a fool to leave you, Chastity . . ."

Her wide blue eyes filled with tears. Regan had always been an extremely proud man. She knew well what the admission had cost him. "Your wife—" she choked out.

He sighed and closed his eyes. "My wife." She could hear the bitterness in his voice as he spoke the word. "My marriage is hell, Chastity. My life is hell without you." He smiled sadly and spoke from his heart. "If I could only relive the last year of my life . . ."

"But you can't!" she cried out. She felt an agonizing, burning tightness in her throat as she drew back from his touch, when everything in her wanted to hold him. "You can't and I can't. We've made different lives for ourselves."

"But neither of us has forgotten what we had together. We'll never forget." He gave up struggling with her and closed his eyes once more. "I need you," he said quietly. "I know that now. I'd give anything to have you. Oh, God, how I need you!" His voice was barely a whisper, but the hurt in it was very real.

Chastity blinked back her tears as she stared at him, at his handsome chiseled features, at his eyes, which were suddenly warm and vulnerable. There was no denying that he spoke the truth. But it was too late. She wiped the tears from her face and took a painful breath. "I—I want to go home, Regan. I shouldn't have met you. It's all wrong."

"No. Please. I'm not asking you to leave your husband if—"

She stiffened at the mention of Jonathon, and felt a terrible surge of guilt. "I want to go home, Regan." Her voice was thin with restraint. "Now." She turned away from him and began to walk toward home. When she reached the steps in front of her home, she paused scarcely a moment to say good-bye, shrugging off his attempted embrace before she hurried up the stairs.

"Chastity . . ."

His tone was so desperate that she stopped short, halfway up the steps, even though she didn't have the courage to turn around, to face him again. She wanted too badly to begin it all over again. She heard him climb to within a few steps of her. She held her breath, but he did not try to touch her.

"I—I can't let you say no to me. You understand that, don't you?"

She squeezed her eyes tightly shut and nodded slowly.

"I love you, Chastity. And if you will only admit it to yourself, you love me, too." He sighed brokenly. "I'm staying at the Crown Point."

She swallowed hard as she heard his feet fall heavily on the wooden steps. He was gone.

For a long time she stood there, trying to sort out her emotions. She still loved him. In spite of everything, she still loved him. And the next time she saw him— She shook her head and hurried up the remainder of the steps, stopping on the porch only a moment to catch her breath. She smoothed her hair and tersely wiped the tears from her cheeks, fixing a smile on her face as she opened the door and entered the foyer. Her smile faded. The gaslight burned low at the foot of the stairs, and there was no light in the parlor, the dining room, or the study. Jonathon had not waited up. She shook off her disappointment and sighed with relief. She needed this time anyway, to think, to plan, to calm herself. She would be much more at ease in the morning, much quicker with explanations should Jonathon question her. And she needed time to deal with her feelings, to decide what to do. She sighed and slowly mounted the stairs, suddenly feeling drained and tired. She quietly opened the bedroom door and closed it softly behind herself. She frowned. All was silent. She strained to hear the sounds of Jonathon's breathing. She heard nothing. From the open shutters poured an abundance of moonlight. It was only a moment before her eyes became adjusted to the light, and then she saw an undisturbed bed. She was alone.

She hurried out of the room and down the stairs in confusion. Jonathon had promised to wait up for her, but he had not done so. The parlor, the dining room, the study, the kitchen. Empty. In near panic, she ran to wake Sarah, who rambled incoherently for what seemed like forever before coming to her senses. "What? Oh . . . yes. Johnny went after you promptly at half past ten. He asked me t' be sure an' remind him o' the time."

"But I told him I was coming home with Mrs. Murphy!" she cried in protest.

"Did you?" Sarah yawned and rubbed her eyes. "Well, then. He'll remember soon enough an' he'll be home." She yawned again as she patted Chastity's arm, but all the while her eyes gazed longingly toward her pillow. Without another word, Chastity rose with a dazed look of defeat and left Sarah to her sleep.

Chastity lit the small parlor lamp and began what would be a long night of waiting. Time and again she felt the tears welling up inside her as the realization struck her: Jonathon knew. She wondered where he had gone, how long it might be before he returned home to confront her with the truth, if he would ever return to this house at all. He might have made a scene earlier this evening; certainly he wasn't afraid to face Regan in a fight. Why hadn't he fought for her? Chastity wondered. Was it possible that he intended to allow his wife her indiscretions and look the other way?

No. Jonathon had his pride, too. He was not capable of living a lie, no matter how much he loved her. And he must have thought . . .

She sighed and wrung her hands. Where was he? Why didn't he come home? Was he alone? For some reason, the thought of Jonathon with another woman tore Chastity's pride to shreds. He couldn't want anyone else, she assured herself. He couldn't. He just needed some time alone, and he would come home to her. She nervously wandered about the parlor debating the possibilities a thousand times over in her head.

Then suddenly she saw it. A package wrapped with brown paper and string and placed in the center of the settee. She frowned and came to examine it more closely, unwrapping it with utmost care until she saw its contents.

She gasped and carelessly let the wrappings fall to the floor.

Their quilt. Far from perfect as it fell across her trembling hands, but patched together with industriousness and determination and affection. She held it to her face and began to cry. Worthless patches sewn tightly together with love. How much warmer and more enduring than even the finest silk! Her fingers shook as they smoothed over the stitches, her mind recounting the special moments which bound her to Jonathon every bit as tightly. The way he stood beside her at her father's grave; the first time he made love to her; the way he laughed when she told him she was with child; the way he held her, and cried with her, after that child had died. Smiles, sorrows, laughter, and tears. And love. In all things, Jonathon had loved her.

She sighed brokenly and bit her lip hard as the tears continued to roll down her cheeks. There was no place for Regan in the life she had made with Jonathon. That part of her life was over, forever. Chastity Stoneworth was not Chastity Morrow. She was a very different woman who had grown with the love of an exceptional man. And what she felt for Jonathon at this moment of her life had nothing to do with guilt or sorrow or wanting to do the right thing. She loved him, more deeply than she had ever loved Regan. And she suddenly knew that she didn't want to go back at all, that she didn't want the life she'd left behind. She wanted the future, with Jonathon beside her. She needed him more than she had ever realized. Why had it taken her so long to see the truth?

She paused at the parlor window and stared at the first gray hues of dawn tinting the eastern sky. After an eternity of darkness, morning had finally arrived. But Jonathon had not come home. She drew a long, ragged breath and dropped into a parlor chair, shaking with utter exhaustion, her hands covering her face in despair. Oh, Jonathon, please come home!

Chastity lifted her eyes in confusion when the silence of the night was abruptly shattered by a jumble of strange, distant noises. The commotion seemed to mushroom instantly. Almost at once, bells were ringing, men were shouting, women were screaming, children were crying. "Fire! Fire!"

She bounded from her chair at the sound and stood at the window, stunned at the sight before her. A gigantic ball of flame had flared from out of nowhere and was slithering about the entire northern side of B Street. The erratic autumn wind, which had howled all night through the house, seemed to splatter the flames from one building to the next. Chastity could just barely make out the scores of men who were attempting to fight the blaze, but it seemed to defy the fire fighters as they feverishly pumped cistern after cistern dry, and the men who joined them in dozens of bucket brigades were forced back time and again as a single gust of wind nullified their efforts. Buildings, many of them flimsy, wooden structures with paper-thin walls of dried stretched muslin, seemed nothing less than tinder boxes, bursting like rockets as soon as the flames touched them. She saw miners running frantically about, throwing dirt and sand atop the openings to the main shafts, trying to keep the fire from spreading to the underground workings. All was madness, disruption, confusion.

In a matter of minutes, C Street had also been set aflame by flying sparks and red-hot cinders carried along in the sudden gusts of crisp dry air. Chastity stared at the flames, awesome as they roared and leapt skyward. They gushed up and out as buildings crumpled and dropped to the ground, one after another after another, illuminating the city in a bright, reddish light. People were running everywhere to escape the fire, jamming the steps that bridged the streets, scrambling helter-skelter toward higher ground. But it almost seemed as if there were no escape. It was spreading so quickly, racing toward the center of town.

The center of town! The office! Jonathon might be there! As soon as the thought occurred to Chastity, she whirled from the window and flew out of the house, running as fast as her feet would carry her in the direction of C Street. She pushed and shoved her way through the crowds of people who were hurrying away from the fire's path.

By the time she reached the B Street steps, the air was so heavy and thick with smoke that she was gasping for breath. But on she ran, trying to ignore the flames jumping magically above her, all around her. It was almost like descending into hell. She stumbled and nearly fell as an explosion suddenly rocked the earth beneath her feet. The crashing of debris and shattered, flaming timbers made her scream in terror. She lifted an arm to cover her face and strained to see what was happening, but what she saw terrified her all the more. Firemen had begun dynamiting in the hopes of creating a firebreak, and the Hotel Crown Point, which had already begun to burn, had been the first building to go. The blast brought a great section of the proud, six-storied building to its knees.

Chastity turned away from the sight, sickened at the destruction of something that had been so grand, so beautiful. She could barely see where she was going anymore for all the smoke. With every breath of the heavy, acrid air, her throat stung with pain and her head became less clear. She sagged limply against the railing and tried to get a firm hold on herself. She had to go on! She had to know if—

"Chastity!"

From out of nowhere, she heard a voice calling her name. She jerked to attention and whirled about, then fell back in despair when she saw Regan coming toward her down the stairs. She hid her face in her hands and broke into hysterical tears.

A rough pair of hands took hold of her shoulders and shook her sober. "What are you doing? Howard Street is still safe! Why aren't you home?"

"Jonathon . . . ," she choked out brokenly. "He . . . he didn't come home! He could be—Oh, no!" She shook her head and tried desperately to free herself from his hold. "Let me go! I've got to find him!"

"Listen to me! There's no chance of finding him now. Go home."

"No!" She screamed at him and pummeled his chest with her fists. "Let me go!"

Regan did his best to force her in the direction of Howard Street, but she wriggled free of his grasp and ran down the last of the steps. When she reached C Street, she paused and looked about in total confusion. The fire was everywhere! Before she could even think of proceeding, Regan was beside her again, spinning her about, his fingers biting sharply into the flesh of her upper arm. "Chastity!" He jerked her body hard against his own and looked down at her face, soot-stained, streaming with tears. She was completely irrational as she fought him with every ounce of her strength. "Stop it!" He took hold of her and shook her until she thought her neck would snap. "I'm not going to let you kill yourself, Chastity. You're coming with me."

Somehow she managed to break free of his hold one last time, and she stumbled on a few more steps. But the heat was so intense that she simply couldn't go any further. She let out an agonizing sob of defeat, then broke off in a fit of coughing as the smoke was drawn deeply, painfully into her lungs. She stood there, weak and helpless, staring dazedly ahead as a false-fronted building creaked and whined and clattered to the ground, sending flames gushing out at her in an army of hungry tongues. She would never find Jonathon now. She felt her skin being scorched with the heat, but as she instinctively drew back from the flames, she stumbled and fell. She could not even breathe. A strange sort of blackness was taking hold of her, numbing the terrible burning of her skin, clouding her fear, overtaking her desire to flee. She closed her eyes and struggled with all her strength to take another breath. She was very sure that she was going to die. And she didn't have the courage to fight anymore.

Chastity was unconscious when Regan found her and lifted her into his arms. He had barely taken a step when the second explosion from the Crown Point sent pieces of flaming debris crashing all around them. The heat was unbearable. Every breath had become a tortured gasp. Re-

gan could feel the fire singeing the tiny hairs on the backs
of his hands, blistering the sensitive skin at his neck and
ears. But he had found her. She would be all right. That
was all that really mattered to him now.

His arms tightened about her as he carried her up the
steps, fleeing from the heat and the smoke and the relentless parade of flames. It was only when he was far above
the fire, when the air had cleared considerably so that it
no longer hurt him to breathe, that he slowed his pace, his
body sagging heavily against the side of a house that had
been spared. As his strength returned to him, Regan gazed
down at the lifeless form in his arms, feeling a tenderness
he had never known for anyone else. She belonged here,
sheltered in his loving embrace. She made him feel as if he
belonged, too. Slowly, slowly, he carried her on toward
Howard Street, ignoring the scores of anguished, despairing faces he passed all along the way. He had found her; he
had saved her life. And the sweet comfort of holding her
again had been worth any risk.

He was nearly at the house when her limp muscles
tightened and she stirred against him, and it was several
moments before she came fully to her senses. "Put me
down." Her voice was quiet, almost expressionless, but
something in her eyes made him do as she asked.

She clung to his arm to steady herself for a time, finding
that the weakness she felt in her knees was slow to fade.
She turned away from him to view the scene below. Yet
another explosion rocked the earth and another building
burst into a million flying pieces of debris. As well as she
knew the city, Chastity could not even distinguish the
streets any longer. It seemed impossible that over half of
the city lay in smoldering ruins after only a few short
hours. And the fire burned on; it was only beginning to die
out. The flames were not roaring quite so ferociously as
before; they were gathering here and there in smaller
patches of fire rather than a single titanic mass.

Her eyes ran dazedly over the destruction for what
seemed like a long, long time. Home after home, church after church, shop after shop. The Crown Point, the Interna-

tional. The heart of C Street. All destroyed. The inferno had been so intense that even the brick buildings had bowed and crumbled in the heat. Her city, the pride of the Comstock . . . in total ruin. Her eyes filled with tears at what she saw, but her mind refused to believe. All along Howard Street, people had gathered to escape the fire. Now, like her, they all stood watching. Families, with nothing but the clothing on their backs, huddled close to one another, drawing solace only from the knowledge that at least they had survived. Chastity searched the clusters of people, her heart going out to those who had lost everything. But her eyes were constantly moving from face to face, seeking out a familiar pair of cool, patient brown eyes. When she did not find them, she closed her eyes and sighed helplessly, feeling totally defeated.

Regan put an arm about her shoulders and she turned to stare at him, wondering why she felt nothing, only a terrible emptiness.

"The Crown Point is gone," he said quietly. "There's nothing to tie me to this place anymore."

She could think of nothing to say in return. It seemed so unimportant now, with everything that had been destroyed in a single night.

He lifted her hand to his lips. "I love you, Chastity."

She knew that he spoke the truth, that he might have died tonight trying to save her, that she surely would have died if he had not risked his life. But somehow his words sounded hollow. They failed to touch her heart as they had just a few hours before.

"Come away with me. We can start all over again. We can build a new life, a better life . . ." Regan's voice trailed off as her eyes drifted aimlessly away from his. She seemed a million miles away, and he didn't know how to reach her.

Suddenly he saw her lift her chin, saw her blue eyes light up with joy and hope and life. He turned his head to follow her stare, and his eyes fell on Jonathon, filthy with soot, his clothing soaking wet, in utter rags on his back. He had no doubt been working long hours with a bucket brigade, but now he was leading over a score of similarly attired people toward the Howard Street house, and the crowd was growing with every step. Regan tensed for a moment when he saw Jonathon's eyes meet Chastity's. But then he looked away as if he hadn't seen her at all. Regan's fingers tightened possessively on her shoulder, and almost in surprise she turned back to face him, the brightness in her eyes fading as she met his. For a long, hard moment she stared at Regan's handsome face, trying to imagine him in the midst of that crowd of needy people, leading the group of homeless souls to his own house. And then she tried to picture him folding programs for a women's suffrage lecture . . . or sitting beside her in a parlor chair, sewing a quilt for the Orphans' Fair . . . or loving her, as Jonathon loved her, without reservation. It was as if she were seeing him for the very first time.

With a joy that surpassed anything she had ever known before, she ran from Regan's embrace and took her place next to her husband. She belonged to him, she was part of him. She smiled at several of the people, offering words of encouragement to others, and even taking hold of Joey Bates's hand. And then she followed Jonathon up the stairs to the house and proudly opened their home to them all.

Regan stared as the last of them hurried up the stairs and crowded into the house, then fixed his eyes on the door, which had closed soundly behind them. Then he bent his head in defeat, and turned to walk away.

Epilogue

The house was absolutely crazy that first day after the fire. Chastity hadn't a moment alone with Jonathon the entire day, and the noise and bustle continued until late evening, when most of their guests had finally found a place to sleep.

Chastity frowned thoughtfully as she readied herself for bed, wondering how much longer it would be before Jonathon joined her there. There had been an emergency meeting called for all city officials to discuss plans to aid victims of the fire, but she had not expected it to last this long. She drew the brush slowly through her hair one last time and set it carefully on the vanity. He might not come home at all, she thought, in spite of her resolution not to consider that possibility. She had to admit that he had acted differently today, and though he had tried very hard to avoid her eyes, she had seen everything in that guarded expression of his. She closed her eyes and sighed. She didn't like to think about how much she had hurt him. And she needed so to talk this out with him, to tell him that it had all been a foolish mistake, to hear him say that all was forgiven, and that he still loved her.

The clock chimed the hour of twelve. She stopped pacing and went to lift the quilt from its new place of honor, folded at the foot of their bed. Her fingers touched it longingly, loosening its folds, carefully smoothing the patches one at a time . . . remembering.

"Chastity."

She whirled about to face him, still clutching the quilt tightly in her hands, tears welling up in her eyes. "Oh, Jonathon, I—I never meant to—" Her voice broke off as he turned his back on her and made his way across the room. He poured himself a glass of brandy from a seldom used decanter. It was a long moment before he finally turned, and met her eyes. "Jonathon, I—"

"No, Chastity. Don't." His expression silenced her more than his verbal order. It was firm, his eyes resolved. "I don't want excuses. I only want you to listen. There's something I have to tell you. I ought to have told you a long time ago, before you agreed to marry me. But then, I wanted to believe that it didn't really matter to us at that point . . ." He took a sip of brandy and she watched him in silence, her heart wrenching with the words of apology and love she needed so to say. But something held her back. A terrible fear that he would not forgive her, that he would not believe she had been faithful to him, after her lie.

"There was a time when Regan Spencer needed money," Jonathon began, pacing before her like a lawyer before a jury. "He asked your father for a loan to finance his hotel. At the time, I was handling most of Samuel's affairs, and he asked me to work out the terms with Regan." He stopped and drew a deep breath before he went on. "Instead of doing what your father asked me to do, I flatly refused to give Spencer the money." Chastity's eyes widened in confusion as he turned to face her. "I did more than just refuse him, Chastity," he continued before she could say a single word. "I lied to him. I told him that Sam's money was all tied up in a trust, that it was impossible to get it out without a long, expensive legal battle."

"I don't understand."

"Don't you see? There's a chance he might have married you, Chastity! But I lied to him, convinced him that he wouldn't get a penny beyond a comfortable living allowance if he did."

Chastity lowered her eyes, feeling a distant stab at her pride. So Regan might have married her, if he'd thought she would bring him Sam's money. But Jonathon had convinced him that there would be no money, and Regan had never really loved her enough to marry her for herself. Somehow, a part of her had known that all along. "But why did you lie to him, Jonathon?" she asked him, needing very much to hear the answer she also knew, deep in her heart.

He sighed, and something like regret settled on his proud, handsome features. "I could say that I was protecting you, that I didn't want anyone to marry you for your father's money. But I'm not going to trade one lie for another, not after what the first lie has cost me . . . has cost us." He met her eyes again and straightened his stance. She was very aware of the courage it took to do that. "The truth is, I wanted you. I've loved you from the first moment I saw you, Chastity."

Her heart skipped a beat and she bit her lip to keep from crying out with joy, while at the same time her eyes filled with tears. Her hand hesitantly stretched to touch his cheek. He stepped away before her fingers touched him, and the light in her eyes died. "Jonathon—"

"I know that you were with him last night, Chastity," he said slowly, once again the Boston lawyer, pacing before her as he spoke. "And I know that you still have feelings for him. But you and I have something more, something deep and lasting that we've vowed to be committed to. We have a marriage, a good marriage—"

"You're damned right we do!"

He blinked and turned in astonishment to face her squared shoulders and raised chin. "What did you say?"

She approached him with measured steps, blue eyes flashing defiantly. "I said, if you have any ideas about throwing away everything we have together, all that we've worked together to build, then you'd better just think again. This is a partnership, remember?"

"Chastity, someone will hear you."

"I don't care if the whole world hears me!" she said even more forcefully. "It's about time women were heard!" She grinned, but that grin faded as she lifted her hand to touch his face. This time he did not turn away. "Jonathon Stoneworth, you really don't know how much I need you, do you?" she whispered tenderly. "I don't think I realized it either, until you didn't come home last night." She drew a long, troubled breath and shook her head. "But suddenly—suddenly I knew that my life would be terribly empty without you . . . that *I* would be terribly empty without you." She put her cheek against his shirt and listened to the sound of his heart. All at once, her throat was stinging with unshed tears. "Oh, Jonathon, don't you see? We're like that quilt, you and I. Sewn together forever."

She felt his hands on her shoulders, forcing a distance between them again. His eyes met hers. "What about Regan Spencer?"

"Regan Spencer is—" Her mouth suddenly broke into a smile, and then she laughed, stopping only when she saw that Jonathon's eyes were still totally serious. "Regan Spencer is a ponycart," she forced out soberly.

He frowned. "A what?"

Chastity closed her eyes and sighed, her mouth curving into a smile. "Something I wanted for so long a time, that a part of my pride doesn't know I've outgrown." Her smile vanished as she opened her eyes, and when she spoke again her words were from the deepest part of her heart. "But I have outgrown him, Jonathon. My life with you is rich and full . . . and happy." She clung to him tightly for a long moment, then kissed him with all the passion and warmth that had suddenly blossomed inside her. Jonathon's love . . . As dependable as the morning, she thought as his tongue took up the gentle game hers had begun. But also glorious as the dawn from the top of Mount Davidson, and warm as the summer's brightest sun!